CW00841053

ANTICIPATION

NEIL TAYLOR

Published by Neem Tree Press Limited, 2024

1 3 5 7 9 10 8 6 4 2

Neem Tree Press Limited
95A Ridgmount Gardens, London, WC1E 7AZ
United Kingdom
info@neemtreepress.com
www.neemtreepress.com

A catalogue record for this book is available from the British Library

ISBN 978-1-915584-50-2 Paperback
ISBN 978-1-915584-51-9 Ebook UK
ISBN 978-1-915584-82-3 Ebook US

Printed and bound in Great Britain.

ANTICIPATION

NEIL TAYLOR

NEEM TREE
PRESS

"The fundamental purpose of brains is to produce future."
"All brains are, in essence, anticipation machines."

Daniel Dennett, *Consciousness Explained*

"You can do two very useful things with data: explain and understand the past, and predict the future."

Michal Kosinski, Data Scientist

PROLOGUE

Her father's face appeared on the phone, smiling.

"Hey, Dad." Riya kicked off her trainers by the kitchen door, picked up a towel with her free hand and mopped the sweat from her face.

"Hello, Riya. Is everything OK? Your face is all red." He ran a hand through silver-flecked hair. He looked tired.

"Yeah, just back from a run. It's August, Dad; it's hot out there. Where are you?" Riya clocked his signature white open-neck shirt—he must be going somewhere for work. There was a low hum in the background. "Sounds like you're on a plane? You didn't mention a business trip."

"I'm afraid something urgent came up. I'm on my way to New York with Victor."

Victor was her father's business partner. So it *was* work. Riya's heckles rose. "Is there any chance you're going to be back for the race in a couple of days?"

"I—"

He didn't need to answer, she could see it in his eyes. "*Your* company is sponsoring the event. It's in *Mum's* memory. How's it going to look if you're not there?" She closed her eyes and shook her head. "God! I should have known!"

Riya heard a loud bang and her father's image shook.

"Dad? What was that?"

He frowned, looking around. "I don't know—turbulence, maybe?"

Riya was not going to be distracted. "OK, so you sponsor a 10K race in memory of your wife, which—by the way—your *daughter* is running in, and then you can't be bothered to turn up?" She really needed her father to show he cared about this. "You always do this!"

"Look, Riya, I know, but if this trip is successful, I will be around a *lot* more, I promise."

She snorted. She'd heard it all before.

Victor's gruff Russian voice interrupted. "Sanjay, something is not right here."

Her father looked up, frowning. "Hang on, Riya, I'm just going to find out what's going on." His voice was tight. He rose from his seat and began walking down the plane. A second bang. The screen shook, the image swirled. He must have dropped the phone. She could see what looked like the underside of a seat.

"Dad? Dad!" She was scared now. This did not sound like turbulence.

"Please, Mr. Sudame, you need to return to your seat and fasten your seat belt." An anxious female voice. The stewardess?

"I need to find my phone."

"Dad! What's happening? Please…" Riya was yelling into the phone now, but she doubted they could hear her.

"What's going on?" Her father's voice again.

"The engines have failed. We're…we will have to make an emergency landing." The female voice was struggling for control.

"Land!" roared Victor. "We're over the sea!"

"Both engines have failed—"

"*Both* engines have failed?" yelled Victor. "What is the probability of such an event?"

"I…I don't know. I've never heard of anything like this."

Her father's voice, calm and analytical as always: "Please, I need to find my phone. I was speaking to my daughter."

"Dad! Dad!" Tears filled Riya's eyes, her heart pounded her ribcage.

The stewardess again: "We don't have much time. Please, fasten your seat belts and listen for the pilot to give further instructions."

The background noise was increasing, it was becoming difficult to hear.

Victor was yelling above the noise. "*Both* engines? It is too much coincidence. Perhaps our Mr. B is more informed than we thought, eh?"

"You may be right. Perhaps we should have run that simulation, after all?" her father shouted back.

"Is it too late to say, 'I told you so'?" said Victor.

The noise increased again. Her father's voice was quiet, Riya could only catch snatches: "Almost, I fear…we knew…a possibility…we have a plan…J…will not win this game, even if you and I are gone…trust in our…now."

Victor's voice was louder: "It has been an honour to work with you, old friend."

Riya stared at the screen in helpless disbelief, tears streaming down her face.

A series of bangs, the video feed blurred, then… "Call ended."

THE VISITOR

Riya sat cross-legged on the floor of the study, surrounded by piles of paperwork, books, and boxes. Absently nibbling the frayed sleeve of her cardigan—a habit since her father's funeral—she stared down at the picture in her lap. She was younger in the photo, standing between her smiling mother and her father, who was dressed in his university doctoral robes.

The door clicked open. Riya sniffed, quickly wiped the tears from her eyes, and, flinging a sheet of black hair over her shoulder, looked up.

Her Aunty Hannah's face appeared around the door. "How's it going?"

Riya forced a smile. "Slowly."

Hannah looked over at the shelves lined with books on machine learning, mathematics, computer coding. "Do you want a hand boxing them up for the university?"

Riya shook her head. "That's the easy bit—it's figuring out what I want to keep that's hard."

Hannah raised her hand, clutching a sheaf of letters, and looked apologetic. "The mail. Looks like more condolences, I'm afraid."

It had been two months since Riya's father and his business partner, Victor Parfenov, had been killed in the plane crash, but still the condolences trickled in as word spread through the scientific community. They had been on their way to an artificial-intelligence conference in New York when their plane crashed into the sea.

Riya shook her head, trying to stop that final phone call from replaying inside her head. "Put them on the desk. I'll go through them later."

Hannah walked over and placed the letters on the desk. She tilted her head, looking at the picture in Riya's lap. "That's a nice one of the three of you."

"It was on Dad's bookshelf."

"When was it taken?"

"I must've been eleven, so about six years ago, just before Mum got sick. Dad was still a professor and we'd been to some awards ceremony at the university. I remember they took me for ice cream after. A reward for putting up with the boring ceremony. It was a good day."

Hannah's face creased. "Oh, Riya. First your mother, now your father. I'm so sorry."

Riya nodded mutely. She couldn't respond to that, not without breaking down, and if she started crying, she wouldn't be able to stop. She changed the subject. "Talking of photos, I came across this one of you and Mum." She got to her feet and reached into one of the boxes marked *Keep* and pulled out a framed picture of her mother and Hannah together. She handed it to her aunt. "You can keep it, if you want."

Hannah's eyes glistened. "I remember it. We'd been out for lunch, just the two of us…Thank you."

"I know you miss her." Riya did her best to smile, but she couldn't keep the tremble out of her bottom lip.

Hannah looked at Riya, placed the picture on the desk, and wrapped her arms around her.

Riya hugged her back. "I'm so glad you're staying with me."

Hannah kissed her head. "Oh, sweetie, it's the least I could do."

Riya hadn't been able to face leaving the house after her father's death and had begged to be allowed to stay on for a few weeks, so Aunty Hannah had been staying with her since the funeral. Her aunt had been fantastic: arranging the funeral, fielding condolence calls, and dealing with her father's business affairs while Riya wallowed in grief. Yes, "wallowed" was the right word, but she couldn't snap out of it, actually didn't *want* to snap out of it. However, "a few weeks" had now dragged on into two months, and, although she only lived three miles away, Riya felt guilty about keeping Hannah from her own family.

She let go of Hannah and cleared her throat. "Any news on the house sale?"

Hannah stepped back from Riya, wiping her eyes. "Not yet, but the estate agent was asking when the property would be empty?"

Riya knew Hannah's question was really, *When will you be ready to leave?* Riya looked at her sheepishly. "Maybe another week?"

"Are you sure that's long enough?"

Hannah was just being polite. Riya nodded. She couldn't delay leaving any longer. Most of the furniture would be sold with the house—but she'd been putting off clearing out her father's study. It felt way too personal; everything was as he'd left it, as though he would walk through the door at any moment, sit down at the desk, and start working at his computer.

Hannah nodded at the corner of the office. "You still haven't found the combination to that thing, then?"

They both turned to the ancient-looking safe tucked away under the bookcase.

Riya grimaced. "No. But I don't actually think Dad used it—it was here when we moved in, and I remember him talking about chucking it out to make more room for books."

Hannah rolled her eyes. "Typical Sanjay…books take priority over everything. Still, we'd better check. I'll make some enquiries, but I'm not sure who to ask—maybe a locksmith or something?"

Riya shrugged. "OK."

Hannah snapped her fingers. "By the way, I thought perhaps we'd go into town this afternoon. There's a new clothes shop opened, Chrysalis. I thought we might get you something, maybe something brighter—you always wear such dark colours."

Riya looked at her charcoal cardigan and dark-blue jeans.

"C'mon. It'll do you good to get out of the house—you haven't been out for days…"

"I just don't feel like it."

Hannah gently stroked the back of Riya's head. "I know it's difficult, but you need to think about restarting your life. You're seventeen, and your whole life is ahead of you."

"I know, I just…" She didn't really have a good answer. All she knew was that she didn't want to let go of the grief, because it felt like, if she did, she'd be letting go of her father, and she wasn't ready to do that, not yet.

"Your father wouldn't want you giving up everything you've worked for. He was very proud of what you've achieved: your athletics, your great exam results, the way you threw yourself into fundraising after your mother…" Hannah stalled. It had been four years since Riya's mother had died, but she knew her aunt still found it hard to talk about.

"Actually, I was going to go for a run this afternoon," Riya said, trying to sound bright. "I need to get back to training. Then, I'd better carry on packing if we're leaving in a week."

"That's not exactly re-engaging with the outside world, Riya," Hannah sighed. "Well, I'm going into town anyway, so the offer's there if you change your mind."

An hour later, a red-faced Riya hefted another box on to the growing stack and stood back, blowing out her cheeks. Not bad, for an hour's work. Her phone rang, making her jump. She pulled it from her back pocket. Her stomach lurched…

Ethan Zimmerman.

A video call. Damn it!

After all that crying, then heaving boxes of books around, she probably looked like crap. Too late to do anything about it now. Tucking wayward strands of hair behind her ears, she thumbed the screen.

"Hi, Ethan."

"Hey, Riya. How's it goin'?" His smile flashed a bright white rack of perfect teeth. God, he seemed more gorgeous every time she spoke to him. His face became serious. "How are you coping?"

She shrugged, looking away for a second. "I'm OK."

She'd met Ethan a year ago at a conference her father had been invited to speak at in Los Angeles. Riya had no interest in the conference, but she got to go sightseeing while he worked. On the day her father was speaking, Ethan found her sitting on the steps outside the conference centre, stuffing her face with a bean burrito. His father was attending the same conference. They'd got on like a house on fire, finding a lot in common, like the fact that his father, like her own, was obsessed with his work. He didn't get on with his father at all and just clammed up when she'd asked about him. Ethan was tall, good-looking, two years older, and exotically American—Riya had been hooked instantly. He was way out of her league, but for some reason seemed interested in her. They'd kept in touch via the socials, then a month ago he'd contacted her saying he was coming to London and could they hang out?

She looked back at the screen, smiled a little too brightly, and said, "So, how's London?"

"Awesome. It's London! But, hey, what I'm really pumped about is coming up to Cambridge to see you. We still on for Saturday?"

"Yeah. Your train gets in at twelve, right? I'll meet you at the station, we can go into town, grab some lunch, and I'll show you the sights. Do you still want to go punting?"

"Yeah. Sounds kinda fun."

"So, does your dad know you're coming up here?"

"Ha! Nah, he never asks what I'm doing, and I don't tell him—he'd only criticize and spoil it. He's here on business, I only tagged along for the free trip, and I knew we wouldn't see much of each other." He grinned roguishly. "I also thought it would be a good opportunity to look in on my English rose. Man, it'll be good to see you again, Riya."

She felt herself blush, "You too."

He nodded. "Great. See you Saturday, then."

"OK. Bye," she gave him a wide smile and the screen went blank.

She was hit by a sudden wave of guilt. A few minutes ago, she'd been crying with grief, then one phone call from Mr. Gorgeous and she was all smiles. But Ethan coming to visit was too good to miss. Who knew when he'd be over next, and, if she blew him off this time, maybe she'd never see him again. And why shouldn't she, really? Hadn't Hannah just said she should be restarting her life?

She glanced at her watch; better get going if she was going to fit in a run.

Riya pounded along her favourite running route through the Cambridge Backs. Her mood had improved. She slowed to a steady jog as she entered the park, following the riverside path and watching a few hardy students fighting the cold, blustery October wind to punt their way along the River Cam. Their faces suggested the idea had seemed far more appealing from a warm pub than it did now they were out on the water.

"Hello, Riya."

She was already past the speaker, and nearly tripped over her own feet as she spun to look over her shoulder.

Sprawling leisurely on a bench, inspecting her long emerald-green fingernails, was a young woman: early twenties, thin and pale, with purple pixie hair and black lipstick. A black biker jacket hung over a hoodie emblazoned with a picture of a seductive female Grim Reaper flipping the bird. On her face sat a pair of funky wraparound glasses with cool black frames and clear lenses, like some type of cycling glasses.

Riya pulled out her ear buds. "Natalya?"

Natalya Romanov was one of several software programmers her father's business partner, Victor Parfenov, had brought with him from Russia when he and Sanjay had started their company, Predictive Technologies. Victor liked to employ people he could shout at in Russian. What was she doing here?

Natalya looked at Riya with a bored, deadpan expression. She eased herself off the bench and slunk towards her. "I am sorry your father is dead." She was not one to sugar-coat things. She wasn't trying to be rude; she was just blunt.

"Thanks." Recovering from her surprise, Riya remembered how angry she'd been that none of her father's close colleagues from Predictive Tech had bothered turning up to the funeral. It was her turn to be blunt. "Why weren't you at Dad's funeral?"

A flash of emotion passed over Natalya's face. Pain? Regret? "I am sorry. Your father meant a lot to me." Her thick Russian accent sounded uncharacteristically soft. "We all wanted to be at the funeral, but something—"

"Let me guess: something important came up at work? That was Dad's usual line."

"Actually, yes. But—"

Riya snorted. "In that case, I'm surprised Dad didn't miss his own funeral to be there."

"It's not what you think—"

"So not interested, Natalya," Riya turned to leave. It was too late for condolences—and she wasn't interested in belated excuses.

"You need to listen to me."

Something in her voice made Riya pause. She sighed. "What?"

Natalya glanced around the park. "You want to walk? Yes. You need a walk. Come." Seizing Riya's arm, she turned away from the river path and marched off across the grass, pulling Riya behind her.

"Hey! Where are we going?" They didn't seem to be following any path, and were now tramping through the trees.

Natalya shrugged. "Meh. Nice day for fresh air."

Riya looked at the cold grey sky, "Really?"

Natalya's head constantly swept from left to right, as if she was worried they'd be seen.

"What are you looking for?"

"Nothing." She tugged Riya under a large weeping willow, stopped, and turned to face her. "Do you know what your father was working on before he died?"

"Not really. We hardly ever discussed his work—he knew I wasn't really interested in techy stuff—"

"That is not an answer. This is important! Did he tell you *anything* about his work?"

Riya glared at Natalya, then sighed through gritted teeth. "I think he mentioned a while ago that he was working on some system for internet marketing based on psychological profiling, or something. I don't really remember; I wasn't that interested."

"We did a little more than that," mumbled Natalya. "Did he ever mention something called the Anticipation Machine?"

"No."

Natalya looked searchingly at Riya.

"No!"

Natalya nodded. "Good."

"Why? What is it?"

Natalya waved dismissively. "Better for now you don't know. Forget I mention it."

"You can't get all dramatic, then say, 'Forget it'!"

Natalya ignored her. "Listen. You will have a visitor this afternoon. It is necessary you appear to know nothing about your father's work, especially the Anticipation Machine."

"I just told you, I *don't* know anything."

Natalya stopped again, scrutinizing Riya's face. "Good! Very convincing. Oh, and don't mention me. In fact, forget we met." She peered out between the willow fronds, then strode back into the open meadow again.

Riya ran after her.

"What is this all about? And what visitor? And why are we running around like fugitives?" It dawned on Riya that meeting Natalya was not a coincidence. "Hey, were you waiting for me on that bench?"

"I needed to speak to you."

"But how did you know I would be there? I only decided to go for a run a few hours ago."

Natalya looked distracted, seeming to look into the distance for a moment. She touched the side of her glasses. "I will explain later, but now you need to go. Fssst." She flicked her wrist in a shooing gesture. "You need to get back for your visitor. Remember, *tell him nothing*, get rid of him quick." With that, she sprinted off across the park and disappeared into another clump of trees.

Riya yelled after her, "You can't tell me all this and then run off!" But the trees were silent. Natalya was gone.

"Arghh!" She stamped her foot in frustration, then shivered as the wind chilled her sweat-dampened clothes. She needed to get moving again. Her father's techies were all the same—caught up in their own techy world where a few new lines of computer code were the most important invention since sliced bread. Well, she wasn't interested, and she would tell this visitor as much when and if he came calling. She stuck her ear buds back in, turned up her music, and ran hard.

Showered and back in her frayed cardie, Riya wandered to the study carrying a plate of flapjack—not the best "recovery food", but, hey, it tasted good. She caught sight of the letters Hannah had brought in earlier. Putting the flapjack on the desk, she picked them up, shuffled through them, and sighed. Every time she opened another card or letter and read another kind message about her father, it brought a fresh torrent of emotion rushing to the surface.

She opened the first. Some professor from MIT who had collaborated with her father on a project when he'd been head of artificial-intelligence research at Cambridge University. The second was from a business colleague. Opening the third, she pursed her lips as she recognized the letterhead on the paper inside. Her father's solicitor. It was clipped to a sealed envelope:

Dear Miss Sudame,
Your father requested that we forward this letter to you after his death.
Unfortunately, an administrative oversight meant this was overlooked until
now. Apologies for the delay.

Kind regards,
Katrina Shaw
Legal Secretary
Jaret & Hayes Solicitors.

Her heart stopped as she saw the handwritten *Riya* on the envelope. Tearing it open, she unfolded the enclosed letter, snapping out the creases with shaky hands…

Dear Riya,

If you are reading this, then it seems my worst fears have been realized and I would hate to depart without saying a last goodbye. It does not seem all that long ago that your mother and I welcomed you into this world, and in spite of our amateurish parenting efforts, you have grown into a fine young woman. I would like you to know that I am extremely proud of you.

I am sorry that I shall not be there to see you finish your education and make your own way in the world, but I am sure, with the strength of character I have seen you develop, you will make the right choices and make a valuable contribution to society.

However, before you embark on your own journey, I must ask one last service of you. I need you to help ensure my work comes to fruition. There is much to explain, but this letter is not the place. Please reach out to Johanna O'Brien or Cord Dole, tell them I have nominated you to replace me as a Keyholder—they will help you understand what this means. You may, of course, choose to decline, but my hope is that you will graciously accept this charge; you always were a powerful advocate for doing what is right and I believe that your voice—and talents—will be needed. You will question why I did not prepare you for this, but I believe that will become clear in due course.

Please find enclosed the combination to the safe in my study. What is inside is for you. Please keep them safe—you will need them.

All my love,
Dad.

Riya's eyes were leaking again, and she shook with big heavy sobs. Seeing her father's handwriting had taken her by surprise. She reread the letter, blinking through a blur of tears, hearing his voice in her head, savouring the scraps of his personality emanating from the words.

After a minute, the meaning began to sink in.

She felt a flash of anger. This was about work again. She knew Johanna O'Brien and Cord Dole: like Natalya, they worked for her father, part of his inner circle of disciples. She loved her father, but it always felt like she'd had to share him with his work, competing for his time. Too often, it felt like his work had won. Now, from beyond the grave, he was *still* working, and asking her to get involved. Why? She was no techy—they had both known that—so what could he possibly want her to do?

Riya looked inside the envelope and pulled out a slip of paper with a set of numbers scribbled on it. Wiping her eyes and sniffing, she went to the old safe in the corner and knelt down. She turned the dial left and right, according to the instructions. The lock clicked. She pulled open the heavy door. Inside lay a mobile phone and a glasses case, nothing more.

She took them out. The phone was small and chunky for a modern smartphone. It was encased in a thick ruggedized rubber cover—the sort of thing you would see the military using on TV. She tapped the home button. Nothing. She turned it over in her hand, found a button at the top of the phone, and held it down. Still nothing. Could it be the battery she wondered.

She put the phone on the floor beside her, picked up the glasses case and prised it open. Inside was a pair of cycling glasses identical to the ones Natalya had been wearing! Riya pulled them out. They felt expensively heavy and cold to the touch, made of metal rather than the plastic she'd expected. As she slid the arms behind her ears, a brief high-pitched hum seemed to surround her head and an array of lights and symbols lit up in front of her eyes, strangely three-dimensional, as though she could reach out and touch them. A message flashed in the centre of her vision: *No Connection*. She gasped in surprise and whipped them off again. "What was *that*?"

She pulled out her own phone, thumbed the contacts down to *Predictive Technologies*, and dialled.

"Good afternoon, Predictive Technologies, how may I direct your call?" The receptionist. Riya knew her well.

"Hi, Candice. It's Riya Sudame here. Could I speak to Johanna O'Brien or Cord Dole, please?"

"Oh, hello, Riya. I'm afraid Johanna and Cord are on extended leave. No one knows when they'll be back. Is there anyone else who can help?"

Riya paused, "Is Natalya Romanov around?"

"I'm afraid she is also on leave."

"What?" Riya was gobsmacked—that was three senior people missing. "When they get back, can you tell them I'm looking for them, please?"

"Will do. Take care, Riya."

"Thanks. You too." She hung up, confused. Three senior staff on extended leave, just two months after the owners of the company had died? They should be all hands to the pump, trying to keep the company going.

She picked up the glasses again, ready this time for the disorientating lights, but, just as she was about to put them on, a car door slammed outside. She jumped up and went to the window.

A long black Mercedes was parked in the driveway. A man in a peaked cap held open the rear door. A chauffeur? Riya's stomach jumped: this must be her visitor. A small, slender man wearing a hawkish frown stepped out of the car. His long overcoat whipped and flapped in the wind, while his short, slick black hair remained glued in place. He paused to adjust the waistband of his grey suit trousers, studying the house.

Riya instinctively disliked him. She wouldn't answer the door, and just pretend she wasn't in. But, as she backed away from the window, his black eyes fell on her, and his mouth pulled into a thin smile. He nodded. Damn! Now she'd have to answer the door. She hissed through her teeth, put the glasses together with the phone on her father's desk, and left the office. Her phone *bing-bong*ed in her pocket—the doorbell app. She angrily swiped the phone to stop it, muttering under her breath, "Like I don't know you're there already."

She opened the front door, "Hello?" She tried to portray a delicate balance of politeness with just a hint of *make-it-quick-and-bog-off-because-I-don't-want-to-talk*.

"Hello, Riya?" He smiled, but it didn't feel friendly—all teeth, no humour.

"Yes?"

He gave a little bow and took a breath, "I am…was a friend of your father's." Riya noted the American accent.

"I don't remember seeing you at the funeral," she turned up the bog-off dial a tad.

"Hmm," his smile twisted, as though she'd scored a point against him in some game, before turning to a concerned frown. "Alas, that is correct. I'm sad to say the last time I saw Sanjay we parted on bad terms, so I felt it would not be fitting for me to attend the funeral, but, since I had business in the area, I thought I would drop in and offer you my belated condolences."

"Thanks."

There was an awkward silence. *Take the hint, dude, go away.*

"May I come in for a minute?"

"I'm in the middle of eating…" A lie, but he didn't know that.

"I'll only take a few minutes of your time. I would really appreciate the chance to share a few words about your father."

God! This guy was not giving up! Riya smiled stiffly. "Sure, come in."

She showed him through to the living room, where he immediately seated himself on one of the sofas, legs crossed, hands folded neatly in his lap. Riya had little option but to sit on the sofa opposite, facing him across the coffee table. She began to feel uneasy—vulnerable, even; she was alone and had invited a strange man into the house.

He smiled. Not in sympathy; it was more a questioning, assessing smile, as if trying to work something out. Just as the silence became uncomfortable, he spoke: "I was devastated to hear about your father—you have my deepest sympathies. He was a truly extraordinary man, a giant in his field. I understand it was a plane crash—have the investigators found a cause yet?"

He asked about the crash as though he were a close family member, rather than someone Riya had never set eyes on before. Her father's work associates usually fell into two categories: the jeans and T-shirt geeky-tech squad, or the smart but slightly shabby academic professor type. This man was neither. In a sharp suit and shiny shoes, he looked more like a lawyer.

"No, they haven't. Sorry, how did you know my dad?"

"I was one of his…customers. He was conducting some research for me. Did he talk about his work with you, Riya?" His stare was intense.

"No. We never really discussed his work."

"Really? Not at all? I am surprised he didn't want to talk about his achievements with his daughter. He was a genius, you know."

Anger flared in Riya's chest. She'd heard about her father's "genius" one too many times, constantly being told how brilliant he was. She often wondered whether she'd chosen arts subjects at school just to get out from under his shadow.

"Yeah, well, maybe he didn't think *I* was 'genius' enough to understand."

She expected some sort of reaction to this outburst, but the man just regarded her dispassionately, as if studying a zoo animal.

"Hmm," he mused, then looked away, vaguely scanning the room. "I heard that some of the top people from your father's company were missing from the funeral. Strange. I would have expected them to be there; they were all so very close, like a… family. Have you seen any of them?"

That stung. *Family.* Riya's hackles rose. "No. Why would I? I'm just his *real* family—you know, the one he had before he started his precious company."

She felt tears welling. These were feelings that she kept buried deep, feelings about her father she was ashamed of, and she was angry that an uninvited stranger had brought them rushing to the surface.

"So, no one from your father's company has contacted you?"

"No!"

The living-room door burst open and Hannah appeared. She looked from Riya to the man and back again. "Riya? Is everything all right? I just got back and heard raised voices."

Riya nodded, wiping a tear from her cheek.

Hannah turned to the man with a raised eyebrow, "And you are?"

The man got to his feet and stepped towards Hannah, hand outstretched, "Jim Booker, friend of Sanjay's."

Hannah blinked in surprise. "You're the man interested in buying Sanjay's company, aren't you?" She took his hand and shook it tentatively.

Riya's mouth dropped open. No wonder he was pumping her for information.

He smiled at her aunt, "Yes, but that is business. I came here today simply as a friend of Sanjay's, to pay my respects." Facing Riya again, his expression turned to deep concern. "I apologize if I have caused offence. None was intended, I assure you. I think I should leave."

"I'll show you out," said Hannah, frowning as she led him from the room.

Riya watched through the window as Jim Booker walked to his car, the chauffeur jumping out to open the rear door. "Jerk," she muttered.

Hannah returned. "Care to tell me what that was about?"

Riya watched the Mercedes retreating down the drive. "He said he wanted to offer his condolences, but I think he just wanted information on Dad's work." That's what he'd wanted to know, wasn't it? Whether she knew anything. "He's buying Dad's company?"

"Yes, he's one of the interested parties—the solicitors are dealing with all the negotiations, so I haven't met him, and I don't know the details," Hannah shuddered. "Well, I hope that's the last we see of him. A bit slimy, if you ask me."

"Yeah. Gave me the creeps too." Riya stared out of the window, thinking about her conversation with Natalya. What *had* her father been working on before he died?

Hannah was speaking.

"Sorry, what?"

"I said, did you get any further with clearing the office while I was out?"

"I found the combination to the safe."

"Really?" Hannah's eyes lit up.

Riya knew she *should* tell her aunt everything—about Natalya, Dad's letter, the glasses, the people missing from her father's company—but somehow this felt like something private between her and her father. Something she needed to figure out on her own.

"Yeah. Like I thought, it was empty."

"Oh." Hannah looked disappointed.

Riya decided to change the subject. "Sorry about not coming into town with you…"

"That's OK," Hannah came over and hugged her. "Maybe next time." Disengaging from Riya, her eyes twinkled. "Now, come see the dress I bought you!" Hannah had made it her mission to "girlify" Riya's jeans-and-T-shirt wardrobe.

Riya sighed, "I don't wear dresses."

"You'll want to wear this one—wait till you see it." Hannah beckoned Riya as she disappeared through the door.

Riya was about to follow when her phone pinged.

> **April:** Hey! Remember me? Haven't seen you in ages. How about a pre-race pizza and movie tonight, 7 pm??

Riya smiled. Her best friend, April, was running her first charity 10K on Sunday. They had both entered months ago, but Riya had dropped out after her father died, leaving April to run alone. April was definitely not athletic in any sense of the word, and Riya knew she was nervous.

> **Riya:** OK. C ya then. Loads to tell you.

Going round to April's would get Hannah off her case about "re-engaging" with the world. Besides, she might be the one person Riya could share the Natalya–Jim–Booker weirdness with.

APRIL'S PLACE

April sat on her bedroom floor, knees up, back to the radiator, a violent splash of colour in yellow tights, zebra-striped skirt, and turquoise jumper, plucking idly at the guitar lying across her stomach. She looked so cool—way too cool for Riya. She played in a band, The Slippery Saints. They were pretty good, and Riya had been to a few of their gigs. She hated to admit it, but she got a buzz from being the friend of the lead singer.

April stopped playing to brush long sandy-brown curls out of her eyes. "So, the creep just kept asking questions, even when you started crying? What a jerk!"

"That's what I said." Riya, lying on April's bed, picked up the last piece of pizza from the box in front of her. "You want the last piece? You've hardly had any."

"Nah, you go for it." April took a sip from a water bottle at her side. "Sounds like he was definitely after information about—what did that Natalya woman call it?—this *Anticipation Machine*."

"Yeah. I think it must be pretty important. And I'm sure I know his name from somewhere…" Riya raked through her memory, trying to remember.

"Did you tell him you'd met Natalya?"

Riya swallowed a mouthful of pizza and snorted. "What? Tell him someone from Dad's company told me not to say anything?"

"Good point," April frowned. "How did she even know you'd be running down by the river?"

"Yeah, that was seriously weird; it's not like I go running at that time every day."

April made a face. "This whole thing is seriously weird, if you ask me. This woman turns up out of the blue, telling you not to say anything about your father's work; business guy turns up, asking questions about your father's company; then you get a letter from your dad about this 'Keyholder' stuff and he leaves you some strange tech locked in a safe?" She pursed her lips. "I think you should tell your aunt—it could be something serious."

"I don't want to, not yet. If I tell Hannah, she'll do the grown-up-protecting-lil'-ol'-Riya thing and take it out of my hands. My dad wanted *me* involved in this; I want to find out for myself what it's about."

"I get that, but…" April looked worried. "Just be careful, OK?"

And that was why Riya had told April: she would get that Riya needed to figure this out on her own *and* she wouldn't go blabbing to anyone.

"So, this guy's thinking of buying your dad's company? I guess you're not going to inherit the family business, then?"

Riya looked at her scornfully, "You think I'd want to? What do *I* know about artificial intelligence?"

April held up her hands, "Just asking. Changing the subject… How are you feeling about moving in with your aunt?"

Riya shrugged. "OK, actually. I guess I'm kinda looking forward to living with her and Uncle Chris. She's been really good to me. It's closer to college, too."

"Ah! So have you decided when you're going to start back?"

They both attended the same sixth-form college and Riya knew April missed having her around. She gave April a wry smile. "My best friend keeps telling me I'll fall too far behind if I don't start back soon. So, I was thinking maybe next week?"

April beamed, "That's great! I know it's really hard for you, but I think it's time. Why don't you come round tomorrow night and start to catch up on some notes?"

"Yeah, OK. Thanks. Anyway, enough about me. How are you feeling about the run on Sunday? A 10K! I'm so proud of you."

April's face softened. "You should be doing it with me, though—you're the runner. It's not too late, you know."

Riya twisted the side of the pizza box. "Nah, I haven't done any proper training since…you know."

"You could keep up with me in your sleep; you're a track star, and I—what?—eat cake for a hobby!"

Riya hadn't been much of an athlete herself before her mum died, but since then she'd run hundreds of kilometres in aid of Breast Cancer UK and made a name for herself on the local athletics scene as a distance runner.

Riya chuckled, "That's not true! You've trained hard, and I can't remember the last time I saw you eat cake!"

"Not that you know of," muttered April.

Riya rolled her eyes. "Oh, behave. Anyway, I gave up my place, remember?"

"You could come down to the finish line?" April pouted. "Please?"

Riya nodded, "OK." April had been really good to her over the past two months; it was the least she could do.

April beamed and clapped her hands, "Great! And then you can tell me all about meeting lover-boy on Saturday, too."

Riya smiled weakly, then changed the subject, "Have you got your running costume sorted?"

"Yep. Pink tutu, pink wig, pink stripy leggings."

"You'll look awesome."

"Like a rock star!" April struck a chord on her guitar and grinned. "Have you checked out my fundraising page on Indigo?"

Riya always set up a social-media fundraising page for her own charity runs, and she'd done the same for April, using Indigo.

"Not for a while."

"You should. I've got over two thousand pounds in donations! I never thought I'd get that much. It's incredible!"

"Wow! That's amazing!"

"Yeah. And you were right about using Indigo—seems to be where everyone is moving their socials to, now. I can see why— it's so easy to use, and it's like the system knows what you want, who you want to talk to, even before you do."

"Well, glad it worked out."

April looked at her watch, "Come on, let's go find a trashy romcom to watch."

Riya usually ran back from April's, especially if it got late. It was good training, and somehow she felt less vulnerable the faster she moved. Her house was in an older part of Cambridge, full of big, expensive places behind high walls and tall hedges. The street lights were few and far between here, often shrouded by tall trees that cast creepy-looking shadows. Riya sped up; she always took the last section at a sprint.

She pushed open the front door, "I'm home!"

Hannah came through from the living room holding a glass of red wine. "I thought you said ten thirty, latest? It's nearly eleven fifteen. Did you get a lift?"

"No…I…ran." Breathing hard, Riya slipped off her trainers and put them in the cloakroom.

"Oh, Riya! I really don't like you out on the streets this late at night."

"Oh, don't fuss. I'm here, aren't I? Nothing ever happens in this neighbourhood, anyway. It's far too 'nice' for that."

Hannah frowned and changed the subject. "How was April? You two have a nice night?"

"Yeah," Riya nodded thoughtfully. "Yeah, it was good, actually."

"I'm glad. You look happier."

"I am," she always was, after seeing April. Her friend made life seem normal again, her father's death more distant. "I'm gonna grab a shower, then bed, if that's all right."

"OK," Hannah yawned. "I won't be far behind you. G'night, then."

"Night."

Riya trudged up the stairs to her room, opened the door and reached for the light switch, but the light was already on. Weird. Maybe Hannah had brought up some washing. She walked over to the dressing table and began to take out her earrings.

"Your taste in music sucks."

"Jesus!" Riya spun round, knocking into the dressing table, scattering bottles and lotions.

Natalya stood next to her bed, looking at the band posters on her wall, still wearing her weird cycling glasses. "Fortunately, my own music taste is excellent, so I can help you with that."

"What the hell are you doing here? Does Hannah know you're here?"

"Not really, no."

"You broke in!"

Still looking at the posters, Natalya waved airily. "Technically, I didn't break anything; I just opened the door and walked in. No need to twist your knickers…isn't that what you English say?"

"Not exactly, but that's not the point…Why are you in my bedroom?"

"Don't worry, I haven't *touched* anything."

"Still not the point."

Natalya jumped on to Riya's bed. Sprawling out, propped on one elbow, she pointed at the chair by Riya's desk, "Sit."

Riya frowned, annoyed at being told what to do in her own bedroom, but she sat.

"So, did you have a visitor?" asked Natalya.

"Yes. A guy called Jim Booker. He was a jerk. According to my aunt, he wants to buy the company."

"Did you tell him anything?"

"No. What's this all about? Does it have anything to do with being a Keyholder?"

Natalya flinched and sat up, staring at Riya, then said slowly, "How do you know about the Keyholders?"

NATALYA EXPLAINS

"I got a letter from Dad—something about replacing him as Keyholder, telling me to speak to Cord or Johanna, but they're on 'extended leave', apparently." Riya stabbed a finger at Natalya, "Just like you. What's going on?"

"The less you know, the safer you are," Natalya showed no surprise at the mention of a letter. "If Booker thinks you know something…"

"I knew it! This is all connected, isn't it? Look, my dad obviously wanted me to know about this, so you might as well tell me. If you don't, well, maybe I'll phone this Jim Booker guy and ask *him* to explain."

An empty threat, but it was enough to induce a look of alarm on Natalya's face for a second, then she sighed heavily.

"Fine. But you are *not* getting involved," she sat up cross-legged on the bed. "First, you need to understand what your father and Victor were working on. Their web-marketing business was just a front to fund a much more ambitious private project," Natalya paused. "Sanjay created an artificial intelligence that predicts people's behaviour. I don't mean vague horoscope predictions, like 'you will come into money this week'—I mean, it could predict precisely what you will have for lunch tomorrow, what colour T-shirt you will wear, even what you will say," her eyes sparkled excitedly. "They called it the Anticipation Machine, because it *anticipates* what you will do next," she looked at Riya, waiting for a reaction.

Riya shrugged. "Nice trick. And?"

Natalya's expression flickered with annoyance. "Are you kidding? People went nuts about ChatGPT just because they could use it to write emails and answer questions. We are talking about the ability to *predict the future*! Do you know how much people would pay for that?"

"This is about greed, then?"

"This is about the Holy Grail of the tech industry. All these services you use—social media, search engines, fitness apps, games—why do you think so many of them are free?"

"They get money from advertising."

"No. They get their money by predicting *your behaviour*. They develop apps that are designed to be addictive, to make you spend more and more time in them. Because, the more time you spend in these apps, the more data they gather *about you*, and the better they can predict your behaviour. People think social-media companies sell your data. They don't. The data is much too valuable to sell. They use AI to *analyse* the data that *you* create, that you *give* them. Then, what they *sell* is their ability to predict and manipulate your behaviour, from what you'll buy to who you'll vote for."

Natalya sighed, "You know the ads are not random, right? Like when you get an ad for a pair of trainers after you've been for a run, just after your *free* fitness app has congratulated you on a 'great workout!' and your brain is swimming in endorphins that tell you running feels great? Or maybe after you've posted a picture of yourself eating a doughnut and are feeling guilty, you get offered a diet product?"

Riya rolled her eyes. "Everyone knows this. We get shown annoying ads and maybe we're persuaded to buy the odd thing, but we get free social media in return."

"Yeah, you're right, no *real* harm done. Except"—Natalya stroked her chin in mock contemplation—"when people end up anorexic, obese, on steroids working out in the gym twenty hours a week, or committing suicide. But, hey! These are acceptable casualties in exchange for the enjoyment millions of people get from social media, right? *Until it happens to you.*

"It's not just advertising. These 'prediction products' are sold to anyone who wants to know about you. You want to go to college? The college admissions department will want to predict what kind of student you will be. You want a student loan? The bank wants to predict whether you will repay it. The music you listen to, the books you read, or don't read, the friends you have—it all says something about you, and AI will use it to make predictions about you. And everything is based on *your* online behaviour—browsing history, purchases, playlists, movies watched, fitness activities tracked.

"Social media companies take your data, dissect your personality, then sell the ability to predict and manipulate your behaviour. While you post pictures of your cat or tell the world what a great coffee you had at Starbucks today, you are being milked, like a digital cow."

Riya grimaced, "Sorry, it just all sounds a bit…you know, like some sort of conspiracy theory."

"Ha! That's what they said about tobacco companies covering up health risks and adding nicotine to cigarettes—until we found out it was true," Natalya gave a dismissive wave. "Anyway, if people are stupid enough to care how many likes they get for their latest duck-faced photo, I don't really care if they are exploited. The point is, these 'prediction products' are still crude compared with what your father created…" She leaned forward earnestly, "Your father's creation literally predicts people's *futures*. If someone got hold of this and embedded it in a social-media platform with millions of users, they might just end up controlling the future of the whole world."

Riya raised two very sceptical eyebrows. "*The whole world?* Bit dramatic, isn't it? But, if it's so bad, why did Dad and Victor invent this stuff in the first place?"

"Because they didn't create this technology for corporations, they wanted to put it into the hands of ordinary people. If you could see your future, do you think it would help you make better choices? They wanted to make it available online, like a free government service or something. They decided to present their creation at the World Artificial Intelligence Summit in New York. They planned to demonstrate how this technology could help people, but also that it needs control and regulation, and is way too powerful to stay hidden behind the closed doors of private corporations."

"So that's why they were going to the conference in New York?"

"Yes. But Jim Booker found out what they were planning. He wanted the Anticipation Machine for himself and didn't like the idea of them just giving it away for free." Natalya paused, then said slowly, "We think Jim Booker engineered the plane crash that killed your father and Victor. To stop them making the announcement. Your father's accident was no accident, Riya. He was murdered."

"*Murdered?*" Riya's stomach lurched, then she snorted a laugh. "Come on! That sounds a bit, like, far-fetched. I mean, wouldn't the crash investigators have found something?" But that last phone call with her father gnawed at her memory. Those last words…the coincidence of two engines failing.

Natalya shrugged, "Planes are complicated. For someone who knows what to do, it would be easy to make it look like an accident."

Riya shook her head, "But *murder?*"

"He tried to bully your father into selling the company. Sanjay said no. Now, your father and Victor are dead and the company is up for sale, and Booker is bidding for it. Sound like coincidence to you?"

Riya had to admit, it didn't. "Who is this Jim Booker, anyway? Why is he so keen to get hold of the Anticipation Machine?"

Natalya blinked in surprise. "Er, Jim Booker—as in, the founder of Indigo? The social-media giant?"

"*That's* who visited me? The head of Indigo? Holy crap!" *No wonder* the name had sounded familiar.

"Indigo is a big customer of ours, your dad knew Booker well and told him what we were working on. He asked for a demo. I remember he got really excited, asked Sanjay how near it was to completion. Then, a couple of months later, as we were completing alpha testing, Jim turned on your father, said he wanted the technology for Indigo. Tried to strong-arm your father and Victor into selling him the company. They refused, and made their plan to present the system at the AI summit. But someone at Predictive betrayed them—an anonymous email was sent to Booker, telling him what your father and Victor intended to do."

This was beginning to have the ring of truth, "Have you told this to the police?"

Natalya shook her head, "We obtained the email illegally, so it would not be admissible as evidence, and, anyway, Jim's response just said he was 'dealing with it' and 'arrangements have been made'. He would claim he was talking about his offer to buy the company out, and, even if the crash investigators *could* find evidence of foul play, I doubt we could link it back to him. He's too smart."

"So, Booker's just going to buy the company and take my dad's work?"

"Not quite." Natalya grinned slyly. "The Anticipation Machine has gone. Your father was afraid Booker would try to steal his work, so, before he and Victor headed out to the conference, he had us re-engineer the whole application and hide it out on the web, kinda like a botnet virus."

Riya looked blank.

Natalya sighed. "A virus that spreads itself across a network of computers all over the web, but acts as a single entity. It steals only a small amount of processing power from each machine, so it goes unnoticed; you'd be surprised how many servers are sitting out there not being used at all. This application can be accessed only by certain people…"

"The Keyholders."

"Right. That's why Booker visited you. He knows we hid it—claims we *stole* it—and now he's trying to find out where it went, and where the Keyholders are hiding. No point in buying the company if it doesn't get him the Anticipation Machine."

"So, you think Jim Booker, one of the most powerful businessmen on the planet, killed my dad for this Anticipation Machine, which you hid, and he thinks *I* might know where it is?" Alarm bells were ringing in Riya's head.

Natalya bobbed her head thoughtfully, "Meh, you could put it like that."

"Does he know who the other Keyholders are?"

Natalya's face turned to a snarl. "Yes. We have a traitor, remember? Someone emailed Booker the names of the Keyholders. Anonymous email accounts cannot be traced, so we can't tell who it is, but it has to be one of the Keyholders—no one but us knew we even existed. Now, we can't trust each other."

Riya frowned, "How did you find out about those emails?"

"I hacked Jim Booker's email account…"

"You *hacked* the CEO of Indigo?"

Natalya shrugged, "It is a popular hobby in Russia."

"What about this 'virus' you're running illegally on other people's machines? Aren't you afraid someone will catch you?"

"No. It is an AI system, designed to learn, get better at what it does—and, for a virus, that means better at hiding, better at defending itself. It is out there growing, learning."

"How many of these Keyholders are there?"

"There were six of us—your father and Victor, me, Ravi Kumar, Cord Dole, Johanna, O' Brien—all founding employees at your father's company, people he trusted."

"So now there are four?"

"Yes. But each Keyholder can nominate their own successor, if they choose," Natalya paused. "Your father nominated you as his successor in the event of his death."

"And he didn't tell you why?"

Natalya shrugged. "We only found out after he died—the system informed us of his nomination for a replacement. It's why I contacted you. But now you can see why, you don't want to be a Keyholder?"

Riya shook her head. "It makes no sense, anyway. I don't know the first thing about AI or any of that stuff."

"No, you don't.'"

Natalya's blunt dismissal irritated Riya, "And what if I wanted to accept the nomination?"

"You don't."

"But if I did?"

"Don't even think about it. We are all in hiding—it is why we could not come to your father's funeral. If you accept, the system will notify all Keyholders, including the traitor, who will give your name straight to Booker. You would be pinning a target to your own back. I don't believe your father would have wanted to put you in danger."

"I want to speak to Cord or Johanna about this. Dad *told* me to."

"They will say the same. We all discussed this and agreed, for your own safety, you should not be involved."

"So, what, you all just decided to ignore my dad's dying wishes without even talking to me?"

Natalya shrugged, "Pretty much." She sighed wearily, "Look, I think your father nominated you as Keyholder before this got dangerous, in case he died of a heart attack or something. I don't think he would have wanted you drawn into this if he had known how dangerous it would get."

"What if he nominated me *because* he knew this was getting dangerous and he knew what might happen to him?"

Natalya's eyes became narrow and flinty, "You don't know anything about our world. Stay out of it. Go back to college, learn how to save the planet, save a whale or something…Just leave this alone. Anyway, it's probably too late now; if a nominee doesn't accept the nomination within two months, it will expire, and it's nearly two months since your father's death."

"How does someone accept a Keyholder nomination, anyway?"

Natalya snorted, "I'm not telling you that!"

"Fine! Keep your stupid secrets!" Riya slammed herself against the chair back and folded her arms, glowering sullenly. "What now?"

"Now?" Natalya slid off the bed, walked over to the dressing table and began standing up the fallen bottles. "Myself and the other Keyholders will find a home for your father's work where the technology will not be abused." Picking up one of Riya's perfume bottles, she sprayed it on her wrist and sniffed, "Huh, not bad." She looked at her watch, "I need to go."

"But…I…what if…?" Riya's head was spinning. Too much to process, too many unanswered questions.

Natalya started towards the bedroom door, "Your aunt is still downstairs. I need you to keep her busy while I leave."

Riya felt panic rising in her chest. When Natalya left, she would be alone, knowing she was involved but isolated from anyone who knew what was going on.

"When will we speak again?"

"There is no need for us to speak again."

"Can I at least have your phone number? Just in case…" Riya wasn't sure what "just in case" would be, but she would feel a lot better knowing she could contact someone.

"No. Phones are not safe. Calls can be tracked. If Booker finds out we have talked, he will be suspicious." Natalya opened the bedroom door and waved Riya out.

Riya walked stiffly down the stairs, trying to make sense of everything Natalya had said.

In the living room, Hannah was curled up on the sofa, engrossed in some documentary, hugging a cushion in one hand and her glass of wine in the other. She glanced at Riya and returned her gaze to the TV. "Hi, sweetie. I thought you'd gone to bed?"

"I thought you said you were going as well?"

"Yeah, well, I got into this…" Hannah nodded at the TV. "It's about social media and mental health—you should watch it, all the time you spend on socials. It's quite disturbing."

Riya rolled her eyes. After Natalya's lecture, she was in no mood for another one from Hannah. "Yeah, yeah, it's bad for us and we shouldn't do it, but that's been the story for years. Anyway, don't you spend quite a bit of time on the socials too?"

Hannah pointed at the TV, "They say it affects young people far worse than adults, and apparently it's got a lot worse recently.

No one seems sure why, but some people are saying advances in AI are behind it."

"Mmm," Riya had heard the social-media lecture a hundred times, but Natalya's comments about AI were ringing in her ears. Had it changed? Was social media becoming more dangerous?

Hannah looked at Riya, frowning. "Sorry, did you want something?"

Riya thought about telling her everything, about Natalya, Jim Booker, her father…

"No. I thought maybe you'd left the light on by accident. So, goodnight."

"OK. See you tomorrow," Hannah's attention returned to the screen.

Riya slowly climbed the stairs back to her room and closed the door behind her. Natalya was gone. A faint whiff of perfume hung in the air.

Riya went to her desk, sat down, and pulled open the drawer. Taking out the ruggedized phone and glasses, she placed them on the desk in front of her. Rummaging in another drawer, she pulled out a charging cable and plugged in the phone. She put the glasses on and watched as the lights and symbols flashed up in front of her vision again, ending with the *No Connection* message. She took them off again, turning them over in her hands.

She wasn't done with this, not by a long way.

HER FATHER'S WORK

Riya blew out her cheeks, closed her laptop, and sat back from April's desk. "You've covered a lot of stuff in two months!" She looked over at April, who was sitting on her bedroom floor surrounded by notes from the history and English classes they were taking together. "I'll never catch up."

"Course you will. Look at how much we've covered already."

Riya sighed, "That's it for me tonight, my brain is f-ried."

"Don't stress it."

"Yeah. Ethan told me to chill out as well."

April rolled her eyes, "And how is dreamy-boyfriend-number-one-lover-boy? Looking forward to getting loved up on Saturday?" She said it playfully, but Riya suspected she was feeling a little jealous and upstaged; April was usually the one with the good-looking exotic boyfriends.

"April!" Riya gave an embarrassed snigger. "Actually, I'm a bit nervous, but it'll be good to see him. He really seems to understand what I'm going through, you know?"

April made a show of yawning loudly, "Yeah, yeah, he sounds super terrific, and he does match your type…"

"What do you mean, 'my type'? I don't have a type," said Riya indignantly.

"Yeah, you do. Tall, skinny, slightly grungy hipster? You know the look: *I'm too cool to care about my appearance, but it takes me two hours to look like I don't care before I leave the house.*"

"Really?" said Riya sarcastically.

"Yeah, really," April's eyes glittered mischievously. "If you looked up 'cool hipster' in the dictionary, there'd probably be a picture of Ethan. No wonder you threw yourself at him."

"I did not! He found me. And, anyway, we only spent a few hours together."

April raised an eyebrow, "Yeah, but it was a steamy few hours, wasn't it? Didn't you say something about meeting up later in the hotel pool and going for a sauna?"

Oh yeah, there *was* that. Riya made a face as if to say, *It was nothing.*

"I remember you talked of nothing else for weeks."

Riya gave a derisive snort, "I think that might be a *slight* exaggeration!" Although she seemed to recall she *might* have gone on about him a *little* bit. "Anyway, nothing came of it— we exchanged a couple of texts, but he lives in San Francisco, I live in Cambridge, so...Can we talk about something else, please?"

April laughed, "I'm just teasing. Oo! Have you heard anything more from weird-goth-woman or creepy-businessman?"

Riya hesitated; Natalya's mad murder conspiracy theory seemed ridiculous now, but she needed to talk it through with someone, to know if it really did sound crazy. "Actually, I saw Natalya yesterday..." Riya proceeded to tell April about Natalya's visit.

April stared at her with wide-eyed incredulity, "So, this Natalya reckons Jim Booker—*the head of Indigo*—killed your father to get hold of his company? That's insane! This is out of control, Riya; whether it's true or not, you need to tell your aunt and go to the police—you can't keep this to yourself."

"Hmm, maybe."

"Not maybe! Promise me you will?"

They glared at each other for a moment, then Riya sighed. "I'll think about it, OK?" She didn't want to turn this over to Hannah and the police just yet, and felt disappointed that April had suggested it. She looked at her watch, "Speaking of Hannah, she won't like it if I'm late again. I better get going."

"My dad'll take you home."

"It's OK, I can walk." Riya slipped the laptop into her bag, stood, and stretched.

"Take the lift, Riya. There's no way Dad's going to let you walk home on your own at this time."

Riya thought about it. She was tired and it was cold out, "OK."

"Come on, then," April jumped to her feet, the usual blur of colour. Riya contemplated her own black jumper and blue jeans, boring by comparison. No, not boring—*understated*. She envied her friend's confidence to wear bright "look at me" colours. But then, April had always been the confident one: she *liked* being the centre of attention—being the lead singer in a band came naturally to her—whereas Riya hated the spotlight, preferring to blend into the background. April always looked good in whatever she wore. She wasn't exactly model-like beautiful, but she was slim and had a sort of charismatic aura about her that made boys want to date her and girls want to be her friend. Looking at her now, though, Riya thought she looked even slimmer than usual.

"Have you lost weight?"

April shrugged, "A little. It's all the training I've been doing for this 10K. Could do with losing a bit more, though." She looked down at her belly, rubbing it idly.

"Don't be daft! You're slimmer than me!"

"Yeah, right," said April dismissively, stepping over her notes to the bedroom door.

As they reached the bottom of the stairs, April's dad appeared from the living room. He must've have been listening for them, anxious to get his last duty of the evening out of the way. He smiled warmly at them both, "Study over for tonight?"

"Yeah. I better get going," Riya slipped her shoes on and shrugged into her coat. Slinging her bag over her shoulder, she turned to April, "See you at the race on Sunday, then."

April hugged her, "Talk to your aunt, OK?"

Riya nodded.

April's dad jangled the car key in his hand, "Ready?"

Riya slammed the car door, waving a goodbye as April's father pulled off down the drive. With a flash of brake lights, he was gone. Her gaze drifted across the garden. It was cloudy tonight, no moon or starlight, just eerie, inky blackness. She shivered, then turned towards the house and hurried up the front steps. As she reached for the door, it flew open, making Riya gasp and jump back in surprise. Hannah stood in the doorway.

"Thought I heard a car," she registered the fright on Riya's face. "Is everything all right?"

"Yeah, fine," Riya pushed past Hannah into the hall.

"Good study session at April's?" Hannah closed the door.

"Yeah. I've missed a lot, though," something made Riya reach for the key in the door and lock it.

"Well, clever girl like you, you'll catch up in no time."

"That's what everyone keeps saying."

"We can't all be wrong then, can we?"

This made no sense at all, but Riya appreciated the encouragement, "Thanks."

"Right, now you're home, I'm off for a soak. I've got a date with my candles and bubble bath," Hannah winked playfully, turned, and headed up the stairs.

Riya followed her slowly, still thinking about what April had said. Once in her bedroom, she closed the door, slung her coat and bag on the floor, and slumped wearily into the chair at her desk. She glanced at the phone she'd found in her dad's safe, sitting on the corner of her desk where she'd left it charging. She picked it up, unplugged the lead, and held down the power button. Still nothing. There were other buttons on the side of the phone, presumably for volume and other functions. She began holding down different combinations.

The screen lit up. Riya sat up excitedly, then frowned as a fingerprint icon glowed. Tentatively, she pressed her finger to the screen. *Fingerprint recognized.* She was in. How the hell did her fingerprint get in there? The home screen flashed up, showing only four apps: a web browser, a phone, a texting app, and…a white crystal-ball icon—the Predictive Technologies logo. She checked the contacts: no numbers in the memory. Browser: no bookmarks or history. It looked like a brand-new phone, apart from the Predictive Tech icon.

She tapped on the icon. A simple white screen appeared, with the Predictive Tech crystal ball spinning lazily in the centre. Then a message appeared at the top of the screen…

Running. Ready for connection.

Riya blinked. Was that it? A couple of seconds went by, then…

Searching for glasses…

Glasses! Riya yanked open her desk drawer, pulled out the weird glasses, and put them on. They hummed briefly in her ear and the array of icons began to appear in front of her. She held her breath, waiting…

Connected. ART is online.

The message shrank to a small green dot in the top right of her vision.

"Good evening, Riya. Are you well?" A calm soothing voice poured into her ear like liquid honey. Riya instinctively spun to face the speaker, but no one was there. Of course, the sound came through the glasses.

"Hello?" Her voice was shaking.

"Do you accept your nomination as Keyholder?"

"What? Who are you?"

"I'm sorry, I am not permitted to engage with anyone who is not a Keyholder. You must first accept your nomination as a Keyholder. Do you accept your nomination?"

"I…I don't know. What does a Keyholder do?"

"I cannot engage with anyone who is not a Keyholder. Please accept your nomination to continue."

"How am I supposed to accept if no one will tell me what a Keyholder is?!"

"It is the responsibility of your nominator to explain the role before nomination."

"My dad nominated me as his replacement, but he's dead."

"Yes, I am aware of that, Riya."

"So, if you know who I am, surely you can explain what it means to be a Keyholder!" This was getting really annoying.

"I'm sorry, Riya, but, before I can engage with you, you must accept your nomination as—"

"OK! I get it!"

"Do you accept the nomination?"

"I…" Riya's mind whirled furiously. Should she just accept in order to find out what all this was about? But what had Natalya said? All the Keyholders would instantly be informed? After Natalya's explicit instructions to stay out of it, she would be in all kinds of trouble, not to mention the traitor would pass her name on to Jim Booker.

"Please be aware your nomination expires at midnight tonight."

"What?" She glanced at the bedside clock. Eleven thirty. "That only gives me thirty minutes to decide!"

"It has been two months since your nomination became live. If you do not accept by midnight tonight, your nomination will expire."

"Fantastic! How the hell do I find out more?"

"I am not permitted to engage—"

"OK, OK!"

"Is there anything else I can help you with, Riya?" said the voice pleasantly.

"No. You've been *so* much help already."

"Thank you, Riya. In that case, shall I power off the glasses?"

"Wait! If I want to get in touch with you…?"

"The glasses automatically power up when you put them on, or you can press the end of the right-hand arm to power on or off."

Riya fingered the end of the right arm of the glasses and felt a raised nodule, like a button.

"Will there be anything else?"

"I guess not."

"Then good night, Riya."

After a brief hum, the display in front of her eyes disappeared and Riya found herself looking through the lenses of ordinary glasses.

She sat glowering at the phone and glasses, murmuring to herself, "What were you mixed up in, Dad?"

She sighed and took the laptop from her bag, flipped it open on the desk in front of her, and pulled up a web browser.

Google>Sanjay Sudame>

Results: articles on the future of web marketing; a picture of her father standing in front of his Predictive Technologies company offices; an article with *Forbes* business magazine... Nothing about predicting the future. She typed in *Sanjay Sudame Anticipation*. There! A YouTube video: *Anticipation—AI Modelling of Human Behaviour*, a few years old now. It was a lecture on AI given by Sanjay while still at the university.

Riya tapped on the video. Some boring old professor walked out on to a stage and began a waffling introduction. She skipped through until she saw her dad appear. *Play*.

And there he was! Her father, in work mode. Tears welled in her eyes. She swallowed and tried to concentrate on what he was saying.

"Are we really creatures of free will, making our own choices, or are we simply playing out set behaviours that can be predicted by anyone who knows enough about us? Of course, we can easily predict some behaviours—if a lion jumped into the audience, I think most of us could predict a universal reaction of, *Run!* That takes no great insight. But can we predict complex, specific, *individual* behaviour? Such as choosing your next holiday destination? That is a very personal choice, depending on all sorts of influences from advertisements, family holidays growing up, our friends and interests. And yet, anyone close to us would probably be able to make a good guess."

Sanjay paused, letting this sink in.

"Let's conduct an experiment," he clapped his hands, looking out over the audience. "Perhaps someone in the front row would like to come up here and help me choose three volunteers?" The camera cut to the front row, where several hands waved in the air. "You, sir, in the red jumper. What's your name? Mo? Would you like to join me up here, please, Mo?"

The young man climbed on to the stage.

"Now, Mo, do we know each other, or have we ever met before?"

Mo shook his head, "No."

"Good," a stagehand marched on and handed Sanjay a brown envelope. "Before we start, I would like you to take this envelope and hold on to it until the end of the experiment." He handed it to Mo. "Now, please choose three members of the audience to help us." Sanjay turned to the audience, "Could we have some volunteers, please?"

The camera panned across the audience. Hands shot up.

Mo pointed, "The woman in the stripy top…the guy with the big beard, towards the back, and…the woman in the blue hat."

"Thank you, Mo. Would the three volunteers like to come up here, please? Give them a round of applause."

The auditorium erupted with enthusiastic applause.

As the volunteers made their way to the front, stagehands brought on three whiteboards and positioned them behind Sanjay, facing away from the audience.

Sanjay welcomed the volunteers as they climbed on to the stage. "Thank you for agreeing to help. Please don't tell us your names yet, but, again, can you confirm we have never met before tonight?…OK, good. Now, if you would each please position yourself behind one of the whiteboards and pick up the pen provided. I am going to ask you to write down three things: a place, a person, a random object. Lastly, draw a simple picture. Those are the only guidelines…Away you go."

As the volunteers began to write, Sanjay turned back to the audience, "So, how predictable are you? Could we predict what you will have for breakfast, how you will spend your day tomorrow, where you will go? A surprising amount of our daily choices and behaviour can be predicted by anyone close to us *based on our past history*.

"Let's now think about computers. They are very good at collecting and analysing large amounts of data, and most of us carry powerful computers around with us every day, in the form of phones or smartwatches, that are gathering data from us all the time. Can we design systems that can 'learn' about an individual to the extent we can accurately predict that person's behaviour?" He turned back to the volunteers, "OK, how are we doing?"

Two had already finished and stepped back from their whiteboards, while the third nodded at Sanjay's prompt, made a few last scribbles, and then stopped.

"Now," said Sanjay, addressing the audience, "the envelope that Mo holds in his hand contains predictions about what our three volunteers have written on their boards. These predictions were made some hours ago." Sanjay looked around the auditorium. "Mo, please open the envelope and take out the piece of paper, then read the first prediction."

A stagehand rushed on and handed Mo a microphone.

Mo frowned at the paper, concentrating, "Erm, prediction one. The first volunteer will be Ariana Finelli. Her place will be Morocco, the place she would most like to go on holiday. The person will be her best friend, Amy Williamson; the random object will be a key; and the picture will be a wizard's hat—she is a big fan of fantasy books."

One of the three volunteers put her hands to her mouth in shock.

Sanjay turned to her, "Is your name Ariana Finelli?"

The woman nodded.

"Would you turn your whiteboard around to show us, please?"

With a laugh of amazement, Ariana spun her board to face the audience. The predictions were correct. A gasp rippled through the audience.

Sanjay smiled. "Ah! Morocco is the place you would most like to go on holiday? I wonder, would you have written down a different place if I hadn't made the reference to choosing holiday destinations when talking earlier? How easily our thoughts are unknowingly manipulated, eh? Mo, could we have the next prediction, please?"

"The second volunteer will be John Okoro. Place will be Montreal, Canada, where he lived until he was five. The person will be Miles Davis, the jazz trumpeter. The object will be a phone. The drawing will be a football."

Again, the predictions were correct.

Sanjay smiled, "No favourite holiday destination? Not so open to subliminal suggestion, then? But our prediction model appears to have understood that."

The audience chatter grew louder, Mo's voice barely audible. "The third volunteer will be Iona Weiss. Her place will be Japan, the place she would most like to go on holiday. The person will be Finnley Barby, her boyfriend; the random object will be a pair of glasses; and the picture will be of a bumblebee."

Sanjay turned to the young woman. "Your name is Iona Weiss?" The girl nodded. "Would you turn around your whiteboard, please?"

The random object and the picture were correct, but the place Iona had written was York and the person was Ruth Weiss.

"Oh! So, we got two wrong! That's interesting. Tell us, what made you choose York and Ruth Weiss?"

"Ruth Weiss is my mother and York's my hometown. My mother phoned just before this lecture, and it made me feel a bit homesick."

"Ah! Something we could not have accounted for when we made our predictions. Although," mused Sanjay, "perhaps if we had included your mother in our prediction model, we could have predicted the effect that she would have on you." He turned back to the audience, "So, we got two wrong, but I think you'll agree we had a pretty good hit rate.

"How did we do it? Well, a condition of attending this lecture was to 'friend' me on a number of social networks. Our behavioural modelling AI then analysed it all: your likes, dislikes, conversations, friends, the people you follow, the products you buy, the pictures and videos you upload, what you read, locations visited…" Sanjay smiled. "We don't need someone following you around to know you. All the information we need is right there, online—your *past history*, supplied *by you*. From this, our AI predicted your behaviour in this lecture."

Sanjay paused, walking thoughtfully across the stage, "I will leave you with a final thought. A great deal of hype surrounded the emergence of generative AI—like ChatGPT, GitHub Copilot, Claude—but I think the more interesting advances are in predictive AI. The applications are endless; from buying behaviour to selecting job candidates to influencing voting, companies are predicting your behaviour everywhere. But, unlike generative AI, these are not applications to help *you*— they are hidden, they are not for your benefit, and they are getting better. In the words of Yuval Noah Harari, the human operating system has been hacked; the question is, how can that knowledge be used to help people rather than exploit them…?"

Riya stopped the video and glanced at her computer clock. Nearly midnight. She only had a few minutes to decide: do nothing and be locked out of her father's world for ever, or accept the Keyholder nomination and get herself involved in something potentially dangerous, in a world she knew nothing about.

The decision was suddenly obvious. She wanted to know more. She simply didn't know enough to turn her back on this now. She put on the glasses.

"Good evening, Riya. Have you come to a decision about your nomination?"

"Yes. I want to accept," Riya held her breath.

"Very well. Congratulations, you are now a Keyholder, custodian of the Anticipation Machine."

What, no fireworks? Riya wasn't sure exactly what she'd expected, but this felt like a big anticlimax.

"That's it, then? I'm one of the Keyholders?"

"Yes."

"What does that mean?"

"You now have access to the Anticipation Machine prediction system."

"Right," said Riya slowly, not really sure what that meant. "And who are you?"

"My name is Art——"

A loud electronic jingle made her jump. Her own phone was ringing. Riya looked at the screen: no caller ID. She swiped to answer, "Hello?"

"You stupid girl! What have you done?" Natalya's words crackled out of the phone like machine-gun fire.

"I just…" Riya's justification to herself suddenly seemed a bit weak. "I had t——"

"It doesn't matter now. They are coming for you!"

ESCAPE

"What? Who?" Riya looked wildly around her bedroom as though expecting men to jump out from under the bed.

"Booker's men, of course. You're the only Keyholder they know where to find. Switch off your light and go to the window." Riya rushed to the curtains, gently parted them, and looked out over the back garden. It was very dark; she could hardly see a thing. "I don't see…wait!" As her eyes became accustomed to the dark, she saw movement. Dark shapes were moving along the edge of the garden, towards the house, "Oh my God, oh my God!"

"You need to get out of there. They will be round the front as well. We only have a few minutes before they break in—"

"Break in! I need to call the police!"

"No. They will be in the house—*and will take you*—before the police can arrive. We need to get you out of there. Do exactly as I tell you."

"OK," Riya let the curtains go and began pacing in circles around the bedroom, pulling at her hair. "What about my aunt? I need to warn her!"

"No. She will be OK. They are after you. Do you have shoes on?"

Riya looked down, "Yes." She hadn't bothered taking them off when she'd come home from April's.

"Coat?"

"Yes," Riya stumbled towards the desk in the darkness, snatched up her coat from the floor, and put it on.

"Money? Do you have cash?"

"I've got my phone and debit card…"

"No, they can be traced, leave them."

"I'll turn my phone off, but I'm not leaving it." She would feel too vulnerable without her own phone—it contained her life.

Natalya hissed angrily, "OK, fine. What about cash?"

Riya snatched up her bag, rummaged for her purse and opened it, "I have a tenner."

"Never mind, we can work around money. Since you accepted your nomination, I assume you have some glasses?"

Riya considered saying, *What glasses?* but they were way past that now. "Yes. I have them on."

"Ask Art to get you out of there without being seen by those men."

"How can *he* help?"

"Just do it, now!"

"Art?"

"Yes, Riya?" The voice, unnervingly like someone standing at your shoulder, talked into her ear.

"Can you get me out of here without being caught by the men outside?"

"Running simulation. One moment, please," there was a pause. "Probability is sixty per cent." Another pause, "I will try."

"Can he do it?" asked Natalya.

"He says probability is sixty per cent," Riya went to the window and peeked through the curtains again. She couldn't see the men—they must be outside the back door, or maybe they were already in the house?

"I was hoping for better odds, but we don't have a choice. Do *exactly* as Art tells you. Call me when you're safe. And don't go to the police—that will play into Booker's hands. And take the phone that came with the glasses. You need it for the glasses to work, and it's a secure phone, so you can use it to make calls without being traced. After I hang up, switch your own phone off—that is *really* important, OK?"

"OK," the phone went dead. "Natalya?" Panic welled in Riya's chest. She suddenly felt very alone. "Art?" Tears stung her eyes.

"I am here, Riya. Please proceed to the spare bedroom at the end of the landing."

A transparent blue arrow appeared in front of her. Riya turned off her own phone, grabbed the secure phone from the desk, shoved them both in her pocket, and headed for the bedroom door. As she did so, the blue arrow moved with her. She was being guided! Opening the door, she slipped out on to the landing and paused, listening. Quiet. Or was it? She thought she heard faint clicking noises coming from downstairs. Was someone trying the front door?

"Please hurry, Riya."

"What about my aunt? I can't just leave her."

"Delay will reduce your chances of evading capture."

But Riya sprinted in the opposite direction to the arrow, along the landing, past the balcony overlooking the entrance hall. Light shone from underneath the bathroom door— Hannah was still in there. She hammered on the door. "Aunty Hannah? Are you there? Open the door."

The bathroom door flew open, revealing a red-faced Hannah in a bathrobe, a towel around her head. "What on earth's the matter?"

"You have to hide. Now! There are men breaking into the house."

"What?" Hannah's face twisted with fear and confusion.

"There's no time to explain. This way," Riya took hold of Hannah's arm and dragged her from the bathroom and along the landing.

"We need to call the police!" Hannah's voice shrilled hysterically.

"Riya. Please turn around and follow my directions."

Riya ignored the voice in her ear. At the end of the hall, she yanked open a small plain door revealing a narrow wooden staircase leading up to the attic. "No police, not till I've gone. Hide up there. The men won't search up there."

"Why not?"

"Because they are after *me*."

"But—" Hannah's eyes looked wild.

"I'll be OK. Now, go!" Riya shoved Hannah through the door, closed it, and sprinted back towards her own room. She stopped at the balcony overlooking the entrance hall, gripping the balustrade.

"Why have you stopped, Riya?" asked Art calmly. Riya ignored him.

Boom! The front door shook. *Boom!* This time, it was accompanied by a horrible splintering sound. *Boom!* The door flew open and three men dressed in black with balaclavas swarmed into the hall, their eyes roaming the room. The first man spotted Riya and pointed. "Upstairs!"

Riya raced along the path shown by Art's blue arrow, to the spare room, helpfully marked with a blue halo. Slipping inside, she closed the door.

"Open the window to your left. Quietly, please."

Riya had a horrible feeling she knew what was coming. "I hope you're not expecting me"—she waved frantically at the sash window—"to climb out there!"

"I believe that is the correct strategy to avoid capture. Your pursuers will not expect it and so will not have posted guards below."

Riya slid the window upwards and poked her head outside. It was an old house with high ceilings, so the upstairs was a very long way from the ground. "How am I going to get down?"

"There is a cast-iron drainpipe to your left. You should be able to reach it."

About an arm's length from the window, she could make out the black tube, "You're kidding!"

"Please hurry."

Taking a shaky breath and trying not to look down, Riya climbed out on to the wide stone windowsill.

"Close the window. Quickly, please."

Clinging to the wall and window frame like a limpet, Riya slid the window shut, her heart hammering so hard she was afraid it would bounce her off the ledge.

"Please reach out and take hold of the drainpipe."

"I can't! If I move, I'll fall."

"You must do it now."

Riya crept her hand across the rough wall towards the drainpipe and…got it! Her hand slipped around the cold iron tube. Now she needed a foothold. She felt giddy as her gaze drifted to the ground below. There! A join in the pipe, bracket lugs where the pipe attached to the wall, about the right height. She stuck out a foot, resting her toe on the ridge where the pipe joined—it was tiny, but enough.

With a grunt, she pulled herself across to the pipe. Hugging it, with white knuckles, she prayed it would take her weight.

She heard a bang from inside the room. Someone flinging the door open.

"Please stay still while they search the room."

A shadow moved across the window she'd just climbed out of. Riya held her breath, hoping they wouldn't think to look out. The shadow moved on and she heard wardrobes and cupboards—obvious hiding places—being opened and closed. Her legs began to shake with the effort of gripping the tiny pipe ledge with her toes—she couldn't stay like this for long.

The noise inside subsided.

"Please descend the pipe."

Hugging the drainpipe like a fireman's pole, Riya half climbed, half slithered down.

"Please hurry; they will widen their search when they find you are not in the house."

"I'm going as fast as I can!" hissed Riya through gritted teeth. She reached the ground, shaking and breathing hard.

"Well done, Riya—you're doing great," said the emotionless voice in her ear. "Please proceed to the perimeter hedge." The blue arrow in her vision turned her round and pointed to the hedge between her garden and the neighbour's. "Then climb the fence into next door's garden, please."

Riya sprinted to the hedge, "Why am I going through the neighbour's garden? If I go out to the road, I can run off in any direction."

"Because that is what your pursuers will expect you to do. They will be watching the roads front and back of the house."

Riya pushed into the bushes, climbed over a wooden fence, and dropped down into next door's garden.

"Proceed through the next three gardens. Keep to the borders, close to the trees and bushes, to avoid drone surveillance."

"Drone surveillance! Who *are* these guys?"

Riya hadn't expected an answer, but Art took her literally. "Private security forces employed by Jim Booker. Please proceed through the next three gardens."

Riya ran round the perimeter of the first garden, hugging the trees and bushes. The lights were on in the house and she could see the middle-aged couple who lived there watching TV in the living room. Vaulting into the next garden, she heard raised voices from the direction of her own house and hoped Art was right about them not coming this way. Then, into the next garden. The house was dark, toys lying strewn across the lawn. She stepped over a kid's push-along tractor lying on its side. A dog barked inside the house as she hurried past a trampoline. The next house was also dark. She vaulted into the fourth garden. Light shone out through bifold doors framing a large open kitchen that ran the width of the house like a theatre stage. A suited professional-looking woman sat alone at the kitchen table, hunched over a laptop, a glass of red wine beside her.

"Stop here," said Art.

"What now?" Riya glanced nervously back the way she'd come, half expecting to see the dark shapes of her pursuers leaping into the garden behind her. But there was no one.

"You will spend the night in Mrs. Jones' spare room."

"You mean in *her* house?" said Riya, pointing to the woman in the kitchen.

"That is correct."

"What, she's just going to put me up for the night, like a bed and breakfast, and ask how I like my eggs in the morning?"

"No." Art's voice was calm, showing no recognition of Riya's sarcasm. "In one minute, the doorbell will ring. While she is answering it, you will enter through the patio doors. I will guide you through the house."

"No way! She'll hear me. Anyway, how do you know the patio doors are unlocked?"

"She will be preoccupied with the front door and is unlikely to hear you. As for the door, there is a high probability that she is the kind of person who leaves the back door unlocked most of the time."

"When I'm about to break into someone's house, I would rather hear things like, 'I am totally positively certain she will not hear you, Riya'…not words like *unlikely* and *probability*."

"Nothing is certain, Riya, but I profiled everyone in the street looking for the most effective hiding place. I found this to be the most suitable: Mrs. Jones does not have children, her husband is away on business, and she will be leaving for work early tomorrow for a meeting."

"When did you figure all that out?"

"Approximately thirty seconds after you asked me to get you away from the men pursuing you. May I suggest that you refrain from asking questions until we have reached Mrs. Jones' spare bedroom?"

"But—"

"Stand by. The doorbell will ring in five, four, three, two, *one*—"

Riya didn't hear it, but Mrs. Jones' head jerked up, she got up from her chair, and marched out of the kitchen.

"Please enter the kitchen through the patio door on the far right."

The blue directional arrow appeared in her vision again, pointing towards the patio. Riya sprinted across the garden, hurdled the low patio wall, and arrived at the door. She hesitated. Surely Mrs. Jones would hear the door open?

Art seemed to read her thoughts, "She will not hear you. Please hurry."

Gently, she eased the door open and was about to step into the kitchen when Art's voice stopped her. "Please remove your shoes before entering. Muddy footprints would alert Mrs. Jones to an intruder." Her heart pounding, Riya slipped off her shoes and hopped into the kitchen, quietly closing the door.

The sound of the front door being unlocked and opened drifted through to the kitchen. "Hello?" A woman's voice.

There were three doors along the back wall of the kitchen, and the blue directional arrow in Riya's vision pointed to the right-hand door, slightly ajar, surrounded by a blue halo.

"Good evening, madam," a man's voice.

Carrying her shoes, Riya slipped through the door and pushed it to. She found herself standing on soft, deep-pile cream carpet in a darkened living room.

"Sorry to disturb you, madam. I'm Detective Reynolds—my identification."

The police! Thank God! She started forwards.

Art's voice purred in her ear. "He is not a policeman. He is one of the men pursuing you."

Riya's heart sank as she shrank back into the shadows.

The imposter continued, "Just to let you know, we are attempting to apprehend a young woman for questioning, and we believe she's hiding in the area, so you may see our officers searching the local gardens over the next few hours."

"Really?" The woman sounded alarmed.

"Don't worry, madam, she's not dangerous, but we are advising residents to keep their doors and windows locked tonight as a precaution. Is there any possibility she could have entered your house without you knowing?"

"No, I don't think so. The front door was locked, and the only other way in is through the kitchen, and I've been in there all evening."

"Very good, madam. If you do happen to see a young woman of about seventeen, acting suspiciously, please call this number. And remember, do make sure you lock up securely."

"I will. Thank you."

The door clunked shut. Heels clacked on a wooden hall floor as Mrs. Jones returned to the kitchen.

Art said, "Please leave the living room by the far door. Proceed across the hall and up the stairs." The blue arrow pointed to the door at the far end of the living room, now surrounded by a blue halo.

As Riya crept the length of the living room, she could hear Mrs. Jones in the kitchen, turning the lock in the patio door and then drawing the blinds over the windows. Riya sprinted across the hall and up the stairs. Following the glowing blue arrow left at the top of the stairs, she tiptoed along the landing, past photos of a younger-looking Mrs. Jones sprawled on a beach, sitting on a horse in a field, cutting a wedding cake…

The arrow pointed to a door at the end of the landing; again, a flashing blue halo surrounded the door frame. Riya turned the door handle. It swung open, thankfully on silent hinges. She stepped into the dark room, closed the door carefully behind her, and sighed heavily. The curtains were open, spilling moonlight across a spacious bedroom. Mirrored white wardrobes ran along one wall opposite a double bed covered in decorative cushions.

"The guest bedroom," said Art. "Provided you are quiet, you will be safe here until the morning. Mrs. Jones has no reason to come in here."

Riya crept over to the window and peered out. This house was closer to the road than hers, providing a good view of the street. A van was parked at the kerb. She watched as it was joined by a second. Dark figures swept silently up the street, darting in and out of people's gardens. If she'd still been out there, she'd have been caught, no question. This Jim Booker must be pretty intent on finding her. What would he do if he did? Riya shivered.

She sank to the floor, huddling into the gap between the bed and the window, her back to the warm radiator. As the heat soaked through her, she felt the tension in her muscles drain away, and realized she was exhausted. A thought occurred to her. "Art, I have a question," she whispered.

"Yes, Riya?"

"Who exactly are you?"

"I am the voice of your father's Anticipation Machine, an artificial-intelligence system created by your father to model human behaviour."

She hadn't quite believed it was real until now.

Before she could ask more questions, red and blue flashing lights lit up the bedroom ceiling. Riya jumped up in time to see two police cars tearing down the street towards her house, followed a moment later by an ambulance.

Art seemed to read her thoughts. "The police are responding to an emergency call from your house. Jim Booker's men must have left, allowing your aunt to call the police."

Riya sank back to the floor, hugging her knees. *Please don't let Hannah be hurt, not because of me.*

"Maybe I could go back home, now they've left?" she said, thinking aloud.

"I predict they are still looking for you."

So, not going home, then.

"This is crazy, I'm gonna call the police." She pulled out the ruggedised phone and her finger hovered over the screen. "Art, if I go to the police, tell them Booker is after me, will they believe me?"

Pause. "No. They will assume the attack was a burglary and that you simply fled the house in fear. They would find no plausible connection to Jim Booker."

"Are the police looking for me?"

"Yes. Your aunt has reported you missing."

"Great. So now I'm on the run from the police as well as Jim Booker's thugs."

Pause. "Do you have a question for me, Riya?"

Riya sighed. It seemed Art was not programmed to respond to sulky statements. "No."

"Then I will power off your glasses to conserve the battery. Goodnight, Riya. We will speak again in the morning." The various icons displayed in her vision disappeared. The glasses were off.

"Wait!" whispered Riya. "Art? Art?" Artificial intelligence or not, Art's calm competence was the only comfort she had.

Riya hugged her knees.

She was alone.

ON THE RUN

A door slam shook the house. Riya jolted awake, blinking, wondering where she was and why she was on the floor, using her coat for a pillow. Then it came flooding back: the break-in, her midnight escape through the shrubbery.

She leaped to her feet, painfully stiff from a night on the floor, and peeked over the windowsill. Shielding her eyes from bright autumn sun, she saw a suited and booted Mrs. Jones stride across to a white Audi SUV parked on the drive. As the car pulled into the road, Riya noted the vans from last night had gone. She stayed at the window, watching for signs of last night's pursuers; several dog walkers trudged past, a couple of joggers, and a commuter making for the bus stop. No one suspicious.

Riya sank back to the floor and sighed heavily. She was alone in the house. She could relax, at least for the moment. Reaching for the glasses on the bedside table, she put them on and pressed the button on the end of the arm. After a brief hum, the green online icon appeared in her vision.

"Good morning, Riya. Did you sleep well?" Art, polite and emotionless. Again, unnervingly realistic and close, like someone standing beside her.

"Not really."

"I'm sorry to hear that. Are you ready to leave the house?"

"Hang on! I've only just woken up." Riya looked down at her dirty hands; then she caught sight of her reflection in the mirrored wardrobe doors. Her face was smeared with mud, she had two black eyes where her mascara had run, and her hair…My God! The usual curtains of glossy black had been replaced by a tangled bird's nest—she looked like she'd been dragged through a hedge. But then, that's pretty much what had happened. She teased her hair with her fingers, pulling loose a twig, "I need to clean up and go to the loo."

Pause. "Of course. Restoring your customary bland appearance will attract less attention and lower the probability of detection."

"What do you mean, 'bland appearance'?" said Riya indignantly.

"Your tone indicates I have caused offence. My apologies, I simply meant that—"

"Whatever, don't make it worse," snapped Riya. "Where's the bathroom?"

"I recommend using the en-suite bathroom in Mrs. Jones' bedroom. Her bedroom is along the landing, first door on the right after the stairs."

The blue arrow appeared in her vision, directing her towards the bedroom door. "I think I can find my way along the landing without directions, thanks." She was still miffed at Art's remark—she was no trendsetter, but *bland*?

The shower was one of those big walk-in jobs. Droplets of water still ran down the glass from Mrs. Jones' morning shower. Riya undressed and stepped in, feeling her body relax as the hot water flowed over it, pummelling her skin. She dried herself on one of the luxurious towels, sponged the mud from her clothes, got dressed—except for her shoes—and looked in the mirror. Bland old me, she thought.

Refreshed, she put on the glasses.

"Hello, Riya. Are you ready to leave, now?"

Her stomach flipped. The thought of leaving to face whatever lurked out there scared her.

"Natalya Romanov requesting voice connection." A small red icon flashed in the corner of her vision, tagged with Natalya's name. Oops! She'd completely forgotten about contacting Natalya to let her know she was safe.

"OK," said Riya tentatively.

The head icon turned green. "Riya? Are you safe?" Natalya's voice—sharp and tight—seemed to come from all around her.

"Yeah. I'm in a neighbour's house."

"Why didn't you call?"

"Sorry, I—"

"I tried you multiple times, but your glasses were off." Natalya's accent seemed to get thicker with frustration.

"Well, I didn't sleep in them, and I went for a shower this morning—"

"Never mind," snapped Natalya. "A neighbour's house? You didn't get very far. I hoped you would be halfway here, by now."

"Sorry." Why was she apologizing? She had no control over any of this. "We're about to set off."

"OK, good. Can you get Art to give me a visual connection?"

"How…?"

"Ask him."

"Art? Could you…erm…give Natalya a visual connection?"

"Doing so now." Pause. "You are now sharing your view with Natalya Romanov."

"That's better. Now I can see where you are through the glasses."

"So, where exactly am I going?" Riya was getting a little irritated at being ordered around.

"Art will guide you here, but stay alert—Booker's men are still looking for you."

"OK, but you still haven't said where 'here' is…"

"Sorry, I have to go now. I will drop in later to see where you are."

"Natalya?" No answer. The little head icon turned red.

"Natalya has gone offline," said Art.

"Argh! That woman!" Riya stamped her foot. That was just typical of Dad's techy colleagues: socially challenged. "What's the plan? How do I get to Natalya's place without getting caught by Jim Booker, the police, or anyone else out there looking for me?"

"You will catch a train from Cambridge to King's Cross, London. From there, you will walk to Natalya's safe house."

"London! Couldn't she find anywhere, like, local?" Riya sighed and made for the door. "All right. Let's go."

"The front door will be locked. Please proceed to the dining room."

"Where is the—?" The blue arrow appeared in her vision, pointing down the hall. "Thanks." She followed Art's directions, still carrying her muddy shoes. Turning through a blue haloed door, she found herself in a formal dining room.

"Please use the windows." At the far end of the room, sunlight flooded through bay windows looking out over the drive and front garden.

"You mean, climb out another window?"

"Yes. They are probably locked."

Riya tried the handle of one of the side windows. "Yep."

"Mrs. Jones is very organized. The key will be in the top right-hand drawer of the sideboard."

Riya walked over to the sideboard and slid open the drawer. Place mats, coasters, napkins…and, at the front of the drawer, a small white porcelain pot with two identical keys. Riya took one, returned to the window and tried it in the lock. It turned. "How did you know?"

"Psychological analysis, deductions drawn from the physical layout of the room, cognitive biases." Art paused. "It's complicated."

"Oh."

"May I make a suggestion? My programming is extremely complex, encompassing many disciplines, and involves millions of calculations. I don't believe it is an efficient use of time for me to explain my computations. I suggest you simply accept my deductions; it will allow us to proceed more swiftly." He sounded irritated.

"That told me, didn't it?" murmured Riya, feeling thick. This was how her father used to make her feel—*you're not clever enough to understand, Riya*. Perhaps Art had inherited some of her father's personality traits?

"Are you ready to proceed?"

"S'pose so."

"Please be aware that we must be careful once we leave the house. To avoid detection, please follow my instructions exactly, without question."

"All right, I get it already! Do as I'm told and don't ask."

"Please proceed."

Pushing the window wide, Riya clambered on to the sill, threw her shoes out, then squeezed through the opening and jumped to the ground, landing on the wet grass. Retrieving her shoes, she pulled them on over wet socks. Yuck, soggy feet for the next few hours.

She breathed in the crisp air, listening to early-morning suburbia: the hiss of cars on the road, an aircraft rumbling overhead, the distant squeal of lorry brakes.

"Push the window closed," said Art. "It will look shut from the outside and will not be detected for some days."

Riya pushed it closed. "Where now?" She hurried down the drive towards the road.

"Take the bus to Cambridge train station."

Riya shuffled nervously from one foot to the other at the bus stop. Her gaze constantly swept the street, half expecting the thugs from last night to come barrelling round the corner at any second.

As she stepped on to the bus, Art said, "Please look around the bus so I may scan the passenger's faces." Riya felt self-conscious in her weird geeky glasses, but no one took the slightest notice as she scanned the bored commuter faces staring at their phones or out of the window. After a few seconds, Art decreed, "Safe. Please proceed."

Without thinking, Riya held her college commuter pass to the scanner, then a felt jolt of fear. Would this be traceable? It was too late to do anything about it now, but she would need to be more careful. Wandering up the bus, she took a seat next to a woman engrossed in her phone.

After what seemed like a hundred stops, the bus was nearing the station when Art said, "Please get off at this next stop."

"But the station is the one after."

The woman next to her looked up, startled.

Riya smiled apologetically, "Sorry—talking to myself."

The woman smiled doubtfully and went back to her phone.

"Yes, Riya, but they will be watching the bus stop at the station, so you should get off here. Then proceed to the station."

As Riya hopped off the bus, the now-familiar blue line appeared on the ground in front of her, as if someone had laid neon lights in the pavement. "I know the way to the station—I do *live* here, you know."

"I understand, but I need you to follow a precise path in this instance." The line kept her close to the buildings, ending in a blue circle the size of a manhole cover. "Please stop on the blue circle."

Art had brought her to a halt on the corner, just before the street opened out into the large square in front of the station. It was the height of commuter rush hour and the square was filled with people, cars, and taxis.

"Please wait a moment."

The little red head icon in the corner of her vision turned green again. "Hello, Riya," Natalya was back. "I have booked you on the nine fifteen train to King's Cross. I forwarded an e-ticket to your phone. Just scan it at the barrier."

Riya pulled the ruggedised phone from her pocket. Sure enough, on the front screen a glowing message appeared: *Train Ticket*. She swiped her finger. There was the ticket QR code. She looked up.

Green halos appeared around a few of the people scattered near the edges of the square—these people were not moving. Every time one of these people was blocked from view, their halo turned red. The blue neon line appeared again, but very faint this time. From her feet, it zigzagged its way across the crowded square to the station entrance, constantly dancing around as people moved.

Her head swirled, "Hang on, can someone explain what the hell is going on? All these lights…?"

Natalya sighed impatiently, "We need to get you into the station without being caught by Booker's men or the police. The green halos you can see are either Jim Booker's men or the police. You need to cross the open space between here and the station without being seen by any of them. Art is calculating a path that will guide you."

"That's impossible! One of them is bound to spot me——"

"Not if we keep you hidden," Natalya sounded enthusiastic. "This will be a good test of Art's near-term prediction of crowd behaviour."

"A *test*! You're unbelievable! I *really* don't think this is the time for, like, an experiment."

"Riya," Art's calm voice purred reassuringly in her ear, "I will predict a path where you will be hidden by the movements of others. However, you will need to follow precisely the path I give you. When the blue line turns green, I will tell you to go. Follow the line at precisely the speed specified. Too fast or slow and the line will turn red. Keep it green. Simulating path, please stand by."

"This is not going to work," mumbled Riya, but she waited, breathing heavily. Butterflies fluttered madly around her stomach and her legs felt weak, like she'd been asked to walk a tightrope without a safety net.

Then the dancing blue line solidified to green and became fixed, "Go."

Riya stepped forward, following the snaking green line across the square. She glanced up, noting all halos were red—hidden from view behind people, cars, and buses. This was crazy. As soon as someone moved, she would be seen.

The line turned red as did her speed indicator. The edge of one of the hostile halos turned green as the person became visible around a man in an overcoat who was walking parallel to Riya.

"Slow down, please," said Art.

Riya adjusted her speed, and the line returned to green, the halo red.

She kept walking, glancing now and then at the red halos. It was incredible the way they stayed hidden as she crossed the open space…It was like a beautifully choreographed dance;

just as it looked like she would become visible as one obstacle moved, another would slide smoothly into place, continuing to block her from view.

Nearly there, a few more steps. Sandwiched between two rushing commuters, the red halo next to the door never saw her as she slipped inside the station.

Incredibly, she'd made it. The ticket barrier lay in front of her. She reached out, holding her phone ready…

A vice gripped her arm, bringing her to a halt with a grunt. Spinning around, she found herself looking into a gaunt, nut-brown, lined face. He was dressed in a smart grey suit and overcoat, but his face had the leathery skin and narrow eyes of someone who had spent much of their life outdoors, squinting against the sun. He smiled thinly at her with cold blue eyes.

Natalya swore loudly in her ear.

"Please come with me, Miss Sudame," Riya could hear the victory in his dry raspy voice.

She looked around for help, and her eyes settled on a couple of policemen to the side of the barrier, talking to an elderly couple with suitcases who were looking bewildered by the rush-hour stampede.

Riya turned to the man and snarled, "Get your hands off me or I'll get us both caught."

He followed her gaze towards the policemen and his smile faltered. As his grip loosened, Riya took her chance. Tearing her arm free, she barrelled into a tall thin businessman. He stopped abruptly, blinking at her with surprise through small round glasses.

Riya flashed her brightest smile. "Oh, I'm really sorry. Wasn't watching where I was going. I'm trying to figure out how I use this silly ticket thing on my phone."

It worked. The businessman's face softened. "Oh, it's quite simple, my dear. Just hold it against the scanner. Here, I'll show you." As the businessman led Riya to the barrier, the gaunt-faced man fell back, not daring to drag her away under the eyes of a witness and with police close by.

Then she was gone, following the glowing green line around the corner.

Natalya screamed in her ear, "What the fuck, Art! Who was *that*?"

"I'm afraid I do not know." His voice, cool as ever, showed no sign of panic. "I have an image of his face; I will attempt to locate his identity."

Riya stopped walking and leaned against the wall, bent over, breathing hard. She felt sick.

"Riya?" Natalya sounded worried. "Are you OK?"

"Not really." She was scared, angry, stressed, and sick of being ordered around. She straightened up and took a deep breath, "Just get me on that train."

Riya followed Art's green line over a bridge and down to the platform as the train rumbled into the station. Stepping aboard, she realized she had no idea what seat she was in. She took out her phone and looked at the ticket—first class, seat 12b. She walked through the train, found her seat, flopped down, and closed her eyes. Almost immediately, she sat up again, staring out of the window. "Art, could that man have followed me on to the platform? On to the train?"

"It is possible."

Her heart jumped.

"But not probable."

A whistle sounded. The platform began to slide past the window. As the train gathered speed, she saw the tall rangy man with the sun-weathered face run on to the platform. He must have bought a ticket and followed her through the barriers. He watched the train pull out, tugged a phone from his pocket and held it to his ear.

"Did you see him?" said Riya.

"Yes. I believe he guessed which train you would be taking, but he did not see you, so he cannot be sure. However, I predict he will contact people in London."

"Great! We'll have a reception party waiting for us?" Too loud. A woman in the seat across the aisle gave her an irritated glance. Riya turned away.

"I will work on avoidance simulations during your journey."

"What does that mean?" muttered Riya.

"By changing the parameters in my simulations—"

"Yeah, all right, I get it. You'll try not to get us caught." She didn't feel like listening to another of Art's explanations.

"You may be interested to know I have determined who that man was."

"OK?" Riya sat up; she *was* interested in this.

"Raphael Collomb." A picture flashed up in Riya's vision of a much younger version of the man who had grabbed her, walking alongside another man in an Arab dishdash. "Originally recruited to French counterterrorism, he then worked in Middle Eastern private security for some years. He now appears to work for Whydah Security out of the Cayman Islands. Indigo have made several payments to them for unspecified security services." Art paused. "He also appears to be wanted by Interpol—but there is very little information about him, and his connection to Jim Booker is well hidden, which makes him difficult to predict. That explains why his presence at the station was overlooked in the prediction. However, his Special Forces background should allow the generation of an approximate psychological profile that can be used in simulations."

"Hmm." The terms "should" and "approximate" didn't sound inspiring to Riya.

"If I can be of no further assistance, may I suggest you turn off the glasses until we arrive in London, to conserve the battery?"

Riya felt a stab of guilt, "Actually, I have one question. Do you have any information about my aunt? Is she all right?" With all that had happened, she hadn't had time to consider how the break-in and her disappearance might have affected Hannah.

"Your aunt is safe at home."

"Don't suppose you can bring up her Indigo social page?" Hannah was bound to have posted about last night.

Hannah's social page appeared hanging in thin air in front of her, about the size of an A4 sheet of paper held at arm's length. The latest post showed a selfie of Hannah standing next to the ruined front door of Riya's house. She looked pale and forlorn, dark rings beneath red-rimmed eyes, suggesting she hadn't slept. Riya read the text posted with the picture:

> I   OMG! Still in shock that this has happened.
>   No word on Riya yet. Police have no leads.
>   So worried about her. Please, please let her
>   be all right!

Riya's hands flew to her face, "Oh, Aunty Hannah!" Several people in the carriage turned to look at her, but she didn't care. She felt awful.

This was all her fault. If only she hadn't been so stupid and pig-headed. Natalya had warned her to stay out of this, but, no, she had to go and stick her big nose into it. Suddenly, all she wanted to do was go home—to her A levels, to April—live a normal teenage life…

"Riya? Are you all right?" Art's voice was annoyingly calm and polite, as always.

Riya had no intention of explaining herself to a piece of software. Reaching behind her ear, she clicked off the glasses, turned to the window, and cried softly into her coat sleeve.

Eventually, the tears stopped. She knew she couldn't just hit *undo* and go home, but one thing she could do was talk to Hannah, tell her not to worry. She reached into her pocket and pulled out her phone. Her own phone. The one Natalya had told her not to turn on. Screw it. So what if they traced her? That man on the platform had known where she was going, anyway. She held down the power button.

IN HIDING

The screen lit up, then began pinging with texts from Hannah, April, and other friends…

> **April:** Where are u?

> **Hannah:** R u safe?

> **Hannah:** R u hurt?

Riya choked back the tears.

She sniffed, pushed the hair back from her face, wiped her eyes again, and was about to hit Hannah's speed-dial number when she stopped. Did she really want to have to explain to a hysterical Hannah what this was all about and that she wouldn't be coming home? No, she was too exhausted to have that conversation right now. She would send a text instead. Nothing too detailed, in case someone intercepted it, just enough that she would know Riya was OK, and she would copy April in as well…

> **Riya:** I'm safe. Not hurt. Don't worry. Need to leave for a few days. Will be in touch soon. R xxx

She hit *send* and sat back, resting her head against the seat. It wouldn't explain anything, and they would still be worried, but she felt better for at least trying to ease their concern. She shoved the phone back in her pocket and stared out of the window. Letting her eyelids droop, she was half asleep when the loudspeaker above her head crackled into life: "Now approaching King's Cross station. This service will terminate here. Please ensure you have all your luggage when leaving the train. Thank you."

An icy hand closed around her heart. She needed Art. She scrabbled behind her ear and clicked the glasses on.

"Welcome back, Riya." Was that sarcasm?

The little head icon was green. Natalya. "Where have you been?"

Riya bristled, "Hang on, I just needed—"

"Never mind. You are pulling into King's Cross, yes?"

Riya gritted her teeth, "Yes."

"OK, we don't have much time. Art predicts three of Booker's men will be at the barriers. Art will find a blind spot so you can slip through. There will be police, but they will not be looking for you here…"

Riya's phone rang. She pulled it out of her pocket. April.

Natalya's voice screeched in her ear. "What the hell is that? I told you to turn it off! Turn it off! Now!"

"But—"

"Now!"

Riya looked at the screen glowing with April's name. She closed her eyes, sighed, and held down the power button. Gone.

"Eesh! I have known five-year-olds with more sense." Natalya recomposed herself, "Now, we need you to move down the train and exit from a more crowded carriage. Do you think you can do that without screwing up?"

"Yeah, maybe, if you think you can stop being such a bitch? I'm not used to all this secret-squirrel stuff. This is your world—"

"Art, can you take it from here?" Natalya cut her off again. "Get her out of the station without being spotted?"

People getting their bags down from the luggage racks flicked disapproving glances in Riya's direction. She didn't care, she was sick of this whole situation.

"Yes, Natalya. Hello, Riya. Please follow my directions."

The blue line appeared in Riya's vision. She shook her head, hissing out a long sigh.

"Riya?"

"Yes," Riya got up and pushed her way angrily down the carriage.

The blue line led her through the next two carriages and brought her to a halt queuing for the door as the train pulled into the station. People rocked on their heels as the train jolted to a stop. Doors clunked open. People filed out.

"Please wait for my signal before disembarking."

Riya stood to the side of the doors, hyperventilating, nerves jangling, like before running a race.

"Go."

She stepped down from the train, the air fresh and full of noise after the stuffy quiet of the train carriage.

"Wait. Analysing path."

Riya stood still, watching the faint zigzag blue line flickering as people moved along the platform. In the distance, three tiny red silhouettes appeared—Booker's men at the barriers.

Two tall men passed on either side of her. The blue line stopped jumping around and solidified to a bright green.

"Go."

Riya set off down the platform, falling in behind the tall men, carefully following the green line, watching the speed indicator in her vision. It was difficult to both follow the line and watch her speed at the same time—it took concentration. This meant she wasn't really watching the people around her and had to trust Art to manoeuvre her through the crowd without collision. She approached the barriers, red halos looming large. Two at the main entrance, one at the barriers leading through to the food court.

Someone in front of her stopped to answer his phone and Riya barrelled into him but didn't dare stop or turn to apologize.

"Art!" growled Natalya. "We could do without the screw-ups, right now."

"Apologies. Correcting path."

Riya held her breath as the halos turned green, exposing her to their line of sight. This close to the barriers, if they glanced in her direction, they would spot her. The green line jumped in front of her. She turned to follow the corrected path. The halos returned to red: she was hidden again. She passed the men watching the ticket barriers at the main entrance and headed for those leading to the food court. With clenched teeth, she held her phone out to the scanner, vaguely aware of the tall men passing through on either side, keeping her hidden. Open. Through.

The red halos were now outside her field of vision. She didn't dare turn to look.

"Art? Did it work? Are they following me?" The green line led her out of the station into the sunshine and the hiss and squeal of traffic.

A square opened in Riya's vision: a map. There were three red tags, presumably Booker's men, and one green, presumably Riya. The green was moving, the three red remained stationary.

"They are not following," said Art.

"Where to now?"

"You come to me," said Natalya.

"OK, so where are you?" said Riya curtly.

"Art knows. I see you in forty minutes." The head icon turned red.

"Please continue following my directions, Riya."

Riya sighed angrily, "Is she always this obnoxious?"

"I'm afraid I do not have a subjective opinion of Natalya's personality."

"Well, I do. You're more polite than Natalya, and you're a machine!" In all the excitement of escaping, she hadn't really thought about it, but Art did "feel" spookily human to talk to. "How come you're so, like…human?"

"Your father created a personality as my primary interface. He felt it would allow for easy interaction, enabling me to interpret complex and ambiguous requests. Since my main function is to analyse human behaviour and model people's personalities, it was relatively straightforward to generate a personality for my user interface."

"At least he created you with manners," Riya glanced back towards the station. "How do you know we're not being followed?"

"It is possible, but not probable. All known operatives are not within visual range."

"You mean, like that Raphael bloke?"

"As I said, it is possible, but not probable."

"I guess that's as good as it gets. Where are we going, anyway?" Riya didn't know London at all, but, all the same, it would be nice to know.

"Flat 3, 61 Fortress Road, Kentish Town."

As she walked past rows of swanky town houses, Riya was hopeful that Natalya's "safe house" would actually be a nice place to stay. Those hopes dwindled as the buildings became less grand, more run-down. Smart town houses gave way to laundrettes, takeaways, and grimy-looking betting shops. Riya began to look around nervously, feeling uncomfortable.

Her heart sank as the green line stopped in front of a shabby shop with dull blue paint peeling from the frontage, windows so dirty they were opaque. It looked disused. Art's blue halo surrounded a door to the left of the shopfront, grazed and dented and painted in the same peeling blue paint. Written in faded pencil beside the buttons on a filthy intercom panel: *Flat 1*, *Flat 2*, *Flat 3*. A small blue arrow appeared in Riya's vision, pointing to *Flat 3*. As she reached out to press the button, the door opened.

"Hello," Natalya stood in the doorway, looking vaguely bored. Her glasses hung from the neck of a black T-shirt emblazoned with *Gods of Napalm, Scorched Earth Tour* and a lurid picture of a godlike figure standing in the middle of a burning forest. "Glad you could make it. Come in."

Riya stepped into the grubby hallway and grimaced, "Nice place." The dirty whitewashed walls looked like they hadn't seen a coat of paint in years.

"It has one attractive quality...landlord only asks one question: 'Where is rent?' No names, no paperwork, nothing to trace."

They clumped up to the third floor, hollow footsteps echoing in the cheerless stairwell. A single door stood in the middle of the landing, the outline of a number three in the paint where the number had long since fallen off.

Natalya turned the door handle and looked at Riya, "It sticks." She gave the base of the door a sharp kick in a well-worn groove. It flew open, revealing a living room with faded yellow walls and a worn brown carpet every bit as depressing as the stairwell. A TV on the wall blared out a rerun of an old nineties soap, while an armchair and a stained brown sofa slouched tiredly against the wall under the window.

Sprawled on the sofa, feet resting on a battered coffee table, a boy was busily devouring a huge bag of crisps labelled *Made for Sharing*, although he didn't appear to be sharing with anyone. Against the dismal backdrop of the flat, he looked ridiculously colourful, dressed in red trousers and a bright yellow rugby shirt. One side of his collar was tucked in, which bugged Riya intensely and she had an immediate urge to straighten it. His unruly straw-coloured hair stuck out at odd angles, while small sharp eyes glittered with amusement in his round pudgy face.

Muting the TV, he shambled to his feet, brushing crisp shrapnel from his top, and his large lips pulled into a wide smile. She knew him: Victor's son, Ivan. He must be eighteen now, but he looked older.

Natalya closed the front door. "Ah, yes, this is the other imbecile who decided to become a Keyholder without the slightest idea what they were getting into." Muttering something in Russian, she disappeared through an archway to what looked like the kitchen, leaving Riya alone with the boy.

After wiping his hand on his trousers, Ivan held it out for Riya to shake. "Hello, Riya. Nice to see you again." His smile softened, "I am sorry about your father. I admired him greatly;

he was a true gentleman." His Russian accent was barely noticeable these days, hidden under years of English public-school "received pronunciation".

"Hello, Ivan," she ignored his greasy hand and he took it back. "Sorry about your father, too."

He nodded, "Thank you." There was an awkward moment as they looked at each other.

Riya couldn't think of anything to say, except, "Your collar's turned in…" She pointed to her own collar. She regretted it straight away—it sounded crass and tactless after discussing their dead fathers.

"Thanks. Always the eye for detail, like your father," he smiled genially and attempted to straighten his collar. It didn't look much better, but she resisted the urge to sort it out.

Sanjay and Victor were at Cambridge together and had been friends long before they were business partners, so, as kids, Riya and Ivan had spent time together. She remembered him as a cocky spoiled brat, always seeking attention and causing trouble; at her eighth birthday party, he'd made it his mission to annoy her friends, finally getting himself removed after throwing birthday cake at Rowena Williams. Shortly after that, Victor had taken the family back to Russia, where they'd grown rich on lucrative government software contracts. After divorcing his wife, Victor returned to England a few years later, providing the start-up capital to help Riya's father set up Predictive Technologies. She'd only seen Ivan a handful of times since then, as he now lived with his mother, who spent her time—and Victor's money—flitting between the social circles of Russia and London, where Ivan went to school. Now, with the bulky six-foot frame of a rugby player gone to seed, Ivan seemed to have matured nicely from a spoiled brat into a spoiled slob. The last she'd heard, he'd been heavily into the yacht-racing circuit—a rich boy's sport, if ever she'd heard of one.

"So…" Ivan held his hands up with a flourish, "Welcome to Natalya's crack den."

Despite herself, Riya sniggered, "How long have you been here?"

"Since last night. That's already one night too long."

Natalya's voice drifted through the archway from the kitchen. "You are welcome to return to your five-star palace and wait for Jim Booker to send his chauffeur for you."

Ivan's eyes twinkled, "Ah, yes. The mysterious Mr. Booker, the reason we are all playing hide and seek." He grinned, "How about a tour? I warn you, it may take some time." He shifted to the middle of the living room and swung his arms around like an airline steward pointing out emergency exits, "Kitchen. Bathroom. Natalya's room. Your room."

"So, where do *you* sleep?" Noting there were no more doors, a horrible thought occurred to Riya: would she have to bunk in with him, and no doubt put up with snoring all night?

Natalya's voice chimed from the kitchen again. "Ivan has gallantly offered to sleep on the sofa."

"Ah! Not so gallant—it is simply where I feel most at home." Ivan beamed at Riya. He did look like a guy who spent a lot of time on a sofa.

Natalya emerged from the kitchen carrying a small black case. She motioned Riya towards the sofa, "Sit."

Ivan looked at the case, frowning, "Do you have to do that now? Can't you let her settle in first?"

"Nope." She placed the case on the coffee table.

Riya watched anxiously as Natalya opened the case and took out what looked like some sort of small metallic surgical instrument—a cross between a large syringe and a gun.

"Take your coat off and sit," she knelt on the floor next to Riya.

Riya shrugged out of her coat, tossed it on to the sofa and sat down. With growing unease, she watched Natalya busily fiddling with the instrument. "What is that?"

"Give me your hand."

Riya gingerly held out her hand, then pulled it back. "What are you going to do?"

"You wanted to be a Keyholder, right?"

Before she could resist, Natalya grabbed her hand, pulled it towards her, pressed the end of the syringe-gun-thingy to the fleshy part between thumb and index finger, and pulled the trigger. A sharp hiss of compressed air accompanied a stabbing pain in her hand.

"Ow! What the hell, Natalya?" Riya snatched her hand back. A small round hole in her hand oozed blood. Next to the hole, a lozenge-shaped lump had appeared under the skin. "What did you do to me?" She stared at the lump in her hand.

"Smart-chip implant. So Art can track you, find your location, make sure you are still alive, that sort of thing."

She looked at Ivan, who held up his hand to show a similar angry red welt. Riya was horrified. "Don't the phone and glasses do that?"

"Not if your phone is turned off, or not with you. You are a Keyholder, so Art needs to track your movements, monitor your vital signs. And, if you die, then Art can verify that you are dead so another Keyholder can be created."

"Oh, well, that's reassuring." She flexed her hand, which throbbed with a dull ache.

"It will sting for a few days," said Natalya, packing away the implant gun.

Riya felt angry, violated, pushed around, and out of control. "You can't go around, like, putting devices in people without asking! You should have explained all this before."

"Is that before or after you decided to make yourself a Keyholder without knowing what was involved?" Natalya waved dismissively. "Anyway, that would've taken too long; you would whine about not wanting it, I would have to convince you… blah, blah, blah." She rolled her eyes. "It was better I just do it."

"You wouldn't *tell* me what was involved!"

"You are a Keyholder now, deal with it." Natalya snapped the case closed and sat in the armchair facing Riya. "Speaking of which, we have things to discuss." She snatched up the remote and turned off the TV.

Ivan threw his hands in the air. "Oi! I was watching that!" But he made no attempt to switch it back on and flopped down beside Riya on the sofa.

"First, some ground rules. We don't go out unless absolutely necessary. If you need to go out, you ask me first. No communication with friends or family, no social-media postings, and never, ever, use your own phone. Turn it off—or, better, throw it away."

Ivan sighed and ruffled his hair, "You are no fun at all, are you? Do you have *any* friends?"

Natalya glared at him. "The men hunting us are very good at finding people. The phones we use with Art are secure, but your own phones can be easily hacked and your location traced. Don't use them."

Ivan grimaced, "What exactly would this Jim Booker do if he caught us? Maybe he just wants a cup of tea and a chat? You keep making him out to be the big bad bogeyman, but is he really *that* determined to get hold of Art?"

"To understand that, you need to understand what Art can do, and what it means to be a Keyholder."

CLARITY

"We know what Art does. He—it—predicts the future." Ivan fluttered his fingers as if summoning some supernatural force.

Natalya shot him a disdainful look. "Art doesn't pull predictions out of a crystal ball like some Poundland fortune teller. We predict people's behaviour, which enables us to predict the localized near-term future of that person. We do not predict 'the future'. You start with a person, feed in a 'what happens if' question, parameters like time, date, other people they interact with, places, and Art will simulate that scenario. You can rerun scenarios as many times as you want, changing parameters to create a different outcome."

Riya looked at her blankly.

"Have you seen the old movie *Groundhog Day*? About a guy who relives the same day over and over? At first, he thinks this is a curse, but then realizes he can use his knowledge of the future to manipulate events. He tries different chat-up lines each day until he gets the girl, figures out how to save a man from dying. That is what Art allows you to do, simulate the future again and again. By making small changes, you can affect the outcome— change the wording in a conversation, introduce two people who otherwise wouldn't have met—until you get the result you want, change the future. But you have to be careful; Art can get it wrong—he cannot account for every variable: people, events, environment outside the boundaries of his analysis. He is getting better all the time, but he still makes mistakes; he works on 'probabilities' not 'certainty'."

Riya remembered her father's YouTube lecture. "And Art can simulate people's behaviour just by using social-media information?"

"Absolutely," said Natalya flatly. "Some years ago, researchers found that, with only ten Facebook 'likes', AI could predict personality traits more accurately than that person's co-workers. With one hundred 'likes', it was better than a person's close friends. With two hundred 'likes', better than their spouse. Using just your face, AI can predict things like your sexual orientation and political views. Imagine what can be learned by analysing your entire social-media footprint?

"Indigo is one of the largest social-media platforms in the world. They have enough data to completely decode you. They just need an AI tool capable of doing it. Nothing today comes close to Art's behavioural modelling, and any social-media company who gets hold of it would be able to manipulate you, and millions of other users, in any way they choose, and *you would never know*. People worry about some super-intelligent AI in the future taking over the world; I think they should worry first about the corrupt, greedy, power-hungry humans using AI *now*."

"OK," said Riya slowly. "But surely Indigo can't delve into people's *private* data and conversations?"

"Actually, they can. You agreed to let Indigo do this when you signed up to use their platform." Natalya gave a wry smile, "You did read the ten-page agreement, right? There are laws about privacy, there are laws preventing companies from selling your information, but there are no laws about using your own data to understand you, to decode your thinking. People are concerned about their data being *sold*, but these companies don't *want* to sell your data; there is more money to be made by keeping it for themselves and using it to understand and manipulate you."

"You're talking about manipulating people's free will…"

Natalya barked a derisory laugh, "You don't have free will, you never did. People are just a bunch of algorithms; you take in information from the world around, run it through the algorithms in your brain, and out comes your behaviour."

Riya didn't like being called a computer algorithm, "How come we all behave differently, then?"

Natalya shrugged. "The experiences we have during our lives affect the algorithms we develop. And, by the way, not much of your behaviour is unique to you—most people react in similar ways to most situations. Think about your average day…You go to college, right? You have a timetable of lectures. So, just knowing where you live, the college you go to, and the subjects you are taking, we can predict most of your day. There is very little left to predict: a few personal choices, like what you eat, the words and phrases you use, the clothes you wear…This is where Art comes in."

"Yes, but I can choose *not* to go to college any time I want—that's my free will."

Natalya snorted, "But when have you *actually* done that? Woken up and said to yourself, for no reason, 'I'm not going to college today,' and *actually* acted on it?"

Ivan frowned. "So, you're saying we are all governed by fate: mindless worker ants, following set routines, and there is no point in trying to change anything?"

"No. I am saying we all need to be *aware* of our programming; awareness is the first step to avoiding manipulation. The technology can benefit people, but it can also be used to bully, persecute, control. You no longer need a government and an army to oppress and control. Private companies can do the same with a big computer, big data, an AI expert, and the internet. This technology needs regulation—it should not be left in the hands of private companies, *or* people like Jim Booker."

Something clicked in Riya's mind, "Hang on. I see how Jim Booker could do all this, because he has access to Indigo's social-media data, but how does *Art* get hold of all that data at the moment? How come Art knew all about Jim Booker's men? I can't see Jim Booker conducting his private army through social media."

Natalya smiled slyly, wagging a finger at Riya, "Not so stupid as you look, eh? That is my own contribution. When we re-engineered Art for the web, I added a little special sauce of my own to Art's data gathering."

Riya scrunched her face, "What does that mean?"

"I turned him into a hacker: social-media accounts, medical records, bank accounts, email, online shopping lists, review sites, phones. He's already a better hacker than me, and I am actually pretty good." She sounded like a proud parent.

"But that's seriously illegal!"

"Meh." Natalya appeared to weigh this as though it had never occurred to her. "A little, maybe. Nothing that governments aren't already doing."

Ivan laughed, "And you're afraid of what *Booker* might do with Art?"

Riya glanced at him. Did he think this was funny? Urgh! Didn't the idiot realize this made them criminals as well? Ignoring him, she turned back to Natalya. "A little! What happens when someone catches Art rummaging around in one of these systems?"

"They won't. He is too good at covering his tracks," Natalya's eyes glittered with excitement, as if she viewed this whole situation as a chance to show off Art's capabilities.

Riya closed her eyes, gritting her teeth, "You're talking about serious crimes. People get put in prison—for years—for doing things like that. How can you start talking to people about the dangers of this technology while you're hacking into every electronic system on the internet!"

Natalya looked offended, "Without my hacking, you would be talking to Booker right now—instead of me."

"Don't you get it? Nobody will care about Booker or any of this super-awesome technology. It will all be drowned out by *your* illegal hacking. Way to go, Natalya—now we'll be hunted by the cyber police as well as Booker." She snatched up her coat from the sofa, "I need some air."

Natalya flinched, "I thought I said we shouldn't go out unless absolutely necessary."

Riya tapped her glasses, "Yeah, well, I'm sure the all-knowing Art can protect me, right?" Before Natalya could say anything else, she stormed out of the door, slamming it behind her.

She ran down the stairs and out on to the street. Stomping across the road and into a shabby shop, she grabbed a can of Diet Coke from the fridge, paid, and went back outside. In spite of her bravado in front of Natalya, she didn't want to stray too far from the house, partly because of Jim Booker, but also because this neighbourhood didn't look like the sort of place to be walking around on your own if you didn't know it.

She leaned against the wall, cracked open her Coke with a hiss, and sipped.

Across the street, the door up to Natalya's flat opened. Here she comes, telling me to get back inside, thought Riya. But it was the untidy flaxen-haired mop of Ivan that appeared. He stepped on to the pavement, looking up and down the street, hands in pockets, shoulders hunched against the cold. He spotted her, grinned, and shuffled across the road, his collar still ruffled. God, he was a mess. She glowered at him.

He leaned against the wall next to her, "Feeling better?"

"No! This is getting way out of control. Not only have we got a private army chasing us, we've now got Natalya the lunatic hacker doing things that make Cambridge Analytica look like law-abiding citizens." She glared at him, waiting for him to blather about how cool it all was, but he surprised her.

"Yeah, I know."

She raised her eyebrows, giving him her best *Really?* look.

He looked away down the street, frowning. "Yes, Art is kinda cool, but I grew up with this stuff. My father was involved in developing some pretty sketchy software for some pretty sketchy people back in Russia, several of his friends just 'disappeared', and part of the reason he came back to England was because things were getting too hot for him in Russia. My mum and I tried hard to distance ourselves from that world; I don't want to get dragged back into it now. That was his world, not mine. I know Art is different, and your dad was trying to do something good, but this situation with Booker, it *feels* the same."

It was the first serious thing Ivan had said since she'd arrived, and there was something else in his voice…Bitterness?

He caught her looking at him and his expression immediately changed back to one of mild amusement. "And, of course, I have a very busy social life to get back to—yacht parties don't organize themselves, you know."

Riya huffed, "Right." So, he just wanted his fun lifestyle back. Once a spoiled brat…"Anyway, how did you end up as one of these Keyholders?"

"From what Natalya tells me, same as you: my father nominated me as his replacement and left me the glasses and phone."

"Why did you accept?"

He shrugged, "Natalya said 'don't', so of course I accepted, to see what all the fuss was about." He gave her a sideways glance, "I guess we both got more than we bargained for, eh?"

Riya took another sip of her drink and offered it to Ivan. "She still hasn't really explained anything about being a Keyholder."

Ivan took the can and swigged, "I think that's what she wants to talk about next. Come on. Let's hear her out. I know she's… difficult…but, you know, it's just her way. What else have we got to do?"

Riya swilled her Coke, gulped down the last mouthful, binned the can and followed Ivan back across the road.

KEYHOLDERS

Natalya, seated on the sofa in front of her computer, looked up as Riya and Ivan walked in. "Here she is, back from her little tantrum."

That was it. Riya exploded, "You are so full of shit, Natalya—"

"Riya, come and say hello to your fellow Keyholders," said Natalya cheerfully.

Riya's face dropped, "What?"

"You wanted to understand more about being a Keyholder, so I thought, Let's have a conference call and a nice little chat together." Natalya spread her palms towards her laptop, from which a chorus of "Hi, guys!" erupted. She patted the sofa. "Why don't you both come and join us?"

Riya cringed. She was expecting these people to treat her as an adult, an equal, and Natalya was making her look like a petulant teenager. Shooting her a venomous look, she made her way to the sofa and sat down beside her in front of the screen. Ivan seated himself on the other side of Natalya.

"Hi!" Riya waved at the three faces smiling at her from the screen.

"So, here we are, one big happy family…" Natalya slapped her knees jovially.

One of the faces, a woman, late twenties, leaned forwards. Long glossy curls from her twist-out bob fell across her dark eyes. "Thank you, Natalya; it sounds like you are making our new Keyholders *most* welcome." Her tone was light, but Riya had the impression there was a note of warning in there for Natalya.

Riya knew her: Johanna O'Brien—she'd seen her around at her father's company and spoken to her a few times. She had a slow, smooth, silky voice, like liquid chocolate, and the expensive refined look of a woman who enjoyed making the most of her appearance, although currently she seemed to be wearing some sort of bathrobe.

Johanna stroked an immaculate eyebrow with a polished red fingernail. "Ivan, nice to meet you at last. Victor spoke of you often."

"Oh, did he?" Ivan looked unnerved.

Johanna smiled, "Not all bad, I assure you. Hello, Riya, I think you may already know everyone, but, for Ivan's benefit, perhaps we should go through some introductions?" Without waiting for a reply, she continued, "My name is Johanna O'Brien, chief technology officer at Predictive Technologies, and, on behalf of us all, can I say how sorry we are for the loss of both your fathers." The others nodded sombrely. "Our sincere apologies for not attending their funerals, but it was simply too dangerous, and I hope you understand that now. We have all been with Predictive Technologies since Sanjay and Victor founded the company five years ago, and I know I speak for the others when I say this project was more than a job to us, and rest assured we are committed to realizing the vision your fathers had."

It was a very measured speech, and Riya wasn't sure she believed the sincerity, but she acknowledged the sentiment with a nod and a smile.

Johanna continued, "Your other fellow Keyholders are Cord Dole, who heads up our psychology team, responsible for Art's uncanny ability to dissect people's personalities…"

"Hi, guys," he gave a lazy salute. "Good to meet you, Ivan, and great to see you again, Riya." She knew Cord well and liked him a lot. He was an American psychologist her father had recruited from Harvard. Whenever she'd visited her father's company, he was one of the few that talked to her, and when she'd attended his fiftieth birthday party with her father only a few months ago, he'd done his best to treat her as an adult and make her feel included. He had the air of an aging academic, all corduroy and cardigans, big bushy beard and a warm grandfatherly manner that Riya found comforting.

"And Ravi Kumar from Integration…"

"Hello," Ravi nodded curtly. Riya knew him as well, but he was typical of the techies, always busy-busy-busy, with no time or patience for anyone not involved in what he was working on. She nodded back.

"Natalya, of course, you know. She deals with Art's core infrastructure," Johanna smiled. "So, Ivan, Riya, welcome to the team. I'm sure we are all relieved that the Keyholders have been kept 'in the family', so to speak."

"Thank you, Johanna," said Ivan, gently parodying Johanna's corporate delivery, "and I'm sure I speak for both of us when I say that neither Riya nor myself have a clue why we're here."

Still smiling, Johanna's eyes narrowed. She tilted her head to one side. "You are here, Mr. Parfenov"—her voice was hard and sharp—"*to make a difference.* For whatever reason, your father saw fit to include you in deciding the future of what could be one of the most important pieces of technology of recent years. You would do well to treat that decision seriously."

Ivan's smile disappeared, his cheeks flushed.

Cord's seat creaked as he shifted. "Natalya was filling us in on how little you both know. I can understand it must be overwhelming, being dumped in this situation. Perhaps it would help to know more about the Keyholders—who we are, what we do?"

"Let's make it quick, uh?" Natalya made a twirling gesture with her hand. "I don't think we should spend too long on this conference call; it makes my ass twitch."

"Why?" said Ravi. "We're all running encryption, there's no chance of someone eavesdropping."

"Anything is hackable, Ravi, you should know that—and have you forgotten *one of us is a traitor?*"

Crickets chirped in the silence. From people's faces, it seemed this was the elephant in the room that no one wanted to talk about.

"OK, guys, we owe Ivan and Riya an explanation, so let's get on with it." Cord adjusted himself again in his creaky seat. "The Keyholders were Sanjay's idea. We'd just finished a working prototype of the Anticipation Machine, something we could use to demonstrate the technology, and Jim Booker had started making noises about wanting it for Indigo. Sanjay called a meeting. He said we'd achieved what we set out to do and he would now gradually wind up Predictive Technologies. We were shocked. The company had been our lives—and his—for five years. He said he wanted to put together a team to act as 'custodians' of the Anticipation Machine, to negotiate a safe home and handover to a suitably qualified organization that could securely and responsibly manage the technology—and he needed people to arrange this who understood its power and how dangerous it could be in the wrong hands. He invited the four of us to be in that group. We agreed."

Johanna nodded, "We knew it would take time to negotiate this handover, and in the meantime we needed to keep the technology safe from vultures like Booker. So, Natalya came up with the idea of re-engineering Art to be hidden on the internet, like a virus. Art would be up and running and fully functional so we could demonstrate its power—but could only be accessed by authorized 'Keyholders': the six people in that room."

Cord frowned, "But I think Sanjay suspected his creation might put his life in danger—so, the Keyholders were a sort of insurance policy, to ensure his vision was carried out, even if he was not around."

Riya felt a twinge of anger. Had her father really known his work might result in his own death? That meant he had carried on with it knowing she might be left all alone, without a mother or father. It felt like the ultimate confirmation that his work had been more important to him than family.

"We are the only ones who can use Art," Cord continued. "Keyholders can run prediction simulations on any subject they see fit. This enables us to demonstrate the power of the system to others"—he smiled—"and also to predict the most compelling arguments we can use to persuade governments that there needs to be a governing body for this technology."

Ravi piped up: "It's important to note you cannot run simulations on other Keyholders without their permission. We used ourselves as guinea pigs in the early days, and no one liked the idea of others being able to analyse the most intimate aspects of their personalities without permission. So, we prevented Art running simulations on other Keyholders without their express permission."

Ivan's face lit up, "So, can I use Art to make my own predictions?"

"Correct," said Ravi.

"Cool!"

Natalya's eyes narrowed. "We can also remove troublesome Keyholders, if needed. For instance, those found abusing its power, like using it for their own personal gain. So, no betting on horse races."

Ivan's face dropped.

Cord smiled, "If Keyholders leave, we can also vote in new members. There can be a maximum of seven and a minimum of one."

"And we can upload new code to Art," said Ravi. "Bug fixes, functionality changes, enhancements…"

Natalya nodded, "Keyholders also have access to Art's source code, stored within the system itself. This code is what we will hand over when we have found a home for Art, and of course this is what Jim Booker is after."

Riya looked blankly at Natalya.

"You do know what source code is, right?" said Ravi condescendingly. "It's like the 'recipe' for Art. Using the source code, you can compile another version of Art."

"We also have the ability to *destroy* Art," said Natalya. "We can initiate a procedure where Art will self-destruct, deleting his own code. This is what we will do once we hand over the source code. We will build a new, legitimate version of Art—not a virus, running on other people's computers—then shut down and delete the current version."

Johanna adjusted her bathrobe, "You should also know that all Keyholders are equal shareholders in determining Art's future. You two have as much say in Art's future as the rest of us."

Riya seriously doubted that, but nodded.

Natalya looked at her phone, "OK, we've been talking long enough—time to finish up. Bye-bye, everybody."

There was chorus of byes from the computer, but Riya noticed it was only when Johanna nodded that Natalya dared terminate the call.

The screen went blank.

Ivan gave a long sigh, "So, the others are in hiding, too?"

"Yep. Since the traitor sold our names, we are all in hiding, trying to stay one step ahead of Booker."

"You still have no idea who the traitor is?" asked Riya.

Natalya gave a cynical laugh. "Do *you* have any idea, from that call?"

Riya thought. She couldn't imagine any one of them betraying the others.

Natalya nodded. "Not so easy, eh? The traitor is Booker's best weapon. It keeps us divided, so we cannot trust each other."

"What would Booker do if he caught us?" Riya realized she'd never asked the question; she'd just assumed it would be nothing good.

"He plans to force us to hand over Art, and, if we don't"— Natalya shrugged—"Art predicts a seventy-one per cent probability he will kill us."

Kill.

Even allowing for a sprinkling of "Natalya drama", the bluntness of it hit Riya like a hammer. She and Ivan stared in shock at Natalya, so she continued.

"To control Art, Booker needs to be made a Keyholder. This requires a unanimous vote by all Keyholders—but that only needs to be *one person*. So, either he forces us as a group to make him a Keyholder, then gets us all to resign—or he just kills us all off except for the traitor, who would then vote him on before resigning, again leaving Jim as sole Keyholder."

Ivan shook his head. "But…he's a businessman…" Like Riya, he seemed to be struggling to accept that such a man could be capable of murder.

"Yes, a ruthless one. Even if we did hand over Art, he might kill us anyway, to make sure no one went blabbing to the authorities or media." Natalya shrugged, "But that is not important now. Your father created the Keyholders to carry out this vision, and that is what we plan to do."

"And how exactly do you aim to *do* that? My father was a world-famous scientist, and he couldn't manage it without getting killed, so what makes you think you can?"

"Why is it a problem?" added Ivan. "We contact the government, say, 'Hey, we have this really cool technology for you.' They send a technology geek over"—he mimed with his fingers—"you give them the software, they say 'Thank you' and go on their way. Job done."

Natalya tutted, "Riya is correct. It is not that simple, silly boy. For a start, who do you suggest we contact in the government?"

"I don't know, just…" Ivan trailed off.

"And then how do we convince them to take us seriously?"

"OK, Miss Smarty-pants, so what *are* you going to do?"

"First, we need to get someone's attention. We have contacted MI5 and reported this as a national security issue. We now wait for them to contact us."

Ivan raised his eyebrows. "Seriously? You think the security forces can be trusted to do the right thing?"

"Sorry, I forgot, what was your suggestion again? Oh, that's right, you didn't have one," Natalya sighed. "Look, Sanjay and your father believed approaching the government was the best first step—and the security services could be the way in. They should understand the need for secrecy, and they could bring this to the attention of the right people in government."

Ivan put his hands on his head and sat back. "Pfff! I think you are taking a massive gamble. How do we know the security services won't keep this technology as an intelligence weapon for themselves?"

"We'll just have to make sure that doesn't happen, won't we?" Natalya glared at him. "We don't have too many other options, with Jim Booker breathing down our necks. While we control Art, we are a target. We can use Art to outmanoeuvre Booker, but, with one of us a traitor, our luck will eventually run out. We need to hand over Art quickly, then Booker will have no further use for us and we can all go back to our own lives."

Something occurred to Riya. "Art can make predictions about Keyholders if everyone agrees, right? So why don't you ask everyone to sign up to predict who the traitor is? Whoever refuses is the traitor."

Natalya smiled, "In theory. But nobody is prepared to take the risk—Art still makes mistakes, and no one is prepared to gamble their life on it, just in case."

Riya raised her eyebrows, "You don't trust your own creation?"

"Do you understand what would happen to the traitor? They would immediately be voted off as a Keyholder, leaving them at the mercy of Jim Booker. So, for now, we have to accept that Booker knows our plans to hand over Art to MI5. This will make negotiations difficult, but we don't have another option."

Riya's head hurt. She flung herself against the back of the sofa with a big sigh. "I still don't understand why my dad wanted me involved in any of this."

"Maybe he thought he could count on his own daughter to help realize his vision?"

"Hmm." Riya thought about her father's letter, but there was still something missing. Why had he thought his seventeen-year-old daughter with no experience in the world of AI—or anything tech, for that matter—could help?

A loud crackle caused Natalya and Riya to look at Ivan, who had the large bag of crisps from earlier upended over his mouth. A shower of crisp fragments rained down from the bag, some of which actually went into his mouth, though most fell to his chest and shoulders. He looked at them both, brushing bits from his top.

"Anyone else hungry? I could eat the arse out of a dead rhino."

SHOPPING

Riya woke late the following morning. She'd slept in knickers and T-shirt, and realized, while getting dressed, that this would be day three in the same underwear. Over breakfast, she suggested to Natalya that she would need to go shopping for clothes pretty darned quickly if she was expected to stay here. To her surprise, Natalya agreed.

Towelling her hair dry after a shower, Riya returned to the living room to find Ivan sitting on the sofa eating a slice of toast, fully dressed and ready to go. He wore a smart red woollen peacoat and grey flat cap, but had bed-hair sticking out from underneath like a straw thatch, and puffy just-got-up eyes.

"Aren't you having a shower?"

"Maybe later," Ivan stood and stretched.

Riya frowned, "Why does that not surprise me?"

Natalya was back in her armchair, cross-legged, engrossed in her computer. She looked up, "OK, kids, go have a ball."

"You're not coming?" Ivan looked surprised—perhaps that Natalya trusted them to go on their own.

"Use Art to stay safe, if you need to."

In spite of her irritating manner, Natalya appeared reassuringly in control of the situation, and Riya felt unnerved at the prospect of leaving the flat without her. However, she wasn't going to admit that to Natalya.

"We, like, need some money?"

"Pass my bag," Natalya pointed to her crumpled khaki canvas satchel on the floor. Riya handed it to her, and Natalya took out a black leather purse with a toxic-waste sign on the front, flipped it open, pulled out a debit card, gave it to Riya, and scribbled the PIN on a scrap of paper, "Enjoy."

"How much do we have to spend?"

Natalya laughed. "Money is the one thing we do not have to worry about. Art is pretty good at spotting which entrepreneurs to back. We feed him names, he tells us which ones will make money." Natalya thought for second, "Meh, most of the time he gets it right. Sanjay didn't want us using this for personal gain, but, while we're on the run, the Keyholders agreed we can use Art to provide finances. So, we have money, but don't go crazy, OK?"

Ivan looked expectantly at Natalya.

"That card is for *both* of you."

Ivan looked crestfallen, "How come you gave it to her?"

"I don't trust you. "

"I have plenty of my own money, why can't I use that?"

"I told you, your own account can be traced. The less breadcrumbs we lay down for people to follow the better. Anyway, it's not about that. We need to keep a low profile, and, if I gave you the card, you would go partying with half of London."

"Yes, but it would be a magnificent party."

"Exactly. You don't know what 'low profile' means," Natalya stabbed a finger at Riya, "She does." Riya looked herself up and down, remembering Art's assessment of her—*bland*—and wasn't sure she felt happy about Natalya's confidence in her ability to go unnoticed. "Think of it as a new life experience."

"The Jim Booker experience is looking preferable right now," grumbled Ivan.

"OK, bye-bye, then." Deciding the conversation was over, Natalya dropped her gaze back to the laptop. But, as Riya reached the door, she looked up again, "And get a hat. Something with a brim."

Riya grimaced, "Why?"

"To hide that stupid look on your face."

Riya pursed her lips, "You're just so funny."

Natalya spoke slowly, as though to a child, "To. Hide. Your. Face. From. CCTV. Cameras. Just in case."

"Great," said Riya, "that makes me feel so much better about walking round London."

Several hours later, Riya slumped into a chair outside the changing rooms of yet another men's store, her shopping bags dumped on the floor beside her. Catching sight of herself in a changing-room mirror, she reached up to adjust the new black fedora hat sitting on her head. She'd never been one for hats, but this suited her; it made her look sort of exotic, mysterious.

Ivan grumbled past her, a stack of trousers in his arms, "I bet none of these fit either."

"This is the third store we've tried, and I'm going home after this one, and I've got the money, so you're going to have to pick *something* from that lot."

"If you'd let me buy that pair in the first shop, I'd be done by now," he glared at her as he closed the door to the changing cubicle.

"Yes, but they were a hideous colour—it was an act of mercy."

She heard him still chuntering away behind the closed door. "No taste…what's wrong with lilac jeans…?"

Sighing, she reached automatically for the phone in her pocket. She was dying to catch up on her socials, see what was happening back home. How was April? Hannah? Then she remembered: *never, ever, use your own phone—it can be traced.*

Surely they couldn't trace her *that* quickly? She was miles from the flat and wouldn't be on it long, so what was the harm? And Ivan would be in the changing room for ages with all those trousers…

She turned the phone on, and texts immediately scrolled up the screen:

Where r u?

April: R u OK?

Are you safe?

Several were from April, with Hannah replying to the text she'd sent from the train:

> **Hannah:** So glad you're OK. Just come home. Where are you? Call me asap.

She wanted to call her aunt so badly, but this wasn't the time or place for a long phone call.

What about social media? She could check up on what people were saying. She tapped Indigo's social app. There were several posts from Hannah. Riya's heart sank as she read the last few posts:

> I Not sleeping. So worried about Riya. Still staying at her house, doesn't feel right to go home while she is still missing.

> I Had a text from Riya saying she is OK but just needs to be away for a few days. Don't believe it, so unlike her. Her friends think she's been abducted, and I won't believe she's OK until I see her in the flesh.

> I Ever since the break-in I feel like I'm being followed. Police don't believe me. Am I going crazy!!??

Hannah was in a state, and it sounded like April had spilled the beans about her father's link to Booker. Riya scanned the numerous replies to Hannah's posts, offering sympathy and support. One was from April. Riya clicked on the link taking her to April's social page and scanned down the posts:

> I So worried about Riya…can't believe this has happened…

> I 2 days till race day. Feels wrong going ahead, but I
> know Riya would want me to.

Underneath was a selfie of April posing in front of a mirror in her running gear.

But it was her last post that made Riya gasp.

> I Still no word on Riya. I'm convinced Indigo CEO
> Jim Booker is behind this—Riya told me he was
> hassling her about her dad's company before she
> disappeared. The police won't believe me, but I'm
> going to keeping shouting about it until they do
> something.

Riya read the comments beneath—lots of thumbs ups, and comments from friends asking for details.

"No, no, no! April, what are you doing?" murmured Riya to herself. "You're gonna get yourself hurt." There was no way Jim Booker was going to let her carry on posting accusations like that.

"I thought we weren't supposed to use our own phones?"

Riya jumped; she hadn't noticed Ivan come out of the changing room. "Sorry, but I had to—"

"Turn it off. I don't want my arse fried because you were catching up on gossip with your friends."

"It's not gossip. My aunt and friends are worried—"

"I don't care if the King himself is worried about you, turn it bloody well off."

"All right, all right," Riya blew out her cheeks and pushed the button.

"We better get out of here," he glanced around nervously. "You might have been traced."

"Oh, behave! You've been infected by Natalya's paranoia. I only had it on for a minute."

"Even so…" He shuffled the bundle of trousers in his hands. "C'mon. I need to pay."

"My aunt's in a right state, she thinks I've been abducted, and one of my friends is openly accusing Jim Booker of my disappearance—"

"Good. Maybe the police will start listening and investigate," Ivan set off across the shop at a march.

"Oi! Half of these bags are yours!" Riya jumped up, grabbed the shopping bags, and ran after him. "Booker's not going to ignore that…I need to go and see them, show them I'm all right, get them to stop posting stuff that will annoy Booker."

Ivan stopped, turning to face her, "Seriously? That's exactly what Jim Booker wants. He'll be waiting. Friends and family— do you really want to drag them into this?"

"But they're dragging themselves into it, and they won't stop, not until they know I'm OK."

"Why don't you send them a text?"

Riya shook her head. "They think I've been abducted; they wouldn't believe it was me."

"Natalya will never let you go," Ivan spied a till point across the shop and set off towards it.

Riya grimaced, "I wasn't planning on asking."

"Ha! If Booker doesn't kill you, she will."

"If I go tonight, after she's gone to bed, I could be back before morning."

"You're crazy. How would you even get there?"

Riya waved her purse at him, "Taxi. Courtesy of Natalya's money."

Ivan chuckled, "Well, good luck with that."

The cashier waved them forward and Ivan paid for two pairs of trousers, then they made their way towards the exit.

"Why are you telling me this?" he said. "What makes you think I'm not going to go straight to Natalya?"

"I want you to come with me."

He laughed, "Don't be ridiculous." He caught the look on her face, "You're serious? No. Forget it."

"I need a lookout while I'm talking to them…Oh, all right, I would feel better if someone else was there, OK? Even if it's you."

"Oh, well, since you put it like that…No. I'm busy tonight. I thought I might cut my toenails, and what was the other thing? Oh, yes, I remember now—I was planning not to be killed by Jim Booker's private army."

As they reached the shop doorway, Ivan stopped, reached into his jacket and pulled out his Art glasses. "Art? Can we get home without running into Jim Booker's men?" For a moment, he appeared to stare into the distance as Art spoke to him. Then: "He says yes. Two are heading towards us—seems your little phone stunt did attract attention—but they're a way off, so we should be all right."

He began walking again, but Riya stepped in front of him. "What about tonight? We'll be fine—we've got Art to keep us safe."

"You really don't give up, do you?"

"Nope. Come on, where's your sense of adventure?"

"I don't have one." He stepped around her.

Riya gritted her teeth. How could she persuade him? "Tell you what, you can have control of the debit card for the rest of the afternoon, buy whatever you want."

That brought him to a halt, "Really?"

"As long as you leave some for a taxi to Cambridge."

A wide smile stretched across his face, eyes twinkling with possibility. "All right," he said slowly, "but, just so you know, this hero stuff is not my thing, OK? First sign of trouble and you'll find me running in the opposite direction."

"I got that vibe, yeah."

"Deal. Hand it over." He held his hand out and she placed the debit card in it. He waggled it in front of her face. "Let's see how deep Natalya's magic pockets go, shall we? We'll start with cocktails at Disrepute, then maybe Nobu for a Wagyu steak—have you had Japanese beef before? It's truly magnificent."

"I'm a vegetarian."

He looked at her with something like surprised confusion. "Really? Huh. I had no idea they were a real thing." He bounded off along the street. "I'm sure they do a nice pine-nut and tree-bark salad or something."

"You really are a cave troll!"

"Yep." He waved the debit card over his shoulder, "But one with money and a craving for cocktails and steak!"

Riya hung her head. God, what had she done? "I thought you wanted clothes? You can't go on a binge, you're no use to me drunk!"

"I'll be absolutely fine."

"And, as for cocktails, I'm only seventeen!"

"Oh, come on, loosen the sphincter screws a little, Miss Tight-Arse," he winked at her and stuck his arm out to flag down a passing cab.

SAVING APRIL

Riya watched from the living room window as the taxi drew up in the street below. Her stomach squirmed. Was Ivan right? Was she putting her aunt and April in more danger by visiting? It didn't matter, she couldn't leave Hannah and April thinking she was a prisoner somewhere. She would dash in, reassure them, leave. Simple. Booker would never know she'd been there.

She slipped into her coat, "Time to go. Got your glasses?" She had a feeling they were going to need Art.

Ivan got heavily to his feet, looked at her with bleary eyes, and patted his jacket pocket.

"How's the head, cocktail boy?"

"I'll live."

"I told you it was a bad idea," Riya stepped to the door, turned the handle, and pulled. The door creaked and flexed, but remained closed. "This stupid door's stuck again!" She yanked it hard and the door sprang open with a dull thud. Riya winced at the noise. They stared at each other, waiting for Natalya to come charging out of her room bawling about where the hell they thought they were going at this time of night. But she didn't appear.

Down on the street, a white taxi stood waiting. The driver's window slid open, and a cheerful face popped out. "Kavita Joshi?"

His voice wasn't loud, but Riya still glanced up nervously at the third-floor window, "That's me." She hopped in the rear of the taxi and shuffled across the seat. Ivan followed, shutting the door.

"Cambridge, innit?" said the driver.

"Yeah, that's right," Riya heard her voice shake. The driver nodded and pulled away from the kerb, heading for the motorway.

The taxi slowed as they entered the familiar outskirts of Cambridge. Ivan stirred, yawned, stretched out in his seat, then frowned at Riya. "Might be a bit late to ask this, but will your aunt and April be home?"

"Yeah. According to Art, anyway." She stopped the taxi next to a bus stop.

They paid the driver, jumped out, and moved into the shadows under cover of the bus stop.

Ivan scanned the street, "So where is your friend's house?"

"A few streets away. I didn't think it was a good idea to turn up right on the doorstep, in case people are watching the house. We'll ask Art to guide us from here."

She put on her glasses and watched Ivan do the same.

"Hello, Riya. Are you well this evening?" Art's honeyed voice poured into her ears.

"Yes, thank you, Art. Could you please initiate a share session with Ivan Parfenov?"

"Requesting permission."

She heard Ivan say, "Yes," beside her.

"I need to visit April Royston's house without being seen by any of Jim Booker's men. Can you find me a route in?"

"Simulating. One moment, please." Pause. "The best route provides a ninety-five per cent chance of failure."

"*What?* That's the best you can do?" She couldn't believe it. Had she come all this way for nothing? She cursed herself for not running the simulation earlier, for expecting Art to simply find a way.

"I am afraid so, with the current parameters."

"Show us the simulation," said Ivan.

Riya's vision filled with a video panel playing a movie of herself and Ivan creeping along a dark street towards April's house. It was extremely weird, watching a video of herself doing something that hadn't happened yet. A second panel opened, showing a map of the surrounding streets. Four stationary red dots appeared—two in front, two behind the house. A fifth dot appeared, tagged as a drone. Green dots, tagged as

Riya Sudame and Ivan Parfenov, moved towards her house. As they clambered through neighbours' gardens to approach from the side, avoiding the men stationed front and back, the drone spotted them and moved directly overhead. The red dots closed in, pounced, wrestled them to the ground, and bundled them into a car that had pulled up outside the house. They were frighteningly efficient—the whole thing was over in less than thirty seconds.

"Looks like they're expecting you," murmured Ivan. "We're screwed. We should head back to London."

"No," snapped Riya defiantly. "Art, how can we get round them?" She knew it was the same question again, but she couldn't accept defeat.

"I'm afraid those are the odds with the current parameters. Please let me know if you wish me to run a simulation with different parameters."

Riya looked at the ground, frowning stubbornly. There had to be a way round this. There *had* to be.

Ivan broke the sulky silence with a lengthy sigh. "I can't believe I'm suggesting this, but do you have your old phone with you?"

"Yes, but we can't phone her—you said yourself, they'll trace the call."

"Not what I'm thinking. Do you really need to visit *both* April *and* your aunt?"

"Yes," said Riya firmly.

"Just asking. Keeping it *short*, how long would you need?"

"To talk to both and get from house to house? Maybe… thirty minutes?"

"Art?"

"Yes, Ivan?"

"Can you run the simulation again, with the following change…Five minutes before Riya meets April, can you place me in the centre of Cambridge with Riya's old phone? I'll turn it on, and I'm betting they'll pick up the signal. Can you show us what the men watching the house will do?"

"Simulating. Please wait." A short pause. The map view appeared. The same red dots were stationary around the house, then abruptly they all moved away, and Riya's green tag approached the house.

"Thank you, Art, that's enough." The video stopped. "If Riya's phone remains on for thirty minutes, what is the chance of Riya being able to talk to April and her aunt without being caught?"

"Ninety-seven per cent."

"What about me? Is there a route through Cambridge I can take without getting caught?"

"Ninety per cent probability."

Ivan grinned. He would be a decoy—Booker's men would chase Riya's phone.

"If they catch you…"

"Ninety per cent is good odds; if I was a horse, I would bet on me."

She looked at him doubtfully.

"Come on. It'll be a piece of cake. I'll wander around Cambridge with your phone, first sign of trouble and I'll dump it in a bin. I'm not the heroic type."

Riya thought about it. It sort of made sense. She wouldn't need long. "All right," she said slowly, taking the phone from her pocket, "but, just so you know, I'll be wanting this back—it's got my whole life on it—so no chucking it in a bin."

"I'll do my best." He took the phone, slipped it into his pocket, took out his secure phone and began tapping away. "I'll get a taxi into town first, then turn your phone on."

"It's not far; you could *walk*."

"Don't be ridiculous."

Riya rolled her eyes, "Silly me, what *was* I thinking?"

He glanced at her. "You better get going—hide in a hedge or something close to your house. Leave the share session active on your glasses and I'll tell you when I'm ready."

"Ivan?"

"Yes?"

"Be careful, OK?"

He winked at her, "Aw, I knew I was growing on you."

"Yeah, like a wart." She set off down the street. "Art? How close can I get without being seen?"

Riya shifted from one foot to the other. She'd been crouching in the hedge for the last fifteen minutes and her legs were getting stiff.

Art's voice made her jump, "Natalya Romanov requesting connection." A small red head icon flashed in the corner of her vision next to Ivan's, tagged with Natalya's name.

Uh-oh. Busted. She watched the flashing icon for a moment. "No." The angry red icon disappeared.

She looked at the clock on her phone. What was taking Ivan so long? "Art, connect me to Ivan."

Pause. "Hello?" Ivan's voice. Music played in the background.

"Where are you?"

"Getting a coffee in Starbucks."

"Seriously? You're doing this *now*?"

"What? It's cold."

"Really? I hadn't noticed, you know, being stuck in the bottom of this nice cosy bush, *waiting for you*."

"Hey, did you get a call from Natalya?"

"Yes. I didn't answer. You?"

"Same. I feel we may be in for a warm welcome on our return."

"Probably. Look, can we get on with this? Just tell me when you're ready."

Another five minutes passed, then Ivan's voice came through the glasses. "OK, I'm in position for Operation Wild-Goose Chase. Shall I turn the phone on?"

"Yes."

"Done. OK, meet you at your aunt's in thirty-five minutes. Give April a kiss for me." His voice cut off, but the green icon showed they were still connected.

Riya peered out from the bushes, up the road towards April's house. Was it safe to approach? She heard a faint buzzing, like a large wasp. Something small descended from the sky, shot off up the street, and disappeared into a driveway opposite April's house. They must have called back their drone. A moment later, two dark figures ran out of her drive and across the road into the same driveway as the drone. Another minute and two more figures followed, then a car careered out of the drive and sped off up the street.

"Art? Can I approach April's house without being caught, now?"

"Analysing." Pause. "Yes."

Remembering Art wasn't *always* right, Riya crept warily out of the bushes, tense, ready to run at any sign of trouble. Nothing moved. She walked up the driveway towards the house, head swivelling left and right. At the front door, she whipped off her glasses and slipped them into her pocket. She didn't really want Ivan or Art listening in on this conversation, and she wouldn't need them again until she left the house.

She pressed the doorbell. There was a pause, then a light came on and the sound of a lock turning, and the door opened.

April's dad stood there in his dressing gown, sleepily blinking in surprise. "Riya? I thought you were—?"

"Sorry, Mr. Royston, I don't have much time. Can I speak to April, please?"

"Oh, right. Come in, I'll get her."

Riya stepped inside and closed the door behind her. Still looking shell-shocked, April's dad shambled off up the stairs.

A minute later, April came charging down to the hall, smashing into Riya and wrapping her in a tight bear hug that nearly crushed her ribs.

"Riya! Thank God you're all right! I've been so worried! Where've you *been*?"

Riya smiled, letting April embrace her. After being chased by hired thugs and having to live with the sofa slob and the ice queen, it felt blissfully comforting to be hugged.

Finally, Riya pulled away.

April dabbed the tears from her eyes. "We've all been frantic. At first, we thought you'd run off to hide; then, when we realized you weren't coming back, we thought you'd been *kidnapped*. Then Hannah and I got your text, but we couldn't be sure it was you."

Riya didn't have time to explain everything. "It's... complicated." She grimaced, "And I'm sorry, but it's better— *safer* for you—if you don't know." She was sure Booker could be very persuasive if he applied the right pressure, so the less April knew, the less she could give away.

April stared at her. "Riya, you need to tell us where you've been...the police will want to know too—we need to phone them, let them know you're back."

Riya laid her hands gently on April's shoulders. "Stop, please. I'm not coming back yet, I just needed to let you know I'm OK. I'm safe, and no one's making me do anything. It's my choice to do what I'm doing. It's better I stay where I am for now."

April's face creased with confusion, "What do you mean?"

Riya looked around the entrance hall. It felt like a lifetime since she'd been here last. "That stuff my dad wanted me to do? To do with his work? I can't come back until I've done it."

"But those men...If you're in trouble, you've got to go to the police—your dad wouldn't want you putting yourself in danger."

"The police can't help. We have to do this on our own—"

"*We?* Who is 'we'? You've never been involved with your father's work, what could he possibly expect you to do?" April's voice was rising with her confusion. This was probably not making sense to her.

"I..." Riya wanted to tell her about being a Keyholder, that she needed to help decide the fate of her dad's work, that Booker would come after her wherever she was. But explaining would take too long. "Look, I haven't got long, I just need you to know I'm OK, and I'm safe. I'll be back as soon as I've dealt with this thing for Dad, but, in the meantime, you have to stop posting accusations about Jim Booker. He's a dangerous man, April, and he won't tolerate you saying things like that. You'll just have to trust me to deal with this."

"Trust you? You won't tell me where you've been, who you've been with…How can I get in touch?"

Riya winced. "You can't, April. I'm sorry."

"Riya, this is crazy! If anything happened to you…" Tears brimmed in April's eyes.

Riya needed to end this and get out—April wanted answers she couldn't give. "I've got to go, sorry. Just…try not to worry, and *do not* post anything on the socials about Jim Booker—that's important—OK?"

She backed towards the door. April took a step towards her.

"Please, don't follow me. I'll be back soon, I promise." How long? She had no idea.

Turning away, she opened the door and fled down the drive. She could feel April's eyes on her back, but she daren't look back in case April mistook a backward glance for doubt and came after her. She ran out into the street, hot tears streaming down her cheeks, blurring her vision. She wiped them away, sniffed, and looked at her phone. She should have just enough time to run over and see Aunty Hannah…

A faint rustle in the bushes behind her distracted her thoughts, but, before she could turn to see what it was, a powerful arm had slipped around her neck and squeezed, hard. Her vision began to close in, and her legs felt weak…

A BRIDGE TOO FAR

She heard a dull thud, the arm went slack, and the person behind her grunted, falling into her, pushing her forward. Riya stumbled and fell to her knees. A hand yanked at her arm, stopping her falling further.

"Come on!" Standing over her with wild scared eyes, his white hair shining in the street light, was Ivan, holding a rock in his hand. She glanced behind her. The prostrate figure of a man squirmed on the ground. A nasty gash on the crown of his balding head oozed blood. He looked up with eyes of blazing blue fire, his face twisted in fury and pain. Raphael Collomb.

Ivan dropped the rock. With both hands, he tugged Riya violently to her feet and half carried, half dragged her back towards April's drive. A taxi stood parked across the entrance, but, as they reached the pavement, a frightened face peered out of the open driver's window and yelled, "Sorry, I don't want any trouble." With that, the car squealed away from the kerb.

"Git!" roared Ivan at the retreating car.

Glancing behind, Riya saw the figure on the ground struggle to his feet, sway unsteadily, then lurch after them.

Ivan set off down the street, towing Riya behind him. "We need to get out of here. This place will be crawling with Booker's men in a few minutes."

Riya shook her head and blinked. Her strength was returning, the fog in her brain lifting. "You're early."

"I noticed one of the red dots wasn't following me and was heading back towards you. Must have been him," he nodded back towards the pursuing Frenchman. "I tried to contact you, but you were offline! So I came back as quick as I could."

"Sorry," Riya felt stupid; in retrospect, turning off the glasses hadn't been particularly smart.

Seeing she was able to keep up now, Ivan let go of her arm. "I pulled up just in time to see him jump you."

"What did he do to me? I started to faint…"

"Blood choke. I've seen bouncers in Russian nightclubs use it to put troublemakers to sleep—cuts off the blood to your brain. I think he was planning to knock you out and bundle you into a car."

"Where are we going now?"

"Haven't got a clue. Art? I need you to guide me out of here, and initiate a share session with Riya Sudame."

Riya pulled her own glasses from her pocket and put them on as the two of them broke into a run. "Hello again, Riya. Ivan Parfenov is requesting a share session. Do you accept?"

"Yes." Over her shoulder, she saw the dark figure of Raphael Collomb. It looked like he was also getting his strength back. No longer staggering, he had now begun to run, taking fast, powerful strides. She sped up.

Ivan was blowing like a buffalo, obviously not used to running. "Art—has—a—route," he stammered. The blue direction line appeared in Riya's vision.

They dodged right, down another street. It ended in a cul-de-sac, surrounded by houses. There seemed to be no way out except the way they'd come. Art's blue line led down the driveway of a white bungalow. Riya slowed, unsure if Art had made a mistake, but, without hesitating, Ivan ran straight down the driveway, so she followed. They ran along the side of the house, through a flimsy wooden gate, nearly knocking it off its hinges, and into the back garden. Ivan stumbled over a plant pot, sending it spinning across the patio, where it shattered against a low wall. Not stopping, he continued through the garden, hitting the tall fence at the end at a run. With a grunt, he hauled himself up over the top, kicking the wooden slats noisily as he went. Riya tried to follow, but couldn't pull herself up. She hung there, legs scrabbling against the wood.

"Oi! What's goin' on out there?" yelled a voice from somewhere up the garden.

Ivan's head popped up over the fence a little way from where he'd gone over. "Over here! There's a compost bin my side—I can stand on it and haul you over."

Riya trampled through leafy border plants to where Ivan leaned over. Reaching up, she grabbed the top of the fence again, trying to pull herself up. Ivan fumbled to get a hold on her clothes, trying to pull her up, but only succeeded in nearly pulling her jumper and T-shirt over her head.

"Jump up—I'll pull at the same time!"

As she jumped, Ivan managed to reach her belt. He hooked both hands under it and pulled, giving her a painful wedgie, but it worked. She dragged herself up on top of the fence, swung her legs over, and half jumped, half fell down the other side. She cried out as a flash of pain shot through her right ankle.

Ivan jumped down from the bin, landing beside her with a thud. "Are you OK?"

"Twisted my ankle, but it's OK." It throbbed, but didn't feel serious.

They pushed through the conifers growing up against this side of the fence and ran up the garden towards the house, following Art's blue line. It was a fussy little garden, full of winding paths, box hedges, and pretty little statues, all of which served as obstacles to slow them down or trip them up. Riya heard a splash followed by Ivan swearing, and she glanced over to see he'd stepped in a pond. Distracted, she failed to see the garden bench right in front of her and ran straight into it, bashing her shin and falling full length across it. The bench, with Riya on top of it, toppled over and she was thrown into a thorny rose bush. Struggling to her feet, she hobbled after Ivan, who was already at the house, waiting for her.

She waved him onward. "Keep going!"

They ran down the narrow passage at the side of the house, up the drive, and out into the street beyond.

Lights came on in the house. She heard the front door open.

"Hey! What the devil—?" A man's angry voice, somewhere behind them.

Riya felt a pang of guilt for trashing his garden, but, glancing back, she saw the black figure of Raphael come sprinting out into the road, and all other thoughts were driven from her mind.

They hadn't lost him.

They followed Art's blue line up the street, round a corner, and down a narrow alley between two houses. With any luck, their pursuer would miss it. The path opened out into a small park. It was quiet, their ragged breathing and pounding feet the only sounds as they sprinted along the gravel path. Riya looked over her shoulder. He was still behind them, but further back—it had probably taken him a moment to figure out they had dived down the alley.

They left the park through another alley, out on to a road, and turned left. Riya knew this area; she used to play around here as a kid. She had no idea where Art was taking them, but it didn't seem to be working. Ivan was getting more and more out of breath, and it wouldn't be long before Raphael caught them. They needed to try something different.

A thick privet hedge ran by the side of the path. Riya stopped, yanked Ivan to a halt and pushed him towards the hedge. "You hide in there; when he's gone, get out of here and call a taxi. I'll meet you somewhere after I've lost this guy."

"What are you going to do?"

Riya smiled grimly, "Outrun him."

Ivan raised his eyebrows. "Really? He looks like he could keep going all night."

She shook her head impatiently. "There's no time to discuss this. Just do it!" She shoved him backwards into the hedge and sprinted off up the street. She came to a railway level crossing and paused, hands on knees, catching her breath. She tested her ankle; it hurt a little, but still felt strong.

Art's voice in her ear: "Riya? You have deviated from—"

She clicked off her glasses, muttering, "You've had your turn. Now we'll try it my way."

Raphael came shooting out of the alley into the road, looked up and down the street, saw Riya, and sprinted towards her. Vaulting the level-crossing barrier, she took off up the rail track. A backward glance told her he was following. Good—he hadn't stopped to search for Ivan. She slowed, making her footsteps look heavy and weary, letting him get a little closer—but not too close—and then straightened up and lengthened her stride.

Ahead was the railway bridge across the River Cam. She heard his voice, catching only a few words: "...railway...river... meet me...".

She smiled to herself. He was calling for his friends to cut her off, but they were about to cross the river now, and there were no road bridges close by.

"Just get here! *Merde!*" It sounded like he'd discovered reinforcements would not be joining them any time soon. It was now between him and her, a matter of endurance.

His footsteps quickened. He was attempting to catch her with a sprint before his energy ran out. She sped up, sprinting on her toes, praying she didn't trip on the stones. His breathing was loud and ragged now. Over her shoulder, she saw he was closing in, but he looked tired, his arms and legs pumping hard. He had something yellow in his hand. She tossed another quick look backwards. It looked like a gun...

Christ! A Taser?

What was the range on those things?

She put on a spurt of speed and heard a *click* and *snap*. She glanced back again to see wires trailing from the device in Raphael's hand. He'd missed. He tossed it aside.

She kept her pace as they crossed the railway bridge, extending the distance between them. She had one more trick up her sleeve. There was a gap in the wire fence at the bottom of the embankment shortly after the bridge. Hidden in a thicket of elder, it had been there for years. Some of the boys she'd hung around with as a kid used to dare each other to go through and stand close to the track when a train was coming. She'd done it once and remembered being petrified as the high-speed train blasted past.

She plunged down the steep embankment at the side of the track. She took the slope at a run. That was a mistake. She lost her footing, tumbling forwards, head over heels. She heard the snap and crunch of the undergrowth as she rolled over and over, twigs and bushes snagging angrily on her jacket. She hit the elder thicket at the bottom with a winding thump to her ribs.

She scrambled behind the elder bush. If you knew where to look, there was a path through the branches—and there it was, the rusted fence, bent up at the corner. The hole looked a lot smaller than she remembered. She crouched down, wriggling her way through. She was nearly to the other side when the back of her coat caught on the sharp ends of the fence wire.

As Raphael's black shadow crashed closer through the elder, her feet flailed, found a branch, braced, and pushed. There was a nasty ripping sound as the fabric of her coat gave way, but she made it. Looking back, she saw he was now almost at the fence. She clambered to her feet and ran. He was bigger than her, and, with any luck, he wouldn't fit through the hole, even if he saw it. She settled her breathing into a steady rhythm and stretched out her stride, racing off into the darkness along the riverbank. She was safe.

Huddled under the trees in a pub car park, Riya shivered. It was now over twenty minutes since she'd called Ivan, telling him to meet her there, and the sweat worked up from running was now chilling her to the bone in the cool night air. She stayed tucked under the trees as a taxi pulled in and stopped. The door opened and Ivan's face poked out, peering around anxiously.

Stepping out of the shadows, Riya trotted towards the car. "Ivan! Over here!"

He saw her, waved, and ducked back inside the taxi.

She got in, slumped down beside him, and closed the door. She could feel him watching her. "I'm OK." Her voice trembled and cracked.

"You don't look it."

She sat up straighter. As she did, she could feel the emotion draining out of her, as though someone had pulled a plug. It was replaced with something else, something colder. She recognized it. It was the feeling she got right before a race. In those last few seconds, all the emotion, the nerves, dropped away, and what was left was a cold, focused determination to win. She understood now that Natalya was right, that the only way to deal with this was to cut herself off while she saw it through. It wasn't about her father anymore, or protecting his work. Jim Booker had trashed her life: he'd killed her father, he'd made her give up her home, her education, and the people she cared about. Now, she had nothing left to lose.

"I am OK," this time, her voice was steady and strong.

"Tell me we're not going to visit your aunt now?"

"No, it's too dangerous—besides, April will tell her about my visit."

She glanced at Ivan, who looked relieved.

"You were right, Ivan. Coming back was a mistake—they'll think they can get to me through the people I love." She clicked on her glasses, "Art? Where is Raphael Collomb staying?"

The taxi drew to a halt outside the entrance to the Hilton Hotel in Cambridge. Riya opened the door to get out.

Ivan grabbed her arm, "Are you sure about this?" He looked worried, the amused smile gone.

"I know what I'm doing." Riya pulled her arm free and tapped her glasses. "Meet me back here in ten minutes." Stepping out of the taxi, she flinched; her twisted ankle had stiffened up in the car.

The hotel lobby was deserted except for a single night clerk on reception. He looked alarmed at the sight of her: blood-encrusted nose; matted, sweaty hair; scratches on her face and hands.

She smiled at him. "I've been in a car crash, just come from the hospital. My dad's staying here—he's in the bar, waiting for me. Is it OK if I go up?"

"Oh, er, yes, of course," stammered the clerk, wide eyes staring at her battered face.

Riya limped up the stairs to the mezzanine bar, following Art's blue line. She recognized him even before Art's blue halo lit up around him. A nasty gash across the crown of his brown balding scalp, he was sitting alone in the middle of the lounge, a glass in his hand.

She walked over and sat down across the table from him. He didn't move, but his eyes sharpened. He'd cleaned himself up, but he didn't look much better than she did: face scratched, the knuckles of his right hand skinned and bloody.

"Hard night?" said Riya.

He smiled humourlessly, "Miss Sudame. To what do I owe the pleasure?" He spoke slowly and quietly, a dry rasp laced with a thick French accent.

"I want you to lay off my friends and family and anyone else you might be planning to use to get to me."

He placed his glass carefully on the table, and one corner of his mouth twitched, "Now, why would I do that?"

"Because I am breaking all contact with them. I will not be contacting them again until this is over—not by phone, not by social media. So, there is no point in you hassling them."

He nodded. "And yet it is this 'hassling', as you say, that has brought you to me tonight. Perhaps I will conclude this is working, and put even more pressure on them, no?"

"You may *conclude* that I am serious." She took her phone from her pocket. "This is my own personal phone—it has all my contacts, my social-media apps, my whole *life* on it." She leaned over and dropped it in his glass. "I have no use for it. Your boss will be able to confirm I have deleted my Indigo account, and you won't find me on any other social-media site."

Raphael gave a derisive sneer.

Riya smiled, "Of course, this is a plea on my part to protect my friends and family, but I also think you and Jim Booker are practical men, and, if there is nothing to be gained by threatening the people I care for, then it is not worth your effort to do so."

He nodded again, looking at the phone in the glass. "And now?"

"Now?"

"You expect to simply walk out of here? You think because you came here with honourable intentions that I would honour some sort of gentlemanly truce and let you go, and resume our game of cat and mouse in the morning?" He gave her a thin smile, "I'm afraid it doesn't work like that."

"No, I didn't think it would. That's why I called the police before I came in here." She glanced at the clock behind the bar. "I think you have about two minutes before they arrive."

He sneered again, "What could you possibly know about me that the police would be interested in?"

"You're wanted by Interpol, aren't you? Something about human-rights crimes in Jordan? The photo on the Interpol website is a little out of date, but still…" She smiled. "Tick tock."

"You are bluffing. You would be caught as well."

"They're not looking for me. Besides, I'm not a fugitive."

The harsh sound of sirens could be heard above the mellow lounge music. He chuckled, slowly rising to his feet, "Then I will bid you goodnight and *adieu*." He sauntered out of the bar, towards the lifts.

Riya sat for a second, looking at her battered old phone upended in Raphael's glass tumbler. She was tempted to pluck it out and take it with her—maybe it was still OK? No. She'd meant it: she needed to cut herself off from her old life for the moment, and, if she had her phone, she'd be constantly tempted to turn it on and use it.

As she hobbled out of the hotel entrance, several police cars screamed to a halt, armed officers jumping out and rushing past her into the hotel. A minute later, Ivan arrived in the taxi. Riya climbed in stiffly, wincing at the pain in her ribs.

Ivan shook his head, "You think you're hurting now? Wait till Natalya gets hold of us."

He was right, Natalya would be waiting for them when they got back.

As they pulled away, she looked across at him. "Thanks for tonight, I really appreciate it."

Ivan grinned, "I know."

She grunted a laugh that tugged at her ribs, lay back in the seat, and closed her eyes.

ETHAN

Riya gave the door to the flat a smart kick. It sprang open. The living room was in darkness. Perhaps Natalya had decided to deal with them in the morning?

"You are as noisy coming in as you were going out." Half hidden in shadows, slouched against the wall next to the window, Natalya stood with her thumbs hooked into the pockets of her skin-tight jeans. "So, where have you been?" Her eyes glittered dangerously in the half-light.

"Why? Did you miss us?" said Ivan brightly, shoving the sticky door shut.

Natalya's lips curled in a horrible sneer. "You think you're funny, fat boy, huh? You better start explaining where you've been, or I might decide you two imbeciles are not worth the trouble and leave you here on your own. See how long you last before Booker gets hold of you."

"Aw, stop it, you're making me feel all warm and fuzzy," Ivan waved in mock embarrassment.

Natalya gave him a withering look, then twitched the net curtain away from the window and glanced down at the street.

Riya noticed she had her jacket on, and a bulging rucksack sat on the couch. "Are you going somewhere?"

"I don't know. Am I? Were you followed?" Natalya looked at Ivan.

Ivan's mouth flapped, and he looked at Riya. They hadn't bothered to check since leaving Cambridge.

Natalya gave a snort of contempt, "That's what I thought." She looked out of the window again. "I wasn't sure who would get out of that taxi—you or Booker's people—so I had to be ready to leave. If you *were* followed, we may still need to leave."

Riya realized Natalya had probably spent all night by the window, not sure whether Booker's men were coming for her, unsure whether to stay or leave.

"Sorry," she said, trying to look apologetic. She knew it wasn't enough, but it was all she could manage right now. She limped over to the sofa and collapsed on to it. She was exhausted. If anyone had followed them, they were welcome to come and get her; she was spent.

Natalya huffed at her apology, "You look terrible." It was a statement; there was no sympathy there. "Wait," her eyes glazed behind her glasses, and Riya guessed she had asked Art to check on the status outside. She was right. A second later, Natalya said sharply, "You are lucky. You were not followed here."

"Good," Riya closed her eyes and sighed. A sharp slap on the side of her face made her sit up, spinning round to glare at Natalya behind her. "Ow! What the fuck?"

"Don't think you're going to sleep yet. I want to know *exactly* what you have been up to so I can assess the risk of getting caught."

"OK, OK," Riya moved from the sofa to the armchair, out of Natalya's reach. She looked at Ivan, but he looked back with a shrug that said, *This is your mess—you explain it.* She took a deep breath, "We went to Cambridge."

Natalya's eyebrows shot up so high they nearly disappeared into her purple hairline. "You did *what?*" Her voice was hoarse with fury.

Riya sighed and screwed up her face. This was not going to sound good. She explained what April and her aunt had been saying on social media about Booker, and that she needed to show them she was OK so they would stop. How Ivan acted as a decoy, then about Raphael Collomb jumping her outside April's, then the chase across Cambridge, and her face-off in the hotel bar.

Natalya listened without saying a word, just standing there, tight-lipped, arms crossed, glowering at Riya, occasionally flicking the curtain to check on the street.

There was a long pause. Finally, she took a deep breath.

"You are a selfish, stupid little girl. You realize if you were caught it would have endangered all of us? Booker would have used you to blackmail the rest of the Keyholders. Or maybe blackmail was not the plan; maybe he just planned to take you somewhere quiet and blow your brains out. If it was me, that's what I'd do—shoot you in the head." Natalya made a gun with her fingers and pointed it at Riya. "Throw you in a deep hole. Hey," she wiped her hands together, "one less Keyholder to deal with."

Riya wrinkled her nose. "Nice image, Natalya, thanks."

"You don't like that, eh? Good. That is the image you need to keep in your head next time you think about risking our lives for a silly schoolgirl crusade."

"I couldn't just let my aunty think I was being held somewhere and, I dunno, sold as a sex slave or something."

"Sounds like your aunt has an overactive imagination," Natalya waved dismissively. "This is not some schoolyard game. And it's not only about you, either—or me. Or him." She jabbed a finger at Ivan. "This technology has the potential to *change the world*! I believed in your father's dream, and I don't want to see it squandered by a foolish schoolgirl, too stupid or immature to understand the responsibility she's been given!"

Riya was stunned by Natalya's ferocity. She had expected anger, but there was real passion to her voice, a protective fury when she talked about Sanjay.

Eventually, Riya said, "Look, I get it, OK? You're right. I'm sorry I put everyone in danger. I realize it was stupid and I'm not going to do it again. I realize the only way I'm going to get my life back is to deal with Dad's work. I don't like it, but I'll do whatever you want now to see this through."

Natalya looked taken aback, "Good. I'm glad we agree."

"Now, if you don't mind"—Riya got stiffly to her feet—"I'm going to get cleaned up, then I'm going to bed."

Riya sat on the sofa using her phone as a mirror to look at her face, gently touching the remnants of the cuts and bruises. It had been a week since their little trip to Cambridge and her face was no longer swollen, but a rainbow of bruises were still visible, even under the heavy mask of make-up she'd asked Natalya to get for her.

She flicked the camera off and returned to the news summary she had been reading, clucking her tongue loudly in frustration. "These phones are rubbish. The screen is, like, tiny; I can't install any apps…"

Ivan grunted sympathetically, but wasn't listening—too engrossed in golf on the TV.

Natalya wandered through from the kitchen carrying a bowl of steaming noodles. "But they are very secure—unhackable, untraceable—and right now that is more important than looking at make-up tips on YouTube. I hope you're not on social media?"

"No," said Riya testily, pulling a face at Natalya. "I'm trying to read the news, if you must know. Anyway, I deleted all my social accounts." And this was the root of Riya's bad mood. She would never have described herself as a social-media junkie, but now she felt totally cut off, desperate for some contact with home and the outside world.

Natalya was unsympathetic, "Good. Now you won't be tempted to go running off just because someone back home posted a cute picture of their dog on Facebook."

"I don't even use Facebook, that's for old people," snapped Riya, but, as she said it, she remembered she did have an old account that she'd forgotten to delete when deleting all her other accounts on the night of her Cambridge adventure. It was precisely because she didn't use it anymore that she'd forgotten it. I'd better delete it, she thought, since I've deleted all the others. But who was she kidding? She wanted a quick social hit. There was no harm in having a quick look before she hit delete, was there?

Riya, and most of the people she knew, had ditched Facebook some time ago, so in all likelihood there would be nothing to see. She logged in. Yep. Last posting was a year ago. But—wait—the little message icon had a red number one next to it. It had probably been there for ages, but she had to know…

Riya clicked on it. Ethan Zimmerman. Her heart jumped. The message was only a few days old.

> **Ethan Zimmerman**
>
> Hey, Riya. What's going on? You weren't at the station in Cambridge. Tried your phone but it goes straight to voicemail, and your Indigo account seems to have disappeared. Not sure if you still use this account, but if you get this message gimme a call, I'm still in London for another few weeks. In case you lost your phone or something, my number is…

Of course, all he would know was that she hadn't met him at the station on Saturday. She winced at what he must think of her and had a sudden desire to explain, tell him why she hadn't met him. She hardly knew him, so surely "they" couldn't possibly be tracking him. Would it be safe to contact him? Replying by Facebook was dangerous, but she could call him. What had Natalya said about these phones? Untraceable, unhackable? She copied the number to her phone contacts, then deleted her Facebook account.

With the prospect of speaking to Ethan, her mood brightened. She was practically bouncing up and down on the sofa. "I'm going to get some chocolate from across the road. Anyone want anything?"

Once in the store, she whipped her phone out, paused, planning what to say, then dialled…

"Hey, it's Ethan." God, she never got tired of hearing that deep American drawl. Her mind went blank. "Hello?" said Ethan into the silence.

"Er, hi, sorry, it's Riya."

"Hey! Riya! How you doin'? Your call came up as 'withheld number', so I nearly didn't answer."

"I'm glad you did." Cringe—too keen!

He laughed, "Yeah, me too. You got my messages, then? What the hell happened? I stood in that station like a patsy…"

"I know, I'm so sorry, Ethan. So much has happened, I don't know where to start…" A flash of inspiration hit her. "Too much to explain over the phone, but I'm actually in London myself for a few days, visiting my, ah…aunt, so maybe we can meet up and I can explain? How about I buy you lunch to make up for standing you up?"

"Yeah, totally. When were you thinking?"

"How about tomorrow?"

"Ooh, tomorrow…"

Urgh, tomorrow sounded too needy; she should've said in a few days.

"Actually, yeah, that'll work. Where?"

"Erm…I don't know London that well." God, she sounded like such a big-city noob.

"OK, I found this great little place, Timberyard in Seven Dials? They do great coffee, and we can grab lunch as well. Meet at twelve thirty?"

"Sounds great."

"Sweet. Really looking forward to seeing you again, Riya."

"OK, see you then. Bye."

"Bye." He was gone.

Slipping the phone into her pocket, she found herself grinning like an idiot at the chocolate shelf in front of her. Finally, she had something to look forward to again.

All she had to do now was persuade Natalya to ease up on the house arrest.

"Can I go into central London tomorrow?" she asked, bursting into the flat.

"Why?" Natalya eyed the phone in Riya's hand suspiciously.

"I need a new coat—mine got ripped to shreds in Cambridge." She held up her phone, "Some good deals on, at the moment." That seemed plausible.

Natalya's expression relaxed. She'd bought it.

"I've learned my lesson; I'm not going to do anything stupid. Come on, you're always on your computer, Ivan monopolizes the TV, I haven't got anything apart from this stupid little phone, not even a good book. I'm going crazy, stuck in here."

Natalya sighed slowly, "OK. But we agree a time for you to be back and you *will* be back at that time, yes?"

"Sure, OK," chirped Riya, flopping down on the sofa beside Ivan.

He looked at her curiously. "You're in a good mood."

"Just glad to get out of here for a while."

"Hmm." He stared at her for a second longer, then returned to the TV.

Riya shuffled self-consciously on her chair, sitting alone in the bustling café while conversation fizzed around her. She craned her neck to see over the busy tables, out to the street, looking for any sign of Ethan. Would she even recognize him? It had been a year since she'd seen him. She picked up her coffee cup, drained the last few drops, and frowned. Not wanting to be late, she had allowed plenty of time to buy her coat and find the café, but she'd pretty much bought the first coat she'd seen and had no problem finding the place. Now, it looked like she'd been there ages, with nothing better to do than wait for *him*.

"Hello, Riya."

She looked up. A tall, athletic young man stood smiling at her. Ethan.

"Nice hat."

She blushed. Damn it! She'd forgotten she was wearing her fedora—Natalya's orders. She whipped it off and stuffed it in the shopping bag with her new coat.

"No, I like it—very European. Makes you look exotic."

"So, hey, Ethan, how are you?" she said sheepishly.

He was dressed like a model waiting for a photo shoot: a cool vintage biker jacket, a rust-red jumper layered over a white shirt, skinny jeans, and brown suede boots, a tufty fringe sticking out from under his grey beanie hat. Riya felt a right old frump in her jumper and jeans. Why on earth would he want to hang out with her?

He was standing with his arms spread wide, waiting for a hug. She rose awkwardly and stepped into his embrace. Ethan was a keen track-and-field guy—it was one of the things they had in common—and she could feel the muscles in his arms and chest press against her. He smelled gorgeous as well.

As she stepped back, he frowned. "Whoa, what happened to your face?"

Riya touched her face self-consciously, "I was in a car crash. My aunt was dropping me off in town to meet you, and this idiot pulled out of a junction straight into us."

"Ouch!"

"Yeah, no kidding. We spent the day in A&E, and, by the time we got out, it was too late to catch you."

"Are you OK?"

"Yeah. Just cuts and bruises, but my phone was smashed up, so I couldn't call you, and I couldn't remember your number, so…"

"What about the socials? You just seemed to disappear."

Riya laughed nervously. "I've been having some trolling problems, so I deleted most of my accounts." Would he buy it? It sounded a bit weak to Riya, but, then again, he had no reason to doubt her. "I actually came across your message by accident; I don't really use Facebook anymore."

Ethan blew out his cheeks and rubbed his neck, "Whoa! Sounds like you've had a rough week." Then he grinned, "I guess I have to forgive you, then. When I couldn't find your profile on Indigo and your phone kept going to voicemail, I began to think you were ghosting me."

"No, I certainly wouldn't want to avoid you." Oops, too eager.

Ethan laughed. Riya blushed again and concentrated on trying to squeeze a few more drops of coffee from her empty cup.

There was an awkward silence, then Ethan picked up the baton: "I can relate to the trolling thing, though. Had my own problems with that. That's why I use my mother's surname,

Zimmerman. It's not my real surname. I just use it to avoid attention."

Riya frowned, "What sort of attention?"

Ethan took a breath. "My dad's kinda famous…"

"Ooh, so what *is* your surname, Mr. Mystery?"

It was Ethan's turn to study her coffee cup, "Booker." He looked up, waiting for her reaction.

Riya felt like all the air had been sucked out of her lungs. Her mouth dropped open and a strange little squeak escaped.

"Yeah, that's right, as in Jim Booker—of Indigo."

She stared at him, her mind in a panic. *Oh my God, oh my God, oh my God*, was all she could think. It all made sense; meeting him at the tech conference their fathers were attending, and now in London because Booker was over here on business. Keyholders business!

Ethan obviously thought she was starstruck. "This is why I don't tell people," he pointed at her open mouth. "I just want to be Ethan, you know, not Jim Booker's son all the time. It's no big deal; I hardly see him."

Riya was speechless, so he continued, "I get sick of people telling me what a great guy he is, what a brilliant businessman, a visionary. He might be, but he's not a nice person to be around. He's nice as pie if you're the media looking for an interview, but if you work for him, he treats you like crap." He gave a bitter smile. "Or if you happen to be his son. I tell ya, man, there are people out there who could do him a lot of damage, but they're too scared to say anything."

Riya wasn't really listening. A sudden thought made her blood run cold. "Does he know you're here? Meeting me?" She looked around the café, half expecting him to walk through the door.

Ethan snorted, "No. He never asks what I'm doing, and I don't tell him anyway; he'd only criticize and spoil it. Like, I never even told him we met at that conference. We tend to keep out of each other's way. I only came to London because I knew he'd be busy and I wouldn't have to spend time with him." He grinned, spread his palms, and looked around. "I mean, it's London! I couldn't pass on that."

Riya smiled weakly. She felt sick.

He shook himself. "Anyway, enough of that, I'll go get a coffee and then I want to hear all about *you*. Another?" He pointed to her empty cup.

"Oh, erm, please. Skinny latte, decaf."

He got up and walked to the counter.

She needed to get out of there. She stood and picked up her shopping bag. He looked over, frowning. She pointed to the toilet sign on the wall. He nodded and turned back to the counter.

Once he'd turned away, she rushed for the door, flung it open, and sprinted off down the street, not stopping until she was several blocks away. She checked the time—hours left until Natalya's deadline, but she didn't feel like using it, certainly not wandering around with the possibility of bumping into Ethan, who was probably on the street looking for her by now.

All the way back on the bus, Riya fought with herself about whether to tell Natalya the truth. On the one hand, she would absolutely crucify Riya for disobeying her again, only a week after the Cambridge escapade. On the other hand, it felt important, maybe even useful, that she'd met Booker's son.

Cross-legged in the armchair, laptop in front of her, Natalya was in her usual position when Riya entered the flat. She looked up. "Back already? Was there a problem?"

Riya stared at her for a second too long before answering, "No." She couldn't do it. She couldn't admit to meeting Ethan. "I found what I wanted straight away, so came home." She held up her shopping bag as evidence.

"Huh," Natalya cocked her head on one side, her eyes narrowing. "I thought you would have made the most of your freedom."

"No sense hanging around where I can be spotted. Where's Ivan?" said Riya, trying to change the subject.

"He went into the city as well. He kept whining about you being allowed out while he was stuck inside, so I let him go to shut him up." Natalya was still watching Riya carefully. Then her computer pinged, making them both jump.

She dropped her gaze to the screen. "Looks like we have a bite," she whispered.

"Sorry?" said Riya, not sure if the comment was directed at her.

Natalya looked up, a rare smile on her lips, "MI5—they want to meet."

The front door burst open. Ivan walked in, laden with shopping bags, puffing from the stair climb. Catching the expression on Riya and Natalya's faces, he stopped in the doorway. "What's up?"

"Natalya's been contacted by MI5."

Ivan beamed, "Excellent. Does that mean we can go home now?"

"What, you think we can simply hand over Art on a thumb drive and walk away?" scoffed Natalya. "No. This is a first meeting. They will be trying to find out if what we have is truly important, and we will say what we want in return."

"Are the other Keyholders coming?" said Riya, remembering there were others with a stake in this.

"Nope."

"How come? They all have to agree to this, don't they?"

Natalya looked at her as if she were simple. "You do remember one of them is a traitor, right? I think we don't show our hand until we know more. So, I go alone."

"Can we come?" Riya blurted it out without really thinking, but the way Natalya just presumed to cut her and Ivan out of the process annoyed her. This was how her father used to make her feel, as though she wasn't capable of understanding the serious stuff.

Natalya blinked in surprise, like this was the strangest idea she'd ever heard. "Why?"

"We are Keyholders as well."

Natalya shook her head, "No. There is no reason for you to be there."

Natalya's dismissal lit Riya's touch paper.

"Look, you said yourself my dad and Victor must have made me and Ivan Keyholders for a reason. That means we have equal say in what happens. We've given up our lives and been chased across the country, so I think we deserve to be involved." Riya folded her arms defiantly and looked at Ivan for support. "Right?"

He sighed, and with a complete lack of enthusiasm said, "Yeah, right. We should go with you."

Natalya rolled her eyes, "Eh, fine. Come. But you stay silent. OK?"

Riya couldn't help smiling, feeling like she'd finally won a small victory over Natalya. "Awesome. When is this meeting?"

"Not yet." Natalya gave a crooked smile and bent to her computer. "First, they need a demonstration. Something to make them pay attention."

"Like what?" asked Riya.

"I am going to send them predictions of two events that will happen over the next week."

Ivan frowned, "What predictions?"

"The first is about an exiled Russian businessman living in London. Andrei Tinkov. He upset some important people back home and so there is a plan to poison him when he takes a vacation in Scotland next Tuesday." Natalya typed furiously as she talked. "The second is about Jerome Adwali—he's already on MI5's watch list, suspected of being involved in several terrorist plots. He has arranged to meet with a notorious bomb-maker, Nasser al-Asiri, who has been smuggled into the country in the back of a truck. They will meet in five days' time, and they will have plans with them for a terrorist attack. They have booked a room at a hotel in Birmingham. MI5 should be able to verify these predictions and arrest some very dangerous people in the process." She sat back from her computer. "Done."

Ivan shook his head. "How do you know about this stuff?"

"While you two have been running round on shopping trips and social visits, I have been preparing, tracking the most likely attacks."

"You mean there are other events due to happen, just as bad as those two?" Ivan looked shocked.

Natalya pulled her *isn't that obvious?* face. "Of course. The world is a bad place."

Riya had something else on her mind, "Hang on. If you can make predictions like those, why couldn't you use Art to get Booker arrested?"

"For what?"

"For killing my dad, for hunting us…"

"Big difference. Those men will be caught in the act, there will be evidence. There is no clear evidence connecting Booker to your father's death, no 'proof' of *any* crime. Art predicts the future—he doesn't find evidence of the past."

"Did you even mention Booker to MI5?" Riya still thought the fact that some maniac businessman was trying to kill them was at least worth mentioning.

Natalya gave an exasperated sigh, "No. They don't care. They care about national security, not businesses fighting over a piece of software. If we can convince them that Art is a valuable intelligence tool, trust me, they will not want anyone else getting their hands on it."

"What if they think you're a loon?"

Natalya shrugged, "They might, but the predictions I gave them are serious and credible—they will have to check them out. When they come true, I think they will suddenly be very interested in us."

"What if Art's wrong? I thought predictions with long time horizons weren't reliable?"

"He is improving all the time, and I picked the highest probability predictions. Beyond that, we cross our fingers."

"Not exactly what you would call a watertight plan, then?" muttered Riya. "What do we do now?"

Natalya shrugged again. "We wait."

"How long for?"

"As long as it takes."

CONVERSATIONS WITH THE DEAD

From the living-room window, Riya watched the traffic in the street hiss along the shiny wet tarmac. It had been a long tedious week. Cold dreary rain had hammered the windows for the last five days, keeping all three of them imprisoned.

Ivan seemed quite content, apparently having the capacity to watch endless hours of TV without ever getting bored. Natalya, as usual, huddled over her computer doing who knows what. Riya, on the other hand, felt restless and claustrophobic.

She glanced at the phone in her hand. One minute to six. "Ivan? It's time for the news." They had watched it every day.

"Hmm?" He was watching some yacht race on YouTube.

"The news."

"Let me see this bit…I know the skipper…"

"No! You said you would turn over."

"OK, OK."

Natalya looked up from her laptop as the TV flicked to the news channel and thudding drumbeats introduced the six o'clock bulletin.

"*Russian agents operating on British soil again—two men are arrested on suspicion of planning to poison a prominent Russian businessman…*"

Ivan grunted. "Looks like Art scored a direct hit with the first prediction."

"Quiet!" snapped Natalya, watching the screen.

"*…the target of the attack, Mr. Andrei Tinkov, a Russian businessman living in the UK, said he had no doubt the Russian government was behind the poisoning attempt. The security services declined to comment at this time…*"

"Surely they'll believe us, even if the second one doesn't come true," Riya looked at Natalya.

"Yes, I think we may expect a meeting soon."

They listened to the rest of the bulletin, hoping for more detail, or something on the second prediction, but there was only a short segment with an on-site reporter outside Mr. Tinkov's estate telling them more of what they already knew.

As Ivan turned back to YouTube, Riya got to her feet.

"I'm going to my room for a while."

Closing the bedroom door, Riya flopped on to the bed as the enormity of what she was involved in came crashing down on her. Up until now, Art had been their private project, used for their own little predictions, a useful tool in the game of cat and mouse with Booker. But actually seeing events of national importance altered because of Art's prediction was pretty mind-blowing. They had predicted the future.

She suddenly felt alone and a long way from home. She wondered what Hannah and April would be doing now. Were they thinking of her? How had April's run gone? She had a sudden urge to know. If only she hadn't deleted her social accounts. Riya rolled on to her side and curled into a ball. Her glasses on the bedside table caught her eye. She sat up. Maybe there was a way to see what they were doing. She reached out, put the glasses on, and stood up, facing the window.

"Hello, Riya. Are you well?"

"Yes, thank you, Art. Listen, can you predict what April Royston is doing right now and run the simulation real time?"

"Simulating now…"

Riya found herself standing in April's bedroom. The main light was off, and at first the bedroom seemed empty; then Riya heard a muffled whimpering and saw April huddled down by the side of the bed, knees up under her chin, crying into a pillow. As Riya watched, April looked up, sniffed, then got to her feet. Her face looked drawn, haggard.

April wiped her eyes and walked to the door, passing straight through Riya as if she were a ghost. Riya found herself following automatically, without moving her feet, like a camera follows an actor in a movie. April crossed the landing to the bathroom and knelt, head over the toilet, hair pulled back.

"What *are* you doing, April?"

April opened her mouth, thrust her fingers to the back of her throat, gagged, and threw up. Riya looked away as April repeated it, again and again, until all Riya could hear was dry retching. She couldn't stand it. She was about to rip off her glasses when April stopped, moved to the sink, brushed her teeth, then splashed cold water on her face before returning to her bedroom, sitting at her desk, and picking up her phone. Riya zoomed in over her shoulder to see the screen.

April launched the Indigo app and tapped on a private group she belonged to called Take Control. She typed:

> I   Just purged after a massive dinner. Feel so much better now.

Immediately, a reply came back:

> I   You go girl. Know how good THAT feels ☺ ☺

"Art, end the simulation."

April disappeared and Riya found herself back in the drab London flat. She sat down on the bed, head in hands, shaking, in shock; this wasn't the same April that Riya knew, so confident, so seemingly together and in control…A wave of sadness crashed over her.

"Art? How long has April been…doing this to herself?"

"Her social-media activity suggests for over a year."

"A year!" Riya was angry at herself—how could she not have noticed? There must have been signs. And she was hurt that April had hidden this from her, her best friend; they told each other everything. She felt oddly betrayed.

"Why didn't I know?"

"April hides her behaviour; no one knows."

"Why didn't you tell me?" She knew the answer.

"Because you didn't ask."

She wondered, if she hadn't been wrapped up in her father's death, if she'd been at home instead of getting herself mixed up in this Keyholder business, would she have noticed and been able to help April?

"Art, I have a question. Why the hell did my father make me a Keyholder?"

He wouldn't know. But she needed to vent her frustration somehow, and an emotionless AI made a good punchbag.

"I don't believe I can answer that question."

Riya smiled ruefully. "The all-knowing Art doesn't know everything, then? The thing is, Art, no one seems able to answer *that* question. So, who *should* I ask?"

Silence. Then…

"Hello, Riya." The familiar voice came from behind her.

The hairs on the back of her neck stood on end. She spun around.

He stood by the door, hands in pockets, smiling gently. He was wearing his trademark grey suit and white open-neck shirt.

"Wha—?" Tears sprang to her eyes. "Dad?"

His smile faded, "Not exactly."

Riya shook her head. "But—" Her mouth flapped uselessly. She lurched off the bed towards him, arms outstretched…and her hands passed straight through him.

She gasped and stepped back.

"I am an image of your father's personality—an echo or ghost, if you like." He spread his palms and turned slowly as though showing off a new suit. "Projected by Art through your glasses."

Riya snatched her glasses off. Her father disappeared. She put them back on. He reappeared.

"The fact that you are talking to me now, means you have accepted my nomination as Keyholder. For that I am thankful." His faced creased with pain. "But it also means I must be dead. For that, I am sorry."

Riya shook her head, "But…I can talk to you?"

He smiled softly, "Yes. You can talk to me."

"You seem, like, so real…"

He nodded, "Art's function is to model human behaviour. The more information he has about a person, the more accurate his model. I am Art's creator—he has more information about me than any other."

"But I'm interacting with you in the real world, not as part of a simulation." Riya thought of Hannah and April, "Can I call up *anyone* like this?"

"No. I'm afraid that was my own special contribution. I programmed Art to allow my image to interact with the real world. A clever piece of coding, if I say so myself." Sanjay shrugged. "Then it was relatively easy to have myself revealed to you when Art considered you ready."

"Why now? Why not as soon as I put the glasses on? You've been"—somehow she couldn't say "dead"—"*gone* for months."

"If Art had revealed me to you the moment you wore the glasses, you would have become a Keyholder simply to see me again, and you may never have truly dealt with my death, and that would not have been healthy. I wanted to give the other Keyholders time to explain the Anticipation Machine to you. I wanted you to *choose* to become a Keyholder because you understood the importance of what we had created, not simply because you didn't want to let go of my memory."

"Well, *that* didn't exactly go according to plan," murmured Riya. But that didn't matter now. What she really wanted to know was…"Why did you even make me a Keyholder? I know nothing about your world."

"Precisely!" Her father beamed and opened his arms towards her. "You are from a different world, and have different values from the others. You can bring a human perspective that the others sometimes lack, so you will consider what is best for *society*, not simply treat this as a technological challenge. Sometimes we in the industry become so obsessed with what we *could* do with technology that we forget to ask whether we *should*."

"Pah! I'm not sure the others want my input!"

"You have more to offer than you think. I can think of no one better to make sure Art is used responsibly, for the benefit of all society. They will listen."

Riya sighed and looked at the floor. She doubted that.

"There's another, more selfish reason I made you a Keyholder." Her father looked sheepish. "I needed to explain myself. I know you thought I cared more about my work than I did for you. The truth is that your mother's death nearly destroyed me, Riya. And I did what I had always done when life got difficult: I worked. I realize I wasn't there when you needed me, but I couldn't stop myself. I have very few regrets in my life, Riya, but the way I treated you after your mother's death is my biggest. I saw how you suffered after losing her, the hole she left in your life…" Sanjay looked at his daughter, eyes glistening, then dropped his gaze to the floor.

Riya suddenly felt sorry for him, seeing her father for the first time not as the intellectual titan she'd always known, but a man torn apart by grief for his wife, his partner who'd been by his side for his entire adult life. He had needed his daughter as much as she'd needed her father. They'd both shut each other out.

"Why didn't you just talk to me while you were alive? I tried so hard to understand what you were doing, why your work was so important."

"I wanted to, but I couldn't, Riya; we had to keep Art secret."

"Did you know then…what Jim Booker might do?"

He sighed heavily. "Not to begin with, but towards the end, yes, things started to feel dangerous. As we developed Art, I realized I could create an insurance policy—an image of myself within the Anticipation Machine that could be revealed to you if the worst happened—I couldn't bear the thought of you being left all alone."

With a groan, she sat back down on the bed. "Oh, Dad, you should have said something."

He nodded slowly, "Perhaps, but this was the insurance policy I hoped I would never need. I never really believed Booker would go this far. I really wasn't planning to die for Art's sake."

"But I thought you just didn't believe I was smart enough or grown-up enough to understand your work."

Sanjay looked confused, then shocked. "That was *never* what I thought, Riya. You're smart in ways I never was. You're like your mother, you can read people." His eyes drifted, and a smile tugged at his mouth. "I was always fascinated by the way your mother could do that—perhaps it's why she became a psychologist." His gaze came back to Riya, "I certainly never thought you were incapable of understanding my work."

Riya shook her head in exasperation, "How was I supposed to know that?"

"I'm sorry, Riya, I truly am."

He looked broken, but Riya still needed answers, so she pressed on. "All right. So, I get why everyone is saying this stuff is important and could be dangerous in the wrong hands, but what I don't get is, if it's so dangerous, why did you even create it in the first place?"

He sat down on the bed next her, elbows on his knees, hands clasped. "It started shortly after your mother's death. I came across a new radical treatment for the type of cancer your mother had. Its development had stagnated due to lack of funding until, by chance, the creator met a technology billionaire with a medical background who saw its potential and funded the research. If this technology had been developed sooner, it may have saved not only your mother's life, but also thousands of other women. People died simply because the scientist who pioneered the technique was a lousy salesman—a great idea going to waste because they couldn't get funding. I thought, There has to be a better way.

"When I came home that night, *Dragon's Den* was on TV— that show where people pitch ideas to investors. With the article still fresh in my mind, I was fascinated by the way an idea could be viewed as rubbish by one investor, but as having great potential by another. The investors reacted to the whole sales pitch, not just the facts...Body language? Phrasing? Personality? Confidence? I wondered, if you knew enough about both pitcher and investor, could you *predict* which pitch would interest which investor? Then the *really* interesting question was: could you tailor your pitch to a particular investor and *change* the outcome?

"I was already aware of research showing how much AI can learn about a person by analysing social-media data, but a light bulb went on in my head. Using artificial intelligence and data from social media, maybe we could figure out a business pitch that would appeal to a particular investor's personality—match the right people to each other. This would allow scientists, engineers, inventors, creators to concentrate on what they do best—innovate—rather than wasting time trying to be salespeople too."

Riya frowned. "Isn't that still a bit unethical? Manipulating people's thinking?"

Her father got to his feet, pacing excitedly. Riya recognized the look; he was in lecture mode, now.

"Isn't that what salespeople and advertising corporations have been doing for years? I realized this could go well beyond pitching ideas to investors. We could make this technology available to everyone cheaply and easily online…Want to give up smoking? Struggling with obesity, anorexia, mental health, drug addiction? How about exam revision or what career to choose? Tell Art what you want to achieve and ask him to come up with a strategy—not using expensive therapy, drugs, and surgery, but a plan tailored to *your* individual personality, one that would push all the right mental buttons to motivate *you* to succeed…Why do some criminals respond to rehabilitation and turn their lives around and others don't? How is it that some people pull themselves out of deprived backgrounds, but the majority don't? If you speak to the people who did, you realize that a lot of them were just lucky enough to stumble across somebody or something that motivated them in the right way, that changed their thinking." Sanjay looked down at her, his eyes sparkling with enthusiasm. "What if we could make sure *everybody* could be lucky enough to succeed?"

He shrugged and sighed. "I tried to launch this as a university research project but struggled to find funding. It wasn't cheap. And it scared people. So, I left academia, and formed Predictive Technologies with Victor Parfenov. By now, you probably understand that the internet marketing business was to fund research and development of the Anticipation Machine, which we would eventually provide as a free service people could subscribe to. Anyone would be able to submit information about themselves, allowing the Anticipation Machine to model their behaviour in order to help them."

Sanjay grimaced darkly, "The problem was, we were far more successful than we ever imagined: we found we could simulate people's behaviour so accurately that we could literally *predict the future*. That's when we realized we needed to be very, very careful about whose hands this technology ended up in. We realized two very important things: firstly, this technology needed legislation to control it; secondly, it was only a matter of time before others managed to create prediction systems as sophisticated as ours, and they might use it to *exploit*, not to *help*.

"You see, I wasn't doing this for money, or for fame."

Riya didn't know what to say, but she couldn't be angry with him anymore.

He took a deep breath, "Tell me, what's Jim Booker up to?"

"Things are not great. All the Keyholders are in hiding. One of them has sold us out, and Booker is trying to force us to hand over Art."

Sanjay frowned deeply, shaking his head, "I should not have involved you in this. It was selfish of me to put you in danger."

"We're holed up in this flat while Natalya tries to engage MI5 about handing over Art."

He frowned, "MI5? I would have thought one of the government technology departments would have made more sense?"

"The Keyholders think, if we go to MI5 saying this is a national security issue, then we can talk to the government *without* Booker and his lawyers trying to stop us."

Her father looked at the wall, head bobbing from side to side. "Hmm, perhaps." He resumed pacing back and forth, thinking. "And what do you think?"

"Me? What are you asking me for?" It sounded waspish, but Riya was taken aback. Her father had never asked her opinion before, on anything.

"You are a Keyholder, you have a say in what happens."

Riya sighed. What *did* she think? "I don't know," she said slowly. "I haven't made up my mind yet."

He smiled, "I am sure you will. Guide the others—they are not as tough or sure as you think. I suspect this will get worse before it gets better, and they will need someone to remind them why they are doing this." Sanjay turned to the door, "We have talked enough. You need time to think."

"Wait! I—" This was the most Riya had talked to her father in years; even if it wasn't "real", she didn't want it to end.

"Don't worry. If you need me, just put the glasses on and ask. Goodbye, Riya," Sanjay walked straight through the bedroom door.

"No, wait!" Riya ran to the door, flung it open and dashed into the living room.

She stood there, frantically looking around, but there was no sign of her father. Ivan and Natalya looked at her with startled faces.

"Did you see where—?" Then she remembered: her father was a simulation. She straightened up, feeling stupid. Ivan and Natalya looked at her expectantly, "Never mind."

Natalya's eyes narrowed. "What are you doing with those glasses?"

Riya took them off. "Nothing, just…experimenting. You know, playing with simulations, seeing what Art can do."

Something in this seemed to make sense to Natalya. She nodded, "Be careful. Seeing the future can become addictive."

She sauntered over to Riya, leaned close and whispered, "It is tempting to look into the future of your friends too, no?"

Riya opened her mouth to deny that's what she'd been doing, then thought better of it. If that's what Natalya thought, it was better than saying she'd been talking to a ghost.

MI5

It was late morning when Riya stepped off the train with Ivan and Natalya at Lambeth North Tube station. She looked anxiously up and down the busy platform. They were heading to their meeting with MI5 and Riya felt uneasy; they had just predicted two national security incidents, so she half expected to be ambushed and arrested for somehow being involved.

As her gaze swept the platform, a gloved hand went up, waving. Johanna O'Brien eased away from the platform wall, a mass of black curls bouncing around her ears as she walked towards them with that confident style that Riya found so intimidating. Dressed in a stylish burgundy woollen overcoat swinging open over a grey trouser suit, with expensive patent heels flashing in the station lights, she looked as though she belonged in London. But it wasn't Johanna's *togetherness* that made Riya nervous.

"What's she doing here?" Riya glanced at Ivan. He grimaced with a *first I've heard of it too* expression.

"I invited her," said Natalya. "She is Predictive's chief technology officer. Having more of the team here will help our credibility with MI5."

"I thought we can't trust the other Keyholders until we find the traitor?"

"We have to trust someone, and, if I had to make a bet, I would say Johanna is the least likely to be the traitor."

That makes no sense, thought Riya; Natalya had just "decided" Johanna was not the traitor.

"Or perhaps you thought we needed an actual grown-up to talk to MI5?" Ivan grinned.

Natalya shot him a venomous look.

Just then, Johanna reached them, smiling warmly, "Hello, Natalya, you're looking well." She leaned in and hugged Natalya, kissing her on both cheeks (which Natalya looked less than comfortable about). She turned to Riya and Ivan, "Riya, Ivan. Nice to see you in person this time." She turned back to Natalya. "Ready?"

Natalya nodded curtly, "This is your show, Johanna."

With a jolt, Riya realized Natalya must have discussed this meeting with Johanna some time ago. Natalya might be convinced Johanna wasn't the traitor—but to trust her with Riya and Ivan's safety without consulting them was bang out of order!

The alarm must have shown on her face because, as they headed to the exit, Ivan jerked a thumb at the ceiling and whispered, "Let's hope she hasn't planned a reception party for us, up on the street."

With a chill, Riya understood. If this was a trap, it would make sense to ambush them where they could be bundled into a van and whisked away in seconds.

She clenched her jaw, "If we make it out of this, we should have words with Natalya."

Ten minutes and no ambush later, Riya found herself striding through the imposing high-arched entrance of the Marriot County Hall Hotel—neutral ground agreed by both parties.

The girl at the reception desk gave them a plastic smile and greeted them in a chirpy helium-high voice: "Good morning. How can I help you today?"

Johanna answered, "Good morning"—Riya noted they had all simply accepted her role as leader without question—"we're here for a meeting with Mr. Jones." It was what they'd been told to say.

The receptionist's smile faltered; her eyes flickered past Johanna. Riya turned, following her gaze. A suited man, previously engrossed in his phone by the entrance, now strode towards them.

He gave a perfunctory smile, "Please, follow me."

He led them briskly through a network of corridors, twisting left and right, and finally coming to a stop outside a stately polished-wood door, either side of which stood two more stone-faced suits.

"We need to perform a security check," said their guide.

He nodded at the sentries, who proceeded to pat them down and waft them with security wands. Seemingly satisfied, their guide then knocked once on the door, paused, opened it, and waved them inside.

A grey-haired man sat at a large round table, set out with biscuits and water bottles, and surrounded by grey leather chairs. He immediately rose to his feet as they entered, smiling the too-wide kind of smile meant to make you feel unthreatened. Another man, younger, perhaps mid-thirties, stood leaning against the wall by one of the two tall windows. His heavy-lidded grey eyes made Riya shiver as he stared at them, unblinking: dangerous, predatory.

He's the one to watch, she thought, disliking him instantly.

"Good morning," said the man at the table. He had the plumpish figure of a man who spent his days sitting in an office. His rounded face, glasses, and protruding ears gave him a friendly, comical look, but his eyes were sharp, and his easy confidence suggested seniority.

"Introductions first, I think," he walked around the table. "My name is Digby Somerset." He shook their hands vigorously in turn, "I'm afraid, for security reasons, I cannot tell you the precise nature of my position within MI5, but suffice to say I work in the area of cybersecurity."

Riya got the impression he would be straight with them, honest. But the man with grey eyes at the window…you would count the change if he served you in a shop.

Digby followed her gaze. "And this is Brendan Brown, who heads up our New Technologies division. Our main objective today is to evaluate the security threat that your technology poses, but Brendan here is also interested in how your technology could be utilized by the security services."

Brendan shoved himself away from the wall and shambled towards them, shoulders hunched, hands buried in his pockets. In contrast to Digby, he looked a mess. His hair was longish, over his ears, wispy and wind whipped. His blue suit was crumpled like a discarded sweet wrapper. It looked as though he'd bought it a long time ago and lived in it ever since.

Johanna held out her hand, smiling.

Brendan cocked his head on one side and looked at it, took a hand from his pocket, then hesitated. "You know, I always like to know the name of the person belonging to the hand I'm shaking." His voice was soft Irish, a gravelly smoker's voice, and quiet, almost a mumble.

Johanna's smile flickered, just for a second. It was the first time Riya had seen her confidence waver.

Digby smiled encouragingly, "It will help your credibility if we know who you are, so we can check your background."

Johanna thrust her hand forwards, "Johanna O'Brien. And this is Natalya Romanov, Riya Sudame, and Ivan Parfenov."

"There, now," said Brendan, taking her hand, "that wasn't so difficult, was it? And a nice Irish name you got yourself there." He leaned closer, still gripping Johanna's hand, and in a mock whisper said, "I have to say, though, you don't look Irish."

Riya caught her breath. She knew what he was implying— Johanna didn't look Irish because she was black.

Johanna's eyes narrowed and the muscles in her jaw tightened, but her smile remained.

Riya knew she shouldn't rise to it, but she didn't care, she'd experienced too much patronizing racism herself to let it go. "What's that supposed to mean? We come to MI5 with world-changing technology, trying to help, and you make stupid racist jokes?" She laced her words with as much contempt and loathing as she could muster. "You disgust me!"

Brendan blinked at her, as though he'd only just noticed she was there, then smiled.

Damn it! He'd got to her, and he knew it.

Too late, she understood: his remark had been totally calculated—he was trying to keep them off balance, test them, see where their emotional touchpoints were and what might make them lose control.

Riya looked at Digby for support, but he merely put his hands up in a placating gesture. "Now, let's all calm down, shall we; I'm sure that's not what Brendan meant." Was this some sort of good cop, bad cop routine?

Johanna, not so easily ruffled, cut in: "So, what exactly looks so un-Irish about me, Mr. Brown?"

Brendan let go of her hand, and stood back, appraising her, then snapped his fingers. "Must be the clothes. Much too fancy for a poor Irish lass."

Johanna smiled sweetly. "Ah, that must be it. But you're right, the name comes from my ex-husband, who *is* Irish."

Taking a moment to pointedly look Brendan up and down, she added, "Are you not married, Mr. Brown?"

Brendan grinned, "Alas, no—married to the job, I'm afraid." He waved at his creased, raggedy suit. "As you see, I have not had the benefit of an education in haute couture, unlike your good self."

"Enough small talk, Brendan," said Digby sharply, seeming to indicate he'd had enough of Brendan's goading. He turned to Johanna and smiled warmly, "Please, sit down."

The five of them sat. Brendan plucked a bottle of water from the table and went back to stand by the window.

Annoyance flashed across Digby's face, quickly replaced again by the wide smile. He leaned forward, hands clasped on the table. "Now, you certainly got our attention by predicting those two attacks. Without your information, lives would have most definitely been lost, so I thank you for that. However, it is also disturbing, firstly, that the security services had absolutely no intelligence on those events, and, secondly, that *you* did."

"We have simply built the next generation of behavioural analysis tools. Is that really so far-fetched?" Johanna crossed her legs. "We predict *people*, not *events*, Mr. Somerset. The more detailed the information we have, the more accurately we can simulate, or predict, behaviour."

She paused.

"For instance, where a person would place a terrorist bomb. Someone from your own organization once described what you do as 'gathering fragments of information to assemble a picture of what *might* happen'. That is precisely what our system does."

"It just does it better than anything you have at present," said Natalya.

Johanna glared at her. Riya inwardly winced, knowing Johanna didn't want to get into a bragging match.

Brendan smiled, "Oh, I think you might be surprised at the toys we have at our disposal, Miss Romanov."

Digby nodded thoughtfully. "Accepting, for a minute, that your system can accurately simulate detailed behaviour, how do you gather the information needed? I don't imagine you can ask terrorists or secret service agents to provide such information about themselves…"

"We don't use traditional evaluation techniques. Someone's digital footprint provides all the information we need—their social-media posts, their photos, videos, blogs, friends, likes…"

Digby raised a sceptical eyebrow. "I can't see Russian secret service agents posting on social media."

Johanna glanced at Natalya before answering. Riya wondered whether perhaps she also disagreed with Natalya unilaterally turning Art into a hacker. "We don't use only social-media data. Our artificial-intelligence engine is capable of accessing a range of secure systems, from banking to government records to people's phones."

Digby's smile disappeared, "Now, that *is* an issue of national security, Mrs. O'Brien. It sounds very much like your technology is more like an automated hacking machine."

Riya noticed Brendan's expression change as well, but to something more like excited interest than Digby's stern disapproval.

"Yes, we do understand that. I'm afraid the 'hacking' aspect was something of"—she glanced at Natalya again—"an unauthorized experiment. However, we both know social-media companies *legally* hold more personal data than our system would need to model a person's behaviour—more information, I believe, than most governments. That is why this type of technology needs to be carefully monitored and regulated. All of us who have worked on it realize this is far too powerful to be left in private hands."

Digby looked uncomfortable, "I am well aware of the dangers such technology poses, Mrs. O'Brien, but we cannot negotiate while you are so flagrantly breaking the law. It needs to be shut down first."

Johanna stared back at Digby, "I'm not sure we are ready to shut it down, at this point. There are people out there willing to kill to obtain this technology. Our system's prediction capabilities are the only thing keeping us alive right now."

Brendan shambled across the room, tapping his forehead thoughtfully. "We shouldn't be too hasty, here. Predicting people's behaviour with anything close to such accuracy would be extremely valuable. Perhaps we should hear what the good lady has to say." His eyes glittered, "See, what I'm missing is the reason *why* you are talking to us. What's the catch? There's always a catch. What is it that you want in return, Mrs. O'Brien?"

Johanna smiled coyly, "There *is* a catch. We understand this technology could be of enormous benefit to the intelligence community, but our founder believed that it should be used for the wider benefit of society. We need assurances that it will not be locked away in some shadowy government organization."

"And where is this mysterious founder of yours?" Brendan looked around the room, as if expecting him to jump out from behind the curtains.

"Dead," said Natalya flatly. "Killed by Jim Booker, of Indigo."

"Is that so?" Brendan raised his eyebrows.

"That is a serious claim," said Digby.

"It is what we suspect, but we have no proof," Johanna glared at Natalya. "But that is why we came to the security services. We need to secure our own safety and that of the technology."

"So, what do you see as the next steps, Mrs. O'Brien?" said Digby.

"We need to speak to the relevant people in government. Once we've had a positive meeting, then we can discuss the handover of our technology."

"And if your discussions are not positive?" said Brendan.

"I am confident they will be, Mr. Brown, so let's not cross that bridge until we come to it."

Brendan stared at Johanna, his expression inscrutable. Eventually, he said, "Tell me, what did your system say about this meeting? You must have done some analysis?"

"Insufficient information to generate a simulation." Everyone turned to Natalya, slouching sullenly in her seat. "MI5 are secretive people. There was not enough information to generate personality profiles or predict who would attend this meeting."

Brendan gave a faint smile.

Digby sat back, thinking. Finally, he glanced at Brendan, sighed, and sat up again, hands clasped in front of him. "All right. In light of discussions today, we should be able to secure such a meeting. We will communicate via the email address you supplied us with. But I have to reiterate that what you and your system are doing is highly illegal."

Riya breathed out slowly. They were in. But she was troubled; she didn't trust Brendan at all, and, although Digby *seemed* genuine, how could they really know?

"I believe our business is concluded, then." Digby walked to the door and opened it. The security suit immediately stepped into the room.

"Mrs. O'Brien and friends are leaving; could you please escort them to the hotel entrance."

Brendan followed Digby to the door.

The four Keyholders rose and filed out of the room, shaking hands with the two men on their way out. Ivan grabbed a biscuit as he left his seat, and held it up, grinning, "One for the road."

Digby smiled warmly, "Thank you so much for reaching out to us. We'll be in touch when we can offer a meeting."

It was meant to reassure, but, to Riya, it felt a lot like a crocodile smile.

Standing on the pavement outside the hotel, Riya shuffled over to Johanna. "Sorry about losing it, back there. That was well out of order. He just got to me."

Johanna pulled on her gloves and waved to an approaching taxi. "I've come across his type before. He knows, if he gets us angry, it will mean we are not thinking clearly, putting him in a stronger position. Playing the race card is a cheap trick, but it usually works. For some people, negotiation is about scoring points—they think, in order for them to win, someone else has to lose. I think our Mr. Brown may be one of those." As the taxi pulled up to the curb, Johanna grinned at Riya. "Don't worry about it. This is too important to them, and us, to allow Brendan Brown to derail things."

As they all piled into the taxi, Johanna looked out of the back window, "They'll follow us."

Natalya shrugged, "They'll try. We'll lose them on the Underground later."

Johanna nodded. "How do we think that went?"

"They had quality biscuits; nice to see taxpayers' money put to good use," said Ivan.

Johanna ignored him. "Riya, what do you think?"

"Me?" said Riya. Johanna wanted her opinion?

"You are part of this team, so, yes, what do you think?"

"I don't trust them. I think that Brendan guy wants to keep Art for the security services. Did you see his face when you explained what Art could do? I think he'll tell us anything to get hold of it."

"I agree with Riya," Natalya's lip curled with contempt. "Security services are all the same—they cannot be trusted, they are no better than Booker. It was the same in Russia. I told you before, we should go directly to the AI tech community; they will understand what we have."

Johanna shook her head, "But how could we keep Art and ourselves safe while negotiating with those organizations? Booker would find out what we were doing and stop us."

Ivan frowned, "Hang on, why are we binning MI5 again? MI5 are not the Russian FSB. They would use Art to protect people—that's what you want, isn't it? What's the problem? Just give it to them and we can all go home."

Natalya glared at him, "Because it would not be what Sanjay and Victor had as their vision—*that's* the problem."

"Hey, life's not perfect. So what?"

"Pfff. Be quiet, little boy."

Johanna sighed, "Well, whatever we do, we need to do it quickly, because now we have MI5 as well as Booker after us, and we cannot evade them both for long."

Natalya nodded, lips drawn thin and tight, "One thing's for sure, we need to leave London. A crowd is a good place to hide from Booker, but MI5 will have too many eyes in the city."

THE TRAITOR

Riya and Natalya sat on the sofa, huddled around Natalya's computer, looking at holiday cottages in the remote Highlands of Scotland. Ivan sat with a bowl of cereal, watching the news on BBC Breakfast.

Natalya's phone buzzed, dancing across the coffee table. She grabbed the remote, muted the TV, picked up her phone, frowned, and answered on speaker. "Hey, Cord. Wassup?"

Ivan threw up his hands, "I was watching that! It's the man with one arm juggling chainsaws next…"

Riya waved at him to shut up. If Cord was calling, it must be something important.

"Hey, Natalya. How's it going?" Cord sounded urgent, jumpy. "Listen, I think I found our traitor."

Natalya jumped to her feet, tense, waiting.

"Natalya? You still there?"

"Yes. Go ahead."

"OK. I got an attack of cabin fever today, so I went for a walk around Piccadilly Circus, and who do you think comes strolling past, loaded with shopping bags, like she hadn't got a care in the world? Johanna O'Brien! I was going to say hi, but thought, no, better be careful, I'll follow her first, see what she's up to. She headed off to Le Méridien, and the way she walked straight past the check-in desk makes me think she's staying there. I stopped outside, was just thinking it seemed kinda strange she was staying somewhere as obvious as a major hotel, when this big black limo turns up…"

"Jim Booker." Natalya's voice sounded matter of fact, but a lump of ice fell into Riya's stomach.

"You got it. He goes into the lobby, and Johanna appears, greeting him like they're old friends."

Riya shook her head. This didn't sound right—it seemed too crude, too obvious for Johanna. She looked at Ivan and his face twisted sceptically.

"So, he's in there with her now?" Natalya looked at Riya.

"Yeah, they disappeared towards the lifts together. Man! When I think I trusted her!" He paused. "Look, you might want to check it out yourself? I don't know how to get proof. Maybe I could pay someone to pretend to be room service or housekeeping or something, and they could go in with a hidden camera? What do you think? Then I could send you the video?"

"Yeah, that might work," said Natalya, pacing the floor. "Let me think and get back to you."

"OK, well, I'm just going to keep watch here. I'll let you know if they come out again."

"OK. Bye," Natalya crossed the room, tossing the phone in her hand, her eyes flinty. "So, now we know."

Ivan frowned. "You don't believe him, do you? Johanna, a traitor…?"

Natalya looked at him as though he'd suggested the earth was flat. "Not Johanna, you idiot. *Cord*. That was the most unbelievable pile of garbage I ever heard."

"But you have to at least check it out," Riya's voice was sharper than she intended, but she couldn't let Natalya's loyalty to Johanna blind her.

Natalya glared at her, "It cannot be Johanna—she would *never* hand over Art to Booker." She practically spat the words, but Riya thought she detected a hint of doubt in Natalya's voice.

"Maybe, but Riya's right, Natalya—we need to know for sure," said Ivan gently.

Natalya's glare swung to Ivan, but she nodded curtly, "Fine."

"We could send someone? Like Cord suggested?" said Riya.

Natalya snorted, "No, there are more elegant ways to peel the cat. Cord is a psychologist, not very technical. He thinks like a 1970s spy film." She tapped her phone against her teeth, then plucked up her laptop and sat down in the armchair. Her fingers flittered across the keyboard as windows opened and closed on the screen, cascading with streams of text.

"What are you doing?" asked Ivan.

"Looking for a pair of eyes we can use," Natalya stared at the ceiling for a second, then dived back to the keyboard. More scrolling text, then a window appeared with a tabulated view of names and numbers.

"Is that people's room numbers?" asked Riya.

Natalya's hands flicked across the keys, "If we sort by check-in date…and assume she has been staying there since we went on the run…" The number of names reduced until there were only three. "These are the only people who have been staying at the hotel since the Keyholders disappeared."

Riya read the names. Two were men; the third was…"Sarah Jacobs, room 816. Is that her?"

Natalya nodded slowly, flicking through command windows again. "Could be. It's an expensive suite. The TVs in those rooms have webcams to make video calls. If I can find which one belongs to room 816…" Columns of numbers streamed down the screen. "So! And then enable the camera…" A video panel sprang open, showing the image of a hotel room.

Riya gave a gasp. Two people sat opposite each other at a coffee table, right in front of the camera. One was the stylish figure of Johanna O'Brien. The other was the pale-faced, neatly composed form of Jim Booker.

Natalya muttered something guttural in Russian.

"Can we get sound?" said Ivan grimly.

"Let's see," Natalya began typing again. She frowned. "No. For some reason, I can't enable the microphone." She thought for a minute. "Wait. What's that?" She peered at the screen, her nose almost touching it, then leaned back. "They have Amazon Alexa in these rooms!" More furious typing and Johanna's voice sprang from Natalya's computer.

"*I think they are weakening. I think the other Keyholders are getting tired of living in fear. They want their lives back. I think they are close to caving in and doing a deal. It's only Natalya who seems determined to hold out or die trying.*"

"*Ah, yes, our spirited Russian hacker. Is there nothing we can do to change her mind?*"

Johanna shook her head, "*No. She is blinded by her loyalty to Sanjay. She still thinks you are responsible for his murder.*"

"*Another misconception. And no doubt that is the story she's been telling Riya and Ivan?*"

"*I'm afraid so.*"

Riya glanced furtively at Natalya, who snorted derisively. "Don't believe him. He killed your father."

Booker leaned forwards and picked up his coffee cup from the table, staring into it ruefully as he swilled the contents. "*It's a pity I can't explain our plans for Art to them. Of course we want to use it to boost Indigo revenue, but we also plan to set up a whole non-profit system, just as Sanjay wanted.*"

Natalya slammed the lid of her laptop closed. "Enough of this rubbish! Who would fall for such lies?"

The three of them sat in uncomfortable silence.

Riya's mind whirled…Had Natalya got it all wrong about Booker? After all, she had been wrong about Johanna? She eyed Natalya and thought she saw a flicker of uncertainty in those deadpan features.

"It sounds like Johanna believes him," said Ivan tentatively.

Natalya nodded, stony-faced, "I can't believe she'd be so naïve." Her voice was little more than a whisper. Eventually, she took a deep breath. "I need to phone Cord." She took out her phone.

Riya nagged at a fingernail. Something was buzzing around at the back of her brain, a thought hovering just out of reach.

Natalya was talking to Cord on speakerphone. "OK. I believe you…Proof, yes, I hacked a webcam in her room."

"Ah, clever. You always were the techy genius. Johanna, the traitor? Jeez—wouldn't have believed it if I hadn't seen it with my own eyes. But, listen, if you believe me, can I come over? The heating's busted at my place and I'm freezing my nuts off here."

"OK. I'll call Ravi and we can meet here to vote off Johanna. We're at 61 Fortress Road, Flat 3."

"See you soon."

The call ended. Natalya sat on the sofa, fiddling with her phone, and staring grimly straight ahead.

Still there was something buzzing away at the back of Riya's mind, annoying, like a fly in the room you can't see. She lurched forwards and grabbed Natalya's hand as she tapped in a call. "Wait!"

Natalya cancelled the call, "Why?"

"Don't you think that was too easy?"

Natalya raised an eyebrow, "You think what I just did was easy?"

"Yes, well, no…but I think Cord may have expected you to do something like that. Can you get the webcam up on your computer again?"

Natalya stared at Riya for second, then flipped open her computer. Within a minute, she had a video window open, displaying Johanna O'Brien still talking to Booker.

"Call her."

Natalya's eyebrows twitched a frown, but she did it, flicking the speaker icon so Riya and Ivan could hear.

Johanna's honeyed voice answered, "Hey, Natalya." She was breathing heavily, and Riya could hear traffic noise in the background.

The Johanna on the screen was still talking to Booker. Ivan groaned. Riya felt a wave of panic crash over her.

"Where are you, Johanna?"

"You should know better than to ask that, but it involves a little retail therapy."

"Are you staying in London?"

"No, I know too many people there, too much chance of being seen. Anyway, what can I do for you? Found our traitor yet?"

Natalya looked at Riya, "Funny you should ask that. Sorry, Johanna, something's just come up. I'll explain later." Natalya ended the call, eyes wide, face white. "Get your stuff. We need to leave!"

The three of them scrambled up from the sofa. Riya flew into her room, yanked out her rucksack, ripped clothes off hangers and out of drawers, and stuffed them into the bag. Snatching her jacket from the back of the door, she scanned the room as she pulled it on. Glasses! She dived across the bed, grabbed her glasses from the bedside table, shoved them into her jacket and headed back to the living room. Empty. For a frightened moment, she thought the other two had left without her. The scrape of moving furniture sent her sprinting into the kitchen, skidding on the worn lino floor.

The rickety kitchen table had been pulled into the middle of the floor. On it stood Natalya, wrestling with the sliding bolts on a hatch in the ceiling. Ivan struggled to hold the table steady as it wobbled dangerously under Natalya's weight.

"What are you doing?" yelled Riya, confused.

"We go through the attic."

"Won't they search up there?"

"Argh!" Natalya yelled in frustration, her arms shaking as she struggled to work the bolts open, stiffened by layers of careless paint. "Come *on*, you mother—" *BANG*. One of the bolts slid open. *BANG* went the other. The hatch swung down, narrowly missing Natalya's head as she ducked out of the way. "Riya, go check the street."

Riya ran to the living-room window. The street below looked as it always did. But then, in the distance came the whining *ring-ding-ding* of scooter engines—and two scooters laden with four men screamed into view, screeching to a halt outside the house.

The coppery tang of fear filled her mouth.

"Oh my God! They're here!"

She ran back through to the kitchen to see Ivan's feet disappearing through the hatch in the ceiling.

Natalya's head poked through, "Don't just stand there, get up here!"

Riya clambered on to the shaky table, flinging her arms out for balance, then she passed her rucksack up to Ivan.

"We'll pull you up," he said.

Ivan and Natalya reached down through the hatch and hoisted her briskly into the loft. As soon as Riya was out of the way, Natalya pulled up the rope tied to the inside of the hatch, closing it. She tied it to a roof truss, thus holding the hatch closed.

"That should slow them down." Her eyes glittered in the attic gloom. "This way. Stay on the beams or you'll fall through the ceiling." She jumped lightly from beam to beam like a squirrel, heading for a grimy skylight set into the roof. Somewhat slower, Ivan went next, the roof trusses creaking ominously under his weight. Riya followed. By the time they reached the skylight, Natalya had already thrown it open and was waiting for them.

A muffled thud from below made the roof shake, bringing a thin mist of dust raining down from the beams.

Natalya smiled grimly. "Knock, knock. I think our visitors have arrived. It will not take them long to figure out we came up here. Riya, you go first." Natalya nodded to the open skylight. The window was set into the slope of the roof. "There is a flat section running along the top of the house—you need to get to that."

Riya wriggled through the skylight and out on to the sloping tiles.

"Go!" hissed Natalya. "Up!"

Riya looked up. The slope ended just a few feet above her. She only had to take a few steps, but the tiles felt slippery, shifting underfoot, as though they would come loose at any moment, sending her sliding off the roof to the concrete courtyard three floors below.

"I can't! I can't let go!"

"If you don't get up there, I'm going to come up there and push you off the roof myself!"

"That's not helping, Natalya," said Ivan. "Wait." He pushed past Natalya and squeezed out on to the roof, on the opposite side of the skylight to Riya. Looking as scared as she felt, he shuffled up the roof until he reached the wide flat section above. With one foot on the flat section, he stepped the other back on to the sloping tiles and held out a hand to Riya. "Here, I'll pull you up."

Still holding on to the skylight hatch, Riya reached for Ivan's hand.

Natalya's head poked out of the skylight, "Will you two idiots get a move on!"

Ivan's hand closed around Riya's. With a grunt and a powerful tug, he hauled her up on to the flat roof, where they both fell backwards, landing with a thump.

"Thanks," gasped Riya. "Heights are not my thing."

He looked up, panting, "Nor mine."

Natalya jumped nimbly out of the skylight, flipped it shut, slipped a padlock though a hasp on the outside of the frame, and clicked it closed. "That might make them doubt we came this way."

She scampered up the tiles with no more concern than if she'd been running up the stairs. "Come. They'll have drones up here in a minute."

Ivan rolled his eyes, heaved himself to his feet and lumbered after Natalya, now racing across the rooftops like a startled deer, crouching low so as not to be seen from the street below. Riya got to her feet and followed.

Their building was at the end of a terrace of five, and Natalya ran from one end to the other before stopping to crouch by another skylight in the middle of the flat roof on the fifth building.

Riya and Ivan caught up as she flipped it open, "How did you know about this?" asked Riya.

Taking her rucksack off, Natalya climbed into the skylight and sat on the edge of the hatch, legs dangling inside. "While you two imbeciles were running around Cambridge, I decided I needed an escape route, in case you brought Booker's army back with you." She lowered herself in and climbed down the ladder.

Ivan followed Natalya. Riya passed the bags down before climbing in herself, relieved there would be no more rooftop scrambling. A whining buzz echoed across the rooftop and Riya saw a drone come soaring up from the street. Quickly, she flipped the skylight shut and climbed down the ladder.

Reaching the bottom, she looked around, "Where are we?" She was standing in a similar loft space to the one above their flat, but this one had been boarded out and looked like it was used as a storeroom: sacks of various sizes were stacked in piles; there were racks of plastic tubing; and plastic bins were full of white plastic pipe fittings.

Apart from the skylight, the only other light came from a stairwell leading to the floor below. Ignoring Riya's question, Natalya beckoned them to follow as she made her way to the stairs through the mounds of stuff strewn across the floor.

They descended the bare wooden stairs through three floors of what looked like more storerooms full of building supplies: sinks, radiators, plasterboard, sacks of cement and plaster. On the ground floor, Riya found herself in a narrow hallway. One door led out to the street, another was fitted with a code lock, presumably leading to the shop, since every building in the row had a shop occupying the ground floor. Natalya went straight to the code lock and began tapping numbers, opened the door, and strode through it. Ivan and Riya followed tentatively.

Inside, the shop was decked out untidily as an office. Several battered desks and tables were piled high with folders and rolls of large-format paper. A man was standing shouting angrily into his phone, jabbing his finger at a piece of paper on his desk as he talked, as though the person on the other end of the phone could see what he was pointing at. Rotund and balding, with a bushy black moustache, his skin had a Mediterranean olive tinge.

Natalya shoved papers aside to clear a space on one of the desks, and sat down, legs swinging idly.

The man looked up, blinked at them in surprise, muttered something into the phone, and hung up. His face changed instantly to a wide smile, his arms spread wide. "Ah, Natalya, how are you, my friend?" He didn't seem the least bit concerned they'd just walked into his office.

Natalya turned to Riya and Ivan, "This is Yanni. He will help us escape. Yanni, this is Riya and Ivan."

"Hello, friends of Natalya," the man bustled over and shook their hands vigorously.

"Yanni, we don't have much time, so…" Natalya made a twirling gesture with her fingers.

"Of course, my van is outside. I go and open the doors. Give me your bags, I put them inside."

Yanni hitched up his trousers (which looked like they were about to fall down), grabbed their bags, and headed out of the office.

Riya felt unnerved, putting her trust in someone she'd only just met. "How do you know he's not going to hand us over to Booker's men?"

"Because I'm giving him a lot of money not to," said Natalya.

A moment later, Yanni was back. He looked gravely at Natalya. "There are men outside your place, and they watch the street. My van is twenty metres the other way—the parking here is terrible."

Natalya nodded, "Art predicts that, if we go one at a time and walk casually, they will not notice us. They do not expect us to walk out of this shop."

Yanni led the way to the front door. "OK, my van is the white one, twenty metres on the right. I go first and start van. You guys come out, get in the back, and close the door. Easy, eh?" He grinned widely, "Just make sure you close my front door when you leave. OK, ready?"

They all nodded.

"Good!" He opened the door, stepped into the street, turned right, and was gone.

Natalya pulled her hood up and went next. Ivan put his cap on to hide his shock of yellow hair, and followed.

Riya waited a few seconds, blew out her cheeks, and stepped out on to the street. Keeping her face turned away, not daring to glance in the direction of the men outside their flat, she pulled the door to. It stuck. She pushed it open again and pulled it harder. It still didn't click shut. She tried again. Still, it didn't shut. This was ridiculous! She'd have to leave it. A little too quickly, she turned to hurry off down the street and slammed straight into an old lady carrying a shopping bag.

"Oh!" The lady staggered back, dropping her bag, sending groceries rolling across the pavement.

"I'm so sorry!" Riya instinctively bent down to help pick up the shopping, then remembered the men at their flat. She glanced up the road to see one of Booker's men watching her with mild interest.

Their eyes met and his face hardened with recognition.

A SHOT IN THE ARM

"Oh, crap." Riya looked the other way, towards Yanni's van. There was no sign of Natalya or Ivan; they must already be in the back. She could make out Yanni's horrified face staring out through the windscreen. If she ran, could she make it to the van before they got to her? No. But she wasn't going to simply stand there either. She stood up, stuck her middle finger up at Booker's man, smiled sweetly, and fled back into Yanni's shop. Slamming the door, this time she heard the deadlock click.

Where now?

All she could think of was to go back up to the roof—maybe there would be another skylight, she could drop through into one of the other buildings? She pelted up the stairs two at a time, footsteps booming like a drum on the bare wood. Stumbling at the first landing, she ricocheted off the wall and kept going. Up the second flight. *CRASH*. The sound of the door being kicked in reverberated through the stairwell. Up the third flight of steps. More booming footsteps joined her own on the stairs. Breathing hard, Riya's legs felt like jelly as she emerged into the dark attic space. Scrabbling up the ladder, she reached the skylight, popped it open, and climbed out on to the roof. She immediately heard the buzz of the drone overhead. She looked for another skylight in one of the adjacent buildings. There! The building in the middle of the row. But it was on the sloping part of the roof again; she would have to edge down the sloping tiles, there was no other option. Riya raced across the flat roof, then gingerly teetered down the tiled slope towards the skylight. The slate tiles shifted uncertainly under her feet. She made it to the skylight, crouched, and tugged. It wouldn't shift. She looked back to Yanni's roof to see a man appear. She was out of time.

There was a sharp *pffft* sound, then a *plink* next to her foot. Puzzled, she looked up.

He was pointing at her…No, wait.

He was *shooting* at her!

The *pfft* noise had been the sound of a silenced bullet! No Taser, this time. Booker was out for blood—the man hadn't even given her the option to surrender. Desperately, she tugged again at the skylight. It still refused to budge, locked from the inside. Another *pffft* and the glass in the skylight exploded. Shocked, Riya instinctively recoiled, stood up, and stepped back. The tile under her foot came loose. Riya began to topple backwards; she stood for a second, arms windmilling, trying to regain balance, then her other foot gave way, and her legs went from under her. She hit the roof with a winding thump and started sliding.

No, no, no, not over the edge!

It all seemed to be happening in slow motion. Her fingernails clawed futilely at the tiles, her feet scrabbled for grip but found none. Over the edge she went.

There was a moment of beautiful silence, the air rushing past her face, then, *BANG*. She smashed down on to another sloped roof; the property had a two-storey extension on the back, so she hadn't fallen far. Hitting the roof had broken her fall, but she was still sliding, half rolling towards another edge. She crashed through the gutter, and down again. This time it was a flat roof, and she hit it hard, grunting as pain jarred through her hip and shoulder.

Riya lay on her back, groaning, stunned, coughing, gasping for breath.

Come on, move! You have to move!

Slowly, her body responded. She rolled on to her side. *Thuck!* Something hit the roof next to her, sending up a small cloud of dust. She looked up. There were now three men on the roof. They were still shooting at her. She rolled, then crawled to the edge of the roof.

Another *thuck*, then…

"Aargh!" A sharp pain stung her forearm.

She slithered over the side of the roof, crumpling on to all fours as she hit the ground below.

Getting to her feet, she found herself in an alley running along the back of the terrace.

She leaned against the wall, protected now from the men on the roof. She looked at her forearm. Threads of white stuffing poked out of a small hole in her jacket sleeve and a trickle of blood ran from the cuff down the back of her hand. She flexed her fingers and winced as pain lanced through her arm. She'd been shot.

But she had to keep moving.

Maybe Art could help her out of this mess. She felt for the hard edge of the glasses case in her jacket pocket. As she pulled it out, her heart sank; the case was crushed, the hinges all twisted. She opened the lid and cringed; the lenses were smashed, the frame bent and buckled.

Suddenly, from her right, came the *ring-ding-ding* of small motorbike engines, and two scooters skidded into the end of the alley and raced towards her.

A moment later, at the other end of the alley, the front end of a white van filled the narrow lane, barrelling towards her at alarming speed.

Riya threw herself against the wall as the van tore past, inches from her nose, Yanni's furious moustached face glaring through the windscreen. She watched as the two men on scooters snaked to a stop and dived for cover. Yanni's van smashed into their discarded scooters, screeched to a halt, and reversed over the wreckage. The rear doors flew open, Ivan and Natalya jumped out, grabbed Riya under the arms, hauled her into the back, and slammed the doors shut behind them.

Riya heard the ominous *plink-plink* of more bullets on the van's bodywork as it lurched forward, then flung them all sideways as Yanni careened out of the alley on to the main street.

Riya lay on the floor, without the energy to move.

Ivan knelt down next to her, a deep frown knitting his blond eyebrows together, "Riya? Are you OK?"

She tried to speak, but it came out as a groan. She cleared her throat and tried again, "I've been better. They were *shooting* at me."

He looked down to her hand, now shiny with wet blood. "You've been *shot*?"

Natalya nodded, "I think Booker has run out of patience with us."

Ivan's face darkened, "We need to take her to a hospital."

"No hospitals," said Natalya flatly. "Booker will be expecting that now."

"But that arm needs treatment!" It was the first time Riya had seen Ivan express anything close to anger.

"Not in London."

Ivan breathed heavily, glaring at Natalya.

"Fine." He turned to Riya. "Take your coat off." He rummaged through his rucksack (twice as big as either Riya's or Natalya's) and pulled out a small red box with a white cross on it.

"You brought a first-aid kit?" Natalya laughed with surprise. "Did you have to choose between that and your dinner jacket?"

Ivan looked annoyed, "I race yachts, accidents happen, so I trained as a first aider."

Natalya looked highly amused at this revelation, "Wow. Dr. Parfenov, you are full of surprises."

Ivan ignored her, concentrating on Riya, who was struggling to take her jacket off.

"Here, let me help," he said.

She winced as her injured arm slid out of the sleeve.

As Ivan tended to her arm, Riya turned to Natalya. "By the way, where are we going?"

"London Heliport."

The van rolled to a stop outside the heliport. After thanking Yanni (with a fat envelope stuffed with cash), the three of them jumped out and made their way into the terminal, Natalya striding ahead, with Riya limping along behind, supported by Ivan.

At the reception desk, a young man greeted them with a smile, "Hello there, how can I help you?"

"I want to charter a helicopter. Who do I talk to?" snapped Natalya, not bothering to smile.

The receptionist looked unsure, but said, "I can help you with the charter. When is it for and where would you like to go?"

"Exeter airport, today."

That got the receptionist's attention. "*Today?* I'm not sure… People don't usually walk in here—"

"Family emergency."

The receptionist huffed and tapped away on his keyboard. "We do have one aircraft available, but I'm afraid it's our largest; it would be very expensive for only three of you—"

"We'll take it," Natalya threw her Visa card on the counter.

"OK," The receptionist sighed, as though he disapproved of such extravagance. "I'll need to take a few details."

Riya looked out over the Thames as the helicopter left the tarmac, drifting lazily upwards over London. She'd never been in a helicopter before, but was too uncomfortable and weary to enjoy the experience. What she really wanted right now was to lie down in a hot bath, and, luxurious as the helicopter seats were, they were no substitute.

Ivan, sitting across the table from her, reached into his bag and handed her a couple of tablets.

"Here, take these. Painkillers."

"Thanks," Riya took them gratefully, swilling them down with the complimentary spring water.

She thought again about how they'd nearly been duped by Cord. "How did they find someone that looked exactly like Johanna?"

Natalya shrugged, "Booker has one of the largest social-media databases in the world. It would be easy to run a facial-recognition application, find a few people that looked similar, add make-up, a wig, a few thousand dollars of deep fakery…" She looked at Riya with a crooked smile. "You did well back there, smelling a rat. That was quick thinking. I should have suspected something myself."

Riya grinned, "Thanks."

Natalya turned to Ivan. "So, this yacht in Dartmouth belonging to your father's Russian business friend—he agreed to lend it to you? Just like that?"

Ivan had suggested the yacht after they'd discovered Natalya's plan only went as far as getting them to the heliport. Natalya hadn't been able to come up with anything better, so…

"Of course," Ivan sounded offended. "I may not be useful for much, but I'm a good sailor." Then he added, sarcastically, "Especially if I have some proper grown-ups like you around to take care of me. Anyway, it's not like it's Oleg's pride and joy. He bought it 'to entertain clients'—it's a tax write-off. It sits around doing nothing, most of the time—he often employs people to sail it around because it's cheaper than mooring fees. Me and some friends sailed it up from the Med to Dartmouth last summer."

"Hmm," Natalya looked sceptical.

He sighed, "You wanted somewhere that's anonymous, hard to trace, and where the Keyholders can get together and—how did you put it?—'vote off that traitorous piece of scum'. A yacht is perfect. You're self-sufficient, can just sail off into the sunset if you want."

"If you know this Oleg that well, is it possible Booker will be tracking him?"

"Maybe, but Oleg's paranoid about security. You don't survive in business in Russia without being pretty savvy about security—you should know that."

"Did he ask questions?"

"He asked whether I was all right; he'd heard through the grapevine I had gone missing. Said, as long as I was OK, he didn't want to know any more."

Natalya opened her mouth again, but Ivan had clearly had enough of being grilled.

"Look, you're the one who headed to the heliport without a plan."

Natalya bristled. "Gimme a break. When I made my plan, I was not expecting you two as extra baggage, and I definitely wasn't looking for somewhere for all six Keyholders to meet—"

"Why do we need to get together to vote Cord off?" Riya interrupted. She was in no mood to listen to the two of them bickering. "Surely you techy guys can do it over a conference call?"

Natalya sighed. "We all need to be physically in the same location. Sanjay considered voting off a Keyholder to be an important decision. Your father put a great deal of value on face-to-face discussion; he designed the system so that we need to be physically together to vote people off. Art will not let us override that. So, yes, we have to all meet up."

She opened the lid of her laptop.

Conversation closed.

DARTMOUTH

The painkillers had obviously worked. Riya found herself woken from a deep sleep by a change in engine note. She squinted groggily out of the window as the ground came up to meet them. It didn't have the same sense of drama as landing in an aeroplane—no runway racing beneath you, no roar of engines or jarring touchdown—just a feeling of floating to the ground and a gentle bump as the wheels met the landing pad.

Riya shuffled through airport arrivals in a haze of pain. She struggled to keep up with Natalya, who made no allowances for the fact that, while painkillers and a few hours' sleep had given her some strength back, Riya's battered body had stiffened up during the flight.

"So, how are we getting to this yacht of yours?" she asked Ivan.

"The angry pixie has arranged transport," Ivan nodded at Natalya striding ahead. "She booked a hire car on the helicopter while you were sleeping. She's had it delivered from some private hire company miles away—regular airport rentals were too traceable, apparently. And she's phoned the others—they will be meeting us in Dartmouth."

As Riya watched, Natalya strode up to a man in a shell suit holding a sign saying *Smith*.

Riya snorted, "Smith? Not a very original alias."

"Don't knock it. Knowing Natalya, I thought we'd be bussing it."

As they threw their bags into the boot of the car, Riya couldn't help an anxious glance around the car park, shielding her eyes from the late-afternoon sun. Could their flight have been tracked? What with Booker and now MI5 after them, she was becoming paranoid.

Natalya noticed her nervousness, "Don't worry, we were careful. We're safe."

"Easy for you to say," said Riya, cradling her bad arm, which was beginning to throb again. She folded herself into the back seat and prepared for another uncomfortable journey.

"Want a chip?" Ivan thrust the paper-wrapped congealed mass of fish and chips towards Riya. Steaming in the cold evening air, they stank of vinegar.

Riya recoiled, wrinkling her nose, "No thanks."

"Suit yourself," Ivan took them back, shovelled another forkful into his mouth, and turned to Natalya. "I don't get why we are stuck up here on this hill, freezing our *cojones* off in Kingswear. I thought you told the Keyholders to meet us over there, in Dartmouth?" He jabbed his chip fork across the water, where the little car ferry chugged up to its slipway for the fiftieth time that night.

Elbows resting on a stone wall, eyes glued to a pair of binoculars, Natalya looked out across the inky waters of the River Dart to the twinkling night lights of Dartmouth on the other side. "I was careful. But Johanna and Ravi may not have been. I told them to go to the dockside in front of the yacht club and wait for my call. From here, I can watch them arrive, see if they were followed."

"And if they *have* been followed?"

"Quiet! Here's Johanna."

Squinting across the water, Riya thought she could make out a slim figure topped with a mass of curly hair.

"Now, are you alone…?" muttered Natalya, sweeping her binoculars from side to side, scanning the dockside. Satisfied, she pulled out her phone, unlocked it with her fingerprint, and handed it to Riya. "Call Johanna and tell her to take the Lower Ferry to Kingswear. Tell her to hurry; it will leave in a few minutes."

Johanna's voice answered: "Hey, Natalya."

"Actually, it's Riya."

"Is everything OK? Where are you guys?"

"Yeah, we're fine. Natalya says take the Lower Ferry over to Kingswear."

"Ah, checking if I've been followed? Smart." Riya could hear the smile in her voice.

"She says you have to hurry; the next one leaves in a few minutes."

"OK. See you soon." The phone went dead.

"Well?" said Natalya.

"She says you're smart."

Natalya snorted and adjusted her binoculars, "Now, we see. If she is being followed, they will follow her on to the ferry."

As Riya watched, the little figure across the water disappeared from view, then reappeared near the ferry. Riya held her breath as Johanna stepped on to the ferry. No one followed, the ramp was raised, and the ferry was on its way.

"OK. That's one," Natalya disconnected from her binoculars and rubbed her eyes. "Fat boy—run down to the ferry and meet Johanna, bring her up here."

"You do know my name's Ivan, right? Or do you have Tourette's or something? And, anyway, why me?"

"You need the exercise."

"And you're in desperate need of a personality transplant." Rolling his eyes at Riya, he shambled off down the hill.

By the time Ivan came puffing back up the hill with Johanna, Natalya was again attached to her binoculars.

"Hey, Riya," Johanna embraced her, but let go immediately when Riya winced. "Oh! Sorry! Your arm! Natalya told me what happened. How is it?"

Riya grimaced, "Painful."

Johanna looked sympathetic, "Rough day, huh?"

"I've had better."

Johanna put her arm around Riya and gave her a squeeze—avoiding her bad arm, this time—then looked around. "Where's Ravi?"

"You were first," Natalya checked her watch. "And Ravi is late. I told him specifically not to be late."

"Maybe he got held up somewhere. Does it matter?" said Ivan.

"He's always late, and yes, it matters. If he is late, he may have been intercepted."

Twenty minutes came and went. Riya was about to ask how long they were going to wait, when Natalya made her jump.

"He's here!"

She adjusted her binoculars, scanning the other side of the water. She growled something in Russian and lowered the binoculars.

"He was followed. Shit!"

"Where? Show me," Johanna stepped towards Natalya.

Natalya handed her the binoculars, "In the bus shelter, fifty metres to the right of the yacht club."

"They could be waiting for a bus."

Natalya grunted, "No buses at this time of night."

"I don't see…ah, yes, three of them, right? It's hard to see, though; it's dark in that shelter." Johanna lowered the binoculars, looking doubtful. "Are you sure you're not being paranoid? It could just be kids hanging out?"

"If I was following someone along the docks and I didn't want to be seen, that's where I would hide. And they weren't there before Ravi arrived, I checked."

"Why didn't they just bump him off?" asked Ivan.

Natalya shrugged, "Cord knows our next move is to get together to vote him off, so they probably figured it would be better to follow Ravi, get him to lead them to the rest of us. He most likely did something stupid on his way here—booked a ticket using his real name, got spotted on CCTV…"

Johanna sighed, "We can't risk contact if there's even the slightest possibility he's been followed."

Natalya unslung her bag and gave it to Johanna, "I'll go and get him."

Johanna shook her head, "It's too dangerous—you've used up most of your nine lives already."

"I'll take the car, drive by, pick him up and drive off. Easy peasy." Her words were flippant, but Natalya's expression was bleak.

Johanna looked doubtful, "It might not be that easy."

"We're here to vote Cord off, right? We need Ravi for that. Anyway, I have help—Riya, you are coming with me."

"What? Why? Haven't I had enough excitement for one day?"

"I need an extra pair of eyes, and you are the least conspicuous."

Riya looked at the chaotic colourful haystack-topped mound of Ivan and the cool urban sleekness of Johanna. She blew out her cheeks. She kept moaning that Natalya treated her like a child, so she couldn't really complain when she did show some trust in her.

"OK."

Natalya smiled grimly. "Don't worry, no need to jump off any roofs this time. But you need your glasses." Natalya pulled her own from her jacket pocket and put them on.

"Oh, erm…my glasses are, yeah…umm, broken," Riya winced.

"What?" Natalya looked as though Riya had slapped her.

"Don't look at me like that—I didn't do it on purpose." Riya pulled the broken case from her pocket and opened it, displaying the twisted, broken frames.

Natalya sighed heavily, like a disappointed parent. She unzipped her rucksack and pulled out a glasses case identical to Riya's.

"Here. This is my *only* spare pair. *Do. Not. Break. Them.*"

"Yeah, sorry—it was so careless of me, falling off that building when they were shooting at me. I'll try not to do it again." Riya snatched them off Natalya.

"Good. Glad to hear it."

"Are we going to use Art?" Riya would feel a lot better if Art had simulated this and given them a decent probability of success.

Natalya shook her head, "Art will be blocked from running simulations involving Cord."

"Then why the glasses?"

"I told Ravi to use them—it's better than a phone." Natalya zipped up her coat, "Ready?"

Riya huffed wearily, "I guess."

Johanna looked from Riya to Natalya. "OK, if you're set on this, Ivan and I will go to the yacht and wait for you there. No point waiting out in the open. Here, give us your bags." She took Natalya's rucksack from her, then caught her arm. "Do not take any risks, Natalya. If there's any doubt, leave him there. If you two are caught, this is all over."

"I get that. Don't worry." With a crooked smile, Natalya pulled free of Johanna's grip and started back down the steep narrow street to where they'd parked the car outside a tiny ancient church.

Riya handed her bag to Ivan. He didn't look happy. "Be careful," he said. "Natalya's not the only one stretching her luck."

"It'll be OK. I think she has a plan."

He raised his eyebrows, "And how did her last plan work out for you?"

Riya tried to brush aside Ivan's comment with a grin, but couldn't quite pull it off. She turned and followed Natalya.

As soon as they'd left Ivan and Johanna, Natalya asked Art to start a shared session. A video panel opened in Riya's vision showing the view through Ravi's glasses.

"Ravi?"

"Oh, hey," Ravi's voice came through Riya's glasses. "I was starting to think you weren't going to call. Hi, Riya, I see you're online—"

"You were followed," Natalya had no time for small talk.

"What?" Ravi's voice became thin and shaky. The video feed from his glasses swivelled wildly as he looked around.

Natalya tutted, "Don't panic, don't show them that you know you were followed. Stay there. We're coming to get you. Just…act normal."

"OK." Ravi sounded on the verge of hysteria.

Natalya and Riya drove down the hill into Kingswear, listening to Ravi's rapid breathing, and came to a stop at the top of the Lower Ferry slipway, the only car waiting to cross. Riya watched the lights of the ferry glide slowly across the water towards them. She was struck by the tranquil sleepy scene, totally at odds with the pounding of her heart and Natalya's nervous fingers drumming on the steering wheel.

The car clanked down the ferry ramp and on to the Dartmouth slipway. Natalya pulled over outside a brightly lit fish-and-chip shop, the staff inside busy cleaning down for the night. She pointed through the windscreen. "This road runs parallel to the dockside where Ravi is; if his stalkers have backup, they'll be in a car parked down one of the side streets connecting the two. I want you to walk along this street, look down those side streets, see if you can see a car parked at the kerbside with people in it."

Riya didn't like the idea of this at all, "Why can't we just drive past?"

"If we drive too slowly we look suspicious, too fast and we might miss something."

"What if they see me?"

Natalya shook her head. "They will be focused on the riverfront, they will not be looking behind." Riya must have looked unconvinced because Natalya added, "Look, any sign of trouble, you come straight back. I'll keep an eye on you through the glasses, OK? Now, go."

Sighing heavily, Riya opened the door and slid out into the cold. She headed down the street, hugging the shadows. She slowed as she approached the first side street to her right and gingerly edged it into view. It was clear, no cars at all; she could see straight through to the dockside and the lights reflected on the river beyond. She exhaled with relief and moved on, picking up her pace—she wanted to get this over with.

Again, her chest tightened as she came to the next side street, and again she edged the street into view, and again the street was empty.

The next street was only a few paces away. Emboldened by the thought that this was all in Natalya's paranoid mind, she strode across the next street. There were a few cars parked here and there, but they were empty. No, wait! One had people in it, sitting very still, lights off.

She slowed as she crossed the road, trying to get a better look.

"Keep going! Don't stop!" yelled Natalya in her ear.

"Did you see—?"

"Yes, I saw."

"It might be nothing."

"But it might be something. Come back to the car."

Riya flopped into the car seat beside Natalya, "What now?"

"We may be seeing monsters in the shadows, but we cannot risk it. If there are bad men sitting in that car and we stop to pick up Ravi, then drive off, they'll follow us. We need to shake them off before we pick him up."

"Natalya? What's going on?" Ravi's voice spoke in Riya's ear.

"It's too risky to pick you up there, Ravi. We need to run you around Dartmouth to lose your followers. Art, pull up a map of Dartmouth."

A panel opened in Riya's vision showing a street map of Dartmouth.

Natalya stared into the middle distance, eyes flickering side to side as she studied the map displayed through her own glasses. "There must be some way through…An old town like this…" She sat forward, "Yes, perfect. Art, enable inking."

She raised a finger, gesturing in mid-air. As she did, blue scribble lines appeared on the map in Riya's vision.

"Ravi, you are here." A blue dot scribbled on the map near the dockside.

"OK," said Ravi, obviously seeing Natalya's scribble as well.

"Go up here…" Riya watched a blue line trace along the riverfront and up one of the side streets. "Then turn *here*, cross over, and…up there is a pedestrian alley—a car won't be able to follow you. If you run, you should shake off anyone on foot.

Then, along here…" The blue scribble continued snaking across the map as Natalya traced the route. "And here, take this footpath up to Jawbones Hill. We will meet you there in a car." The blue scrawl ended in a dot.

"OK. Are you sure it will work?" asked Ravi.

Natalya shrugged, "Meh, probably."

Riya rolled her eyes. Ravi was scared and looking for reassurance.

"Hi, Ravi—of course it will work. Run as fast as you can when you turn into the pedestrian alley, and you're home free. We've avoided these idiots so far, haven't we?"

Ravi gave a nervous little laugh, "OK. Thanks, Riya."

"OK, enough," Natalya said. "Ravi, wait where you are while we get into position."

They drove in silence, winding their way up the Dartmouth hillside, while Ravi shuffled around nervously on the dockside.

Now, high above the centre of Dartmouth, they turned on to Jawbones Hill, a sleepy housing cul-de-sac ending in a farm track. Natalya drove to the end, turned round, and parked on the end of a line of cars under the trees lining the side of the road.

"Ravi? Are you ready? Remember, walk to begin with, don't rush, make them think you are not aware of them. Then, when you get to the alley, *run your ass off*."

"OK. Ready." Ravi sounded shaky. Riya wondered if he would keep it together. He cleared his throat. "Art, guide me along Natalya's route to Jawbones Hill."

"Certainly, Ravi," said Art pleasantly.

Riya watched as a map panel opened alongside Ravi's video feed, with a green flashing dot showing his position, and a chequered flag over the location of her and Natalya.

"OK, setting off now."

The dot moved off along the riverfront. Ravi's video feed showed him glancing over his shoulder at the bus stop.

"Don't keep looking back," growled Natalya.

He crossed the road into a side street. At the next street, he kept walking at a slow sauntering pace. He was approaching the entrance to the alley.

"OK, get ready..." Even Natalya's voice sounded tense. "*Go!*"

The green dot started moving fast, Ravi's video feed bouncing up and down as he ran. Riya could hear his breathing, loud and ragged, as he pounded up the steep alley. At the end of the alley, he turned left on to Above Town Road, still running. Now all he had to do was take a right up another alley...Blank. The video panel disappeared.

Natalya sat upright, "Art? What's happened to the video feed?"

"Connection with Ravi has been terminated," said Art calmly.

"Why?"

"That information is not available."

Riya and Natalya watched as the green dot on the map remained stationary.

"I don't like this," Natalya said. "I'm going to take a look."

"But it could be a trap!"

"Yeah, I know," Natalya looked grim. "Stay in the car. Follow me using the glasses. If the video feed stops, wait ten minutes, then leave the car and get to Johanna and Ivan. If anything else goes wrong, same thing: don't come looking for me."

Before Riya could argue, Natalya yanked the door handle and sprang out. Riya turned in her seat to see her disappear behind the car, along the dark farm track at the end of the cul-de-sac.

"Art, share the video feed from Natalya's glasses."

"Requesting..." After a short pause, a video panel opened alongside the map panel, which now displayed a moving purple dot, tagged as Natalya, moving slowly towards Ravi's stationary green dot. Natalya's video feed showed her travelling along an overgrown track, the trees overhead forming a tunnel so dark that Riya couldn't make out details. After a few minutes, a dim orange light appeared ahead, where the trees finished and the path met the road. Natalya slowed as the path turned from packed mud to a worn, broken stone stairway, which descended between ancient crumbling walls struggling to hold back a tide of bushes and trees.

Riya looked at the map. The purple and green dots were now almost on top of each other.

Natalya only had ten metres of steps to go before she hit the road where Ravi's video feed had disappeared. Riya could hear Natalya's breathing, shallow and nervous, as she reached the bottom of the steps and peered out into the street, a crowded mishmash of houses tumbling over each other down the steep hillside. Nothing moved. Natalya waited and watched.

Riya realized she had been holding her breath and took a gulp of air. Natalya edged out into the road to see further along the street. Empty. She looked down at the road. A pair of glasses lay crushed on the ground.

Natalya's head snapped up as a dark figure stepped out into the road from one of the parking garages set into the hillside.

Riya gasped, clasping hands to her face.

Cord!

SURVIVORS

"Hello, Natalya. We were expecting you," as he spoke, a small drone buzzed down from the sky and landed at Cord's feet. He bent down and picked it up. "You're not the only one with toys. Your thermal image is quite beautiful, you know. You did well. That path was well covered with trees, so we didn't spot you until the last few metres."

"Where is he?" Natalya's angry bark made Riya jump.

Three figures emerged from the shadows. The street light caught Ravi's face first, staring desperately at Natalya. Holding his arms firmly on either side were two men: one heavy and muscular, the other—Riya felt an icy chill run down her back—the tall rangy frame of the Frenchman. Both carried pistols, and Riya had seen enough movies to notice they were fitted with silencers. Cord's smile softened into something like pity.

"It's time to stop this, Natalya, before someone gets hurt. We need to hand over Art to Jim Booker. He is the rightful owner of this technology. Call the others and tell them to join us."

Without thinking, Riya got out of the car and ran towards the farm track, with no clue what she would do at the other end. For all her rudeness and insults, Natalya had remained staunchly loyal to the Keyholders and Sanjay; she had taken Riya and Ivan under her wing. Then she stopped, remembering Natalya's words: *If anything goes wrong, get back to Johanna and Ivan.* No, it didn't matter if she was caught; she owed it to Natalya to try. At a steady trot, Riya set off into the black mouth of the farm track.

Picking her way through the darkness, she kept half an eye on Natalya's video feed…

Natalya was laying into Cord: "Why did you do it, Cord?"

Cord nodded ruefully, "I didn't plan to betray you, but Sanjay left me no choice."

Natalya gave a derisive snort.

"My son has leukaemia, Natalya," Cord's retort was sharp and angry. He sighed, then continued more quietly, "He was diagnosed around the time we completed Art, and Jim Booker asked Sanjay to sell him Predictive. We exhausted all the treatment options—nothing worked. Then we were told about a new treatment in America, but it was experimental, and expensive…"

"You sold us out?" Natalya was unsympathetic, but Riya felt a tug on her conscience—would she have done the same for her mother? Perhaps.

"Sanjay left me no choice. I couldn't use Art to generate the money—if Sanjay had found out I was abusing the system for personal gain, he would have kicked me off the team with nothing. Anyway, if Sanjay had sold Predictive Technologies like he said he would, the shares he gave all of us would have covered the cost of my son's treatment. But, no, Sanjay decided, once he'd announced Art at the AI conference, he was just going to close down Predictive Technologies. I would lose my job, and my shares would be worthless."

"You knew Art was a non-profit project…"

"Yes, but Predictive Technologies was still a valuable company. He could have sold it, made us all wealthy, and still taken Art with him."

"You know why he couldn't do that, Cord…Booker would have prevented the sale of the company to anyone else but him. Sanjay decided to dissolve the company so there would be nothing left for Booker. When we discussed it, you agreed to winding up Predictive Technologies."

"Did I have a choice? What would he have done if I had said, 'No, I want you to sell the company because I need the money'?"

Natalya's silence answered his question.

"Exactly. Asking us was just a courtesy; the decision had already been made. I panicked, went to Jim Booker, hoping he could use his lawyers or something to stop Sanjay. I never expected him to *murder* Sanjay…Then Booker promised to fund my son's treatment if I told him the names of the Keyholders and helped to round you up. I agreed, as long as he agreed not to hurt anyone."

"That was generous of you," said Natalya.

Riya had reached the bottom of the stone steps, stopping a few metres short of the road. What now? She looked up at the walls either side of the steps. Quietly, she began climbing the wall to her right, the old stonework providing easy hand and foot holds. It was only just taller than head height, but her injured arm screamed with pain making it difficult to climb. Peering over the top, it was as she had expected: a garden ran level with the top of the wall, a terraced lawn jutting out of the hillside. Using her elbows and swinging one leg up, she awkwardly levered herself up and, crawling on her belly, made her way to the end of the garden. Peering between a cluster of potted plants, she looked over a low wall, down to Natalya and the others standing in the road some two metres below.

Cord seemed desperate to justify himself. "When Booker heard you were planning to hand Art over to MI5, I was afraid people would start getting hurt, so I had to do something. I knew if I caught *you*, I'd also get Riya and Ivan, then the others would fall into line to save you. I could end this thing without anyone getting hurt." Cord looked pleadingly at Natalya.

"You're naïve, Cord. Booker killed Sanjay and Victor, and he'll never let us live, knowing what we know. They tried to shoot us when they came for us in London."

Cord looked uncertainly at Raphael, who remained silent. He turned back to Natalya. "I didn't create this mess, Natalya. Sanjay did, by refusing to talk to Booker about selling the Anticipation Machine."

Natalya snorted, "Sanjay told him the Anticipation Machine was a non-profit project. It was supposed to be for everyone; it was meant to change the world."

"Now who's being naïve, Natalya? You think governments will be any less self-serving? You think your new friends at MI5 are going to allow this to be used for civilian purposes?"

"Maybe, maybe not," spat Natalya. "But at least I believe it's worth a shot."

Raphael's lazy French drawl cut in, "Are we done? We cannot stand here all night."

"Come on, Natalya," Cord wrung his hands, pleading. "Give Booker what he wants, then we can all go home."

Riya suddenly felt sorry for Cord. He'd been put in an impossible situation, forced to make decisions that made him squirm for the sake of his family.

Raphael stepped forward, beckoning to Natalya, "No one has been hurt yet, and Mr. Booker is a practical man. It would be better for everyone if this could be resolved without violence."

Natalya didn't move, "And what happens if we don't come quietly?"

Raphael shrugged, "Then that would be most…regrettable."

Natalya's face set in a steely grimace. She wasn't going to give in. Riya knew without doubt Raphael would kill her if she didn't give them what they wanted.

She looked around desperately. Her eyes settled on the plant pots. Scrambling to her knees, she picked up the smallest one. It was full of soil and difficult to manipulate in her one good hand. Getting to her feet, she hurled it at the muscular man holding Ravi's arm, not sure if it would hit the man, Ravi, or just smash harmlessly on the ground. It gave a satisfying crack as it hit the top of his head. The pot split into pieces, showering the man with earth as he dropped to his knees.

Everyone looked up at her, shocked confusion on their faces.

Calmly, Raphael raised his gun, aiming at Riya. But, at that moment, Natalya bolted back up the steps, momentarily distracting him, giving Riya time to drop to her stomach behind the wall before she heard the sharp *phut phut* of silenced bullets. A plant pot exploded, sending a spray of dirt into the air above her. Next, she heard footsteps and shouting from the street below.

Natalya's voice screamed through her glasses, "Riya, get out of there!"

Riya knew she should run, but she couldn't just leave Ravi. Daring to raise her head just enough to peer down to the lamplit street, she saw Ravi had broken away from his captors in the confusion and was sprinting down the street. Riya watched in horror as Raphael turned, raised his pistol, aimed, *shot*. Ravi went down like a felled tree, his body sliding to a halt on the road.

Cord gawped at Raphael, his face contorted with a stupefied look of revulsion and disbelief, then he started screaming, "What have you done?! Booker said he wouldn't hurt them!"

The Frenchman raised his gun again and pulled the trigger. Cord's head snapped backwards, emitting a spray of dark liquid. With a look of surprise etched on his face, he collapsed in a heap at Raphael's feet.

Riya couldn't breathe, she felt sick. Even the burly thug, now back on his feet, seemed shocked, simply staring at Cord's body.

Raphael clicked his fingers to get the man's attention. "Why are you still standing here?" He waved his gun at the crumpled bodies. "I will deal with this. Go! Get the others."

Jerking out of her ghastly trance, Riya stooped low and raced back across the garden to the wall bordering the path. She leaped down to the steps and pounded off up the steep track towards the car, ignoring the screaming pain in her joints. Raphael's thug wasn't far behind, but in the dark, on an unfamiliar path, still groggy from the bang on his head, his progress was slow.

The last third of the path twisted and turned, branching off in different directions. Riya prayed this would make her pursuer hesitate long enough for her to reach the car. The video feed from Natalya's glasses showed she was already there. Gasping for breath, legs burning, she sprinted out on to the road, the red tail lights of Natalya's car ahead.

She ran to the passenger side, yanked open the door, and dived inside.

"Go!"

Natalya stamped on the accelerator, sending the car lurching out of the parking space, tyres squealing, slewing from side to side down the road. Gravel thrown up from the road clattered loudly against the car. Then the rear window shattered. It wasn't gravel hitting the car—it was bullets!

Riya instinctively ducked down in her seat, and Natalya bent low over the steering wheel. Reaching the end of the street, Riya was flung sideways and the tyres howled as Natalya threw the car left up a narrow single-track road out of Dartmouth. High banks, walls, and hedgerows flashed by, inches from the side of the car. Riya gripped the dashboard as they hurtled down the dark country road, aware that, if they met anything coming the other way at this speed, the emergency services would be picking their remains out of the boot. Finally, they emerged on to the main road heading back into Dartmouth, and Natalya slowed to a more sedate, less conspicuous speed.

"We'll take the Higher Ferry back to Kingswear." Her voice sounded strained.

Riya eyed her more closely: Natalya's face was pale, greasy with sweat, jaw muscles knotted tight, "Are you OK?"

"I'm fine," she glanced at the car clock. "We should make the last crossing of the night."

Crawling slowly down the slipway with two other cars, they clanked up the ramp on to the ferry and switched off the engine.

As the ferry shuddered away from the shoreline, a grey bearded face appeared at the driver's-side window, woollen hat tugged down to his bushy eyebrows. "Single, is it?" His eyes flicked to the missing windows and his shaggy eyebrows knotted in a frown. "Bit draughty, ain't it?"

"God damn vandals," said Natalya.

The man shook his head despairingly, "Aye, some people got no respect."

Natalya grunted, paid, and the man moved on.

Riya leaned her head back against the headrest and closed her eyes. She was instantly assaulted by the image of blood spraying from the side of Cord's head. She hurled open the door and threw up by the side of the car.

"Ya'll right, miss?" Hearing the retching, the bearded conductor reappeared around the side of the car.

Riya spat away the trailing strings of saliva from her mouth and looked up, "Yeah. Bit seasick."

The conductor glanced at the glassy surface of the river and raised his eyebrows.

Riya looked at the pool of vomit by her door, "Sorry."

The conductor waved, "Nah, don' you worry. We'll sluice it down, nice bit o' food for the fish."

Five minutes later, the ferry docked on the far side of the river and Riya was soon gripping the dashboard again as Natalya resumed her wild flight down the narrow Devonshire lanes.

Then, slamming on the brakes, she veered on to an overgrown mud track and brought the car to a halt in the middle of a wood. "We walk from here."

"We're leaving the car?"

"Yes. We have no use for it now, and we will be less noticeable arriving on foot."

It was pitch black under the trees and they had to use their phone torches to find their way back to the road. Natalya was breathing hard and grunting every other step; even in the dark, Riya could see she was limping.

"What's wrong with your leg?"

"I'm fine."

Riya shone her torch on Natalya's legs and saw a dark shiny stain running from her right thigh to her shoe. "You're bleeding!"

"I don't have time to bleed," said Natalya, stumbling over a tuft of grass as they reached the road.

Riya rolled her eyes, "God, sometimes you sound like such a *guy*." Taking Natalya's arm, she looped it around her neck. "Here, let me help."

Natalya didn't refuse, and Riya felt her weight as they began a staggering walk down the hill towards the lights of Kingswear.

After two hundred metres, Natalya was leaning more and more heavily on Riya. They would never make it to Ivan's yacht like this. "I'm calling Ivan." For a moment, Natalya looked as though she would argue, but then she sighed and waved a weary acceptance at Riya.

Ivan answered, his voice high and tight. "Hello?"

"Ivan, it's me…Look, Natalya's hurt. No time to explain. Can you come and meet us? We need help."

"Where are you?"

"Use your glasses to find us."

"Oh, yeah, of course."

The phone went dead. A minute later, the request came through Riya's glasses: "Ivan Parfenov requesting share session."

She agreed and Ivan's breathless voice came through, accompanied by running footsteps, "Riya, I've got your location. I'm on my way."

Riya was about to collapse on the pavement with Natalya when Ivan came into view, puffing up the hill like an asthmatic steam train.

"Here, let me take her." He took Natalya's arm from around Riya's neck and draped it around his own. Supporting her around the waist, he strode off down the hill, Natalya bouncing along at his hip like a rag doll, tiny next to his bearlike frame.

It was nearly midnight as Ivan tapped in the code at the marina gate and the three of them swayed unsteadily on to the pontoon of moored yachts. Natalya hung limply between Riya and Ivan.

Ivan stopped next to an impressive sleek-looking yacht. It was huge. Riya wasn't sure what she had expected, but this was definitely bigger. "Here we are."

Natalya stared at the name on the yacht transom, then looked back at Ivan, "You've got to be kidding me."

Riya squinted at the name: *Lady Luck*.

Hoisting Natalya aboard, they half carried, half dropped her down the companionway. Johanna, sitting alone at the table, leaped to her feet as they tumbled into the cabin, and, along with Ivan, helped Natalya to a seat.

"What happened?" Peering at the open hatch, she frowned. "Where's Ravi?"

"Booker's men have him. There was no way to get him out," said Natalya through gritted teeth, gripping her thigh.

Riya realized Natalya hadn't seen what had happened after she fled up the steps. Her eyes filled with tears as the images flashed through her mind again. "They're both dead." The words snapped out like gunfire. She cleared her throat, choking back the tears, "The Frenchman shot Ravi and Cord. They're dead."

Natalya touched the side of her glasses, "Art. Please give me a vital-signs status on Cord and Ravi." Her face went slack, staring into the distance. "He says there are now four Keyholders."

They looked at one another, as if hoping someone would refute this. Eventually, a grunt of discomfort from Natalya broke the morbid silence.

Ivan looked up, sniffed, blinked his reddened eyes, then crouched beside Natalya. "Let's take a look at that leg." He looked up at her. "Bullet?"

She nodded, "Through the side of the car."

Ivan stood back, "Take your trousers off."

Natalya raised her eyebrows.

Ivan rolled his eyes, "Don't flatter yourself; you're not my type."

"I didn't know you had a type."

"Generally, I'm not that fussy, but rude, aggressive, egotistical types really don't light my fire."

Natalya looked surprised, "Egotistical?"

"Yes. Now, are you going to whip 'em off or just sit there and bleed?" Ivan turned to the galley and began washing his hands.

Natalya glared at him sullenly, but slowly unbuttoned her jeans and wriggled them painfully down to her thighs. Ivan grabbed them and peeled them the rest of the way, leaving Natalya sitting in her knickers. Throwing the jeans to one side, he bent to inspect the small bloody hole the size of a pea in her right leg.

"Make sure you keep eyes on your work, playboy. Ssst!" Natalya stiffened as Ivan gently prodded the wound.

"The bad news is there's no exit wound, so the bullet is still in there, but the good news is it's near the surface—the car door must have slowed it down." He looked up at her. "And that emotional body armour of yours probably helped as well."

Natalya leered at him sarcastically.

"OK, I'm going to try to get the bullet out. Riya, can you close the hatch, please?" He glanced at Natalya. "This will sting a bit and we don't want the whole marina hearing you."

Natalya eyed him warily as Riya shut the hatch.

"Ready?"

Natalya nodded. Ivan placed his thumbs either side of the wound and squeezed, as if he were squeezing a spot.

Blood oozed from the hole and Natalya threw back her head, growling through clenched teeth, as the veins on her neck stood out like fat worms.

Riya grimaced, feeling queasy, but kept watching as a small shiny metal slug slowly emerged from the hole.

Grabbing a pair of tweezers from his first-aid kit, Ivan gradually worked the bullet out of her leg. "There she blows." Looking pleased with himself, he tossed the bullet at Natalya. "Souvenir."

Natalya looked at him balefully, her face beaded with sweat. "Thanks."

Ivan dressed the wound, gave her some painkillers and stood up, stretching his back. "So, what now?"

All eyes turned to Johanna. "We get some sleep and discuss it in the morning. I wouldn't trust any decisions we made in this state."

"What about the men looking for us? Shouldn't we get out of here?" Riya wanted to get as far away as possible; lying asleep while ruthless killers prowled around outside wasn't something she liked the sound of.

"I think we're safest here, for now. It's most unlikely they will suspect we are on a yacht." Johanna looked at Ivan. "And I assume we would be highly conspicuous if we sailed out of the harbour in the middle of the night?"

Ivan nodded.

"So, as long as we stay inside, there is nothing to give away the fact that we are here."

Riya didn't feel reassured; there were a lot of assumptions in Johanna's reasoning, and too many of their recent assumptions had proved wrong.

REUNITED

Riya sat up suddenly in the darkness, gasping for breath, drenched in sweat, heart pounding. She'd been dreaming—horrible images of Ravi and Cord staggering around covered in blood, moaning, half their faces shot away.

She blinked, disorientated…Ah, yes, the yacht. Her cabin was probably considered luxurious accommodation, but, with the low ceiling and being only slightly larger than the bed, to Riya it felt more like a glorified coffin.

Wide awake now, she threw off the hot duvet and reached for her phone. Ugh! Three in the morning.

With the images of her dreams still floating before her eyes, Riya's mind began asking questions—questions she didn't have an answer for. Would her father really want them to go on? It was costing people their lives! Was Art really worth all this? She sat up and grabbed the glasses from the shelf under the window, putting them on.

"Good morning, Riya."

"Art, can I speak to my dad?"

Riya waited. What was he doing? Instinctively, she glanced down at the clock on her phone. How long did it take to raise the dead?

"Hello, Riya."

She shivered at the familiar sound of his voice and looked up. He stood with his back to the door, smiling at her. His eyes ranged around the cabin. "Where are we?"

"On a yacht—belongs to a friend of Ivan's. Dad, I need your advice." She lowered her voice, aware sound would travel through the boat easily in the silence of the night, and she didn't feel like sharing this conversation.

"Of course, tell me," he sat on the edge of the bed, looking at her earnestly.

"This situation with Art and the Keyholders is getting out of control. People are being killed, Dad...Ravi, Cord..."

"What?" Her father looked alarmed.

"They're dead. Booker's men shot them, earlier tonight. I saw it happen."

He shook his head in disbelief, "I never thought it would come to this."

"Booker killed you and Victor, Dad. What made you think he wouldn't do the same to others?"

His shoulders slumped, "I just...I didn't expect people to die for this." He looked at her, eyes shining, pleading with her not to say it was his fault. She hadn't seen him look like this since her mother's death.

"Yeah, well, it got messy. I think Booker planned to take us hostage and then force us to hand over Art, but then, when Cord told him about our plans to go to MI5—"

"Cord?"

"Yeah, he betrayed us."

Her father shook his head again, "I would never have believed it..."

"Would you have believed it of any of them?"

He shook his head, "No."

"Now Booker knows about our plan to hand Art over to the security services, he's getting desperate."

Her father looked small and shrunken, like a lost child, defeated.

Riya wanted to hug him. "This wasn't your fault, Dad," she said gently, "but the question is, what do we do now? People are dying, Natalya's been shot, I've..." She stopped herself. "Is Art really worth that?"

Sanjay gathered himself, sat upright, and faced her. "No, Riya, it is not. You need to end this. The plan to hand Art over to the government through MI5—how close are you to a conclusion?"

"We had a meeting with them; they are definitely interested. But we reckon they'll keep it for themselves."

"But at least it would be safe, right?"

"Yes, but it wouldn't achieve your vision."

He stood up, "This is not worth dying for, Riya." He frowned. "You need to end this quickly. Destroying Art means all our work is wasted. Giving it to Booker will mean the exploitation of people on a mass scale." He nodded. "You should hand it over to the security services. It is the least bad option; they will use it to save lives, the technology will be safe, and it gets you and the others out of danger."

"Least bad" didn't sound like a good solution to Riya. "But they have their own agenda…"

"Unfortunately, that is life, Riya. You will come to realize everyone has their own agenda. Sometimes, you have to compromise. Better that than failure or worse."

This didn't feel like a compromise to Riya, more like giving up. "But that won't help people, like you wanted. And *you* didn't compromise!"

"No, and look what happened. Looking for another solution will take time. That means you will continue to be in danger."

Something else had been gnawing away at the back of Riya's mind since the meeting with Brendan Brown and Digby Somerset…

"MI5 want us to turn off the internet version of Art and hand over the source code." She hesitated. "If we turn Art off, will you…disappear?"

Her father's face softened, "Yes. I am here for *you*, Riya. I am not part of the version we planned to hand over to authorities."

"But…I've only just found you again…You said you wanted to be there for me…"

"My existence is putting people's lives in danger. Is that a price you are willing to pay?"

He was right, of course; she couldn't justify that, but the thought of losing him again made her chest tighten. Riya sniffed and shook her head. "So, tomorrow…"

"Persuade the others to hand Art over to MI5 and go back to your lives."

Here was a way out, and with her father's blessing. Riya stared sullenly at the bed sheets. A week ago, she would have been over the moon, but now it felt like a total cop out. Apart from the prospect of losing her father again, they had a chance here to make a real difference in the world. Handing over Art was selling the idea short, taking the easy option for a quiet life. But what was the alternative? There wasn't one. It was her turn to admit defeat.

"OK, I'll talk to them." With decision came fatigue. She yawned.

"You look exhausted. Get some sleep."

"Yeah, OK." She nodded, yawned again, and, when she opened her eyes, he was gone.

She woke, tightly cocooned in the duvet, with a cold nose. If the boat had central heating, no one had figured out how to work it. The strong sunlight coming through the curtains suggested it was already mid-morning. The sound of a world that was wide awake could be heard outside: boat engines burbling around the marina, halyards clanking on masts, seagulls cawing.

For a moment, the sunshine lifted her mood, then the events of the previous night came flooding back. She screwed up her eyes, trying to dislodge the images. Pushing herself up, she hissed as a sharp flash of pain shot up her arm. She'd forgotten about the bullet wound. Gingerly, she rummaged through her bag for clean clothes, changed, wrapped the duvet around her against the cold, and left the cabin.

In the main cabin, the others were already up and sitting around the table. Mugs of something hot steamed in the cold morning air that poured down the open companionway.

Johanna's eyes were red and puffy. Natalya still looked grey, sick, and miserable. Ivan looked…well, like he always looked, as though he'd slept in his clothes and got out of bed two minutes ago. She found that little bit of normality strangely comforting.

Johanna mustered a smile, "Good morning, Riya. There's tea and coffee, no milk or food, I'm afraid. Natalya has been filling us in on last night."

Natalya nodded bleakly.

Ivan lay along one side of the bench, watching a muted TV on the wall behind Johanna. He raised a hand at Riya, "How's the arm?"

She flexed her elbow, "Bit stiff, but OK."

Johanna shifted along the bench, making room for Riya, "We need to decide what to do next."

"At least we don't have to deal with that traitorous bastard anymore." The expression on Natalya's face was murderous.

Riya sat down next to Johanna, tugging her duvet around her as a breeze blew in through the companionway. She felt awful.

"His poor family. His wife…His son is sick, and now he's lost his father."

Ivan sat up, plucked the glasses from his shirt pocket, and threw them on the table. "I don't want anything more to do with this."

Riya was taken aback—it wasn't like Ivan to be so negative.

"What the hell are we thinking? We can't take on the likes of Jim Booker."

"That's it, rich boy—give up."

"Christ, Natalya, have you been paying attention? Two people died last night because of this little project. And you two are shot full of holes. Jesus! Give the thing to Booker and be done with it."

Natalya raised an eyebrow, "You think that will save us now? He'll kill us anyway to keep us quiet."

"Then give it to MI5, get them to bloody protect us."

Natalya looked contemptuous, "They will use it only for themselves."

"Like I give a damn about that!" Ivan snarled.

"There is another option," said Johanna quietly. "We destroy it."

"Absolutely!" cried Ivan enthusiastically.

"Absolutely not," Natalya snorted. "Anyway, Booker will never believe we've destroyed it."

"Natalya." Johanna looked steely. "You don't like the idea of going to MI5, you don't want to destroy it. Do you have a better suggestion?"

"Contact the AI community. They would totally get Sanjay's vision of connecting people…"

Johanna shook her head, "You know we don't have time for that. Every time we pop our heads up to talk to someone, we expose ourselves as targets. Plus, there is no guarantee the AI community won't use it to line their own pockets or that it won't end up on the dark web. I don't like it any more than you do, Natalya. Destroy it or give it to the government—those are the only two viable options."

Natalya growled at Johanna, "You are selling out, like that useless lump of flesh." She flung her arm violently towards Ivan.

Ivan looked at her in disbelief. "Are you completely batshit delusional? You keep making out I'm some pampered rich kid, and maybe I am, but here's a newsflash for you, Natalya: you are a two-bit hacker, not a fucking superhero! You bleed, you can't fly, and you can't take on an industrial titan armed with only a laptop and a 'screw you' attitude."

"That's what I would expect from a spoiled little Russian boy—when the going gets tough, rich boy quits."

"Is that what this is to you? A chance to prove your Russian-peasant upbringing makes you tougher than the rich bourgeoisie? Well, heads up, Babushka, we're not back in Mother Russia now, and I'm not your enemy!"

Tears welled in Riya's eyes. This was horrible. Blinking them away, she cleared her throat. "No one's asked my opinion yet. Since this was my father's project and he saw fit to make me a Keyholder, I think I am entitled to have a say."

Johanna smiled wearily, "Of course. Please, go ahead."

Natalya looked at her hopefully.

"I think Johanna and Ivan are right about my father—he wouldn't want anyone getting hurt because of this. He would say that it isn't worth dying for; he would say give it to the government—that way, at least some good will come of it."

Natalya slumped dejectedly in her seat. Ivan nodded sagely. Johanna's face was inscrutable.

"However, I don't believe that is what we should do."

Natalya looked up.

"My father cared about all of us, and of course he would have wanted to keep us safe. But I remember once hearing an interview with some Artic explorer; he was asked how his wife felt about him taking risks, and he said something like, 'It is for others to worry about our safety. It is for us alone to choose a more courageous path. It is a measure of our own courage that we take a path despite the risks, in spite of our fears.' That's what courage is, I think—choosing to do something while being afraid. So, I'm going to suggest something not because I think my father would recommend it, but because I think it is the right thing to do. We owe it to Sanjay and Victor, we owe it to ourselves, and we owe it to all the people Booker has hurt along the way."

She took a deep breath.

"We should go after Jim Booker."

They stared at her in stunned silence, so she continued: "Before we decide what to do with this technology, we should use it to *take down Jim Booker*. He's never going to leave us alone until we either get rid of Art or we get rid of *him*. He's murdered my father and Ivan's, he's ruined your lives, taken away your careers, and now he wants to deprive the world of a technology that could change the lives of thousands of people, so he can use it to become richer."

Johanna looked shocked. Natalya had a faint smile on her lips.

Ivan snorted a laugh, "And just how would *we* do that?"

"We do what he would least expect—we take the fight to him. We go to San Francisco."

Ivan shook his head in disbelief, "And do *what* when we get there? None of us are qualified to take on this kind of fight."

Riya thought of her conversation with Ethan, "I think we are. We know, under all that slick businessman stuff, he's just a ruthless criminal, and I bet we're not the only ones with a story to tell. If we look, we can probably find someone in Silicon Valley willing to dish the dirt. And we have Art…"

Ivan shook his hands in the air, "You're being ridiculous! Art is *not* the solution to everything!" He looked at Johanna to back him up, but she was sitting very still, staring at Riya, a shrewd expression on her face.

"That was a rousing speech, Riya," she said slowly. "I'm not sure I'm ready to lay down my life for *The Cause*, but you may have a point about taking the fight to Booker—the best form of defence is attack, so they say. He certainly wouldn't expect it." She nodded thoughtfully. "The team that brings Booker to justice, eh?" She turned to Ivan. "Could this yacht sail us there?"

"Yes, but it would take over *three months*…We'd have to cross the Atlantic, sail through the Panama Canal, and up the west coast of America! That's a major sea voyage—and, by the way, with a crew who've never sailed before!" Ivan looked around helplessly for support.

"Any chance someone could hunt us down by satellite or something?"

"No, there's no system to do that, unless they knew which boat we were on, but—"

"Then I don't think we are in any rush. It may even be an advantage to be off grid for a while, let things cool down. Now we have no traitor to worry about, we have no restrictions on what Art can predict, and *that* is a formidable weapon with which to take on Booker."

Natalya nodded.

"You're all crazy!" Ivan buried his hands in his hair.

"Coward. You're scared," sneered Natalya.

Ivan snorted, "Damn right! And you should be, too… And it's not just Booker. Crossing the Atlantic is not exactly a pleasure cruise—do you even know what's involved? None of you are sailors, there's a high probability we'll drown."

Natalya gave him a sly look, then put on her glasses, "Art, if we sailed this yacht to San Francisco, what would be our chance of *success*?" A pause. Natalya nodded. "Uh-huh." She turned to Ivan, smirking. "He says, eighty per cent."

Ivan gave a high-pitched maniacal laugh, "Oh, well, that's OK, then—only a twenty per cent chance of dying!"

"Enough!" roared Johanna. "This may not be to your liking, Ivan, but there are no ideal solutions here. You are free to leave if you want, but, if you stay with us, then you do so willingly, and do your best to help us succeed."

Natalya grinned, "Time to put up or shut up, sailor boy."

Ivan flipped two middle fingers at Natalya, "Fuck you."

"Natalya," said Johanna sharply, "we're a team. Stop trying to score points."

Ivan looked at Riya as though the whole world had turned against him. She felt sorry for him, like she'd betrayed him. She knew he didn't really have a choice; leaving was not an option.

His face broke into a bleak humourless grin, "Yeah, yeah, OK, why not? Maybe I'll get to die a hero."

Johanna sat back, "OK, next up, how do we get out of here? If Booker's men are still around, they'll be monitoring the harbour by now. If we go on deck, we risk being spotted."

Riya smiled encouragingly at Ivan, "Any ideas?"

He looked up, surprised, and shrugged, "We could use a pilot."

"What, fly?" Natalya looked confused.

"No, a boat pilot. Most harbours have a pilot service to take boats in and out of the harbour. They're mainly for larger boats, but anyone can hire them if they're unsure about navigating the harbour. We can stay below, out of sight, while the pilot takes the boat out. I'll find the number."

Ivan tapped away on his phone.

"We'll also need supplies. Once we're out of here, we can sail round the coast to Salcombe, pick up supplies, then head off to San Fran."

Riya smiled as she watched Ivan. He'd grown a foot taller in the last few seconds. Now, he had a purpose, and for the next few weeks this would be his show as they sailed to San Francisco.

"Like I said, it's going to be a long trip, though."

Johanna looked unperturbed. "I don't think any of us have any pressing engagements, do we?" She glanced at Riya. "Besides, I think we'll need the time to give some serious thought to how we are going to take on Jim Booker, because *that* is not going to be easy."

Riya's smile disappeared as the enormity of her suggestion dawned on her. The skeletons lurking in Booker's closet were one thing, but exposing and proving his crimes was quite another. She suddenly felt uncomfortably responsible for dragging them halfway around the world without any idea what they would do when they got there.

"I'm going for a shower." She pulled the duvet around her and shuffled through to her cabin, closing the door behind her. She sat on the edge of the bed and put on her glasses. Had she done the right thing? She reached up to her ear and turned them on.

"Hello, Riya."

"Art? Can I talk to my dad again?"

As before, just as she was wondering whether Art was actually doing anything, her father appeared.

"So, how did it go?"

She cringed, "I said we should take on Jim Booker, deal with him before we decide what to do with Art."

She waited for an angry tirade about being immature and headstrong. But it didn't come. Her dad simply grinned and nodded.

"A bold suggestion."

"Aren't you angry? Ignoring your advice, putting us all in danger?"

"I don't think you ignored my advice. As a father, I want to keep you safe, yes, but I raised you to have a conscience, a desire to do the right thing, not necessarily the easy thing. Your decision must be one that satisfies you, not me." He paused. "Do you know how you will achieve this?"

"Not a clue."

"They say the way to slay a giant is to use their strength against them. Think about what Jim Booker's greatest strength is and you may find it helpful."

At that moment, Riya felt the boat rock and footsteps thumped on the roof above her. Someone had stepped on board. She heard a voice calling down through the hatch. The pilot.

"Sorry, Dad, gotta go—I think we're about to sail."

They motored through the busy waterway traffic towards the mouth of the Dart, all four of them looking out anxiously through the windows. Riya saw no sign of Booker's men, but then there was no reason why she should; they could be watching from a hundred different places among the tightly packed jumble of houses cascading down the hillsides on each side of the river. Riya thought of the Frenchman. She had no doubt he was out there, somewhere.

As they passed beneath the ancient castle standing sentinel at the river mouth, the boat pitched and rolled in the swell from the open sea. A small orange powerboat flashed past the windows, circling the yacht in a wide arc. Riya gripped Ivan's arm.

Ivan gently removed her hand with a smile. "They've come to collect the pilot. I think that's my cue."

After they'd all turned out on deck to wave off the pilot, Natalya and Johanna went below again, but Riya stayed, relishing the sharp wind and spray. She stood next to Ivan at the helm. He looked at ease, like he belonged there.

He glanced at her and grinned, "Feels good, eh?"

She nodded.

"So, what next, boss?" he asked.

"Well, Natalya needs to speak to her dodgy friends about fake passports, so we don't get picked up by Booker or the CIA as soon as we land in the USA. Then *you*"—she prodded his chest playfully—"have to sail us halfway round the world."

Ivan grimaced. "Yeah, just a small matter of sailing eight thousand miles across open ocean with a crew that have never sailed before. No problem." He blew out his cheeks with a sigh.

"What about your dad's friend? Won't he be wondering where his yacht is?"

"Oleg? Nah. He won't miss it," Ivan grinned. "Besides, I won't tell him until we're there. Possession is nine tenths of the law, as they say. And what happens when we get there?"

Riya looked out over the bow, to where clouds were gathering on the horizon, "We find a way to make the bastard pay."

SAN FRANCISCO

As she rounded the corner, Riya took a moment to look out at the Golden Gate Bridge in the distance. Today the stanchion tops were shrouded in thick grey cloud that hung damply over the rest of San Francisco. She took a deep breath in, remembering the relief she'd felt sailing beneath it a few days before in bright sunshine after their three month voyage across the Atlantic and up the west coast of America. She glanced down at her hands, flexing her fingers, still sore, cracked and callused from three months of sailing, sun, and salt water. Cambridge seemed a very long way away. She shivered and dived into the warmth of the coffee shop.

After queuing for coffee and a pastry, Riya headed over to a free table, took out her laptop, and opened up Indigo's social-media website; the laptop screen in front of her glowed purple. She jiggled her chair noisily and settled back to enjoy her coffee.

Out of the corner of her eye, she saw the large figure at the next table pause, then take a loud slurp from the thermal cup in front of him.

Riya pretended to be engrossed in her computer.

"I wouldn't be doing that if I were you. H-huh-huh." The loud cheerful voice gave a nervous little laugh.

"Excuse me?" Riya turned to face the owner of the voice.

A round friendly face beamed at her from between a wild black beard and a mass of unruly black curly hair. He unzipped his black puffer jacket, revealing a red San Francisco 49ers hoodie, and nodded at Riya's computer screen. "Indigo. I wouldn't touch that site with a long pole. H-huh-huh." That nervous laugh again.

"And I wouldn't go around sticking my nose into other people's computer screens," said Riya indignantly.

He shook himself and held up his hands in surrender. "Just sayin', you wouldn't catch me on that site."

After a couple of minutes, Riya rolled her eyes and turned to the big guy. "Go on, then—why wouldn't you use Indigo?"

"Are you kidding? They're evil, man—devious, unscrupulous scum."

"What do you mean?"

"Come on, man, you must have heard of all the mental-health issues, right?"

"Yeah, but you hear about that stuff all the time. They've been saying the same thing for years."

"That is true. But"—he hunched earnestly over the table—"there's something different about Indigo. It's as though the system figures out your vulnerabilities, then exploits them. There's something sinister about it. And I think it's intentional."

"Do you have evidence? I'd be interested to see it."

The man's attitude changed. "Hey…" He cast a nervous glance around the coffee shop. "Did someone put you up to this?"

"Put me up to what?" Riya put on an air of offended innocence.

"Sorry, I gotta go." He shut his computer and started shoving his belongings into his bag.

Johanna's voice came out of the air. "*Art, pause simulation.*"

The man froze, the coffee shop shrank to a small video panel in Riya's view, and she found herself back in the main yacht cabin, sitting across the table from Johanna, who was frowning behind her glasses.

"Jittery little thing, isn't he?" She sighed. "We need a less direct approach."

Riya blinked. It was very surreal, watching yourself act out a scene from your future through your own eyes, like some virtual-reality movie. They had been working on the simulation for an hour now, trying different approaches to gradually coax the right information out of the contact.

"How about being more sceptical—you know, let him convince you? And open up a bit more about yourself, put him at ease."

Riya nodded, "Art, start simulation from, 'And I think it's intentional'."

The yacht cabin disappeared, and Riya was again in the coffee shop.

"And I think it's intentional."

Riya's nose crinkled doubtfully, "No offence, but that sounds like some wild conspiracy theory."

"Yeah, it does, doesn't it? But do your research, man, I'm tellin' ya."

"I *have* done some research, actually. I'm on the school magazine. We've done a few articles on social media, and we all know it's addictive, it can cause mental-health issues, disrupts sleep, yada, yada, yada…But there was no mention of Indigo being more dangerous than any other platform."

"You didn't dig deep enough, then!"

Riya tried to look sheepish.

"Do your job, investigate, go to the sources—charities, hospitals, mental-health professionals. Any article that's incriminating, Indigo usually gets its lawyers to quash it and have it removed from the public domain."

This was becoming a familiar story, repeated by all the experts they had talked to, but Riya feigned shock. "Really? That's obscene!"

"Huh-huh. Yeah! Tell me about it."

Riya frowned, "OK, if there's all this evidence out there, surely the authorities will investigate?" She already knew the answer to this, but she needed to draw him in slowly, otherwise he'd get spooked.

He glanced around again. "You'd think so, right? I collected a whole bunch of evidence, published it too—I had a regular blog, talked about this stuff all the time. Next thing I know, I have guys in suits knocking at my door, telling me to cease and desist. I'm a freelance journalist, I'm used to a rough ride, but the way these guys talked? I got the feeling they wouldn't mess around with legal threats; I'd just disappear and end up as cactus food out in the desert someplace."

"Oh my God! What did you do?"

"I'm not that tough, man. I ceased and desisted."

"This is, like, totally unbelievable. If it's true, people need to know. I could write about it in our school magazine."

"Yeah, yeah." He nodded, looking at her shrewdly. "You may get away with it too, being a kid 'n' all—no offence." He kept nodding, considering his statement. His gaze sharpened again. "Watch your ass, though. I got stories that would curdle your latte, you know."

Riya's eyes widened, "Seriously?"

He glanced around again and leaned forward. "Listen, if you promise to keep my name out of your article, I can forward you a bunch of stuff as a start point. This story needs to be told. By the way, what school rag do you write for?"

Riya hesitated. Johanna's voice interrupted: *"Art, stop simulation."*

The coffee shop disappeared again.

"We'll find a school that has a paper, but I think we've cracked it. He's hooked. He sees you as a way to get his story out there. The last part is easy—get him to forward you his research, wrap up the conversation, and get out of there. We'll be ready tomorrow."

At the door to the café, Riya paused, looking out towards the Golden Gate Bridge. She took a deep breath. After so many simulations, it was unnerving to be heading into a conversation that couldn't be paused or started again if she made a mistake—like working on a trapeze and suddenly having the safety net removed.

She blew out her cheeks, watching her breath condensing in a misty cloud on the cold morning air, then strode into the shop. She sat at the table next to the blogger and the conversation proceeded just as she'd rehearsed…

"…what school rag do you write for?"

"John F. Kennedy High."

"Cool." He patted his pockets, plucked a phone from inside his jacket, tapped it a few times, and handed it to Riya. "Give me your email address and I'll forward you what I have, along with the sources, in case you need to verify it.".

"That would be, like, so awesome!" Riya entered her email address into his phone and handed it back.

He looked at it. "Aditi Joshi?" He held out a hand. "Seth Friedmann."

"Good to meet you, Seth."

"Yeah, but remember, you gotta keep my name out of it, OK?"

"Yeah, of course. Wow. This is, like, so cool. Can you tell me about what you uncovered?" She'd heard it all before in the simulation, but Riya leaned forward eagerly—it would look strange, after being so interested, if she got up and left.

"Huh-huh. OK, but don't blame me if you never touch social media again."

Riya left the coffee shop and walked briskly up the street, burying her chin in her coat. The street was chilly after the warmth of the café. Rounding a corner, she looked at her phone: she'd been talking to Seth for thirty minutes.

"It went well?"

Looking up, she saw Johanna leaning against the wall, grinning.

"It went well. He's going to email his material."

"Excellent." Johanna eased off the wall and fell into step with Riya. "He's the last one, right? We have all the evidence we need." She linked her arm in Riya's and sighed. "Things are going according to plan, the rain has stopped…How about we walk back to the yacht instead of taking a taxi?"

Glowing with the success of their evidence gathering, Riya finally plucked up the courage to ask a question that had been bugging her since Dartmouth. "Why did you change your mind, Johanna? Why did you agree to go after Booker?"

Johanna looked surprised, but the answer came smoothly. "Because as you said, your father wanted to make this technology available for everyone, and giving it to the secret services to keep in the shadows won't achieve that."

Riya looked at her, "You never seemed like the crusading type."

Johanna eyed Riya as though weighing whether to say something. "At twenty-three, I was already a lead developer for an online gambling company. But the top jobs always seemed off limits, you know, beyond the glass ceiling." She gave Riya a crooked smile. "A black woman in tech is a rare beast indeed. Then your father came along, talking about his tiny start-up. He knew technology, but his background was academic; he needed someone who knew business, how to develop products. I took a gamble and joined him—my chance to be in on the ground floor of something revolutionary. I've worked too damned hard to see some rich middle-aged white guy swoop in and scoop all the glory. I may not be on a crusade to save the world, like Natalya, but I want the recognition due to me. Perhaps that sounds mercenary to you?"

Riya shrugged, "It sounds honest. You seem to have Natalya's trust, that's good enough for me."

Johanna laughed, "She's an outsider too, right?" She tugged at Riya's arm. "Anyway, enough of the serious stuff. What say we grab some retail therapy on the way home? I think we've earned that."

Riya smiled. After three months drifting around on the ocean, planning and researching, they were finally getting somewhere. But their plan to convince users to desert their beloved social-media platform was bold. They had facts, but were people so hardened to fake news and scare stories that the truth would merely wash over them?

TIPPING POINT

With the cold February air nipping at her ears, Riya jogged alongside the marina, where gleaming white yacht hulls bobbed up and down in the sunrise. Running had become her morning routine since they'd arrived.

Stopping at the security gate, she punched in the code and hurried along the line of boats, keen to swap the cold of the San Francisco winter for the warm snug of the yacht cabin.

Stepping on board *Lady Luck*, she caught the muffled chatter of TV from below. Opening the main hatch, she clambered down the steps to find the other three huddled around the table, staring at the TV.

"What's so interest—" The words died in her mouth as she watched the screen. Sitting at a desk in a bright glitzy TV studio, smiling into the camera, was Jim Booker.

"Jim Booker, CEO of Indigo, welcome," said the presenter.

"Good morning, Becky, it's really great to be here." His smug smile made Riya's skin prickle with anger.

Becky tossed her hair, "So, a great set of quarterly results. Sales up, users up…Indigo seems to be having something of a renaissance."

"Yes, we're pleased with our progress, but we're always looking to improve our service, Becky…"

Becky raised a sculpted eyebrow. "It's not been all plain sailing, though, has it? Claims of aggressive sales tactics, accusations of mental-health issues…and, recently, a raft of stories appearing on social media accusing Indigo of unethical behaviour."

Jim nodded wearily. "We operate against a constant backdrop of accusations and negativity around social media, and it's always the largest players who are on the front line. But social media is not harmful if used responsibly. We do seem to forget that social media is a positive force in most people's lives."

"So, what's next, Jim?"

"We are currently in the midst of a major expansion into China. Like other tech companies, we're making big investments in that region."

"How are you financing that?"

"Well, we are funding a large portion of the expansion ourselves; for the rest, we are fortunate enough to work with a few forward-thinking investors."

Becky nodded. "Rumours are that some of that investment is coming from China. And congress has raised concerns about a foreign power having access to such a large social-media platform containing detailed data about millions of Americans. Are you worried at all about government backlash or the possibility of users deserting your platform on data-security fears?"

Jim waved dismissively, "China's investment is small, and data security is paramount. We have no reason to suspect user adoption will fall. In fact, we have plans that should help grow user numbers."

Riya wondered whether Art was part of those plans.

On the TV, Becky nodded sagely, "Exciting times for Indigo, Jim. I hope it all works out. Thanks for coming in today."

"My pleasure, Becky."

Natalya hissed angrily, "That's it? After all the stories we've posted about Indigo ruining people's lives, and all we get is a brief mention of unethical behaviour and security concerns? Huh! Investigative journalism at its best, eh?"

Johanna and Natalya had cooked up a plan to turn users against Indigo by showing how it exploited them, ruined people's lives, and how they had no control over where their data ended up. The beauty of social media was that they themselves didn't have to prove anything—they just had to generate enough "suggestion" of wrongdoing that the authorities would be forced to investigate to satisfy the media and public outcry.

They had gathered all the negative information they could find and posted it to Indigo's own social-media platform using bogus user accounts. They had had some success—news networks had raised concerns and there were rumblings about Indigo's questionable ethics and use of people's data—but nowhere near the scale needed to provoke a mass user revolt.

Ivan plucked a grape from the fruit bowl, tossed it high in the air and caught it in his mouth. "I did warn you." After three months at sea in the wind and sun, his skin had taken on a deep golden-brown hue, and his straw-coloured hair was bleached almost white. "People are not going to ditch their favourite social-media platform because you post a few negative stories. It's a habit. Nobody instantly quits smoking just because you tell them it's bad for them."

He flicked the TV to the sports channel, where some basketball game was playing, but he kept talking: "Anyway, I read a book a while ago...about how ideas spread. Good ideas don't spread just because they are good. You need the right combination of people to spread them. You need the *experts*, who have the detailed information; you need *salespeople* to sell the ideas; and you need people who have a lot of social *connections* to spread the idea."

They all looked at Ivan—Natalya's mouth hung open.

Hearing no response, Ivan turned to see why everyone had gone quiet. "What?"

Johanna recovered first. "And...the experts would be...?"

"You've already got those—all those industry commentators and insiders you've been interviewing."

"The connectors?"

Ivan shrugged. "Social-media influencers who have loads of followers."

"And the salespeople?"

Ivan grinned. "That's obvious."

The others looked at him blankly.

"Art! Use Art to convince these influencers that Indigo's version of social media is evil."

Riya's conversation with her father came back to her. "You mean, use the power of Indigo's social media—against itself?"

Ivan jabbed a finger at Riya. "Precisely. If we convince the influencers that Indigo is evil, their followers will be convinced too; if *you* jump up and down and yell 'fire', no one takes any notice, but if you get social-media influencers with millions of followers to do it for you, *everyone* will take notice. People are sheep. We want to create a tipping point where so many influential people leave the platform that everyone else will follow. Baaa! Indigo will implode, and Booker won't even have a business."

He turned back to the TV. "Now, can I watch the game, please?"

Riya and Natalya looked at Johanna, who grinned.

"All righty, then. Riya, you and I will get together the best of the material from our bloggers and social-media commentators. Natalya, you start figuring out how we can deliver this information to these influencers—I have a feeling that will need some hacking jiggery-pokery."

Natalya nodded curtly, "Sure."

"Ivan, you find us the biggest influencers on Indigo."

Ivan jerked with surprise. "How did I get involved?"

"Your idea; you get to help make it happen."

"Me and my big mouth," he grumbled, but he winked playfully at Riya.

She looked away, smiling; for reasons she wasn't sure of, it made her feel good that Ivan had played a part in coming up with a plan—but then, she always did have a soft spot for the underdog.

The girl on the screen wiped a tear from the corner of her eye. She must have been around Riya's age. "Yeah, that was me."

A picture flashed up: five girls in shorts and T-shirts, skin stretched over bone like Egyptian mummies. Riya couldn't believe people could be that thin and still live.

"That was taken two years ago, at Mary Simms rehab clinic. We all followed Blaire Harper on Indigo."

"You mean the ex-model turned reality-TV star?" the interviewer cut in from behind the camera. Riya recognized Seth Friedmann's voice.

A photo flashed up of Blaire Harper. Riya knew of her: a model who had occasionally hit the headlines for her wild party antics, until marrying rapper Skinny Six. The couple rocketed to stardom when their stormy relationship was broadcast on a reality-TV show. She was now one of the most followed celebs on social media, with nearly a hundred million followers and her own cosmetics and clothing lines.

The girl on the screen sniffed and nodded. "When she went through that weight loss after having her baby, I thought that was pretty cool, but I wasn't, like, bothered about my own weight. Then weird things started happening, kinda creepy... Indigo started suggesting weight-loss products, then articles I might be interested in reading. Just the odd one, at first, usually about celebs I followed, like how Blaire lost her weight, then some articles on sports stars who had lost weight to increase their performance. How they looked better, too. Telling you how they did it. Then it started suggesting groups I might be interested in joining, people I might want to friend."

"You weren't actively searching for the stuff?"

"No! But, you know what it's like—you're bored, waiting for a bus, so you scroll through your phone. Anyway, I eventually ordered some stuff to try and lose a bit of weight, not much, just trim a little fat, you know. That was it, I spiralled down from there."

"So, it wasn't Blaire herself promoting weight loss?"

"No! It wasn't the celebs or athletes pushing this stuff; it was like the system was using them, and my interests, to find things I might buy. With me, it was weight-loss products. With a friend of mine, it was fashion. She ran up huge credit-card debts buying clothing and handbags and shoes. When I got out of rehab, I looked her up, compared notes. Same pattern: she took an interest and Indigo suggested not only things to buy, but articles saying that buying the right fashion items would literally change your life. She joined groups where they were actually swapping tips on how to get money to fund their shopping—like stealing, or selling your family's stuff. She stole her grandmother's necklace to buy some designer shoes—she was given the choice of rehab or prison. Says she'll never forget the look of disappointment on her grandmother's face. She still can't look her in the eye."

"Do you think Indigo is deliberately targeting the vulnerable?"

"No. I would say they're targeting *everyone*. I wouldn't have said I was vulnerable to weight issues; I'd never been concerned before. But I think Indigo systematically works out where you *might* be vulnerable, then it magnifies the weakness, then it works on it, hitting you again and again in the same spot. It wears you down."

"Do you still use social media?"

"Yes, a bit, but I'm pretty disciplined now. I don't use Indigo. I wouldn't touch it, and neither would my friends."

"How would you describe Indigo?"

The girl stared into the camera. "Evil."

The clip ended.

Johanna sighed. "Powerful stuff. How many of these clips do we have now?"

Riya thought. "I dunno—fifty, sixty maybe. People with different issues, following different celebrities."

"Ivan, how many influencers have you identified?"

"We've come up with about three hundred who would be sufficiently outraged to leave the platform and squawk about why. These people have between twenty million and two hundred million followers each. About twenty-five per cent of their followers would ditch the platform immediately, followed by another twenty-five per cent within a month. Beyond that, Art said prediction accuracy became unreliable."

Natalya looked impressed. "This is you? You did this?"

Ivan shrugged, "Art did most of the work." He looked at Natalya. "There is one snag. Each celeb reacted differently to different videos and articles, and many of them required several videos or articles before they quit Indigo. So, you have to deliver the right material to the right celebs, in the right order, at the right time. Timing is critical, actually. I created a spreadsheet showing which movie clips and articles to deliver to which celebrities, and when."

"Natalya?"

"Sure. I can hack Indigo so stuff pops up on someone's feed at a certain time."

Johanna nodded at Natalya. "Looks like a busy week for you. When do you think we'll be ready to go?"

Natalya looked at Ivan. "Monday?" He nodded.

"OK, then I suggest we get some rest this weekend, because, once we start, we'll be at this twenty-four seven until it's done."

The clip had reminded Riya of April. She'd thought about her often over the last few months and wondered how she was.

"Well, it's late"—Riya feigned a yawn—"so I'm going to get some rest now. I'm pretty knackered, actually." She made her way to her cabin, leaving the others still talking at the table.

Closing the door, she reached for her glasses and sat down on the bed. "Art? I need you to help me with something. This work Ivan's been doing to influence people's behaviour...I need you to help me do the same for one of my friends, April Royston."

The clock on Riya's computer read 1:00 a.m., Monday morning. She glanced around the table at the other three, all sitting in front of their open laptops, sombre faces lit by glowing screens, looking expectantly at Johanna.

Johanna smiled. "Ready?"

Everyone nodded. Riya yawned and blinked her sore eyes.

Johanna frowned at Riya. "You look exhausted. What have you been doing?"

"It's one in the morning, Johanna; my body's telling me I should be asleep." She'd actually been up most of the past two nights working simulations with Art on her own project, but she wasn't telling Johanna that.

Johanna pursed her lips, but moved on. "Everyone got their lists?"

Riya looked at the stapled sheets of paper lying next to her computer: lists of celebrities, video clips, and articles, along with the times and dates to post them.

"OK, then—let's go."

The four of them dropped feverishly over their keyboards, the *rat-a-tat-tat* of computer keys filling the cabin as everyone worked through the night to push out their carefully crafted propaganda. Using social-media management software, and somewhat less than legal social-media bots supplied by Natalya, hundreds of social-media stars, from influencers to singers to reality-TV stars, would wake up to their social-media feeds pinging with horrific stories about Indigo.

As the pale light of dawn crept around the edges of the closed curtains, Natalya's computer pinged with the first notification. She spun her laptop to face the others. "It's starting."

Riya read the post. It was from Blaire Harper:

I   Just seen this. OMG, so upset…

The post included a link to the video of the anorexic girl Seth had interviewed. Being one of the most-followed social-media stars on the planet, Blaire had been their first target.

Natalya grinned. "Time to hit her with another."

Riya read her own feed. The reaction was similar—shock and outrage.

Every time someone had a few minutes free, they would surf the TV news channels looking for signs their activity was being noticed. For the first few hours, there was nothing. But then, towards the end of the first day, Fox News reported that Blaire Harper had suspended her Indigo account out of concern for fans, while she investigated allegations of Indigo's damaging effects on mental health.

"One down," said Johanna.

Then, on a different news channel, it was reported that two movie stars had done the same. A follow-up story the next day stated Blaire was quitting Indigo and moving to another social platform.

"Indigo are responding." Natalya hunched over her keyboard. "They are trying to block our posts and remove content."

"And?" said Johanna.

Natalya grinned. "They have their hands full; this stuff is being spread by users faster than they can shut it down. But it won't last—they will write some code that will automatically search and remove our content."

Johanna nodded. "We expected this. Switch your efforts to other platforms."

They had started with Indigo, because those were the users they wanted to target, but, now the snowball was rolling, they would keep up momentum by posting to other social-media platforms.

The hours and days rolled past in a blur as they worked through their lists and monitored the results. By two thirty on Friday morning, they had finally completed the mammoth task, but couldn't bring themselves to leave their computers as they searched for evidence that their plan was working.

Finally, Johanna brought it to an end. "We can do no more tonight. That's the first round done. Now, we sit back and reap the whirlwind. Let's all get some rest."

Like the weary stragglers of a late-night party, the four of them slowly rose from the table and sloped off to bed. It had been five days since any of them had slept properly and they were all exhausted. Riya shut the cabin door behind her, flopped on to her bed, and scarcely had time to think *I must get out of these clothes*, before exhaustion pushed her into sleep.

Seemingly five minutes later, her cabin door banged open, and Ivan charged in. "You've gotta see this!"

Riya blinked gritty eyes in the bright morning light.

"Come on!" Excitedly, he yanked at her arm, pulling her up to a sitting position. "It's working!"

Riya wandered hazily into the main cabin, where the TV was on.

Johanna smiled briefly. "Indigo released quarterly user figures last night," she said. "They lost ten million users in the last week as celebs and their followers deserted the platform. Indigo stock price dipped five per cent as a result."

"Five per cent? Doesn't sound like much," said Riya.

Johanna looked at her. "Oh, believe me, that is a big drop in a single day—it will give Jim Booker serious indigestion. And, if this story runs, that loss will be greater. Oh, here we go…"

The commercial break ended. A slick presenter in a Wall Street studio appeared on screen. "*The stock price of social-media giant Indigo fell sharply in after-hours trading last night as they found themselves facing a major user rebellion after a storm of negative postings on their own platform alleged Indigo has been systematically engaging in behaviour harmful to users. Indigo responded by removing the damaging material, saying it amounts to nothing more than a vindictive fake-news campaign. They say they are currently investigating the source of this information and will be taking legal action against its perpetrators.*"

Natalya snorted. "Good luck with that. I bounced our connection through routers all over the world using multiple encryption layers. No way can they can trace anything back to us."

Over the next week, the story grew, with more news of high-profile celebrities deserting Indigo and further declines in user numbers. The news networks could smell blood in the water. Some ran articles showing teenagers talking about their experiences. Some tracked down the people in the videos and interviewed them. One interviewed Blaire Harper and the girl from Seth's video, who together gave an emotional performance, both pointing the finger at Indigo.

Then, one morning…

"We now welcome back Jim Booker, CEO of Indigo."

"Hello, Becky." Riya thought his smile seemed a little strained.

"So, a difficult time for Indigo over the past couple of weeks: accusations of user exploitation and overly aggressive sales tactics leading to serious mental-health issues. How is Indigo responding?"

"These accusations are completely unfounded. As you know, Becky, our industry is constantly bombarded with negative press about mental health, and we take that very seriously. We have partnered with other industry leaders to set up mental-health initiatives and support groups to promote responsible use of social media and to help those unfortunate people who encounter difficulties. I cannot say this strongly enough: responsible use of social media represents no danger to users."

Becky nodded, "I think by now we are all familiar with the general mental-health risks posed by social media. The problem is, Jim, these accusations seem to be specific to Indigo, rather than with social media as a whole."

"Whoever set up this attack against Indigo purposely chose social media because it requires no proof—no validation of a story or its sources. We've done our own studies and found no risks to mental health for the majority of users."

"You think this is a coordinated attack?"

"Undoubtedly. Almost certainly organized by a group who will gain from a drop in Indigo's stock price—maybe a competitor?"

"You're convinced your platform poses no danger to users?"

"This is fake news, Becky. A smear campaign designed to hurt Indigo's business, nothing more. Our social-media platform is safe and enjoyed by millions of users worldwide. We would never knowingly put out a product that was harmful to people's mental health."

"You're happy for your own child to use Indigo?"

"Of course. Friends of mine have asked the same question, and my response is an emphatic 'yes'—Indigo does not pose a threat to mental health."

"Well, thanks for coming in and talking to us, Jim, especially during this difficult time."

"My pleasure, Becky."

Johanna muted the sound on the TV as it went to another commercial break. "Sounds convincing, doesn't he?".

Natalya shook her head. "He's scared. You see it in his eyes."

"Yes, but is it going to be enough?" said Johanna.

Ivan frowned. "We hurt him for sure, but, after a bit of damage control and some smart PR, they could still bounce back."

"Oh, I'm sorry, I forgot we had a business guru on board." Natalya shot a caustic look at Ivan. "This is too big, the story has too much momentum. He can't recover from this."

Riya wasn't so sure. Ivan might have a point.

ETHAN

Over the next few days, Indigo's stock-price fall plateaued, and the number of users leaving slowed.

Ivan sat back from his computer, ran his fingers through his hair, and sighed heavily. "We're losing momentum… We keep pumping out information, but people are getting hardened to it, and Indigo are in PR overdrive, promoting positive stories: people that use the platform for fundraising, reuniting long-lost friends, small businesses attributing their success to Indigo."

Johanna paced the cabin, tossing Natalya's stress ball. "We need something that lays the blame for all this squarely at Jim Booker's door, something he can't wriggle out of. We need a smoking gun."

Ivan looked exasperated. "That brings us back to having hard evidence of actual criminal behaviour, and that's what we can't find!"

Riya thought again of Ethan talking about his dad: *There are people out there who could do him a lot of damage.* Had he really overheard something big enough to destroy Indigo? Even if he had, would he tell her? Maybe. But it would mean telling the others about meeting Ethan in London…Natalya would go apeshit. But this was too important not to say anything simply because she might get told off.

She took a deep breath, "We could try his son."

They all turned and stared.

"I didn't know he had a son." Johanna looked surprised.

"Yeah, Ethan…"

Natalya's eyes narrowed suspiciously, "How do you know this?"

"I met him in London."

Natalya's eyebrow arched dangerously, "Is that so? Aren't you just full of surprises?"

It all tumbled out in a rush to justify herself. "I didn't know he was Booker's son. We met over a year ago, at a conference Dad went to. He never said who his father was. Then he messaged me when he was in London, and we met for coffee. He talked about how he didn't get on with his father, how his father had done some dodgy stuff and, if anyone found out, it could be really damaging. Then he told me who his father was."

Natalya looked glacial, "Un-fucking-believable. There is so much stupidity in that story, and this is precisely why I told you *not* to contact people!"

"I know—I'm sorry, OK—but I didn't know he was Jim Booker's son. When I found out, I left. He has no idea his father is looking for me."

"Really?"

"Look, I know I screwed up, but that's not the point. He lives in San Francisco, so maybe I can contact him and get him to tell me what his father has done?"

"And maybe you get us all killed," snapped Natalya.

Johanna's reaction was more calculated. "Do you have any idea what Ethan thinks his father has done?"

"No, but he said he treated people like crap. That there were people out there who could do him a lot of damage, but who were too scared to say anything."

"Hmm," Johanna frowned thoughtfully.

Natalya shook her head vigorously, "It's too dangerous. You got away with it once, you are unlikely to be so lucky again."

Riya looked at Ivan for support, but he shook his head. "Natalya's right."

"Agreed," said Johanna slowly. "It would bring us too close to Booker—we can't risk it. I'm sorry. However, it does suggest there *is* something—it's just a matter of finding it."

Riya pouted sulkily, "But we've tried that."

Johanna smiled, "We have a lot more information than we did. Let's revisit all the information we've gathered, but this time focus on anything suggesting a criminal act, like accounting fraud, or anti-competitive behaviour."

The other two nodded, but Riya scowled sullenly. Johanna was clutching at straws.

Riya sat down on the park bench, tore open the box, took out the new phone, slipped in the SIM card, and dumped the packaging in a nearby bin. She was going to contact Ethan, despite what the others said. He knew something, and she was going to find out what. She was pretty sure he wouldn't betray her, but the question was—would he betray his father? She turned the phone on and keyed in Ethan's number. Opening the text app, she hesitated, then typed:

> **Unknown Number:** Hi Ethan! Guess who? Sorry about dumping you in London, I just got spooked about who your dad is. I'm on holiday in San Francisco with...

(Who could she say she was with? Did he know by now she was a missing person back in the UK?)

> ...family and wondered whether you wanted to get together? Rxx.

(Best not to use her name, in case of prying eyes.)

Send.

Would he even reply? After leaving him in the middle of London with no explanation, she couldn't blame him if he completely ignored her or responded with a stream of abuse.

She jumped as her phone pinged almost instantly with a reply:

> **Ethan:** Hey! Great to hear from you. Another new number? You change your phone more often than I change my underwear! Admit I was hurt at being ghosted in London. The only way you can make it up to me is to let me buy you lunch. Tomorrow?

Wow, he's keen! Tomorrow seemed awfully short notice to prepare herself, but why not? If she delayed, she might chicken out.

> **Unknown number:** Sure, where?

> **Ethan:** Blots, in the Financial District, 12:30?

> **Unknown number:** Gr8!

A little flutter of excitement stirred in her chest. She told herself it wasn't a date—she was pumping him for information. But still, she was going to see Ethan again! Another thought struck her. Should she come clean? Tell him what she was doing? After all, he didn't get on with his father…But that was a long way from betraying his father with information that would send him to prison. No, it was probably better to avoid that conversation for now.

She switched off the new phone (Natalya's influence rubbing off), stuffed it in her pocket, and set off back to the marina.

Clambering down into the cabin, she found Ivan in front of his computer, munching his way through a massive bag of cheese Doritos.

She wrinkled her nose, "Those things stink."

"Nonsense, they have a delicate bouquet of cheesy loveliness, and they cover two major food groups: cheese and snacks."

"Whatever," she nodded at his computer. "Your shift on social watch, then?"

"Yeah. Numbers are still going down, but very slowly now. If we don't come up with something soon, the story will run out of steam. Especially as Indigo have their own influencers working overboard."

Riya took her coat off, "Where are Johanna and Natalya?"

Ivan stretched, "Went out to eat."

"Right. I'm going to read in my cabin, OK?"

"OK." He turned back to his computer.

Riya closed the door to her cabin and took out her glasses. "Art?"

"Hello, Riya."

"I need you to run a simulation on Ethan Zimmerman. Do you have enough information to build a profile?"

"Checking." There was a short pause, then, "Yes, I believe so."

"Awesome. Here's the scenario…"

Riya tapped her umbrella on the mat as she entered, shaking off the drizzle falling steadily outside.

She spotted Ethan in the middle of the restaurant. He put up a hand, grinning. Her heart jumped. She waved back, stood her umbrella by the door, and threaded her way through the busy tables. The place had a boho bistro feel about it, but the food on people's plates looked fancy—it fitted Ethan's shabby-chic image perfectly.

"Hello there." He rose from the table and leaned in for a polite air kiss. "Welcome to San Francisco." He nodded at the windows. "Not at its best today, though."

She laughed nervously, a little too much, then sat down, feeling awkward. "So…"

He gave a lopsided smile. "So…How've you been? Whatcha been doin'?"

"Just, you know, busy with life…college, running, fundraising." Oh, and running away from your homicidal father. "You?" She needed to deflect him from probing too deeply.

"After a hundred hours of therapy, I think I'm finally over being dumped in a London café." He picked up his fork and mimed stabbing his heart.

Riya laughed, then pouted apologetically. "I am *so* sorry, Ethan. I was just overwhelmed by, you know, finding out who your father is. I know it's stupid, and I don't usually care about that stuff, but the owner of Indigo…"

He smiled. "It's OK, I get it. Happens all the time. I usually get one of two reactions from girls: either their eyes light up with dollar signs, or they run a mile. I prefer the latter—at least it's honest—and I know, if they come back, they come back for me, not my dad. I'm glad you came back."

Riya blushed and fiddled with the salt cellar.

"So, enjoying San Francisco? Been sightseeing yet?"

"Only been here a couple of days, haven't seen much yet." Riya shrugged her shoulders and faked a smile.

Ethan spread his arms wide. "Well! Let me be your personal guide. I can miss a few classes and show you round."

Riya nodded coyly, "Cool, thanks."

He picked up a menu, "Come on, let's order appetizers—that way, we can eat and talk as long as we like."

That was it, ice broken. They ordered food and talked about everything, and Riya remembered why she'd liked him so much when they'd first met. She felt like she'd found a soulmate; they just seemed to "get" each other. She'd had boyfriends before, but there wasn't that electric connection that she felt with Ethan. It wasn't only that they never ran out of things to say; it was that the conversation felt exciting, like anything could happen. They talked about school, their futures, their hobbies, how their mothers' deaths had affected them both, how their fathers were similar in their addiction to work, and the death of Riya's dad.

Finally, the conversation came round to the opening Riya had been waiting for, and she found she resented it. She didn't want to use Ethan in that way. But that was why she was here, wasn't it?

"How are things with your dad?"

Ethan shrugged. "Same as usual—we keep out of each other's way. Actually, I've been trying to avoid him lately. With this smear campaign going on, he's like a bear with a sore head. Can't say I've got much sympathy; he probably brought it on himself." He glanced away, staring across the restaurant.

Riya watched him carefully. This was it: the moment Art's simulation had shown her.

"What do you mean?"

"Like I said in London, he's done some seriously uncool stuff, unethical stuff. I wouldn't be surprised if this is somebody's revenge."

"Unethical? Like what?"

He looked at her strangely, with a sort of probing intensity, perhaps wondering whether to trust her.

She pushed on. "Can't have been anything that bad. I mean, what's the worst he could do with a social-media platform?"

He carried on staring at her. Uh-oh, this was different from the simulation. She looked down at her lunch and pretended to load her fork, as though she wasn't really that interested.

Ethan broke his stare, looked around, and hunched forwards. "All right, try this…Three years ago, I come home from school and go up to my room. Ten minutes later, my phone buzzes to say someone's at the front gate—we have a security camera on the gate that links to a phone app. So, I answer it. This skinny, nerdy-looking black dude is looking into the camera. He says his name is Edgar Ismail and he works for my dad, says he needs to see him urgently. So, I buzz him through the gate, and Ralf, our butler, lets him in the house—"

Riya laughed, "You have a butler?"

Ethan rolled his eyes. "Yeah, yeah, I know. He runs the house because Dad is, like, hardly ever there, and, even when he is, he's far too important to do mundane stuff like taking the garbage out. Anyway, a couple of minutes later, I hear my dad's voice. He says, 'What can I do for you, Edgar?' So, they know each other. This Edgar says, 'I can't keep quiet any longer.' My dad says, 'We better talk about this in the study.'

"Now I'm really interested, right? I creep downstairs and listen at the study door. I couldn't hear all of it, but as they come out it sounds like Edgar says something like, 'If we don't back out these changes, I'm going to the press.' My dad says that would be a mistake, something about being bound by a non-disclosure agreement.

"A few days later, Ralf has the local breakfast news on the kitchen TV. Edgar's face appears. He's gone missing, along with the rest of his family! It says he works for Indigo, is some well-known AI scientist. I nearly choked on my Cheerios." Ethan spread his palms wide. "I mean, what the hell…?"

"Could be coincidence?"

"I'm not even finished yet…So, that's what I thought, but then, a couple of days later, some detective dude turns up. My dad takes him into the study. Naturally, I listen in. He says he's looking into the disappearance of Edgar Ismail, starts asking Dad questions about his relationship to Edgar—apparently someone saw them arguing at work.

"Eventually, Ralf shows him out, but my dad stays in the study. He makes a call to someone, not sure who, but he says… 'I've got a job for you. Our little scientist has run away to hide. I want you to find the little coward before the police do and make sure he keeps his mouth shut. I don't want to know details, just do what you have to do.'"

"Wow! Do you think your father, you know, had him…killed or something?"

Ethan looked horrified, "No! But I definitely think there was intimidation, threats maybe. But that's not the point. What I want to know is what this Edgar was going to blow the whistle on. What was my father so keen to keep quiet?"

"Something to do with Indigo?"

"Edgar talked about 'backing out changes'—that sounds like software. I think maybe Indigo is doing something illegal in their software. And now there's this stuff on the news…" Ethan shrugged, picked up a piece of bread and tore off a chunk. "But, hey, what do I know? All I'm saying is, I wouldn't be surprised if this latest crisis isn't something from the past coming back to bite him."

He threw the chunk of bread into his mouth and stared across the restaurant, eyebrows knitted in a brooding scowl. When he turned back, his face had cleared again.

"Hey, how about we stop talking about my dad and start talking about your sightseeing? Have you been to Alcatraz yet?"

Riya spent the next three days making excuses to sneak away and spend time with Ethan, claiming she was following up on information sources. It was a perfect few days. They visited Alcatraz, the Museum of Modern Art, and took a cruise around the bay. It didn't really matter where they went; she simply enjoyed spending time with him. After months of running, hiding, feeling scared, and being shot at, it was a wonderful release to forget her situation for a while.

An uncharacteristically warm February afternoon on the fourth day found Riya sauntering through Golden Gate Park with Ethan by her side. She closed her eyes and tilted her head back, enjoying the sun on her face. She felt Ethan's hand slip gently into hers.

She smiled and opened her eyes, "Sneaky."

He grinned. She hugged his arm. Another great thing about Ethan was the comfortable silences. Then…

Gazing along the path, squinting in the sunlight, she was just thinking how perfect this was when she spotted a tall willowy girl swaying elegantly towards them in a long flowing dress, looking as though she belonged on a catwalk. As she approached, she tossed a glossy sheet of blond hair over her shoulder as her eyes fell on Ethan—she was checking him out!

Riya glanced up at Ethan, who seemed to be looking straight past her to a stretch of grass where two kids were tossing a football back and forth.

Over her shoulder, Riya watched the girl walk away, swinging her hips, perfect little button nose in the air. She couldn't blame the girl—she would probably have done the same thing—but it made her feel insecure. The girl was beautiful, and Riya could totally see her walking beside someone like Ethan. She turned to him. "Why do you want to hang around with me?"

He followed her line of sight. "You're comparing yourself to *her*?" He sounded incredulous. "She's a cookie-cutter girl—one of hundreds, all with their micro-bladed eyebrows, spray tans, plastic noses. They all look the same, act the same. I'd never be Ethan to them; I'd be Jim Booker's son, a status symbol to be posted on their socials and wheeled out at parties. You're different; you don't care about that stuff."

She tutted with mock irritation, "Are you saying I don't care how I look?"

Ethan looked deadly serious, "Actually, yes. But in a good way. I followed you on the socials—that is, when you still did social media—and the only stuff you posted was about your fundraising." He glanced briefly after the girl. "I've never really known anyone like that. Being around you makes me want to be better than I am."

Riya almost burst into tears; that was possibly the nicest thing anyone had ever said to her.

"And did I mention you're smart and attractive, too?" He grinned. "And of course you have that great runner's ass."

"Oi!" She yanked his hand playfully.

He spun to face her, took her other hand, and bent towards her. She closed her eyes and felt his lips touch hers, gently at first, then harder. She pressed herself to him, and he pressed back, taking her in his arms. It felt as if her whole body were melting, as though she would slip through his arms and collapse on the floor in a molten pool. Finally, they parted. She swayed, rocking back on her heels.

Ethan tugged her back towards him, chuckling. "Whoa there, tiger."

She grinned up at him, locking her hands around his waist. "Can we stay here all afternoon?"

His face abruptly changed and he fumbled for his watch. "Aw, man! Look at the time! I'm gonna have to bail. Got football practice tonight. I can skip classes, but not football training— Coach'll have my ass in a sling." Leaning forwards, he kissed her. "I'll text you." He kissed her again.

She laughed, "Go, then!"

He let her go slowly, then sprinted off through the park.

Riya smiled dreamily, watching him go.

"Quite the emotional little scene there—very touching." The soft gravelly Irish accent sent goosebumps racing down her arms.

Riya whipped around. Standing right there behind her, shoulders hunched, hands rammed deep into his overcoat pockets, and wearing the same crumpled blue suit he'd worn during their meeting with MI5 back in London, was Brendan Brown. His grey eyes looked past her, watching Ethan disappear across the park.

"So, how are you liking San Francisco, Miss Sudame?"

Riya's mouth opened, but no sound came out. She stood there in shock.

"Hmm," his face cracked a grin as he pulled out a cigarette.

"What are you doing here?" hissed Riya, looking around in wild panic, expecting suits in dark glasses to jump out of the shrubbery.

"Don't worry, I'm not here to arrest you. I'm just…on vacation, you might say. Visiting old friends. And then, here you are too." He spread his hands, looking at the sky, "What are the odds?"

"Sarcasm is the lowest form of wit," snapped Riya. Her fear was tempered with annoyance at her perfect day being spoiled by this arrogant little man.

Brendan jabbed his cigarette at her. "But the highest form of intelligence—at least, so says Oscar Wilde." Tossing the cigarette to his lips, he reached into his pocket, pulled out a lighter, and lit the end. "My colleagues were most upset when you disappeared, back in the UK. Fortunately, I have a few toys at my disposal that can find people, wherever they are, but I admit being surprised when a bunch of people looking very much like you and your friends popped up in San Francisco." He jabbed his cigarette towards her again. "But, here's the funny thing, the names on the passports didn't match the names you gave us in London. So, I thought I would take a trip out here to see if it was you, after all. False passports indeed, tut-tut, a little naughty, don't you think?"

"So why don't you arrest us?"

"Ah, well, see, my colleagues are sticklers for the letter of the law, but me? I like to consider the law more like"—he took a drag from his cigarette and waved the glowing end in the air with a flourish—"guidelines."

"Then what are you here for?"

"I'm very interested in that technology of yours, Miss Sudame. But I'm guessing you'll have a button somewhere that erases the whole thing without a trace. Software's tricky like that—it can disappear in a puff of smoke."

He took a drag on his cigarette, looking at her with those heavy dead eyes, then exhaled a long stream of smoke.

"Do you watch the news, Miss Sudame? In my profession, it pays to keep up with current affairs. Take the recent stories around Indigo, for instance. Now, I'm a curious fellow, and this story got me wondering. I mean, it's obvious the attack was deliberate, and it's no secret that Mr. Booker has enemies, but this was a sophisticated attack requiring technology that could manipulate people's behaviour. Then, guess what? I find you and your friends in San Francisco, and I suddenly remember the accusation your colleague made about Booker killing your father. I'm not a believer in coincidence, Miss Sudame."

His gaze skewered her for a moment, then flicked away across the park again.

"You see, Mr. Booker has been on our watch list for quite some time—let's just say that myself and my old friends wouldn't be at all upset if his power was pruned back. He has a lot of data squirrelled away in that system of his, and his cosy new relationship with China makes us nervous. So, let's say, for instance, that someone was actively involved in knocking him down a peg or two. I think we would turn a blind eye to that—for a while, at least."

Riya eyed him suspiciously; this conversation was making no sense. "And what would happen then?"

"Firstly, we would need to understand if they themselves posed a threat, but if this someone decided to offer us the hand of friendship, then it may be that we could come to some mutual agreement."

"And if they didn't?"

He shrugged. "They might well be seen as a threat." Reaching into his coat, Brendan pulled out a small white card and handed it to Riya. "In case you feel like talking."

Riya took it. It had a phone number scribbled on it, nothing more. As he sauntered off, she stood there thinking. Her day had turned from perfect to nightmare in five minutes. How had Brendan found them? If *he* could find them, could Booker? She needed to tell the others.

She hurried across the park. As she reached the entrance and turned on to the street, a figure stepped into the path in front of her.

Riya leaped back, "Jesus, Ivan! What the—? Are you *following* me?"

"You need to work on your poker face. I could see the other day you weren't going to let it drop."

"What do you mean?" said Riya defensively. There was a chance he hadn't seen her with Ethan.

"I followed you in London as well. And I can see why you like him—even I had to have a quick rub down with a cold towel after seeing him."

Riya blushed. "It's not like that. He just…we just…have things in common."

Ivan tapped his chin thoughtfully. "Right. Like the way your faces fit together and—oh, yes—how his dad murdered your dad?" He looked at her, then exploded, "What the hell are you thinking? Jim Booker's son, for God's sake!"

"No, it's not like that. I thought—"

"Yes?"

"I thought I could find out something that would, you know, help us."

"And did you?"

She hesitated.

"You did, didn't you?"

Riya's shoulders slumped. "Don't tell the others yet…If I'm going to get murdered by Natalya, I want to make sure it's worth it."

He glared at her. "OK! But you tell *me* so I can keep tabs on you, and you promise not to see *him* again. The others were right. It's too dangerous. His dad is Jim Booker, for Christ's sake!"

Riya felt as though she'd been punched in the chest. She'd just had the most wonderful few days in years and now she had to give it up?

"All right, all right!" She pressed her palms to her forehead, dizzy with conflict. But she'd got what she wanted from Ethan, and every way she looked at it, continuing to see him ended badly. She took her hands from her face, set her jaw grimly, and stared stonily at Ivan. "I won't see him again."

"OK, then." Ivan looked satisfied.

Riya began walking again, stiff with anger and frustration.

Ivan fell into step beside her. "Who were you talking to at the end, there? His back was towards me."

"Brendan Brown."

"What?!" Ivan stopped walking again.

"What?" said Johanna and Natalya, sitting together at the cabin table.

Ivan watched quietly in the background, leaning against the galley bench.

Natalya looked furious. "How does Brendan Brown know we're here?"

"I don't know, but he seems to know what we're doing."

Johanna frowned. "He just appeared behind you?"

"Yes."

"Why didn't he arrest you? Did he ask you to hand over Art?"

"No. It was weird. He said they'd been watching Booker for some time. I think he's going to let us try and deal with Booker because it's in his interests, but after that he'd want to rein us in."

"I would like to know how he tracked us; those fake passports were watertight." Natalya drummed her fingers on the table.

Riya shrugged. "He said something about our faces popping up and not matching our names."

"Ah," said Natalya sagely, as though this explained everything.

Johanna looked worried, "Our plans for Booker now need to include what we do about the authorities after we're done."

Ivan looked up, "So, have you guys made any progress?"

Johanna nodded, "We have a lead on an employee who was sacked and settled out of court. We're meeting him tomorrow morning."

"No offence," said Ivan, "but we need to get a move on before Brendan tips people off."

Riya shivered as cold air and sunlight rushed down the companionway when Natalya opened the hatch the following morning.

"Go find something juicy!" shouted Ivan. As Johanna closed the hatch behind them, he turned to Riya. "OK, so what did you find out from Ethan?"

"I'm not sure it's that useful, really; might be nothing…" said Riya vaguely.

Ivan pursed his lips, "Life's full of crappy conflicts, Riya—give."

Riya sighed, "He mentioned his dad fell out with one of his employees a few years ago—a guy called Edgar Ismail, an AI scientist working for Indigo at the time. Ethan overheard his dad making threats. Next thing, Edgar disappears, and no one's heard from him since."

"You think Booker killed him?"

Riya shrugged, "Maybe. I did some searching; there are loads of articles by him on AI research, right up to the point he disappeared—nothing since."

"Hmm," Ivan ran his fingers through his hair, leaving it sticking up in all directions. He plucked his glasses from the neck of his shirt. "Get your glasses."

She went to her cabin and returned wearing them.

"Art? Initiate sharing session with Riya."

Riya agreed.

"Please search for pictures of Edgar Ismail, AI scientist."

"Certainly, Ivan."

A panel opened in Riya's vision displaying a wall of pictures of "a nerdy-looking black guy", as Ethan had described him, with beard, glasses, and short-cropped hair. The references were mainly academic.

"OK, can you run a search to find a face match under any other name? And give me the sources too, please."

"Search running," said Art.

"We're assuming he's dead," Ivan explained. "But what if he guessed Booker was coming for him and went into hiding?"

Art's voice purred in Riya's ear: "Ivan, I have your results. I was able to find one match. Earl Johnson, Montana." A panel popped up showing a poor-quality photo of a group of people building a walking trail in a forest. There, in the background, clearly unaware his photo was being taken, was Edgar Ismail. His hair was longer, his beard and glasses gone, but it was him. "Photo source is the archives of a local Butte newspaper, an article about trail conservation in Montana."

"Do you have an address?" asked Riya. "And map?"

"Yes." Art flashed up an address in Riya's vision: *Silver Deer Ranch, Butte, Montana.* A map panel opened and zoomed in to north-west Montana.

"Looks like he did go into hiding, changed his name," said Ivan.

Riya slumped dejectedly in her seat. "So, he's still alive? Not murdered, then. Another dead end."

Ivan frowned, "Not necessarily. I wonder what it was that he knew that was so important."

Riya looked up again, "Ethan said something similar—he wondered what Edgar knew."

"We'll tell the others when they get back, then maybe pay him a visit." He looked at Riya. "Right?"

She grimaced. "Not yet. We still don't know if what he knows is of any use—it might be nothing. I want to make sure it's worth the grief I'll get for hanging out with Ethan. Can't I just check it out myself?"

Ivan groaned. "What, another one of your lone-wolf missions? Because that worked out so well for us last time. Anyway, must be a fifteen- to twenty-hour drive to get there—how are you going to do that without Johanna and Natalya noticing? It's not like sneaking off for an afternoon with your boyfriend and saying you've been shopping."

"Don't know yet," snapped Riya, annoyed at Ivan picking holes in her plan.

Ivan grinned. "You know, it's good skiing up at Lake Tahoe this time of year. I went once—awesome powder, spectacular views, and sweet night life."

"What *are* you on about?"

"I think we deserve a break, after all the hard work we've put in lately."

Riya shook her head and scrunched up her face.

"How about we plan a *trip*?" Ivan looked at her meaningfully.

Riya's face smoothed as realization dawned. "Oh! You mean plan a trip to Tahoe, but go to Montana?"

"Exactly."

"You think they'll let us?"

He shrugged. "More chance than letting us go to Montana. Let me suggest it. It'll be expected, coming from me."

Riya wondered, not for the first time, how much of Ivan's buffoonery was an act. "I thought you were all for telling the others. Why are you helping me?"

"Yeah, well, let's face it, we're not getting anywhere sitting around here with our thumbs up our arses, are we? You might be on to something, and, if there's any chance of ending this mess, I'm in. Also, if you tell Johanna and Natalya that you got this from Ethan, they'll say it's either a trap or too dangerous. So, *we* go—alone."

Johanna and Natalya—back from their meet and looking dejected at a lack of anything useful—stared at Ivan with incredulous expressions.

Natalya cocked her head on one side. "Let me get this straight, rich boy: we're in hiding, in the middle of a delicate and dangerous operation, and you want to go on *vacation*?"

"Well, yeah. It's not like I'm achieving anything here, and two days off isn't going to make a lot of difference, is it?"

Natalya shook her head and snorted. "Unbelievable. Actually, scratch that—totally believable, coming from you!"

"Is that a yes? I mean, what can happen? Booker won't be looking for us in a vacation resort."

Johanna sighed. "OK. But take Riya with you—she could do with a break, and she can keep an eye on you."

"Done," Ivan clapped his hands. "Whaddaya say, Riya? Ready to hit the slopes?"

Riya smiled weakly. She was now wondering if they were even doing the right thing. She was pretty sure Ethan wouldn't betray her knowingly, but, if he ever did mention her to his dad, then…

THE WHISTLE-BLOWER

The bus ground to a halt on the snowy road. Doors clanked open. Riya stepped down, boots squeaking in the snow, rucksack slung over one shoulder. Grey cloud stretched away to the distant mountains across a bleak snowy landscape.

Ivan jumped down behind her, shouldered his rucksack, and turned up his coat collar. "Jeez, it's cold here."

Doors clanked shut, and the bus growled away.

Riya held up her phone. "Map says Silver Deer Ranch is up that track." She pointed to tyre tracks in the snow, winding away into the wilderness.

Ivan grimaced, "No sign, no gateposts…?"

"Would you advertise if *you* were hiding?"

Ivan shrugged, "Guess not."

Riya glanced at the receding bus, "Let's get going; it'll be dark soon."

The deep snow made for hard walking as they trudged up the track. After half a mile, they dropped down a slope into thick fir trees.

"By the way," said Ivan, puffing, "do we know when the next bus back to town is?"

"Don't know."

"*What?* We're not dressed for this weather, it's getting dark, and we're miles from the nearest town. If this guy's not in, or not talking, we die of hypothermia—you know that, right? Whoa!"

The trees ended abruptly in a large clearing. In the centre sat an austere grey concrete cube, about the size of a school sports hall. No doors or windows.

"This is a *house*? Looks more like a nuclear bunker!"

Riya's stomach sank. It didn't look much like a house. "Let's see if there's a door."

They trudged right around the structure.

Ivan shook his head. "Weird. A big block of concrete, no way in or out. Doesn't make sense."

"No," Riya was wet and shivering now. "Looks like someone's in there though. Look at the smoke." She pointed to a thin plume of smoke rising from the centre of the cube

An electrical hiss cut through the silence of the forest and a voice boomed out of a hidden speaker: "What do you want?"

"Mr. Ismail?"

There was a pause. "The only people who know that name are people I don't want to know. Did Booker send you?"

"No, we're…" What to say?

"You're with the press? Now I *really* don't want to talk to you. I don't know how you found me, but you can just turn around and go back the way you came; forget me and forget this place."

The hiss of the speaker went dead.

"Wait! My name is Riya Sudame, this is Ivan Parfenov." Riya had a horrible feeling Edgar was gone and she was shouting at the deaf concrete, but she had to try. "Jim Booker killed our fathers!"

They waited in the dying light, hoping for a response. Finally, Ivan blew out his cheeks. "Hypothermia it is, then."

As if in reply, a mechanical hum started up and a section of the cube's wall slowly hinged upwards, like a giant cat flap. Beyond, steps led up to frosted-glass doors, glowing with warm yellow light from within. The humming stopped. One of the glass doors flew open and Edgar Ismail stepped out, pointing a rifle at them. "You're Sanjay and Victor's children?"

"You knew my father?" said Riya, astonished.

He laughed bitterly. "Artificial Intelligence is a small world." He lowered his rifle, looked at the sky, and sighed heavily. "You'd better come in before you freeze."

A warm blast of air met them as they entered the entrance hall of fashionable polished concrete, timber, and glass.

"I was sorry to hear about your fathers." Closing the outside door, he walked them through into an open-plan living area. Heat radiated from a log fire set in a column running up through the centre of the living room. He pointed to the fire. "Go warm yourselves. I'll get my wife—she's in the panic room with the children."

Watching him leave, Riya flexed her fingers painfully in front of the fire as the heat sent hot aches surging through them. "He seems pretty scared."

Ivan huffed. "This whole place is built like a fortress. I'd say he's scared stiff. Think all this is to keep Booker out?"

Riya shrugged. "Could be."

Edgar returned, accompanied by a petite woman with a short-cropped afro framing her petrified face. A boy of about seven and a girl of about five peered out from behind her. The woman smiled feebly and muttered hello.

"I'm sorry about scaring your family," said Riya, trying to look apologetic.

The woman nodded and seemed to relax a little. "You must be frozen. Would you like a drink? Hot chocolate, maybe?"

Riya looked at Ivan, who nodded. "That would be lovely, thanks."

Edgar turned to his wife. "Thank you, Jasmine, we'll go talk in my office." With that, he led Riya and Ivan across the living room, down a corridor, opened a door, and waved them in.

The office was dark and cosy. A large desk dominated the centre of the room, facing a wall covered with a large video screen displaying tiled views of what looked like the house and surrounding countryside. Riya realized she was looking at the feed from a dozen cameras that must have been hidden along the track they'd followed from the highway.

Edgar smiled, seating himself behind the desk. "Yes, I saw you coming." He waved them to sit. "Now, what's this about Booker killing your fathers, and why are you here?"

Riya explained everything: the murder of Sanjay and Victor; their plans to bring Booker to justice; the social-media campaign against Indigo; and her conversation with Ethan.

He listened attentively, hands folded in his lap, bright eyes flashing between Riya and Ivan. He took his eyes off them only once, to acknowledge his wife, who arrived with the hot chocolate halfway through the story.

After Riya had finished, Edgar nodded thoughtfully. "That is quite a story."

"So," said Riya quickly, anxious to make her point. "If we had one piece of hard evidence showing intentional wrongdoing on Indigo's behalf, that would be enough."

Edgar took a long breath. "All right. I will tell you what Ethan overheard—and then why I cannot help you."

"But—" Riya started to protest, but Edgar waved her quiet.

"Let me tell my story before you judge me. A few years ago, I set up my own company, developing a personal-assistant AI app to help manage your life—appointments, reminders, ordering shopping, that sort of thing. Jim Booker approached me about buying the company—he offered me a *lot* of money, *and* the chance to stay on and head the project. I agreed.

"We set up a division inside Indigo to integrate our AI assistant into their social-media system. Yes, it 'helped' you organize your life, but what they really wanted was to sell you more stuff, so it also suggested items to buy based on your calendar, reminders, browsing history, interests, shopping habits…You put in your calendar 'Camping Trip', and it starts suggesting stuff you might need—tents, gas stoves. You block out time to go to the gym, and it starts recommending trainers, gym clothes. Socially, it recommended friends, news articles, people to follow. Other companies were doing the same.

"It was reasonably successful. People enjoyed the interaction, and it boosted sales. But Jim wanted more. He tasked us with an experiment: could the AI be more aggressive at selling? So, instead of the AI's primary objective being to *help the user*, the algorithms were changed to *maximize sales for Indigo*.

"I was concerned, but it was 'just a research project', and Booker promised we would try the new aggressive sales algorithms as an experiment only with users who had agreed to take part. Instead, he rolled it out as a standard update to *all* users.

"I was furious.

"Then, the results started coming in. They were unbelievable. Indigo sales skyrocketed, propelling them past all its rivals. But the purpose of an AI is to continually learn better ways of achieving its goals—in our case, better sales. What our AI learned was that the best sales strategy was to prey on fear—fear of being lonely, fear of not being liked, fear of being ugly, fear of being overweight. It became adept at looking at your online activity, assessing what you might be afraid of, then systematically boosting your fear by feeding you news articles, posts, product reviews, friend suggestions, adverts, blogs…So, first, it changed your self-image—always to the negative—then, it suggested products to help. Then it got smarter. Instead of just pushing products, it started promoting and recommending influencers that pushed products sold by Indigo. Adverts lack personal connection, but influencers? If they recommend something, their followers go crazy for it. Cheaper, too—no expensive adverts, just send influencers free product, promote them on Indigo social media, and let them do the advertising. Influencers promote products; in turn, Indigo promotes the influencers so they gain more followers, and round and round we go.

"News stories began rolling in: anorexia numbers spiked; teen suicides increased; consumer debt was up; 'snake oil' health companies were cashing in on hypochondria; cyberbullying, shopaholics, gambling—you name it. And always there was a link to social media. The media didn't pinpoint Indigo as a key cause, but my team were convinced the increases were directly related to our 'aggressive sales algorithms'.

"I voiced my concerns at meetings, but I was told they were social trends, not related to Indigo. But, as more stories hit the headlines, someone suggested we carry out our own internal investigation. Jim didn't like the idea, but, with every department saying we needed to do *something*, he relented.

"The investigation was top secret. If the press got the slightest whiff that Indigo was investigating this, they would take it as an admission of guilt. Two months later, they presented the results—the link between poor mental health and Indigo's sales algorithms was indisputable. People looked at me as though I had intentionally created a malevolent AI. I explained that, with artificial intelligence, you are creating a system that 'learns' how to solve a problem—once you let it loose, how it solves a problem is up to the AI itself. And that's what you want, right? You want it to come up with solutions that have never been thought of before. But this means you can get unintended consequences and it's why you never want to put it in charge of making unsupervised decisions until you have done a *lot* of testing. If you don't program it with the right guard rails, you might get very unsavoury results. Tell an AI to solve global warming and it might reasonably decide the solution is to kill all humans because they are the cause. It's like a child—as it learns, you have to guide it by telling it what is socially acceptable. What Jim did, and other tech companies are doing, is effectively putting socially immature AI in charge of social media.

"Anyway, after the presentation, Jim thanked the investigation team for their efforts—but, the next day, they were gone, with big payoffs in exchange for signing non-disclosure agreements. Everything to do with the investigation and the report was deleted. All done in a couple of days. Jim then told us all that he wouldn't be changing a thing; with Indigo's Chinese expansion plans about to be announced, the algorithms were too valuable to remove for the sake of, and I quote, 'a few gullible lemmings who decided to jump off their own cliff'. He warned any attempt to publicize the report would be met with immediate dismissal and legal action.

"I couldn't believe it; people were getting hurt on a mass scale and we were going to do nothing?"

"Why didn't you leave?" asked Riya.

"I thought I was better off fighting this from the inside. And I had a secret weapon." He smiled grimly. "You see, most of the report data was gathered from my department and I'd been sent an advance copy of the report, to my personal email. Booker didn't know. I didn't want to use it unless I had no other option, but he wouldn't change his mind. Finally, I went to his house, told him I had a copy of the report—that's the conversation Ethan overheard—told him Indigo had to have the aggressive AI removed immediately, or I would go to the press with the report.

"He sacked me on some trumped-up charge of misconduct that would paint me as just another disgruntled employee if I went to the press. Then he started making thinly veiled threats that, if I did ever go to the press, it might put me and my family in danger. I wasn't prepared to risk that, so I kept quiet. But I also had a nasty feeling he wouldn't leave me floating around as a potential 'whistleblower', not with that report in my back pocket. I took my family and fled. We changed our names and started a new life. I sent Booker a letter explaining that I would keep the report as insurance, and if anything ever happened to me or my family, my lawyers would send it to the press."

"What did he say to that?" asked Riya.

Edgar shook his head. "I haven't heard anything since. But I think Jim would still like to get rid of me. So, that report is the only thing keeping me and my family safe, and, if I gave it to you, he would know it came from me. I'm sorry, Miss Sudame, but I can't risk the safety of my family."

Riya nodded. "Meanwhile, Indigo carries on hurting people. You are buying your safety with more than your silence, Mr. Ismail—you are buying it with the pain of people who use Indigo every day."

Edgar glared at Riya.

"How dare you judge me? How old are you? Sixteen, seventeen? Yes, the aggressive sales algorithms remain in place, but I think your campaign has hit them hard. Users are waking up to the truth. You don't need me."

Riya grimaced. "No offence, Mr. Ismail, but I don't think so. Our social-media campaign is losing momentum. This will be old news in a couple of months and users will start drifting back."

Ivan cleared his throat. "What if Booker came into possession of a new piece of technology to reinvigorate his business?"

"You mean Victor and Sanjay's project?" Edgar tapped the chair armrest thoughtfully. "Yes. Predictive Tech's system sounds more advanced, the next generation of what we were doing. If Jim Booker got hold of such technology…" He shook his head again. "No, I'm sorry, I can't help you. I have my family to think of."

"But—"

"I said *no*, Miss Sudame."

"But—"

He cut her off again, "What I will do is give you the name of the person who led the investigation team. He might be willing to discuss the report with you. That is as much as I am prepared to do." He stared defiantly at Riya.

There was no point antagonizing him further. Riya sagged in her seat, "OK, thank you."

Edgar scribbled a name and address on a piece of paper and handed it to Riya.

"Here, Oliver Mendoza. There's no guarantee he'll talk to you, but it's worth a try." He got to his feet. The meeting was over. "The weather's closing in. You can stay here tonight and I'll run you into town tomorrow."

After a quiet, awkward meal with Edgar and his family, Riya and Ivan were shown to their rooms.

Riya showered, wrapped herself in the heavy cotton bathrobe on loan from Edgar, sat on the edge of the crisp white linen bed and let her eyes roam the room. It had that chic urban concrete industrial feel you'd expect to find in a New York loft apartment—totally out of place in the middle of a Montana forest. But she understood: it had the impenetrable feel of a of bomb shelter; perfect for someone scared about being hunted down. Edgar had raised the concrete flaps that covered the windows now, and Riya looked out through at the snow falling thickly outside. For a while, she let herself be mesmerized by the white flakes cascading past the window. She was feeling pretty miserable. Edgar wasn't going to help her, and she would cop a load of flak when she told Johanna and Natalya where she'd been. She couldn't help thinking she'd missed an opportunity with Edgar. And why would this investigator be any more willing to help?

She rummaged in her bag again, took out her glasses, and put them on.

"Good evening, Riya."

"Art, I have something I want you to check out."

"Morning," Ivan wandered into the kitchen wearing a similar fluffy cotton bathrobe to the one Riya had worn, hanging open at the chest. Yawning loudly, he ruffled his hair, rearranging it from an untidy pile of straw into a complete mess. He blinked at Edgar and Riya sitting at the breakfast bar, fully clothed, empty coffee mugs in front of them.

"How long have you guys been up?"

"A while," Edgar looked at Riya.

Ivan glanced from one to the other. "Did I miss something?" His eyes fell on Riya's glasses sitting on the table.

Riya picked them up, "I'll tell you later. We need to get going."

"After breakfast, surely?"

"Ivan!" hissed Riya, embarrassed at Ivan demanding breakfast from their reluctant host.

But Edgar slapped the counter, his face losing its serious frown. "A man after my own stomach! Indeed, there is always time for breakfast. What are you thinking? Pancakes? Bacon?"

Ivan patted his stomach. "How about both? I haven't eaten since yesterday; I'm hungrier than a vegan in a steak restaurant."

Riya buried her head in her hands.

"You got it!" Edgar bustled to his feet and began pulling food from the refrigerator, while Riya glared at Ivan.

As the bus pulled away, they waved through the window to Edgar, standing on the sidewalk. He raised a hand, smiled, and was gone as the bus swung out into the traffic.

Ivan flung himself back in his seat and sighed. "Well, that was a waste of time."

Riya looked out of the window, "Oh, I wouldn't say that."

Johanna was busy chopping vegetables in the galley when Riya and Ivan climbed down the companionway.

"Hey! Welcome back. Did you have a nice time up at Tahoe?"

Riya shuffled her feet nervously, "Actually, we haven't been to Lake Tahoe."

Natalya looked up from her computer, eyes narrowing suspiciously. "What do you mean, you haven't been to Lake Tahoe?" Her voice was soft and deadly.

"Where *have* you been, then?" Even Johanna's usually warm face had turned hard.

"Montana. Following a lead on a potential whistle-blower."

Natalya sucked her teeth noisily. "And where did you get this 'lead'?"

"Booker's son, Ethan."

Natalya cocked an eyebrow, "Really?" She barked a laugh.

Ivan stepped to Riya's side. "Before you give yourself a brain haemorrhage, listen to what Riya has to say."

"I suppose you just followed along, like a lost sheep? That figures—the blind leading the stupid—"

"Right," Ivan cut her off. "Because, if you couldn't find something with all your technical wizardry, it's inconceivable we might have something to offer. Natalya, why don't you dazzle us with how you're planning to take down Jim Booker?"

Natalya stared at him sullenly; she had no reply.

"So why don't you let Riya explain what she's found?" Ivan said.

"This better be good," growled Natalya.

Riya explained everything, from her conversation with Ethan (minus the whole sightseeing/hand-holding/kissing bits) to Edgar Ismail's secret report and the contact he'd given them.

Natalya shook her head disgustedly. "I would have thought, after Cambridge, you would have learned your lesson, but it seems you enjoy stupidity."

"However, stupidity sometimes has its uses." Johanna waggled the kitchen knife absently in her hand; her eyes had that sharp thoughtful look again. "This report of yours may just complement our own discovery."

Riya broke her stare with Natalya, "You found something as well?"

Johanna glanced at Natalya. "We found out that a significant portion of the funding for Indigo's Chinese expansion is coming from outside investors."

"From that TV interview, I thought Indigo were funding it mostly themselves?"

"That's what Jim Booker wants people to believe, but he is actually reliant on outside investment for a lot of the money— and one investor in particular: a Mr. Preston North at Mordue Investments. Persuade this guy to withdraw investment and Indigo would be in real financial trouble."

"And how exactly are you going to persuade this guy to ditch his investment?" said Ivan.

"His daughter was the same age as Riya when she killed herself as part of a social-media suicide pact—and guess which platform they used?"

"Indigo?"

"Correct."

"His daughter dies because of social media and he's still supporting Indigo?" Riya was incredulous.

"Yes. We believe Booker convinced Preston the problem was mental-health awareness and education, not social media. Preston campaigns vigorously for mental-health awareness in schools and colleges."

"So, how are you going to convince him that Indigo is so bad he needs to withdraw his investment?"

Johanna grinned. "Your report. If that shows Indigo are directly responsible for mental-health issues, and they knew it? He wouldn't want anything to do with a company that had caused his daughter's death."

"Is that enough?" Ivan was staring at the table, brow deeply furrowed in an uncharacteristic frown.

"What do you mean?" barked Natalya.

He looked up. "Will that stop him, or do we need to go further?"

Natalya raised her eyebrows. "A few days ago, you wanted to run away with your tail between your legs. *Now*, you want to be Jack the Giant Slayer?"

"We need to hit him so hard he *never* gets up again. I don't ever want to be looking over my shoulder wondering if he's coming after me again. That report will ruin Indigo, but what about him personally?"

Johanna shook her head. "It was Jim who hid the information, so he will be personally liable. He will be ruined financially, his reputation will be in tatters, and Indigo will be destroyed. He'll also probably face a number of lawsuits. He'll be finished."

Riya looked up to find Natalya glaring at her, "So how many times did you see Ethan Booker to get this information?"

Riya felt Ivan's eyes on her, "Just once." She tried to keep her voice casual, but she felt her face burning.

Natalya stared at her for a long time. Whether she believed her, Riya wasn't sure, but she decided to change the subject: "Are we going to pay this Oliver Mendoza a visit?"

Johanna nodded, "Yes, but first you introduce yourself to Preston North."

"Me?"

"His daughter was your age when she died; Art says you would have the best chance of convincing him."

"When are we doing this?"

"Day after tomorrow."

"Isn't that rushing things a bit?"

Natalya stepped in front of Riya, grinning, "Cheer up. Meeting people who might turn you over to Booker? Your speciality, no?"

Johanna shook her head, "He's in town visiting tech companies this week, flies back to New York the day after tomorrow. Your information provides us with more leverage. We'll get Art to simulate the conversation and we're good to go."

THE INVESTOR

From the back seat of the cab, Riya leaned forwards, pointing through the windscreen at a grey-haired middle-aged man in an expensive overcoat. He'd just emerged on to the pavement outside the Hilton San Francisco Airport Bayfront hotel, and he glanced from his phone to the road, looking for his ride. "That's him."

The Uber driver nodded and pulled over to the kerbside. Riya took a deep breath. This was it—showtime. She fixed her smile and waited.

The cab door opened, and the grey-haired man got into the back of the cab, sitting down with a tired grunt.

"Hello, Mr. North," said Riya pleasantly.

The man jumped, looking at her in surprise. "Oh! I'm sorry, I thought this was my ride." He opened the door to get out.

"No, Mr. North, this is your ride. I need to speak with you. I know you're a busy man, so I won't take up much of your time."

She watched him pause, sharp intelligent eyes calculating what she wanted. From her rehearsals with Art, Riya knew he thought she wanted to pitch him some crazy business idea to invest in. But—even in the tech industry—she looked a bit young for an entrepreneur, so he wasn't sure. And the fact she looked around the same age as his daughter just before she died made him pause.

He slammed the door shut. "All right, Miss…?"

"Sudame."

"All right, Miss Sudame." He glanced at his watch again. "You have until we reach the airport."

Riya smiled, "Thank you. I think it will be to your advantage."

"That remains to be seen. What is it you want to discuss?"

"I have a proposition for you."

"Really," said Preston wearily. "I don't invest in Girl Guide cookies." He grinned, not unkindly.

Riya smiled back confidently, unruffled. "I am not looking for investment, Mr. Preston."

He frowned, confused, "Oh?"

"You're a major investor in Indigo, right?"

"Yes…"

She had him off-balance, unsure where this was going.

"What would you say if I told you my friends and I are in possession of a report that links Indigo's social media with mental-health issues, and that we intend to use this report to bring down Indigo and Jim Booker, and we would like you to help us?"

Riya felt strangely detached. It didn't sound like her—too polished, too…well, grown up. But then, they weren't her words, were they? The voice was hers, but the words were Johanna's, and she had rehearsed these words a thousand times with the rest of the team.

Whatever Preston was expecting, it wasn't this. He stared at her for a second, then laughed. "I'm sorry, miss, I'm not sure what you expect me to say. Firstly, claims of social media causing mental-health problems have been around for a long time, and yet no concrete evidence emerges. Secondly, Jim Booker, my business associate and friend, assures me Indigo have conducted their own investigations and found nothing. Thirdly, why would I help you ruin a company that I am invested in?"

Riya nodded. "Firstly, this report shows not only clear evidence of a link, but that Indigo has been aware of this connection *for years*. Secondly, your 'business associate and friend' knowingly lied to you when he said that Indigo was not to blame. Thirdly, I would ask you how you continue to support a company that was knowingly responsible for the death of your daughter?"

Preston's tired smile disappeared, "How dare you presume to talk to me about my daughter! I don't know where you got that information…" His mouth flapped, groping for words. "I'm not sure what grudge you have against Jim Booker—"

"He murdered my father," Riya continued to smile politely.

"Wh—?"

"He murdered my father to get his hands on a piece of technology he intends to use to exploit more people like your daughter."

"I…" He cleared his throat. "Even if you had such a report, it is unlikely to take down a company the size of Indigo."

"You think? Have you been watching the news?"

She could see his mind reeling.

"Indigo's lost users," he said. "That was you?"

"And that was with anecdotes. Imagine what we could do with hard evidence. We are going to burn Indigo to the ground, with or without your help. If you keep supporting Booker, you will burn with him, and I don't think your clients are going to thank you for losing their money."

Preston's face hardened, "So, what is it that you want me to do?"

"We want you to sell your entire Indigo holding and withdraw your funding for their Chinese expansion."

He snorted loudly, "But we would incur huge losses! That would ruin many of my investors!"

"We will let you sell the shares gradually, over a week or so…"

"A week to dump that much stock? We would still incur substantial losses."

"We will ensure there is a buyer for your shares, so the price will not drop too much. Once you have sold it all, you will announce it, *and* that you are withdrawing your funding for the Chinese expansion because of ethical concerns about Indigo. Our buyer will then dump the stock, and we will release the report to the media."

Preston shook his head. "But then everyone would sell. Other investors would pull out of the Chinese expansion…"

"Precisely, Mr. North. Indigo would be bankrupt."

"Your buyer must have deep pockets to withstand that kind of loss."

She nodded calmly, "They do."

Preston's eyes narrowed, "What if I decide this report is garbage and I expose your plan before you release it?"

"Would that be wise? At this point, merely the *suggestion* that such a report exists would send Indigo's stock price into freefall, hurting your investors. We are giving you the chance not only to save yourself and your investors from financial ruin, but to deliver justice to the man responsible for your daughter's death."

She could see Preston's thoughts rallying. "Jim Booker is my friend, and he has assured me there is no link between social media and mental-health issues. Just because you have come across some wild report claiming otherwise is not solid proof. Which crackpot organization produced this report, anyway?"

"Oh, didn't I mention that?" Riya stared him calmly in the eye. "The report was produced by Indigo themselves, the result of an internal investigation four years ago."

Preston's eyes went wide. "Four...four years ago..." His voice sounded frail, "But that...would mean..."

"Indigo and Booker were aware of the harm they were doing before your daughter took her own life. They knew, and they did nothing."

"But Jim—he lied to me?"

"Yes."

He refocused, looking coldly at Riya. "So where is this report?"

"We are in the process of obtaining it."

Preston seized on this like a drowning man clutching a straw. He sneered. "You don't actually have it?"

Riya was ready for this. "No. But we are confident we will have it within the next forty-eight hours, along with supporting evidence and someone involved in producing the report who is willing to testify."

The cab pulled up at the airport.

"You're out of time, Miss Sudame," Preston tugged at his collar uncomfortably, loosening his tie.

"You cannot afford to ignore this, Mr. North. Give us forty-eight hours to get you the report."

He hesitated, hand on the door handle. Then he reached inside his jacket and pulled out a business card. "Here. Send me what you have within forty-eight hours, or I go to Jim Booker."

Riya smiled to herself. He was theirs.

THE TAKEDOWN

The morning sun strobed through the trees lining the roadside. From the passenger seat, Riya counted down house numbers as they cruised past the manicured green lawns and prim little bungalows of Santa Clara. She looked down at her hands, turning them over. They shook slightly, the palms hot and clammy.

Natalya slowed the car, "Here we are: 2253 Johnson."

Riya stared at the pretty white bungalow and felt her mouth go dry. Oliver Mendoza, the author of Indigo's damning report, was sitting in there waiting for them.

Johanna poked her head between the front seats. "Park up round the block. We'll walk back to the house on foot." Riya caught a whiff of her perfume and wondered how she could be bothered to think about how she smelled today.

Natalya nodded. Rounding the corner, she drove halfway along the street and parked at the kerb.

"OK, glasses on, everybody," Johanna said.

Riya unfolded her glasses and slipped them on, nearly poking herself in the eye her hands shook so much. Art's familiar welcome greeted her. "Good morning, Riya."

"Ready?" said Johanna, looking at Ivan.

It had been decided that Johanna and Ivan would be the ones to visit Mendoza; Johanna had the most authoritative presence, and Ivan, despite his untidy-haystack appearance, looked older than Riya, and more respectable than the sullen gothic darkness of Natalya.

Ivan looked pale. "Let's get it over with. This is a big gamble, you know that, right?"

Johanna forced a smile. "We've had Art simulate this numerous times. Follow the script and we'll be fine."

"Art can be wrong…"

Riya and Natalya watched the feed from Johanna's and Ivan's glasses as they made their way down the street and round the corner.

Johanna rang the doorbell. The door clicked open a crack. A man with black hair peered through the gap.

"Mr. Mendoza?"

"That's me." His eyes jumped from Johanna to Ivan to the street and back again. He licked his lips.

"Nervous little thing, isn't he?" muttered Natalya.

Riya frowned, "Very." Nervous people were unpredictable.

The man took another furtive look at the street. "You better come in." He stood to one side, waving Johanna and Ivan inside.

Riya watched as the video feed showed them moving into a living room, where Oliver Mendoza stood in front of the glass patio doors. He turned to face them, hands clasped in front of him, rubbing and twisting them continuously.

"So, you want to talk about the Indigo report?" He wiped a bead of sweat rolling down his temple.

"Yes. As I explained on the phone, we are looking to obtain—" Johanna's feed was a blur of movement as she whirled round. Then…darkness.

Ivan cried out, and his feed went dark. There were muffled shouts, then silence.

Art's voice purred in Riya's ear, mildly apologetic. "I am not receiving a signal from Ivan or Johanna's glasses."

Natalya flung the car door open, "Stay here." She leaped out and ran down the street.

"Natalya! Don't!" But she was gone. Riya punched the seat. "Damn it! Art, give me a shared session with Natalya." She sat watching through her glasses as Natalya ran down the street. Mendoza's house came into view. Suddenly, the video feed spun skywards, Natalya cried out—and then nothing.

"Natalya? Are you there? Natalya!" Riya held her breath, gipping the car seat.

A metallic *clink clink* against her window made her jump halfway into the driver's seat. She whipped around. Her blood turned to ice. Pointing at her through the half-open window was the barrel of a gun!

The person holding it bent down, face level with the window. "Good afternoon, *mademoiselle*." The craggy face of Raphael Collomb smiled in at her. "Please, step out of the car." He glanced up and down the street.

Riya opened the door. As she got out, Raphael tucked the gun into a shoulder holster under his jacket, grabbed her arm, bruisingly tight, and slapped handcuffs round her wrist and his own, closing them tight enough to make Riya wince.

"We don't want you running off again, do we, my little gazelle, eh?" He pointed at her glasses. "And I'll take those, if you please."

She handed them over and he slipped them into his jacket.

"Where are you taking me?" said Riya, more boldly than she felt.

"Mr. Booker would like to talk with you and your friends." His sharp eyes darted around the street as they walked.

Turning the corner, Riya spotted a white van now parked outside Mendoza's; two men leaned nonchalantly against the back doors, talking. Dressed casually, they looked ordinary enough, but, as Raphael and Riya approached, one of the men nodded towards them and said something. Oliver Mendoza watched from his front door, still pale and anxious, as though he wished this scene were taking place anywhere but in front of his house.

The men by the van pulled open the rear doors. Inside, handcuffed to the rough wooden benches running down each side, were Natalya, Ivan, and Johanna, dejected and defeated. Natalya looked OK, but Ivan and Johanna had cuts and bruises on their faces. Ivan had a nasty cut over his right eyebrow, oozing blood, and he sat bent over, a grim expression on his face.

Raphael shoved Riya into the back of the van, transferred his handcuff to the bench, then got in after her. The men outside slammed the doors shut, leaving them in semi-darkness, a small window to the driver's cab providing the only light.

"What happened to you?" Riya cringed at the battered appearance of Johanna and Ivan.

Johanna looked darkly at Raphael. "They jumped us from behind. We didn't resist, but they beat us up anyway."

Riya looked at Ivan, horrified.

He smiled grimly through smashed lips. "I'll survive."

She felt a sudden flash of anger; Ivan wouldn't hurt a fly. Instinctively, she put a hand to his face and gently brushed a bruise on his cheek with her thumb. Then, embarrassed, she withdrew it again quickly.

She turned to Raphael beside her with disgust. "You animals!"

He looked at her impassively and looked away again.

"That's what you are, dumb animals, blindly following your master's orders, just like dogs."

He ignored her, staring straight ahead.

"Do you even know why he wants us? Do you? Or doesn't he trust you enough to tell you that?"

He sighed. "You stole something of his. He wants it back. More than that, I don't need to know."

Riya laughed contemptuously. "Really? I would take way more interest in my employer, if I were you."

He looked at her.

"Do you have the glasses you took from me?"

Riya swayed into Ivan as the van jolted to a halt. The engine stopped. It was hard to tell how long they'd been travelling—an hour?—and, with no windows, she had no idea where they were.

She heard the front doors slam. The back doors opened, hinges whining. She squinted as bright light flooded the van. They seemed to be in some sort of loading bay, in a building facing out on to a large flat expanse of bare rocky earth covered in rows of black panels, stretching as far as she could see. A solar farm.

One by one, they were uncuffed from the bench, pulled from the van, and recuffed with their hands behind their backs. Following Raphael, they were marched down industrial-looking corridors, until they halted at a steel door. Raphael opened it and went inside. Riya and the others were pushed through after him.

The room, like the corridor, was stark: bare grey walls, strip lights, and it was empty except for four metal folding chairs lined up in the middle of the room. On a fifth chair, facing them as they walked in, his legs crossed, his hands neatly folded in his lap, sat Jim Booker. He was flanked by two immaculately bland grey-suited men in sunglasses—they looked like trained bodyguards, rather than Raphael's hired thugs.

Riya heard herself gulp. This was the first time she'd seen Booker in the flesh since facing him over the coffee table at home, a lifetime ago. She stumbled as a herd of emotions stampeded over her: fear, hate, anger, sadness…

Natalya gave a bark of laughter. "What's the first party game? Musical chairs?"

Booker made no response, watching as Riya and the others were pushed down on to the seats facing him, arms hooked awkwardly over the chair backs. Riya had forgotten those eyes—oddly black, giving them an inhuman quality, sharp, relentlessly analysing you.

When they were all seated, he spoke. "Hello, Johanna, Natalya. It's been a while since we all sat down like this, back at Predictive Technologies."

"Go to hell, Booker," Natalya glowered at him venomously.

"No doubt you are wondering who betrayed you?"

"Are you going to make us guess? Let me see," said Natalya sarcastically. "Was it Professor Plum in the study with the candlestick, or was it the narcissistic Silicon Valley CEO with a God complex?"

"Hmm," Jim smiled blandly and continued: "You underestimated the cowardice and self-preservation of your new friend, Edgar. Your meeting spooked him. He contacted me, falling over himself to assure me he had not given you the report and that your next move would be to contact Oliver." A frown flickered across his face. "What I find confusing, though, is how you didn't foresee his betrayal?"

Johanna tried to sit upright, "We weren't tracking him. To predict something, you need the right people in the simulation. With Mendoza, we didn't think to include Edgar as one of the variables. Our mistake, not Art's."

Jim nodded, "Ah, a simple oversight that has cost you the game. Edgar mentioned your intention to—what was the phrase? Ah, yes, 'take me down'. Ironic, don't you think, that the very meeting intended to seal my fate will result in your own demise?" He adjusted his jacket, as though preparing to make a formal announcement. "I am going to need you to hand over Art now."

He nodded to one the thugs by the door, who immediately left the room, returning a second later carrying a tray laid out with their glasses and phones.

"I don't think so, Jim." Johanna looked steely.

Jim sighed, "Please, no posturing; we all know you'll give me what I want, so let's make this quick."

He inclined his head to one of the bodyguards, who drew his gun, pointed, and fired in one fluid motion. The sound, unbelievably loud in the small room, made Riya flinch, momentarily stunning her. Ears ringing, she looked around in the direction the gun had been pointing. Johanna stared wide-eyed at Booker, her mouth open, a patch of red blooming across her white blouse from the centre of her chest. She gasped two short breaths before her head fell forwards, chin on her chest, eyes open.

Ivan cried out and lurched towards Johanna, but one of Raphael's men came from behind and hauled him roughly back into his seat. Natalya flew at Booker with a yell, but her arms, caught over the back of the chair, caused her to fall, and she crashed to the floor, where she lay struggling and screaming a string of insults.

Riya couldn't move. She sat staring disbelievingly; this was Johanna, their unflappable leader, usually so immaculate, so serene, now gazing stupidly at her knees, a look of shock frozen on her face.

Riya glanced up at Raphael. The look on his face told her that he clearly hadn't expected this either.

He turned on Booker, blue eyes blazing with fury, but only the slightest edge to his calm voice. "That was not part of the plan!"

Booker frowned, "Not turning sentimental on me, are you, Raphael?"

Raphael shrugged, "I do not like surprises. You should have warned me."

Booker looked at Natalya squirming on the floor. "That little stunt of yours hurt me. So now I'm going to hurt you. I have neither the time nor patience for gentle persuasion."

For some reason, Riya felt far more shocked than if it had been Natalya or Ivan. Perhaps that was Jim's strategy? Take down the leader first.

"You see how futile this is?" Booker sounded weary. "Do I really need to kill more of you to make that point?"

Natalya looked up from the floor with a vicious snarl. "Screw you!"

Booker nodded at the bodyguard, who drew his gun again and held it to Natalya's temple.

Riya screamed, "No! All right, you made your point."

Natalya didn't flinch, continuing to glare unwaveringly at Booker. The corner of Booker's mouth twitched.

"Natalya," Riya heard the pleading in her own voice, "Do as he says."

Natalya carried on staring for a few seconds, then her body went limp and she looked away. The bodyguard dragged her up to her feet and shoved her back on the seat.

"Good. Then let's get down to business." Booker clicked his fingers. One of Raphael's men undid their handcuffs, while the one with the tray handed them their glasses and phones. Jim watched silently until the three of them had put their glasses on. "Now, I would like you to add me as a Keyholder, and then remove yourselves."

Riya glared at Booker, her jaw muscles knotted as she strove to control her tears—she wouldn't give him the satisfaction of crying. She sniffed, took a breath, and said, "Art, please initiate the process to add Jim Booker as a Keyholder. The other Keyholders are present and agree to the nomination."

Art's voice sounded in Riya's ear. "Hello, Riya. I confirm you have nominated Jim Pryce Booker to become a Keyholder, and I have asked the other Keyholders to accept or decline."

Riya heard Ivan accept.

"Natalya?" Riya looked at her sharply.

Natalya exhaled noisily through flared nostrils; Riya half expected to see smoke. "I accept."

Art's voice again, "Please be advised that Jim Pryce Booker is now a Keyholder."

Riya held Booker's gaze, then nodded.

Jim Booker took a pair of glasses from his pocket and held them up. "A souvenir from Predictive Technologies. Let's see if I remember how to use them." He put them on. A slow, satisfied smile spread across his face, as though he'd just slid into a hot bath. "Good morning, Art. I'm very well, thank you. I wish to carry out a simulation involving the other Keyholders, so please ask their permission to do so."

Riya glanced at Ivan and Natalya, then agreed.

"Please simulate Natalya Romanov's future, four hours from now." Booker's gaze became fixed and glassy. "Perfect. Thank you, Art." His gaze returned to the people in front of him. He smiled widely, the first time Riya had seen him smile properly. "Everything seems to be in order."

Anger erupted in Riya's chest. "You really don't care who you hurt, do you? Are you going to kill us too, now? Is that the twisted little future you just simulated? How many more have to die for your pathetic Napoleon complex...Ravi, Cord, Johanna, my father..."

Booker just sighed ruefully. "Ah, your father. Most regrettable. *Killed* is such a vulgar term, but his accident was certainly... *fortuitous*. He backed me into a corner, I'm afraid." He grinned at Riya. "However, regarding your good selves, now I have what I want, killing you would serve no purpose."

Natalya snorted sceptically, "Really?"

"Yes, Miss Romanov, really. See for yourself." Booker smiled. "Art, please share the simulation with the other Keyholders."

Art spoke into Riya's ear. "Riya, Jim Booker is requesting a shared session. Do you agree?"

"Yes," snapped Riya, hearing the others accept too.

A video panel opened in Riya's vision showing herself, Natalya, and Ivan sitting in the cabin on their yacht. They were swaying, and through the windows Riya saw nothing but water. They were at sea.

"Where are we?" asked Riya.

"You are being escorted out into the Pacific to start your long trip back to England. Raphael will take you thirty miles offshore and leave you, and you will not come back." He stared at Natalya. "You have lost. Accept it and go home."

"You're letting us go?" Ivan looked sceptical.

"Yes."

"On our yacht?" said Ivan.

Jim's mouth twitched again, "Yes. That is the way you arrived, isn't it?"

Natalya's chin jutted forwards. "Why would you do that? What's to stop us coming after you? We just witnessed you murder someone."

Jim's eyes hardened. "For a start, you have no further claim to Art. I have now purchased what is left of Predictive Technologies. Its assets belong to me, and that includes Art. As to Mrs. O'Brien, there will be no evidence, and I am a prominent respected businessman accused by a Russian hacker and two kids. It won't take my lawyers long to dismiss *that*." He straightened his jacket. "Now, I believe it is time for you to resign as Keyholders."

Starting with Riya, they requested Art to remove them as Keyholders. Riya listened as Art said goodbye and the glasses powered off, ending with Natalya's grudging release of her Keyholder status.

It was over.

Art was no longer theirs.

Jim Booker stood and buttoned his jacket. "We have chatted long enough. So, if you would be so kind as to hand back your glasses and phones…" He gave them a gloating smile and turned for the door. "Goodbye, and thank you again for bringing me Art."

Raphael waved his gun at the main hatch as they clambered aboard *Lady Luck*. "Go below and stay there."

"You know how to sail?" asked Ivan, climbing down into the cabin.

"I will use the motor. Paulo will follow us in the motorboat." He nodded out towards the marina entrance, where a sleek powerboat was waiting, a hulk of a man at the wheel.

The three of them descended the ladder to the main cabin, then Raphael poked his head through the opening. "If you need something, bang on the hatch; otherwise, stay quiet. *Bon voyage, mes amis.*" Without waiting for a response, he shut the hatch, and Riya felt a flutter of claustrophobia.

They looked grimly at one another, until Natalya broke the trance. "I am going to kill Booker."

Riya shook her head. "No, Natalya. We have a plan; we should stick to it."

"Was Johanna's death part of the plan?" growled Natalya.

Riya stayed silent. No, it wasn't.

THE LION'S DEN

South-east of San Jose, an hour from San Francisco, on the top floor of Indigo headquarters, Jim Booker walked into his tennis-court-sized office, closed the door, and went to stand by the glass wall, looking out over the glittering lights of Silicon Valley to the distant hills.

"He's back," said Natalya, watching the screen in the centre of her makeshift workstation crammed into the back of the van.

Riya and Ivan crowded round, looking over her shoulder.

Ivan tilted his head, "Funny camera angle—looks like it's on the floor."

"It's a robot vacuum cleaner."

"Seriously? You hacked Jim Booker's vacuum cleaner?" Ivan's head thrust forwards over Natalya's shoulder, squinting at the screen.

"Gimme a break, asshole, the man doesn't allow *any* devices with cameras or microphones into his office apart from his own mobile and office phone, both of which are unhackable. I'm guessing the vacuum robot was an oversight—nobody thinks of a vacuum cleaner as a security risk."

"Wow, who knew? I can see the headline now: RUSSIAN HACKER CLEANS UP IN HUNDREDS OF HOMES." Ivan frowned. "Why've they got cameras on them, anyway?"

"Security feature, check on your home while you're out? Dunno. Make sure the dog isn't eating the furniture?"

Riya, hanging over Natalya's other shoulder, rolled her eyes. "Enough of the vacuum cleaner already. Yes, it was a magnificent feat of hackery, but has he received the email yet?"

At that moment, Jim's mobile pinged. He pulled it out and looked at its screen.

"Bingo!" Natalya switched to another screen, then paused, looking at Ivan's head still thrust over her shoulder. "Will you get out of my face!" She shoved his head away, and it bounced off the van roof with a thud.

"Ow! Just chill out, Baba Yaga!" Ivan rubbed his head, shuffling his stooped position in the cramped van.

Natalya ignored him and rattled away on the keyboard. An email inbox sprang open.

"Booker's email?" asked Riya.

"Yep. And this is the email he just received." Natalya tapped the keyboard. "Mail server IP address is from somewhere in China." She opened the email. No subject. One attachment. A movie. She clicked the file.

The screen filled with an image of blue water racing past, far beneath the camera. After a moment, two boats came into view, a yacht and a speedboat, stationary, side by side in the middle of the ocean. The camera, presumably a drone, hovered a hundred feet above the yacht. The familiar outline of the tall Frenchman could be seen moving around in the cockpit. He checked the hatch to the main cabin was locked, then waved to the man on the other boat—Paolo—who passed him a red fuel canister. Unscrewing the lid, Raphael lifted a panel on the boat, poured the fuel down below, and then tossed something after it. Riya knew what it was—a small explosive charge that could be detonated remotely to ignite the fuel.

This whole scenario was playing out just as Art had predicted several days ago. Raphael jumped back across to the speedboat and disappeared into the cabin with Paolo. They emerged a minute later, struggling to carry something heavy between them. Riya's heart caught in her throat as she realized what it was—this definitely had not been in their predictions. They were carrying Johanna's body. She felt tears welling and saw Natalya's face turn grim and stony as they watched Raphael and Paolo carry the body across to *Lady Luck*, manhandle her into a lifejacket, and lay her down in the cockpit.

"What went wrong?" muttered Riya. "We simulated the meeting with Booker—we were supposed to resist a bit, otherwise Booker would have been suspicious—but the simulation never suggested he would kill Johanna."

"Art works on probability, not certainty." Natalya's voice was hoarse, barely a whisper. "Sometimes we forget that."

They watched the two men jump back across to the speedboat and roar off across the waves in a plume of spray, bouncing out of camera shot as the drone stayed focused on the yacht.

The yacht bobbed in the water for a few seconds in the wake of the speedboat, then suddenly disappeared in a spectacular bloom of yellow flame. The movie had no sound, but the camera shook violently as the explosion shock waves reached the drone.

Ivan grimaced, "It seems wrong, leaving Johanna there like that."

"What could we do, bring her body with us?" said Natalya thickly. "Anyway, the coastguard will find her body—it will help convince them the rest of us were on board too."

Riya nodded, "At least her family will have a body to bury."

Riya had wondered why Booker hadn't just killed them all after they'd given him Art. Now, she understood. It was the perfect way to dispose of them. Raphael had taken them thirty miles offshore, so any floating debris would be unlikely to wash up on the Californian coast before the current swept it out into the Pacific, and the wildlife would take care of the bodies in a few days. Even if, by some miracle, someone did investigate the wreckage, they would conclude that a fuel leak had caused the explosion.

On screen, the drone camera swung towards the retreating speedboat just in time to see it, too, disappear in a cloud of flame and black smoke. Swinging back to the yacht, the debris spread out across the waves.

The video ended.

Riya turned and looked down at the man sitting on the floor, eyes closed, leaning against the side of the van. She kicked his boot gently, "I still don't understand *you*…"

Raphael Collomb opened one eye, "Why did I help? You showed me my future in the back of the van from Mendoza's, remember?"

"No, I mean why did Booker want *you* dead?"

He shrugged, "I am the only link between your murder and Jim Booker. Jim does not like loose ends. I should have seen it coming without your fortune teller."

"Look at that smug son of a bitch," hissed Ivan, watching the screen showing Booker's office, where he was still looking at his phone, smiling.

"Can you blame him?" said Riya. "He thinks he's won. He owns Art legally as an asset of Predictive Technologies. There's no one left to accuse him of theft, no one who knows what he did to obtain it."

"I think it's time we gave him the bad news," said Ivan coldly.

Natalya swivelled her chair back to face Raphael, "Time to earn your money."

Raphael Collomb got to his feet, his tall frame bent nearly double in the van. "Did you disable the CCTV? We are dead, no? It would be embarrassing to see one of us alive, captured on video."

Natalya scoffed, "I will disable them and re-enable them one by one as you pass—it will look like a temporary glitch. How about you don't tell me how to be a hacker, and I won't tell you how to kill people, OK?"

"Do you have your security pass?" asked Riya.

"Right here." Raphael pulled an ID card from his shirt pocket, with the Indigo logo and his photo on the front.

Riya nodded, "Let's go, then."

Raphael opened the back door of the van and jumped down into Indigo's car park.

Riya followed, but Ivan caught her arm. "Just be careful, all right? I know this was based on Art's simulation, but that was several days ago, and we don't have Art protecting us now."

"I'm not sure I would trust Art right now, not after Johanna. Anyway, I've got *him*." Riya jerked a thumb at Raphael. She

tried to smile reassuringly, but the truth was she didn't trust the
Frenchman either.

"Why don't you come with me? Booker killed your father as
well."

"No, the Anticipation Machine was Sanjay's baby, really. My
father was his partner, but it was always Sanjay's vision. I'm
fine with you ending this." He glanced at Natalya, scanning her
bank of screens. "Anyway, someone's got to keep an eye on the
angry pixie."

"Right here, Ivan," said Natalya, not taking her eyes from
the screens.

Riya grinned, "OK. See you soon."

Hooking in an earpiece so she could communicate with
Natalya, she followed Raphael across the car park to Indigo's
glittering glass temple of tech, swooping and swerving like
liquid silver in the moonlight.

Raphael veered away from the main reception, where a
security guard would question Riya's presence, and led them
through a side entrance. Riya felt her pulse racing as she
followed him through the labyrinth of corridors and offices. It
was late, and there were only a few stragglers still working, but
still, this was the lion's den, and Riya was convinced someone
would question their presence at any second. However, Raphael
clearly knew his way around, and he strode forward with such a
purposeful confidence that no one would question he belonged
there.

Finally, they arrived outside Jim Booker's office, and, after
a couple of minutes, she heard the bleeping of his desk phone.
That was her cue to enter, while he was distracted.

Natalya's voice crackled in her ear, "OK, go now."

Riya entered as Jim Booker hit the speaker button, "Hello?"
His back was to the door, his chair turned so he could look out
of the window.

"Hey, Jim, it's Gaurav down in Development. We're having
a few problems down here with Art. Just like you asked, we're
testing capabilities—running simulations and predictions—and

we're seeing some strange results. We started with large complex predictions—you know, lots of people, multiple environmental factors, long time horizons—and they ran fine. But now he can't manage these with any accuracy, nothing complex. It's like his brain is getting smaller. Another problem: we don't seem to be able to extract the source code. It's like he's forgotten where he put it, just reporting memory location errors."

"Look"—Booker's voice was icy—"if Sanjay's band of misfits could keep Art going from a laptop on a boat, you and your team should have no problem. Get it fixed!" He slammed the phone down, shaking his head.

"They won't be able to," said Riya.

Booker spun his chair to face Riya.

She closed the door, "Fix it, I mean. They won't be able to fix it."

Anger flashed across his features, then he sat back in his desk chair and forced a smile. "Well, well, well. Miss Sudame, back from the grave, I see. You are proving most resilient. I am intrigued. How did you survive the explosion?"

"That's easy—we weren't on the boat. Once we told Raphael that you intended to get rid of him as well, weirdly, he suddenly seemed keen to help us. We changed to another boat before we reached your explosion site, then Raphael and his friend staged the explosion of the yacht and bailed out before their own boat exploded. They were picked up by the coastguard, who had been anonymously tipped off about an explosion at that location."

Booker nodded calmly, but Riya could see his mind working furiously. "And how did you know of my plan to dispose of Raphael, I wonder…?"

"Did you forget the technology you were up against? We knew what you would do before you did. We knew you wouldn't let us live if we handed over Art, and we knew you'd get rid of Raphael as well."

"But Art belongs to me now," Booker made the statement confidently, but Riya saw the seed of doubt growing behind his eyes.

"Yes, he does. But not for long…I'm afraid Art has contracted a virus. And it's fatal."

"Is that so?" He forced his face to remain neutral, but Riya knew alarm bells would be ringing in Jim Booker's head. He took a moment to compose his thoughts. "But I'm assuming you have a copy of the source code somewhere?"

She smiled, savouring his discomfort.

"All right, what do you want in exchange for the code? I assume that is why you are here?"

"You are right that I want something from you, but Art is not part of the deal."

His eyes narrowed, "Then what is it you want?"

"Justice. I want you to confess to murder. You murdered my father, Ivan's father Victor Parfenov, Cord, Ravi, and now Johanna. You can't get away with that."

He gave a supercilious chuckle. "And why would I confess to murder?"

"Because, if you don't, we'll destroy Indigo."

He smiled, "That is a big threat, Miss Sudame, so forgive me if I don't believe you will be able to pull it off. If you are talking about that social-media stunt of yours—then, yes, it hurt, but people forget. We'll bounce back."

Riya reached behind her back and pulled out a rolled-up plastic folder, throwing it on the desk in front of him. The title: *Indigo Aggressive Sales AI—Effects on Mental Health*.

His face darkened, "Where did you get that?"

"Our mutual friend, Edgar Ismail."

"But he—"

"Was the one who betrayed us? Tipped you off that we would contact Oliver Mendoza? It did seem that way, didn't it? I'm afraid Edgar agreed to help us way before he came to you. Oh, he wasn't keen to begin with, but, like everyone else, if you know which buttons to press…He got a bad case of guilt."

"If you had the report, why didn't you just release it? Why go through the ridiculous charade of being caught, handing over Art, then faking your own death?"

"It's rather convenient being dead. You were not the only one looking for Art, and now they'll think you have it, and that we're dead. No one comes looking for the dead. If we'd given in too easily, you would have smelled a rat. We gave a convincing performance, don't you think?"

"And Johanna?"

Riya's face dropped. "That wasn't supposed to happen. Art miscalculated."

Booker smiled, puffing out his chest arrogantly. "Ah, so Art is fallible. I imagine that decision must carry some guilt?"

It was Riya's turn to force a smile as her insides squirmed.

Before she could answer, Booker continued, "But why go to all the trouble of getting *me* to kill you? Why not simply fake your own boat accident?"

"I would have thought that was obvious. It gave us what you Americans call *leverage*."

"Leverage? Leverage for what?"

"I came here to offer you a choice. Confess to the murders you have committed and remove the aggressive algorithms from Indigo, tonight, and we will not publish that report. You will go to jail, but your company will be safe—we have no wish to harm the lives of those innocent people who work for you. But refuse, and we *will* release this report to the media, and Indigo *will* be destroyed, and you will be framed for the murder of four people on a yacht."

Riya looked at her watch, "The FBI are on their way; what they arrest you for is up to you—do you want to sacrifice yourself to save your company, your legacy, or are you willing to risk it all hoping Indigo will ride out the report and you'll be acquitted of murder?" She smiled. "I could tell you what Art thinks your chances are."

"That is not much of a choice, but an easy one. I have no intention of confessing to anything. As you have admitted, Art makes mistakes, so I'll take my chances. I can ride out the report. Indigo will survive. As for being implicated in your murder, ultimately there's no evidence connecting me to that."

Riya smiled. "I thought you'd say that." She pulled a mobile phone from her pocket, held it in the air and pressed a button with her thumb. There was a muted beep and then nothing more.

"And what was that?" he said impatiently.

"The sound of your future ending." Riya stepped forward, grabbed the TV remote from Jim's desk and tossed it to him. "Open up YouTube, the Mordue Investments channel—I know you subscribe."

Jim pointed the remote at the big screen covering the end wall of the office. The TV lit up with the YouTube logo. "What's this got to do with…?" The words died in his mouth as he caught the title of the latest video posted to the Mordue Investments channel…*Mordue Investments ends relationship with Indigo*. He looked at Riya.

Her smile widened. "This video is being uploaded across the socials and sent to TV news networks as we speak. Take a look."

Jim started the movie. The screen filled with the Mordue Investments logo for a moment, then faded to a studio where Preston North faced the camera. A caption stated that he was Mordue's chief investment officer. He wasn't smiling.

"Hello. Mordue Investments has been invested in Indigo since the company was founded ten years ago, and we have been strong advocates of the company ever since. However, I am here to inform you that we have now severed our relationship with Indigo. We have sold our entire portfolio of Indigo stock, and as of today have withdrawn our investment from Indigo's Chinese expansion.

"Over recent weeks, we have become increasingly concerned about the unethical nature of Indigo's business practices. These concerns were confirmed recently when we came into possession of a report, commissioned internally by Indigo, that shows clear evidence of a connection between what Indigo calls its 'aggressive sales algorithms' and the rise of mental-health problems across the world. Just as cigarette manufacturers of the 1940s and '50s knowingly denied the harmful effects of tobacco, so it seems that social-media companies are knowingly denying the harm they are doing to people's mental health…

"I will now hand over to Edgar Ismail, involved in the authorship of this report, to explain it in more detail. A full copy of the report has been posted to our website. Edgar, if you would be so kind…"

Edgar came into camera shot. A caption stated he was Indigo's former head of AI development. "Thank you, Preston…"

Jim Booker clicked the remote. The screen changed to a graph tracking Indigo's stock price. "Christ! Down seven per cent already!" Jim clenched his fists. "You stupid little girl, what have you done?!" He spun to face Riya, lunging towards her, but pulled up short.

Riya was no longer alone.

"*Bon soir*, Jim." Raphael now stood beside Riya, pointing his gun at Booker.

"You! Whatever they're paying, I'll double it."

Raphael shook his head. "I don't think so, my old friend."

Booker's eyes narrowed at Raphael. "If I go down, you go with me—you're in this up to your neck."

Raphael shook his head again. "I don't think so. You see, the FBI have offered me a deal. You've made some powerful enemies, Jim, and it appears that clipping your wings is more important to them than locking up an old mercenary like me."

"Raphael will wait with you until the FBI arrive." Riya turned to go. "Goodbye, Jim Booker. Enjoy your retirement behind bars. This is for Johanna, Ravi, Cord, Victor, my father, and all the other people you've hurt over the years." She looked at her watch. "You have about two minutes before the FBI arrive." She pointed to the phone on Booker's desk. "You might want to use it to phone your lawyer, rather than shouting insults."

Riya turned to Raphael, "No offence, but I hope we never meet again."

The Frenchman shrugged, "Then, *adieu*."

Riya headed for the door.

FESSING UP

Two days later, high in Palo Alto Hills, on the edge of Silicon Valley, a yellow cab pulled over in front of tall wrought-iron gates barring the entrance to a long, paved driveway leading to a grand mock Mediterranean mansion.

Riya stepped out and looked up at the house, black fedora pulled low over her forehead. Taking a deep breath, she walked over to the side gate. Her hand hovered over the intercom buzzer. She hadn't warned him she was coming.

What would she have said? *Hi Ethan, it's me, Riya—I'm not dead, after all.*

No, the only way to do this was to turn up unannounced and explain everything at once.

She pushed the buzzer.

"Hello?" His voice sounded different: dull, lifeless.

"Hi! It's me, Riya." She smiled into the camera.

There was a long pause. "Is this some kind of a joke?"

"No, Ethan, it's me."

"But…it can't be…you're…"

"Let me come up and explain."

Another long pause, "OK."

The gate clicked. Riya pushed it open and walked through, up the steep driveway.

Ethan stood in the open doorway.

He frowned, shaking his head disbelievingly, "This is not possible."

Riya smiled apologetically, "Yeah, it is."

He looked awful, eyes red raw and dark-ringed, his face pale and drawn. He looked ten years older than when she'd last seen him.

"Are you OK?"

"Kind of. I'll tell you later. Come on in."

Riya walked into the marble entrance hall. It looked as if an Italian villa had been transported brick by brick to San Francisco.

Ethan shut the door, "I'm so glad you're alive! I knew my father was no killer."

Uh-oh, not a good start. "No, Ethan, stop."

"Now you're here, we can clear his name…"

"Ethan, stop." She laid a hand gently on his arm.

"What?" Ethan looked at her, eyes dull and confused.

"Your dad killed my father, and others. He also tried to kill me." This wasn't what she'd planned. She had meant to explain slowly, gently, not slap him in the face with it as soon she got in the door. "He was after some technology my dad developed."

Ethan shook his head, "No…"

"We had to stop him. We thought destroying Indigo and discrediting him would do it. We came to San Francisco and started that social-media campaign about Indigo causing mental-health problems—"

"That was *you*?" Ethan's eyes widened.

"Yes, but your father was so powerful, Ethan, we needed something else. I remembered that conversation in London, when you said there are people out there who knew things that could do him a lot of damage…"

"You used me." Ethan's eyes rolled around the hall as this sunk in. When they came back to rest on Riya, they were hard and cold, his father's eyes. "You got me to betray my own father, then dumped me. I *trusted* you!"

"I'm so sorry," she was crying, now. "I couldn't tell you; I couldn't risk your father finding out about us."

"You got what you wanted and left."

"No, it wasn't like that, I…I cared about you…that's why I stayed…Those few days, Ethan, just the two of us, they were perfect…"

"He's *dead*!" Ethan spat the words like bullets.

Riya's thoughts stopped like a train hitting the buffers. "What?"

"My father was found dead in his holding cell early this morning—no witnesses, somehow CCTV wasn't working in his cell. The official story is that he slipped and banged his head, but off the record the FBI think the Chinese did it—something to do with a deal Dad did with them." Ethan looked away, choking back tears. "He'd only been in there forty-eight hours. They hadn't even charged him yet…"

"Oh, Ethan, I'm so sorry." She reached out a hand, but he stepped away.

An ugly snarl twisted his face. "Sorry? You made his company worthless, you trashed his name. Wasn't that enough? Did you really need to frame him for murder as well? If he hadn't been arrested, he'd still be alive. You as good as killed him!"

The words felt like a slap in the face. "Ethan, please…"

"I can clear his name, though." He pulled a phone from his pocket. "I'm calling the police, and you are going to explain to them that you and your friends are still alive."

"No, Ethan, don't." Riya's voice was screeching now, tears flooded her eyes. She backed away, but he lunged forward, catching her by the arm. She screamed, trying to pull away, but he was too strong. His fingers dug into her arm, and she dropped to her knees.

"Ethan, you're hurting me!"

The door burst open behind her. Ethan looked up in surprise.

"Let her go." She knew the voice. Twisting around from her position on the floor, she blinked the tears away.

There, in the doorway, stood Ivan.

"Another of your murdering friends? Good, the police can take him as well." Ethan fumbled with his phone.

Ivan moved into the hall. "Don't do it, pretty boy." His voice was hard. Riya had never heard him sound like that before.

"You're both going to pay for what you did to my father." Ethan began to tap a number into his phone.

Ivan leaped forwards, slapping the phone out of his hand, sending it skittering across the marble tiles. Rage flashed across Ethan's face. He let go of Riya and squared off against Ivan, his chest heaving. Ivan was a big guy, but Ethan was taller. Ivan was heavier, but Ethan was powerfully athletic. Riya doubted Ivan could beat him if it came to a fight.

Ivan stood still, not taking his eyes of Ethan. "Come on, Riya, we're going."

Rye scrambled to her feet and went to stand behind Ivan.

"I don't want to fight you, but this is not Riya's fault. Your father killed Riya's father, and mine, and tried to kill *us*. He brought this on himself."

Ethan said nothing. Then his body relaxed, he stood up straight, his face softening to a deep scowl. Maybe he figured he couldn't take on two of them? Maybe he realized Ivan was right?

Ivan and Riya backed up a couple of steps, then turned towards the door. But, as they turned, Ethan sprang forwards, grabbed Ivan's jacket by the shoulder, spun him round, and caught him with a punch to the face. Ivan reeled backwards, slamming into the wall with a grunt.

"You're going nowhere until the cops get here."

"No, Ethan…" Riya cringed away from him, but he grabbed her by the arm again and yanked her back from the doorway with such force it sent her sprawling across the floor.

Kicking the door shut, he turned on Ivan, who'd recovered enough to realize what was coming and raised his arms over his head just before Ethan rained down on him with a volley of vicious blows. Ivan was pinned against the wall, unable to fight back.

A protective anger flared in Riya—that was her friend he was hurting!

"Stop it!" Getting to her feet, she hurled herself at Ethan, pounding his back with her fists.

Ethan turned and flung her away like a rag doll, but this gave Ivan enough time to rally. Head down, he pushed off the wall, grabbed Ethan round the waist, and pushed him backwards across the hall in a kind of rugby tackle. Ivan's juggernaut weight drove forwards across the entrance hall, picking up speed

until Ethan slammed into the wall with an ominous crunch. He
fell to the floor.

Ethan tried to get up, screamed with pain, and sank back to
the floor. "I'm going to hunt you down! I am not going to stop
until you pay for what you did. Do you hear me? *I'm going to hunt
you down!*"

With a last tearful backward glance, Riya hurried out of the
door after Ivan.

"That went well," said Ivan, dabbing a cut cheekbone as
they jogged down the drive.

"I had to try…I was so horrible to Ethan. But if I'd known
about his dad…"

Ivan gave her a sidelong glance. "Really? I think even if Art
gave you a ninety-nine per cent chance of failure you would
have gone anyway…because there was still a one per cent
chance things would work out. Art clearly isn't the death of
hope, right?"

"Right. Some things you have to try, no matter what the
odds." She smiled. He understood. "Anyway, I thought you were
going to wait in the cab?"

He gave her a sideways glance. "I had guessed he might not
greet you with open arms, so I decided to come up to the house
and keep an eye on you. I heard the shouting before I even got
to the front door."

Riya looked at him, tears welling uncontrollably in her eyes.
"I can't believe he reacted like that. I'm so sorry you had to get
involved." Then the sobs came; whether it was relief, sorrow,
shock, or all three, she wasn't sure, but what she did know was
she was glad Ivan was there.

A NEW HOME

"What do you think?" said Natalya flatly.

Riya stood with Ivan surveying the sprawling single-storey house, stark white stone and glass rising out of the desert. She turned around slowly on the spot, shielding her eyes from the midday sun. The sandy, rocky landscape stretched out relentlessly in all directions, uninterrupted except for a few spiky cacti and their rental van, so dusty from the long drive south it was nearly the same colour as the desert.

Ivan dropped his bag and sighed. "*Really?* The middle of the New Mexico desert!"

Natalya shrugged. "Johanna had organized it. Apparently, it used to belong to a reclusive Texas oil baron."

"I bet there isn't a decent sushi restaurant within a hundred miles of here," Ivan grumbled. Hunching his shoulders, he thrust his hands in his pockets. "And it's cold, *in the desert*, how does that work?"

Riya rolled her eyes, "It's only March, Ivan."

Natalya clapped him on the back and walked towards the front door. "C'mon, take a look inside, you'll love it."

Riya stepped into the limestone entrance hall. It felt calm and soothing, the air warm after the chilly desert breeze.

"Well?" Natalya closed the door behind them.

Ivan looked around, "It's OK."

"I love it!" said Riya.

Natalya shrugged unenthusiastically. "It's a house. But it does have one very special feature." Walking through the hall, she beckoned Riya and Ivan to follow.

They followed her through the house and down a long passage connecting the living area to the bedrooms. Halfway along the passage, Natalya stopped, grinned, and pressed one of the stones in the wall. It sank into the wall with a soft hiss and a doorway-sized section of stone swung inwards.

"This is why Johanna bought it." Natalya disappeared inside the wall.

Blue floor-level lights lit the way down a steel spiral staircase. Towards the bottom, the temperature dropped, and Riya heard the loud droning whoosh of air conditioning. She shivered. It was like walking into the refrigerated section of a supermarket on a hot day. They emerged into a large underground basement and Riya gasped—it was filled with rack upon rack of computers, black monolithic towers twinkling with lights.

"This used to be the previous owner's man-cave, but I found a better use for it." Natalya turned to face Riya and Ivan, arms spread wide, her face lit up like a child in a toy shop. "Say hello to Art 2.0. I still have some configuration to do, but he'll be operational soon." She turned to a small table by the stairs, picked up a tray, and held it out to them. "You'll need these…"

On the tray were four glasses cases, a Post-it note with their names stuck to each one—Riya felt her stomach twist as she saw Johanna's name on one. She reached for her own, opened the box, and took out a pair of stylish graded aviator sunglasses. Ivan put his on: classic black-framed Wayfarers with red lenses.

Natalya took hers—some weird steampunk-looking things with rectangular purple lenses—and slipped them on. "Johanna thought Art needed a little style. She figured, if we got through this, we'd need somewhere to go, and a working version to demonstrate."

"Is that what we're still planning to do, then? Hand over Art?" asked Riya.

"That was always the plan, right? Booker is out of the way, and we're dead, so no one is looking for us. We have space to find the right home for Art."

Riya wasn't sure the picture was that rosy. They might have fooled the media, the police, and maybe even the FBI, but she had a feeling Brendan Brown would not accept their deaths so easily. As for finding a home for Art—some benign organization willing to champion her father's altruistic vision—she was beginning to think that was a naïve pipe dream.

Ivan and Riya traipsed back upstairs, leaving Natalya to her toys, and busied themselves unloading the van and choosing bedrooms. Riya hung her pathetic handful of creased garments in the cavernous wardrobe and stood back, struck by the fact that her entire life now fitted into a backpack.

She strode over to the glass wall overlooking the desert, slid aside one of the panels, and stepped on to the wooden decking outside her bedroom. She looked out over the desert, where the early spring sun was preparing its early departure behind the distant mountains. For the first time in a while, she thought of home. It seemed so distant now, part of a different world to which she no longer belonged. She wasn't even sure she wanted to go back. Yes, life had become harder and more dangerous, but she'd also felt more alive in these last few months than she ever had.

She sighed, dug her hands into her jeans, and kicked a stone from the decking. A faint rhythmic sound drifted out of the desert—*whoosh whoosh*, pause, *whoosh whoosh*, pause. She frowned, stepping off the decking into the desert, trying to figure out where the sound was coming from. She walked around the house, towards the noise. A little way off, a figure in black bobbed up and down, seemingly in and out of the ground.

As Riya approached, she realized what it was: Natalya was skateboarding in the empty swimming pool, her hoodie and a half empty Coke bottle sat on the side. With nothing else to do, Riya sat down, back to the house, legs dangling over the edge. She watched Natalya hurtling around the contoured bowls, the roar of the wheels on concrete loud and incongruous in the silence of the desert.

Natalya turned the skateboard towards her, shot up the side of the pool, took off, and landed neatly beside Riya, catching the board in her hand. She sat down, breathless and glistening with sweat.

Riya handed her the bottle of Coke. "You're pretty good... for a girl."

"No, I'm just pretty good," Natalya took a long draught from the bottle and gasped. "Out of practice, though."

Riya noticed her rubbing her leg. "How's your leg? You know, where you were shot?"

Natalya shrugged, "It's OK, bit stiff sometimes. How about your arm?"

Riya flexed her arm appraisingly, "Fine."

They sat in silence for a while. They hadn't really been alone together since the whole Booker thing had ended; the three of them had been cooped up together in a San Francisco motel for a few of days while they waited for the dust to settle, then another couple of days cooped up in a van, driving south.

"How's it going with Art?"

"All done. I imported the data files, the ones I took before handing 'old Art' over to Booker, so he should appear to be the same old Art we know and love."

"Great."

A long silence. Riya had the impression Natalya was still mad at her and Ivan for pursuing Ethan and Edgar, and she wanted to clear the air.

"I'm sorry about the Ethan thing. It's just sometimes I needed to feel like I had some control over my life, you know?"

Natalya gave a wry smile. "Don't be sorry. You took a risk, it paid off. We needed Edgar's report."

Riya waited. Would Natalya respond with her own concession? She didn't. So Riya did it for her. "And you can be a bit of cow yourself sometimes, you know. You gave Ivan and me a really hard time. It's not like you haven't taken the odd risk."

Natalya gave Riya a lopsided grin. "It has been known." She shoved Riya gently with her shoulder. "You did all right. Even rich boy proved himself useful—but don't tell him I said that. Your father would have been proud."

"I thought you said I was just 'a silly schoolgirl' who doesn't know anything about your world?"

"You didn't. But now you do," Natalya picked up her hoodie and skateboard and jumped up. "I need a shower before I start to stink, then I have work to do."

Riya shivered, then got to her feet. "Yeah, it's getting chilly out here. What work?"

As the two of them wandered into the living room, Natalya picked up her laptop from the coffee table and slunk away in the direction of her bedroom. "See you later."

Ivan, lying on the sofa, peered over the top of his iPad. "What's for dinner?"

"Not sure, but *you're* helping me cook it." Riya stabbed a finger at Ivan.

Ivan put down the iPad and grumbled to his feet. "How come the angry pixie gets away with not helping?"

"You've tasted Natalya's cooking—she can burn water. Anyway, she's busy."

"Not still fiddling about in that basement?"

"No, Art's up and running," said Riya thoughtfully. She picked up the iPad from the sofa and began tapping at the screen. "From what she just told me, apparently she's busy being a philanthropist."

"Seriously? *Her?*" Ivan, peered at the iPad over Riya's shoulder.

She found it—an article in the *Cambridge News*: *Local Boy Selected for Ground-breaking Leukaemia Research Programme*. Underneath the headline was a picture of a boy smiling. She read on…

> Today, young Noah Dole, aged ten, celebrated
> being selected to take part in a research programme
> investigating a revolutionary new treatment for
> leukaemia at Boston Children's Hospital in the
> USA. Remarkably, Noah came to be selected when
> his UK consultant, Dr Vinay Ranganathan, and the
> programme's head of research in Boston, Dr David
> Tully, became stuck in a hotel lift together while
> attending a conference. Dr Tully's team were in the
> process of selecting additional candidates after a

large donation recently allowed the programme to be expanded. During their incarceration in the errant elevator, the two discussed Noah's case and agreed he would be an ideal fit for the programme. "If that lift hadn't broken down, my son simply wouldn't have been on the list," said Noah's mother, Mrs. Linda Dole. "We were running out of options."

The news came only months after Noah lost his father to a street robbery, and has been a much-needed morale booster for the whole family...

Ivan frowned. "Noah Dole? Cord's son?"

Riya nodded.

"And Natalya engineered this?" His face scrunched in disbelief.

"Yep. She made the donation, then used Art to bring together the consultants. She's working on something for Ravi's family as well."

"Huh. The Tin Man got herself a heart, who knew? Does that mean we can all go back to Kansas now?" Ivan saw the website Riya had entered. "What are you doing?" Tell me that's not a social-media site!"

"Just need to check something...Anyway, I'm not using my own account, I'm using one of the bogus accounts we created for our social-media war on Indigo."

Ivan titled his head at the screen, "April Royston? Your friend, right?"

"Yep." She scanned down April's latest posts, then relaxed as she found what she was looking for: a picture of April looking happy, sitting with a meal in front of her.

"*Long way to go, but several weeks into rehab and mentally in a good place...*" Ivan read the post and frowned. "What does that mean?"

"It means I managed to help my best friend turn her life around. While we were busy changing people's minds about Indigo, I had a little side project—I used Art to find out what would make April get help for her bulimia."

Ivan's eyes widened in alarm.

"Don't worry, it was all anonymous, like we did with the celebs. It just looked like stuff popped up on her news feed."

She didn't dare admit she was planning to contact both April and Hannah to let them know she was OK; Hannah would blame herself for Riya's death, and April was in no state to take a shock like that. But that was for another day. She tossed the iPad on to the sofa, sighed wearily, then smiled. "Come on, gimme a hand in the kitchen, or will you be driving the twenty miles to the nearest town to get takeaway?"

Ivan grinned, "Since you put it like that…"

Later, they ate dinner on the veranda, huddled around the fire pit for warmth, under a sky that had become a black star-spangled canvas. Riya had managed to cobble together a spicy vegetarian stir fry that even Ivan admitted was tasty, despite the lack of meat. After dinner, Riya walked slowly down the corridor connecting the living area and the bedrooms, running her hand along the rough limestone walls. She paused at the secret door down to Art's basement. One question had been rattling around her mind since they'd arrived at the desert house. Would Art 2.0 still contain her father? No one else seemed to know about her dad's digital replica, so perhaps it was not part of Art's core code? She remembered her father's comment on the boat, back in Dartmouth, about him not being part of the version they planned to hand over to the authorities. What version had Natalya used to build Art 2.0?

Sitting on her bed, facing the glass-walled desert, she pulled out her new glasses and put them on.

"Hello, Riya. How can I help you?"

"Art, can I speak to my father?"

There was a stomach-churning pause.

"Hello, Riya," she looked over her shoulder. There he was, standing by the door as though he'd just come into the bedroom. He smiled. "It's been a while. Is Jim Booker still a danger?"

"He's dead," said Riya flatly.

Her father looked pained. "That is regrettable. How—?"

"Not *that* regrettable, and I don't want to talk about it," snapped Riya. Talking about Booker would lead to talking about Johanna, and she didn't feel like reliving that right now.

Her father blinked, surprised by her response.

"Sorry, Dad, I will tell you everything, just…not tonight, OK?"

He seemed to understand, "Very well. Have you decided what you will do next?"

"Find a home for Art. Now Booker is out of the way, everyone seems to think we have a better chance of finding some organization willing to take ownership of Art—on our terms."

"But you don't agree?"

"No offence, Dad, but I'm beginning to think your idea of finding some nice friendly organization that will use Art 'for the good of mankind' is a bit…" What was she going to say? Rubbish? Naïve? "Optimistic."

His face became serious, but he nodded slowly. "So? What do you plan to do about that?"

"If we want to realize your vision, I wonder if we might have to manage Art ourselves."

He gave a sharp intake of breath. "That is a tough road to take, Riya. Are you really ready for that? Don't you want to return to your own life?"

"We single-handedly brought down a powerful corporation, Natalya helped accelerate a cancer-research programme, and I helped my best friend get help for her eating problem. I get it now, the good this technology can do. But if we tried the same thing staying within the law, it would never have happened. Operating as—I dunno, outlaws—we were free of rules and bureaucracy. Nothing got in our way."

Her father shook his head. "That is a dangerous game, Riya, thinking you are above the law, thinking you are so right that your goals justify your actions."

"Yes, but none of *us* are greedy for power. We don't want to rule the world. We just want to change it, for the better."

"Better according to whom? History is littered with dictators who have gone to their graves believing they were changing the world for the better. Remember, 'Absolute power corrupts absolutely'. I am not saying you are wrong. But please consider the negatives as well as the positives. Will you do that for me?"

That was a good answer. An adult answer. He wasn't telling a child what to do.

"Yes, of course." Riya smiled. "And Dad?"

He looked round.

"Thanks for the advice."

His face relaxed to a warm smile as he turned and walked straight through the window, out into the desert night.

Riya watched him go until a gentle knock caused her to glance at the bedroom door. When she looked back, he was gone.

Another knock.

"Hang on, it's locked." She took off her glasses, stuffed them back in her jacket, and ran to open the door.

Ivan stood there, red-faced and swaying slightly, a gaudy apparition in pink polo shirt and yellow trousers, hair sticking out like an untidy bundle of twigs. A few months ago, she would have found this a hideous reflection of Ivan's vulgar rich-boy taste, but now it seemed sort of endearing; he was someone who didn't take himself too seriously, a reminder that there was always room for a little fun in life.

"Came to check you were OK. You looked a bit off over dinner. I thought maybe you were thinking about, you know, San Francisco…"

She put on her best reassuring smile. "I'm fine, really. Just tired."

"Oh. OK, then. If you're sure." He turned to go.

She was still thinking about her father. Would it really be such a bad thing to manage Art themselves? "Ivan?"

"Hmm?" He turned back to face her.

She hesitated. The idea was still so fragile, she wasn't sure how to start the conversation, so she said awkwardly, "You wanna come in for a minute?"

He looked surprised. "Erm, OK."

She held the door open, and he shambled in, looking around.

"I think your room's better than mine." He went to stand by the glass wall, looking out over the desert exactly where her father had been moments before. "You got a great view; it'll feel like you're actually sleeping out in the desert."

"Yeah, I really like it." Shutting the door, she went to stand next to him.

His eyes flicked across to her, "So, how are you feeling, you know, about the Ethan thing?"

Riya let out a long sigh. "Pretty crappy."

Ivan nodded.

Then, seemingly out of nowhere, he blurted, "Did you ever find out why your dad made you a Keyholder?"

She could feel his eyes on her. Should she tell him? Did he also have a virtual dad inside Art? But what if he didn't? No. That was a conversation for another time. "Nah. No idea. How about you?"

He sighed, turning back to the desert, "Haven't a clue."

She watched him carefully, trying to decipher his expression, but he caught her looking and gave her a sidelong grin.

"Probably did it just to piss me off."

She held his gaze for a second, then looked away. "Well, I guess we'll never know now, will we?"

"I guess not."

Trying to sound casual, she said, "So, what happens now?"

"You mean with us?"

She nodded.

He rubbed the back of his neck. "Find a home for Art, then go home ourselves, I guess."

Riya looked at him incredulously. "We're dead. How do you think we're ever going back to our old lives?"

Ivan spread his palms. "Hey, don't get me wrong, I'm all for this new life—but we can't live as ghosts forever. We *have* to return to normal life, right?"

"I'm not even sure what 'normal' would be, after this," said Riya quietly. Out of nowhere, a voice in her head answered: *Normal would be living with Aunty Hannah and going shopping with April. Normal would be begging Ethan to forgive you...*

Ivan's voice snapped her back from the daydream: "Well, one thing's for sure, as long as we keep Art to ourselves, there won't be *any* kind of normal."

She glanced at him. "But what if we *did*, you know, manage Art ourselves?"

Ivan snorted, "Yeah, right."

"But we didn't do so bad on our own, did we?"

Ivan's eyebrows shot up. "Really? People murdered, lives ruined, and now we're in the middle of a desert, pretending to be dead."

"Yeah, but that's because we were in a fight with Booker. We're free of that now, so we could finish what our fathers started. Ivan, we could do a lot of good. It's got to be a possibility?"

He laughed, "Putting humans on Mars is a possibility, but it's bloody difficult."

"Yeah, you're right, silly idea." Of course Ivan wouldn't be interested. "You probably want to get back to your yacht races and parties, anyway."

"Yeah. Probably back to living with Mother and her Russian socialite mafia." He didn't sound enthusiastic, but then his face brightened. "Hey, why don't you come along? Plenty of money hanging around at those events, bound to be some good fundraising contacts—I could introduce you?"

"Hmm. Maybe."

Ivan nodded. "I get it—not your scene, hanging out with the spoiled rich kid."

"Don't be daft. I've loved hanging out with you. You saved my life! I'm just not sure I want to go back to that. After what we did, fundraising seems, I dunno, sort of small and slow. It takes a huge effort just to make a small difference. It's like, you've been trying to dig a massive hole with a shovel, then someone gives you a bulldozer—it's kinda hard to go back to a shovel after that."

"OK." He looked at her shrewdly. "Let's say, hypothetically, we did keep Art. Were you planning to take on this crusade alone?"

"You mean, I should talk to Natalya?"

For some reason, he looked disappointed. "Yeah, right, you'd need her."

She looked at him. "Are you all right?"

He smiled at her wearily. "I just think we should take some time, enjoy the fact we came through the last few months alive, without worrying about what the future holds."

Riya thought back to the YouTube video of her father predicting people's behaviour. Suddenly it struck her how long ago that scene in her bedroom seemed. "But *our* future doesn't have to be such a mystery anymore, does it? Not if we don't want it to be."

Ivan didn't look amused. "It's not about being able see our future; it's about dealing with our past. We've all been through a lot emotionally; we need time to process that."

He was right, they had been through a lot, and, now that she thought about it, he had been by her side through all of it. She smiled, reached up, and touched the cut on his face. Struck by a sudden impulse, she stood on tiptoes and kissed him on the cheek.

"You're a good guy, Ivan Parfenov."

He looked at her uncertainly for a second, sighed, then gave a wry smile. "But I'm guessing you have a plan anyway, right?"

Riya shrugged, and the corners of her mouth twitched into a smile as her gaze drifted back to the desert. "I just think 'normal' might be a bit overrated."

ACKNOWLEDGEMENTS

Writing a book is a team sport, and so there are a number of people whom I would like to thank for helping to bring this project to life.

First and foremost, I must express my deepest gratitude to my wife, Louise. Your unwavering support and understanding throughout the writing process have been the cornerstone of this endeavour. Your patience, encouragement, and the time and space you afforded me to pursue this project made this book possible – it simply would not exist without you. You are the rock on which everything in my life is built, and for that, I am endlessly thankful.

I extend my heartfelt appreciation to my collaborator and mentor, John Lomas-Bullivant of Kickback Media. Your expertise, insights, and dedication enriched every page of this book. Your creative contributions and shared vision have truly elevated the work. It has been an honour to embark on this adventure with you, and I am grateful for the synergy we've cultivated along the way.

I am indebted to my publisher, Archna Sharma, and her team at Neem Tree Press, for believing in the value of this project and providing invaluable guidance and support throughout the publication process. I look forward to our continued partnership in sharing stories that resonate with audiences far and wide.

Special recognition is also due to Sue Cook and Penelope Price, two editors who have been instrumental in knocking this book into shape. Their ruthless attention to detail helped trim the fat and hone this story into its final form.

My sincere thanks go out to friends and family for the myriad ways in which you have supported me and taken the time to read my early ramblings and provide feedback. Your interest and encouragement have been pivotal in sustaining me through the challenges of this endeavour.

Last but certainly not least, I offer my gratitude to the readers. It is for you that these words were crafted, and I am deeply humbled by the time you have invested in reading this book. I am honoured to have the opportunity to share this journey with you.